RAZORBACK by Dick Stiv...
A weekend of wild-boar h... buddy pits Gadgets Schwa... razorbacks. Caught in a w... cabal selling hijacked mili~~tary hardware~~ to street gangs and fanatics, the Arkansas woods become a killing ground for high-stakes booty as Able Team moves out—armed and dangerous.

SURVIVAL RUN by Gar Wilson
While on a goodwill tour of the Middle East, the U.S. Secretary of State is kidnapped by terrorists who plan to stage the ultimate world television premiere: the execution of their hostage. The terrorists are unwilling to discuss any terms—so the U.S. sends in a commando team whose negotiating techniques are tough and to the point. The Phoenix Force warriors fight fire with fire—and take no prisoners.

ZEBRA CUBE by Robert Baxter
North Vietnamese officials offer to release high-level American POWs in exchange for the notorious General Tran, believed locked in an underground Saigon prison chamber, the Zebra Cube, named for its mind-bending black-and-white interior. Unable to strike a deal, the enemy storms Saigon to take the jail by force. Special Forces meets the action head-on—and runs up against a VC sapper team led by a mysterious woman with a blood vendetta.

BOOK 1

HEROES

**RAZORBACK
SURVIVAL RUN
ZEBRA CUBE**

A GOLD EAGLE BOOK FROM

WORLDWIDE®

TORONTO • NEW YORK • LONDON
AMSTERDAM • PARIS • SYDNEY • HAMBURG
STOCKHOLM • ATHENS • TOKYO • MILAN
MADRID • WARSAW • BUDAPEST • AUCKLAND

First edition July 1992

ISBN 0-373-62404-2

HEROES: Book I

The publisher wishes to acknowledge the following authors
for their contribution to the individual works:

David North—RAZORBACK
Mike Linaker—SURVIVAL RUN
Nicholas Cain—ZEBRA CUBE

Contents

RAZORBACK
by
Dick Stivers

An Able Team novel

PROLOGUE

The group of men worked hard to finish the prefabricated structure in the Arkansas backwoods. They heard the cries for help as the construction crew from Metairie, Louisiana, struggled to set the large corrugated panels into place.

The foreman of the crew looked at the shorter of the two uniformed officers. "What the hell was that, Sheriff?"

The balding, stocky man took out a rumpled cotton handkerchief from his back pocket and wiped the perspiration from his face. "Dunno. Sounds like somebody's in trouble. Probably a hunter."

The other uniformed officer, whose badge identified him as a deputy sheriff, lowered his voice. "You think he's over in the refuge or around here, Judd?"

The sheriff replied in a whisper. "Don't rightly matter, does it, Stanley?"

Stanley Ruddle, his chief deputy and closest confidant, nodded in agreement. "Guess not. No telling what he's seen."

Judd Bushnell turned to the foreman of the construction crew. "Keep going. I want you finished and out of here before nightfall. We'll be back."

Turning away from the workmen, the two men listened to the cries for help coming from the other side of the pine stand, then followed the sound of the voice into the woods.

THE FURIOUS RAZORBACK continued to attack the small tree savagely with its flailing tusks. Each assault seemed to anger the huge creature.

Phil Rainey knew the tree couldn't withstand many more attacks. He looked down at where he'd dropped his rifle. There was no way he could get to it without being impaled on the slashing tusks.

Suddenly, through the trees, he heard the crack of fallen branches. He stared in the direction of the sound, terrified it might be more wild boars coming to tear him apart with their tusks. But his eyes filled with tears of relief when he saw the two men approaching him. Both were wearing the uniforms of law-enforcement officers, and they were carrying weapons.

The two men stopped at the edge of the pine stand and glanced up at the man in the tree, then turned their weapons on the razorback. Calmly they emptied their barrels into the massive creature until it finally toppled, profusely bleeding from the gaping holes in its skull and body.

Rainey glanced at the carcass. There was no way he could use the head of the razorback as a trophy, but right now that didn't matter as much as it had earlier. He was just grateful to be alive.

"Thanks," he said. "I don't know what would have happened to me if you hadn't come along."

The two men stared at him silently, then looked at each other.

"What do you wanna do, Judd?" the taller officer asked.

The short, stocky man turned his combination rifle-shotgun on the treed hunter and squeezed the trigger three times as his answer.

The deer slugs tore into the stunned man's chest. Screaming, he released his hold on the limb and tried to cover the huge, bleeding cavity as he crashed into a pile of dead leaves.

Bushnell walked over to the still form and knelt. He felt the vein in the neck for a pulse. There was a faint rumble as blood rushed through the artery and poured out of the wounds onto the dark green leaves. He pulled out his .44-caliber Smith & Wesson, pressed it against the man's ear and pulled the trigger. A discharge of bloody tissue and bits of bone exploded through the fallen man's nostrils.

Ruddle bent down, picked up the dropped Weatherby and handed it to Bushnell.

"Must have been real scared to bring something as heavy as this to shoot a razorback," the sheriff commented, handing the rifle back. "Might be worth something to someone. Put it in inventory."

"What about him?"

Bushnell stood then reached down and grabbed the dead man's legs. "Swamps come in real handy for things like this."

Together they heaved the body into the middle of the soupy muck.

Ruddle looked at the sheriff. "Think he came here alone?"

Bushnell hitched up his pants as they watched the body sink into the muddy porridge beneath the water. Then he grinned. "Don't matter much if he did. They'll call the sheriff and file a missing person's report."

1

"You're one dead son of a bitch!"

Hermann "Gadgets" Schwarz heard the words explode from the mouth of the huge bare-chested man who stood a mere ten feet from him. He smiled back at him, knowing the smile under his thick dark brown mustache would infuriate the other man.

Inside, Schwarz felt a touch of nausea in his stomach as the pain from his recent wound surged through his body. The other man had already landed a number of punishing blows. Under his skin, Gadgets could feel his muscles aching from the merciless pounding, especially when the still-healing wound in his right side was hit. He could have avoided most of the blows, but he had agreed to let the other man best him for most of their duel.

The angry attacker rushed him again. His thick hand slashed at Gadgets's sun-bronzed head, and the Able Team warrior stepped inside the arc of the swing at the last possible moment. Wincing with pain, Schwarz twisted away from the furious punch and turned quickly on his heel to face his enraged opponent.

Sergeant Ben "Bull" Crowley continued to press his attack, leaping into the air and throwing his full weight at Gadgets's head. Gracefully Schwarz moved out of the sergeant's path, like a bullfighter stepping to one side of a charging bull.

He had played cat and mouse with the bull-like soldier. Now the game was becoming tiresome, and the pain from his wound was beginning to cloud his thinking. So he tried to think of a way to end it and still accomplish the purpose for which Chan Lao had asked him to come down to Fort Campbell for a few days.

To the observers the two men were mismatched. The sergeant was at least four inches taller. Well-developed muscles bulged on his massive frame. His opponent was older—probably by at least ten years—and slender. While Crowley's expression made it clear he considered this a duel of honor, Schwarz bounced around the dirt area as if he were practicing for a rock-and-roll dance demonstration. His casual attitude infuriated the other man, who was determined to make it clear to the men watching that no one could get away with making a fool out of Sergeant Ben Crowley.

What had started out as a friendly demonstration of martial-arts skills for a company of 101st Airborne Division recruits was turning into a personal battle of honor by the arrogant noncommissioned officer. The more Gadgets easily dodged the other man's moves, the more determined the young sergeant became to maim him.

Crowley paused and sneered at Schwarz, then croaked, ''What's your nickname again? Gadgets?'' He gulped in a chestful of air. ''Is that because you like to play with toys?''

''Save your strength, Sarge,'' Schwarz replied, grateful for the opportunity to rest for a moment. ''I'd hate for you to have to stop because you ran out of breath.''

"Don't worry about me, Grandpa," the sergeant snapped. "Save your own ass."

"After I kick yours, sonny," Gadgets replied, smoothly stepping out of the way of a sudden attempt at a throat jab.

Bull Crowley had expected Chan Lao's civilian friend to fight back harder. But instead the man seemed content to let him do all the work. The sergeant knew he was coming perilously close to losing total control, so he forced himself to calm down.

He could feel the eerie silence around them. The fatigue-uniformed men who crowded around them on the remote athletic field watched quietly as the two slowly circled each other. Even without looking at them Crowley knew he was rapidly losing their respect.

Finally, snorting angrily, Crowley lunged again, directing his left foot at Schwarz's head. Gadgets pirouetted quickly, and the soldier's foot stabbed empty space. Falling to the ground, the furious noncom jumped up immediately and twisted so that he was facing his opponent again. This time he had murder in his eyes.

THE GAUNT-LOOKING MAN in his early forties, dressed in work boots, Levi's and a long-sleeved patterned work shirt, stood at the edge of the crowd, hypnotized as he watched the two bare-chested men square off. But it was the shorter of the two—the brown-haired man—who shocked him. He thought he was seeing a ghost from his past. For a moment Jimmy Joe Masters thought the late-August sun that scorched this

godforsaken Army post sixty miles north of Nashville
was playing tricks on his eyes.

The more he studied the man the more convinced he
became that he was watching the same wisecracking
Hermann Schwarz with whom he'd served in Vietnam. The guy's hair had some gray in it and was cut
shorter than he used to wear it, but it was still mostly
dark brown. His face looked harder, but it was still the
same face, and the same slender build.

Inchworm Masters smiled as he remembered
Schwarz's pet name for him. He knew it wasn't because of the slight difference in their heights. Jimmy
Joe had loved to inch his way along the ground when
he moved in on Vietcong snipers rather than rush at
them head-on and shouting, as some of the gung-ho
types on their reconnaissance team had done.

There was an air of maturity in Schwarz now that he
didn't remember when they'd served together in Vietnam. Back then Schwarz had been the lighthearted
member of the team, always making jokes about everything—the enemy, the land, politicians, the
weather, themselves. Sometimes it was only his wise-
cracks that kept the others going, even when they were
facing almost certain death.

Masters was sure it was the same man. But what was
Hermann Schwarz doing at Fort Campbell, standing
inside a ring of soldiers, wearing a pair of fatigue
pants and fighting with a huge, half-naked man who
looked ten years younger than him? He wouldn't have
been surprised if he'd run into the guy at MIT. But not
here, and not in a fight.

He remembered the nickname—Gadgets—the team
had given Schwarz. When the guy wasn't making some
smartass comment, he would fool around with the

sophisticated electronic gadgets shipped over from the States, somehow making them more effective. Now he was across the field inside a circle of fatigue-dressed soldiers, wrestling with a great bull of a man. But despite the difference in heights and builds, Gadgets seemed to be holding his own against the GI goliath.

Jimmy Joe would have liked to wait until the fight was over so that the two men could catch up on old times, but he had a long drive back to Arkansas. It would have been worth the long hours of hard driving if only his sister, Martha, hadn't been so stubborn. Now he had to go back and tell Judd Bushnell that she'd refused to sign over her share of their jointly owned land.

Masters decided to move closer and waste a few minutes watching Gadgets handle himself. He tapped the shoulder of a husky young soldier standing next to him. "Who's winning the wrestling match?"

The soldier turned and stared at him as if he were a creature from outer space. "They're not wrestling, mister. It's a martial-arts demonstration."

Judo? Of course. Jimmy Joe remembered where he'd seen those movements. Back in Nam and on television, whenever they showed an old Bruce Lee or Jackie Chan film.

The young soldier smiled as he glanced quickly into the circle. "I'd say Sarge Crowley was a little ahead. But that other guy isn't doing so bad, what with him being at least ten years older than the sarge."

SCHWARZ WAS TOO BUSY to look around and see who was watching him. Ben Crowley was a dangerous opponent. His body ached from the blows the sergeant had landed. For a moment he wondered if he'd chosen the wrong path to accomplish Chan Lao's goal.

Chan Lao's request for assistance, delivered through channels, had come at the best of times. The three Able Team warriors had come off a mission the past month that had almost cost them their lives. Gadgets had been the most seriously wounded of them, absorbing slugs that narrowly missed destroying his kidney and liver. Under orders from Hal Brognola, their chief, they were confined to Stony Man Farm until they were fully recovered.

Three weeks of doing nothing had brought them to the point where they were starting to behave like animals caged in a zoo. With permission from Brognola, and a toss of a coin, Gadgets had won the right to pack an overnight bag and call Chan Lao to tell him he was on the way.

The Oriental martial-arts expert had outlined his problem to Gadgets shortly after he arrived last night. "There is an Airborne sergeant on this base who could become a *judorka,* like yourself, but for one problem. His arrogance and pride. He must be taught a lesson in humility."

Gadgets had been surprised. "But you can do that better than any of us."

Chan Lao had nodded. "Naturally. But I am considered to be different by men like Sergeant Benjamin Crowley. You are the same as him. And since you are so much older, he will consider you unsuitable as a competitor."

Schwarz had smiled. "I think I can hold my own."

"Absolutely," the small Oriental had said. Then he'd added, "At least against him. However, you must lose to him, and in losing, you must win."

It was the typical conundrum Chan Lao had posed to his students over the years. He never explained how to accomplish the goal. And Gadgets had spent a sleepless night at the small motel located just outside the main gates to the military reservation, trying to figure out how to win against the sergeant by losing. He had been prepared to leave in the morning rather than try to solve the puzzle of Chan Lao's riddle.

What had stopped him was his respect for the diminutive martial-arts master. And the fact that Stony Man Farm, the complex hidden in Virginia's Shenandoah Valley, had begun to feel like a prison.

Like his two Able Team partners, Carl Lyons and Rosario Blancanales, Schwarz had trained with the Oriental martial-arts master and, over the years, had become a *judorka,* a near master in the strange mixture of kung fu, Kodokan judo and Korean karate that Chan Lao taught.

Chan had no idea what Gadgets did. He knew better than to ask. All he knew was that Gadgets and his colleagues were warriors whose lives might depend on how well they learned the unarmed-combat skills he taught.

Gadgets knew the elderly Oriental thought of the three of them as "barbarians." Rosario Blancanales, whose slick manner had earned him the nickname "Politician," used to try to charm the martial-arts master, but with little success. Carl Lyons, whose hard-nose attitude had earned him the dubious honor of "technically" being the team leader, and the nickname "Ironman," would bristle whenever Chan Lao called him a savage. Only he, Schwarz, didn't seem to care what the martial-arts master called him, as long as the *sensei* also helped him to improve his skills. After all, Gadgets used to tell the other two, Chan Lao felt the same about anyone who wasn't from his home village in China's Sinkiang Province.

CROWLEY KEPT STARING at the brown-haired man, concerned about why he wasn't fighting back as the sergeant suspected he could. All he seemed bent on doing was to turn the match into a comedy routine.

It was one thing when Chan Lao easily brushed away his attempts to pin him to the ground during their drills. Everyone knew that Orientals had a bag of dirty tricks they unleashed on their opponents to beat them.

He decided to use a leg hook, followed by an over-the-shoulder throw. Trying not to look too obvious, he moved diagonally toward his older opponent. Turning quickly, he lashed out his right leg, hoping to unbalance Schwarz. Gadgets seemed to move slowly, but before Crowley's leg could come close, he moved away again.

Exploding with fury, Crowley threw himself at Gadgets, concentrating his anger into his two massive arms. Finesse was no longer important. All that mattered was winning.

Gadgets started to pivot away, then let his body go limp as the massive man lifted him into the air with both hands, spun him around and threw him to the ground.

Schwarz lay still for a moment, tempted to jump up and teach Crowley what judo was really about, as he'd had to so many times in the past. He was getting tired of the game. The stitches that held his wound together were starting to tear.

He ached to end the contest with a simple neck chop. It would be so easy to use the angry soldier's steamroller energy against him.

Gadgets got up slowly. Crowley was standing, waiting for him to move, his face still flushed with anger. He watched as Schwarz glanced at Chan Lao, who shook his head slightly. The civilian stared back for a moment, then shrugged and turned back to face his adversary, lowering his arms to his side.

Crowley saw his opportunity and hurled his body at Gadgets before the man could defend himself. For a moment he wondered if he'd been drawn into a sucker move as the smiling man lightly jabbed his hand at Crowley's heart cavity.

It was too late to worry about that, though. Besides, he had hardly felt the blow. He forced his leg behind the visitor's right knee, twisted his arm and threw him to the ground.

Gadgets lay there, seemingly unable to get up. Then he raised a hand in surrender. "I guess I'm getting too old for this," he admitted.

"Help him up," Crowley ordered a young Airborne trainee. He waited until Schwarz was on his feet, then bowed. Gadgets returned the obligatory gesture that marked the end of a bout, then watched Crowley turn and walk away, accompanied by two admirers.

Gadgets brushed the sunbaked dirt from his Army fatigue pants and smiled at the dozen or so young men who still gawked at him.

Finally one of them asked, "You okay, Mr. Schwarz?"

"Fine, soldier," he said as he straightened. Then he turned and winked at the elderly Oriental, who nodded back, expressionless.

"Tried to hold back," Crowley loudly called out over his shoulder. The soldiers glared at the sergeant's back, then turned back to Gadgets. He didn't appear to be upset by his defeat.

"The sergeant sure landed some mean blows," the first soldier said. "Thought for a moment he was going to kill you."

"It looked that way, didn't it?"

"Crowley's as good a fighter as we got on this base," a soldier added with a Southern drawl.

"Maybe he'll learn something from today," Gadgets said, smiling.

"Sure stopped you from landing many blows," another man commented.

"Quality not quantity, son," Schwarz replied.

The soldiers looked at one another skeptically. The visitor now sounded like Sergeant Crowley.

One of them shook his head. "Better get our butts back to work before the sergeant chews our ass for goofing off," he announced to the others.

As the soldiers slowly walked away, Gadgets glanced at the fragile-looking Oriental standing next to him, then turned and looked across the field to where his recent opponent was proudly parading.

"You look worried," Chan commented.

"I might have hit him too hard," Gadgets replied, turning back to the Oriental. "I didn't come down to Fort Campbell to kill a man."

"You have not," Chan said calmly.

The two of them turned when they heard shouts across the field. Gadgets showed his concern again.

"Only a fool worries needlessly," Chan chastised as he led the way to where the soldiers were gathered.

Pushing through the crowd, they saw the huge sergeant lying unconscious on the ground.

"He just collapsed in the middle of a sentence," one of the two soldiers who had been walking with him said, looking stunned. "I better go get the medics."

"No!"

The soldier stared at Chan Lao.

"He will be in good health in a minute," the Oriental said.

"Yeah, but look at him lyin' there," the soldier protested.

Gadgets knelt beside the unconscious braggart, who started to move his head. Slowly Crowley opened his eyes and looked up at Schwarz. "I was just walking when I blacked out," he said, sounding confused. "It must have been the hot sun."

"No, it was not the sun." The voice was Chan's.

Gadgets and Bull turned and looked at the elderly Oriental, who was staring down at them coldly.

"Your heart could not sustain your false pride," Chan said. He turned to Gadgets. "Come. Follow me."

As they walked away, the martial-arts master looked straight ahead.

"You were right about my not having made a mistake," Gadgets admitted.

"Naturally," Chan acknowledged. "Have I told you about the master and the braggart?"

Gadgets smiled as he nodded. Chan had told him the story so many times that he could quote it from memory.

Chan proceeded as if he hadn't seen Gadgets's nod. "There was once an elderly master who was attacked by a young braggart for not acting subservient to him.

He beat him mercilessly. The master could only land a few light blows. Finally he lay still on the ground. The young braggart walked away, convinced he had destroyed the master's reputation and could now replace him. After he left, the elderly master got to his feet, seemingly unharmed, smiled at those who had witnessed the merciless assault and went home.

"Several days later the sister of the young braggart came to the elderly master's humble home and begged him to come with her. The young braggart had suddenly collapsed for no reason and was near death. The elderly master followed her and examined the young man, who was in a coma. He gently massaged the heart of the young braggart, and the man slowly came back to life. Then the master told the young braggart—"

"Your heart couldn't sustain your false pride," Gadgets interrupted.

"Good," Chan said. "I am pleased you remember something of what I have taught you. Actually, those were not his exact words. But it is the closest I can come to translating the true wisdom of the master into the language of the barbarians."

"But it wasn't his false pride," Gadgets said. "It was the master's carefully aimed heart thrust that almost killed him."

"Some secrets should not be shared," the elderly Oriental murmured.

Schwarz started to say something but was interrupted by a familiar voice behind him.

"Gadgets?"

The Able Team warrior turned and did a double take. "Jimmy Joe Masters?"

Jimmy Joe nodded and grinned as he held out his hand. "I wasn't sure, but I thought it was you getting your ass whupped back there."

2

The oil-stained yellow forklift groaned as it lifted the heavy wooden crates of military assault carbines and slowly moved them through the cavernous warehouse to where Pete Danko, the night warehouse manager, was standing.

"Get a move on, kid," Danko snarled. "I'm not planning to spend all night watching you get tomorrow's shipments set up."

Perched on the hard seat of the vehicle, Tim Hurwich was getting fed up with the gray-haired man's complaints. For the two weeks he'd been working here all the old man had done was find fault with everything he did.

"I'm doing the best I can," he snapped back at Danko. "I'm sweating bullets as it is."

"Then take off that ugly T-shirt," the older man replied. "There ain't no girls around to make fun of your body."

The two uniformed guards cradling automatic rifles broke out in laughter. Hurwich had almost forgotten they were around. One of them was sitting on a wooden chair inside the barred security bay, while the other leaned against the open side door that led to the loading dock. Before the night was over Hurwich promised himself he'd be the one laughing at them. Or at least their dead bodies.

Hurwich had been needled by Danko, the other warehouse workers and the security guards all day about his T-shirt. He'd bought it on a whim at a truck stop. It had a cartoon of a short man flexing exaggerated muscles next to a topless girl who pushed out her gigantic breasts above the words Muscle Beach. He knew he couldn't take off the T-shirt. Not in front of the security guards. The moment they saw the large outline of a hooded figure in front of a large white cross tattooed on his back, they'd know what he really was and yell for the cops. Just like they'd freak out if they knew he had a 10 mm Colt automatic hidden under his shirt.

Hurwich was proud of the design. It made him feel powerful, knowing that it was the tattoo every member of the most feared biker gang in the South wore— the symbol of the White Knights. There wasn't a black or foreigner who didn't shake when they heard that name.

He knew the gang trusted him, even though he'd only been with them a few months. Steen himself had given him the Colt and shown him how to use it.

Hurwich had gone through a series of hellish initiation tests to earn the right to wear the tattoo. This was his final test. If he passed it, Paul the Pig, the gang's tattoo artist, would fill in the outline with the gang's colors—black, green and bright yellow.

Tonight was supposed to be the end of the final test. That was what Steen had promised when Hurwich called the gang's Ozark Mountains hideout before he'd left his motel for work. But so far none of the gang had shown. Hurwich wondered if they were planning to back out of their promise and leave him stranded here.

Another thought raced through his mind. What if one of them had taken a fancy to the chopper Steen had made him leave behind? But Hurwich dismissed the thought immediately. He was sure they'd show up sometime before morning.

"How about me taking a short break, boss?" Hurwich asked.

"Not until you get the rest of those stacks lined up for the pickups."

"Aw, c'mon."

"Don't bitch to me. You're the one who begged me to let you pick up some extra money working overtime tonight. If it wasn't for your old man and me being friends for so many—"

"Okay," the long-haired young man interrupted. "Where do you want this stack to go?"

Danko pointed to a chalked outline of a rectangle on the concrete floor. "Right here where I wrote the shipping numbers."

Hurwich eased the forklift over the chalk marks and lowered the lift to the ground. The chain on the lift slipped, and the boxes made a loud noise as they landed, but Hurwich didn't care.

The slim young man on the forklift hadn't busted his back for Steen and the others to become a warehouseman. His old man had worked in the arsenal warehouse for thirty years before he'd died of a heart attack, and all it had gotten his mother was a lousy little pension check every month.

In a way he was grateful to his dead father. Even with the faked military records Steen had somehow gotten, he wouldn't have been hired so quickly if

Danko and the old man hadn't been friends for so many years.

The forklift stopped, and Danko, who was in charge of the work detail, checked the stamped numbers on the crates against a manifest he held in his hand. Satisfied that the numbers matched, the supervisor pointed to where he wanted the crates placed.

"Watch what the hell you're doing!" Danko shouted angrily. "Them ain't Tinkertoys you're bouncing."

"I know what they are," Hurwich answered wearily. The markings on the crates were self-explanatory. The crates were filled with CAR-15 assault carbines and ammunition. As best he could calculate, he'd already moved more than five thousand guns and at least two hundred thousand rounds of ammunition.

"You bounce them the wrong way and you could blow us all to hell," Danko added.

"Lay off, Pete," the guard inside the security bay called out. "You gotta load these babies with ammo before they can cause trouble."

Hurwich smiled to himself. Before morning the White Knights would have enough guns and ammo to raise a lot of hell, all thanks to his hard work. Of course, most of the guns would be sold, but he was sure they'd keep a few crates for themselves.

"Get the next load so we can start thinking about going home," Danko said, letting the fatigue show in his voice as he worked his way past the forklift.

Load after load, Hurwich absorbed the verbal abuse the older man kept dumping on him. As the hours passed, the two other warehousemen who were working overtime waved good-night as they left.

"Hey, Hurwich," one of them called out as he let the guard near the door go through the formality of checking his ID badge, "that babe on your T-shirt. Can you make her knockers wiggle?"

The other warehouseman laughed. "Stand you a beer before you head home," he told the first man.

"You're on," the wisecracker said. He turned to Hurwich. "Hey, join us when you're through and we'll see if we can help you get your girlfriend excited." Before Hurwich could snap a reply, the man slipped through the door.

Hurwich took a deep breath, then turned to Danko. "What's the big rush about these guns, boss?" He knew he was less angry at the comments from the two men who had departed than he was at the still-missing Steen. But he also knew it was dangerous to get mad at Steen, even in his head.

Steen was like nobody he'd ever met before. He stood six foot five. His shaven head and short black beard made his deep-set eyes seem even more penetrating than they were. Some of the guys in the gang swore Steen was able to read their thoughts.

Hurwich didn't believe in black-magic hokum. But it wasn't smart to take chances. He had seen Steen take a dislike to someone without provocation and twist the man's head with his thick hands until the guy's neck was broken.

"Replacements for the Pine Bush Arsenal," Danko finally replied. "They had to ship their inventory off to Columbia. Something to do with the President promising guns to help knock off the drug barons down there."

Hurwich nodded. Privately he was rooting for the drug dealers. Without the good stuff they shipped,

most of the gang's parties would have been pretty
boring. There was no way to get the gang's mamas
turned on to a wild night of partying without an am-
ple supply of coke. Especially Mary Ellen, who had
been given to him by Steen.

"Now get those six crates from the security bay and
put them here," Danko ordered, pointing at a chalked
outline he was drawing.

Wearily the frustrated younger man spun the forklift around and headed for the security area.

"And be damn careful with them. They're special," the older man shouted.

The guard pressed a switch and let the gate slide
open. "You think it's smart to take these crates out
before the special truck comes to pick them up, Pete?"

"I was assuming both of you were going to be on
duty all night," Danko replied sarcastically. "You
afraid you can't handle any big bad men who try to
steal them?"

Embarrassed, the guard stepped aside and let Hurwich roll his vehicle into the barred area.

Carefully Hurwich positioned his forklift next to the
stack of wooden crates and worked the teeth of the
vehicle under the stack. Then he turned to Danko.
"What's so special about these boxes?"

"None of your damn business, kid. Just move them
over here."

Hurwich couldn't figure out the meaning of the
numbers and words printed on the sides of the six
crates. The only words that made any sense were Top
Security and Experimental.

He eased his foot off the brake and started moving
out of the security bay when he heard the muffled

sound of bikes. Trying to hide his growing excitement, Hurwich forced himself to remain calm.

"What's taking you so damn long?" Danko snarled.

"I don't want to shake up whatever's in these—"

"Any of you hear that weird noise outside?" the guard near the door interrupted.

"What noise?" Hurwich asked, forcing himself to look puzzled.

"Yeah," the guard in the security bay answered. He pressed the button to slide the heavy door shut, then stepped out of the enclosed area to join the other armed man.

Hurwich heard the rapid sequence of explosions. Steen and the others had arrived! He hoped they'd remembered to bring a truck big enough to carry out all the crates he'd moved.

"Hit the alarm!" Danko shouted to the guard at the door.

Hurwich jumped from the forklift and yanked out his Colt. Facing the door guard, he pumped two shots into the man's chest. With a muzzle energy twice that of a .45 ACP, the hollowpoints tore two huge craters in the man's chest. As the guard slid down the wall, Hurwich spun around and pumped two hollowpoints at the second guard.

A fountain of blood spurted from the uniformed man's neck and left eye as he tried unsuccessfully to lift his M-16 to his shoulder.

Danko stared at the fallen bodies, then turned to Hurwich. "What the hell are you..."

Hurwich stopped his question with a 3-shot burst. But the burst of rage continued to pour through the young gang-member's body. He aimed the weapon at

the still body of the hated foreman and yanked the
trigger again. The loud echo of metal on metal enraged him. He dropped the now-empty gun and
yanked the M-16 from the hands of the dead security
guard.

Standing over Danko, he pressed the rifle against the
gasping man's ear and squeezed the trigger. He shuddered for a moment as he watched bits of soft brain
tissue and cartilage shoot out from the ruptured head
cavity. Then he ran over to where the other guard was
slumped against the wall and pointed the M-16 at the
body.

"Hey, Hawkeye, he's dead. Don't go wasting
ammo."

Hurwich recognized the voice and turned toward it
to see Steen standing in the open doorway, grinning.

As he always did in the gang leader's presence,
Hurwich moved away from him as if he were afraid to
get too close. There was something unsettling about
Steen. His dark, deep-set eyes seemed to have a life of
their own. Hurwich wondered if, as some gang members claimed, Steen could kill a person just by staring
at him.

Steen was a huge man, weighing at least three hundred pounds. His massive body, which seemed to
spread in all directions, dominated every place he
went. As usual he was dressed entirely in black, except for the gang's symbol, which was stenciled in
white on the huge T-shirt he wore.

Behind him Hurwich recognized Snake and Dirtbag, Steen's two lieutenants. Right behind them was
Bagman, the kid Steen treated like his own kid
brother.

Like himself, Bagman was younger than most of the others in the gang. What made him important to Steen was that he seemed to know exactly where to find drugs no matter where they were. It was as if Bagman could smell who was dealing drugs, even in the middle of nowhere.

"Good work, kid," the huge man said, dropping his thick hand around Hurwich's shoulder. "What've we got?"

Hurwich pointed at the stacks of crates. "Those are all brand-new CAR-15s." Then he pointed at another row of crates. "And those are filled with the newest ammo for them." Hurwich saw a truck backing up to the loading dock. "Nice truck."

"Almost brand-new," Bagman replied. "It's even got a CB."

"Guy who owned it won't be bullshitting with other truckers where he's gone," Dirtbag added with a cynical laugh.

Steen turned to his men. "Let's get these crates loaded and blow this pop stand." He looked at the forklift. "And load this thing, too. We can use it later."

"I got us a bonus," Hurwich told the gang leader. He pointed at the stack of crates he'd moved from the security bay. "Some kind of experimental weapons. They were supposed to go up to Aberdeen for field-testing."

"Good. We can talk about them later," Steen said.

"Yeah," Snake added. "We ain't gonna be alone for long."

"I'm not sure what's in them, but they're top secret."

Sixteen more White Knights poured into the warehouse, rushing past the bleeding bodies as if they were invisible.

Steen turned to the rest of the gang. "Let's get the stuff loaded up. We got a customer with hard cash ready to pay for them."

Hurwich decided this was a good time to remind the gang leader that he had passed his final initiation test. "I guess the next step is for me to get the gang colors filled in on my tattoo," he said proudly.

Steen looked disappointed as he slipped a hand to his waistband. Swiftly he pulled out a long, slim stiletto and jabbed it into Hurwich's belly, pushing it upward until the entrails popped through the stomach wall.

Hurwich was stunned. "Why?" he whispered.

"Because you failed the test, kid," the giant man said as he pulled the bloody stiletto out and let Hurwich fall to the concrete floor. "You're supposed to let me tell you that you passed."

He turned to the rest of the gang members, who gaped at him. "The cops would have figured he was the inside man if he came with us. This way they'll have a hell of a time trying to find out who did it."

The gang members grinned. As always, Steen made good sense.

Steen turned to Bagman. "Get that nose of yours working. We're gonna need us a mess of happy powder as soon as we get this stuff delivered."

Bagman grinned. "We gonna party after we make the delivery?"

"Soon as you get us some stuff."

"Just tell me where we're heading and I'll make some calls."

Steen liked the kid. But he was still too new with the gang to be completely trusted with their destination. "You know anybody along 285 with some high-quality blow we can pick up on the way?"

"Soon as we get to a pay phone I'll make a few calls."

Steen slapped him on the shoulder. "Don't disappoint me, kid."

"Have I ever, Steen?"

Steen grinned. "Not yet." He turned to the rest of the gang. "Let's get the stuff loaded onto the trucks. We got a long way to drive before we can collect our money and have us a party."

3

Gadgets stared through the window of the coffee shop at the sparse traffic moving along Kentucky State Highway 104. Freshly showered and wearing a pair of jeans and a thin windbreaker to hide the modified Colt Government Model .45 he was carrying, he could still feel the dull ache caused by Bull Crowley's punches. As he sipped his coffee, Jimmy Joe Masters rambled on endlessly, recalling in great detail their adventures in Vietnam.

Outside, Schwarz saw a quartet of tough Airborne soldiers driving by slowly. Each man wore the patch of the famous Screaming Eagles—the 101st Airborne Division—on his sleeve. From what he'd heard they were probably heading for classes at Austin Peay State University, the small school located in Clarksville, Tennessee, where many of the flying soldiers worked on earning college credits.

As tough as they looked, they were a far cry from the soldiers he'd known fifteen years ago, men who would have spent any spare time they had drinking, chasing available females or fighting. The military had certainly changed, Gadgets thought. For the better, he decided, if the four young soldiers were a sample.

He could still remember the excitement Politician and he had felt back in Vietnam when they saw the

Screaming Eagles fall from the sky to assist their group in a battle. It had been many years ago, but the memory was still fresh. The two of them had brushed aside certain death more than once, laughing about it later.

Their friendship had survived the pain and hopelessness of their deep penetrations into enemy territory and had lasted right up to the present. Their special relationship had broadened to include Carl Lyons, the street-hardened LAPD cop, when all three were invited to join Hal Brognola, a tough, seasoned Justice Department agent who was putting together an antiterrorist group called Able Team.

As Brognola had explained to them, Able Team would operate outside the normal rules that other law-enforcement agencies had to follow. At the will of the President, they could use any means they had to neutralize or eliminate any individual or group who threatened the security of the country. The freedom to operate as necessary carried with it the burden of never being acknowledged officially.

Thrust into a dark world most people never knew existed, the three Able Team warriors could only depend on one another for survival. In a world contaminated by politics and self-interest, where the lives of innocent people were only numbers to be reported in newspapers as casualties, Able Team functioned as an undercover "sterilizer," eradicating the vermin who threatened to pull down civilization.

Gadgets was glad to escape the violence temporarily. He was in no hurry to rush back to Stony Man Farm. But he did miss the two hell-raisers with whom he'd kicked mud in the face of the devil. He began to wonder what they were doing to spice up the inactivity at Stony Man Farm.

Knowing Pol, he could imagine the smooth-talking Hispanic thumbing through his thick black book of attractive women, looking for a companion to help him escape boredom. And Ironman? Probably the former college football player was pumping iron in the gym of the secluded compound the three called home. Or challenging Cowboy Kissinger, himself a former football lineman, to a wrestling or martial-arts bout—anything to keep his body ready for battle.

Just then Joe's voice broke into his reverie. "Remember ol' Sam Mercurio?"

Gadgets turned and nodded, hoping Jimmy Joe would finally stop talking so that he could hitch a plane ride back to Stony Man Farm.

"Remember when that crazy ol' coot found those two VC hiding in the tall grass and decided to get himself a medal by wiping them out single-handedly? Poor dumb bastard got himself blown away by the other ten VC who were hiding behind a tree." Masters's eyes misted over as he laughed uncontrollably at the memory.

Gadgets stared at the man, wondering what had twisted him since they'd parted company in Vietnam. There was a deadness in Jimmy Joe's eyes that made Schwarz uncomfortable.

As Masters babbled on about people who had died a long time ago and events that Schwarz didn't want to remember, Gadgets looked around the coffee shop. Except for the waitress and a young girl behind the cash register, there were few customers. Two booths away two young men sat facing each other. Both of them wore baggy jeans and thin golf jackets over T-shirts despite the heat outside.

Gadgets studied them carefully. There was something familiar about them. Schwarz had seen the expressions in their eyes before—cold, unemotional, dead. Every thug he'd ever stared at on the wrong side of a gun barrel had had the same look.

One of them noticed that Schwarz was studying them and stared back. Gadgets turned back to the gaunt man sitting across the table from him. Jimmy Joe continued to ramble on, oblivious to anyone or anything except his nostalgia. Each anecdote was accompanied by another pull on the aluminum flask he carried in his hip pocket.

"That calls for another drink," Jimmy Joe decided yet again. He reached into his hip pocket and took out the flask, which he offered to Gadgets, who waved it away. "Best sippin' whiskey in the South," Masters announced, smacking his lips at the taste. "Remember that hooch I made in Da Nang?" Masters shook his head at the memory. "Did the best I could with canned corn, but it never did turn out. Put two guys in the hospital with gut poisonin'." He slapped the Formica table in the booth as he chuckled at the thought. "Yeah, that was a time of heroes. Our days of glory," he said, finally relaxing. "My great-great-grandpa would've been real proud of me."

Gadgets smiled grimly at the observation. "He would have been among the few. As I remember it, not too many people thought of us as heroes back then."

"He would have. A full-blooded Cherokee he was. Real fighter. Killed himself a mess of settlers and soldiers up in North Carolina before they finally stopped him. Must have been close to seventy when they ambushed him."

"What happened to you after I left Nam?" Schwarz asked.

"Decided to re-up and get me a few more VC. Figured there wasn't much to look forward to back home. Both parents were dead. And my sister, Martha, had run off to attend college. No kin left, so there was nobody around to take care of the land Grandpa had left her and me. Not that there was much you could do with it. Mostly wooded and hilly. Sorrier than a sheep tick in a tar barrel far as farmin' went."

"So you reenlisted?"

Jimmy Joe shook his head. "Wouldn't take me back. Said it was time for me to go home and get some rest."

"Rest?"

"Shipped me back to the States and shoved me into a hospital. Claimed I was suffering from some kind of trauma." He made a face. "What do those damn doctors know? Just 'cause they found some mementos in my duffel bag I wanted to bring home from Nam."

"What kind of souvenirs?"

"A couple of scalps like my great-great-grandpappy used to take. Packed them in a small bottle of sour mash so they wouldn't stink."

As sick as he felt at the revelations, Gadgets felt compassion for the man with whom he'd served for three years. So many had cracked at the sight of the wanton killing by both sides. How many dead children and women could anyone look at without falling apart?

Gadgets remembered how close he had come to falling apart toward the end. Few had made it home resembling the men they were when they first arrived in Nam. "When did they release you, Jimmy Joe?"

"'Bout seven years ago. My sister, Martha, came and got me and took me back to Grandpa's place. I thought me and she would try to make something of the land. But, no, she decided to join the damn Army. So I come up here to talk to her about an idea I have."

"Is she stationed here?"

Masters nodded. "With the 101st Airborne."

Schwarz showed his surprise. "Paratrooper?"

"She's got some kind of job running the office." He looked disgusted. "They wouldn't let a woman fight with them. Not someone as tiny as her." He took out his wallet and found a photograph of the two of them taken the last time Martha had come home on leave.

Schwarz studied the picture. The setting was in front of a small wooden house. Gadgets suspected it was where Jimmy Joe lived. The woman in the picture was half a head shorter than her brother. Despite her short hair and the Army fatigues she wore, he could see she was a natural beauty. Even in the small photograph he could see her large eyes, staring wide and questioning right into the camera. He could easily imagine her standing her ground with a group of tough, battle-hardened Airborne soldiers.

Jimmy Joe saw the expression on Gadgets's face. Like most men who saw her picture, it was obvious he thought she was pretty. What he didn't know was that she hated men. She'd been like that since she was fifteen and their parents had died. Something had twisted inside her. But Jimmy Joe had no idea what it was.

He hated the woman—Loretta—with whom she shared an apartment off base. Loretta looked more like a heavyweight wrestler than a woman, and she shared Martha's dislike for men.

He wouldn't have cared less what his sister had become if Grandpa hadn't left the twenty thousand acres of wooded land to both of them. But as half owner Martha could veto what he was planning to do with the land.

He would have kept brooding about her if Gadgets hadn't asked, "You getting a pension?"

Masters pushed Martha from his mind and nodded. "And I make a little money on the side."

"Doing what?"

Jimmy Joe started giggling, and fondled his hip flask.

"Brewing that corn whiskey you've got in that flask?"

"That's one of the things I'm doin'."

Gadgets didn't want to push the other man. If what he was doing was illegal, it was up to the police to arrest him.

Masters looked at him. "What are y'all doin' down here at Campbell?"

Gadgets explained about the invitation.

"You still in the Army?" Jimmy Joe asked warily.

"I own a part interest in an international security-consulting firm," Schwarz explained.

"You always was a smart one. Got you some fancy clients?"

"We do all right." Pol and Gadgets had set up the consulting firm several years ago to occupy their time between Able Team assignments. The day-to-day operations of the Minneapolis-based firm were supervised by Pol's sister, Toni.

"What kind of stuff do you do for them?"

"Anything that involves their safety or the continued safe operations of their business," Gadgets replied, quoting from the sales brochure Toni Blancanales had written for the firm.

"Somebody threatens them with murder and you come runnin'?"

Gadgets smiled. Several more violent versions of that specific example had occurred in the past. "Something like that."

"We should keep in touch," Masters said.

"You have somebody trying to kill you, Jimmy Joe?"

Masters thought of how Judd Bushnell would respond to the news and shuddered slightly. "No, not me," he answered rapidly. "Who'd have any reason to kill me?"

Gadgets stared into his friend's dead eyes. "Then why'd you ask?"

Jimmy Joe answered quickly. "So you can send me some of your clients when we get the place set up for hunting."

Gadgets looked puzzled. This was the first time Masters had mentioned anything about setting up a hunting preserve. "When and where is this all going to happen?"

"Soon. On the twenty thousand acres Grandpa left us. I came up here to discuss the details with Martha."

She'd rejected his idea, even after he'd driven more than ten hours, all the way from Gobbler Station, to discuss it with her in person.

"If we turn the whole place into a private hunting preserve, I can get all them wealthy hunters to come down and try their hand at shooting a wild boar," he'd explained, just as Judd had instructed him to.

She'd almost chewed his head off from the moment he'd opened his mouth with the idea. "Grandpa didn't leave us the land to have a bunch of fat, chicken-livered hunters running wild with their guns and shooting at everything that moves," Martha had yelled. "If it's not illegal, it's immoral."

"Hell, everything Grandpa did was illegal," Jimmy Joe had said, trying to reason with her. "Remember the whiskey still he had hidden in the woods? Hell, it's still standing."

"If you want to get rid of the land, let's give it to the federal government to add on to the national wildlife refuge next door."

"Give it away?" Jimmy Joe remembered how stunned he'd been at her suggestion. Give away thousands of acres? He hated to think what Judd Bushnell's reaction would be to her suggestion, if he ever found the courage to tell him.

Martha had suddenly announced that she had to get back to her office. "I've got to go." She'd looked at the worried expression he couldn't keep off his face and patted his shoulder. "Tell you what. I've got some time owed me. I'll come home this weekend and we can talk about it some more," she'd offered before leaving.

Gadgets coughed, took out his wallet and handed Masters a business card. Jimmy Joe was getting spacier by the moment. He seemed to drift off into his own world with increasing frequency.

The man studied the card carefully, as if he were having difficulty making out the words. As he continued to stare at it, he wondered how Gadgets could help him. Getting customers? That was much later. With Martha? He might be able to help him convince her.

No, it was in handling Judd that he needed help. Jimmy Joe was nervous about having to face Bushnell with bad news. Having someone like Gadgets around might convince Judd to give him some more time to work on Martha. Especially with the large automatic tucked in Gadgets's waistband that Jimmy Joe had seen when Gadgets's windbreaker opened momentarily as they sat down.

"How about you coming down and getting some firsthand experience at wild boar hunting?" Masters asked.

Gadgets had called Stony Man Farm before he'd faced Crowley that morning. But there was still no action on the horizon. Although he had no desire to kill an animal needlessly, he dreaded facing the tedium of hanging around the complex with nothing to do.

"When?"

"How 'bout right now?"

"You mean drive back with you?"

"Sure. Why not? I've got me a house with extra rooms. And Martha is coming down for the weekend."

He'd have to clear it with Hal Brognola. But unless something had come up since this morning, spending a few days at Jimmy Joe's place sounded a lot more exciting than being bored. Especially if the woman in the photograph was also going to be there. He stood and reached into his pocket for change. "Let me make a call first."

Jimmy Joe watched Gadgets walk over to the phone booth in the back of the coffee shop. The man he had known back in Nam had changed dramatically. The lighthearted kid had become a man. Somehow Schwarz had become stronger and more self-confident. And the Colt Government Model .45 he'd seen tucked into a waistband holster suggested that Gadgets was more than he claimed to be. Jimmy Joe hoped he was enough to make Judd think twice before getting violent.

He knew Bushnell was expecting him to come back with the signed agreement, and he was worried about disappointing the sheriff. A disappointed Judd Bushnell was someone he didn't want to have to face. He'd seen how the stocky man sometimes reacted to disappointment in the past. Like when Tom Milder, one of his deputies, had announced he'd made all the money he needed and was quitting. Judd had gotten that too-sweet smile on his face, patted old Tom on the back and wished him luck. Only nobody had ever seen Tom Milder after that. He had vanished suddenly, like a jug of corn whiskey at a country party.

Jimmy Joe didn't want to disappear like Milder. Judd had a good thing going—buying up guns from hijackers and storing them until they found a buyer who was willing to pay three to four times what they'd paid for the weapons. And he always cut in Jimmy Joe for a share—as a sign of appreciation for letting him use his land to hide them.

The best thing about Judd's business was that there were no cops to bother them. Jimmy Joe laughed at his private joke. Sheriff Judd Bushnell was the law, and his deputies were all in on the deal.

Glancing across the coffee shop, he could see Gadgets finishing his conversation. Schwarz hung up the receiver, turned and smiled at him. Judd was sure his luck was improving. With ol' Gadgets along for the ride, he was safe.

Sliding out of the booth, Masters moved toward Schwarz, just as a burst of gunfire shattered the large glass window where he'd been sitting.

Gadgets's Colt .45 automatic cleared leather as he dropped to the floor. Rolling at an angle from the shattered window, he saw two forms spraying steady bursts of hot lead from the AK-47s they brandished as they charged toward the coffee shop.

The stench of gunfire permeated the small restaurant. Behind him Schwarz heard the sole waitress scream as a ricocheting slug drilled into her throat. There was another scream from the young woman who worked as cashier, but there wasn't time to check if either one was dead. Gadgets pointed his automatic in front of him and squeezed off two shots at the nearest hit man. The first round slammed into the guy's face, shoving him backward. The second tore into his chest.

Swinging his gun at the second thug, the Able Team Commando pulled the trigger three times in rapid succession. The heavyset punk spun around before he could fire the automatic rifle. He fell facedown on the front hood of the gray vehicle.

A sudden sense of danger from behind saved Schwarz's life. He threw himself into a shoulder roll and spun around just as one of the young men in the booth pumped searing rounds of Teflon-coated rounds from the 9 mm Glock automatic in his hand.

Jimmy Joe screeched and threw himself under the table. Gadgets pushed his Colt out toward the new assailant and fired up toward his chin. The young punk's face exploded in a shower of bloody tissue.

The second punk had revealed the massive Desert Eagle he'd hidden under his thin jacket. He jumped to his feet and stared down at Gadgets, hate pouring from his eyes as he began to squeeze the trigger. "Die, bastard," he shouted as he sprayed lead at Schwarz.

Anticipating the path of the huge slugs, Gadgets rolled in the opposite direction. The tiles exploded as lead from the powerful handgun drilled into them. There was no time for Gadgets to aim. He pointed the Colt at the thug's wide chest and fired two shots in rapid succession.

The expression in the would-be killer's face didn't change as the hollowpoints tore through his breastbone and exploded into dozens of searing fragments inside. Even as blood oozed from the huge cavity created by Gadgets's Colt, the killer tried to fire back.

Throwing himself at the young punk, Schwarz fired again, this time at the would-be killer's stomach. The impact of the two rounds pushed the man backward even while he was squeezing the trigger of his gun. A pattern of scorched holes appeared in the ceiling tiles as the man fell back onto a Formica table, then slid to the ground and became still.

Gasping from the thick, acrid cloud of burned cordite, Gadgets struggled to his feet and looked around the demolished room. Jimmy Joe was groaning on the floor, grasping his forehead. He looked up at Schwarz, pulled his palm away and held it up for the Able Team warrior to see. It was red. "I been hit," he groaned.

Gadgets glanced at the gaunt man writhing on the floor. He could see the long, open slice along Masters's scalp. Painful but not dangerous. He helped

Masters to his feet and handed him a paper napkin from a nearby table.

Slowly surveying the damage, Gadgets saw the waitress slumped across the counter, a jagged hole in the side of her head. Without having to examine her he knew she was dead.

Moving carefully around the four fallen attackers, he kept his Colt .45 pointed at the bodies, just in case one of them was feigning death. He used his foot to push the AK-47s and the handguns out of reach before he knelt and felt the killers' necks. They were dead.

Who were they, Gadgets wondered, and what were they after? He looked at Jimmy Joe. "Anybody want to kill you?"

Masters was sitting in a booth, trying to stop the superficial cut from bleeding with the blood-soaked napkin. Still shaking, he shook his head. "Nobody I can think of. How about you?"

Gadgets knew a lot of people who would have liked him dead, but most of them were dead themselves, killed in battles with Able Team. No one came to mind. Even if someone was gunning for him, how would they know he was in Kentucky when he hadn't known himself until thirty-six hours ago?

His musings were interrupted by the wail of police cars rushing up to the building. Six state troopers wearing Kevlar vests and led by a sergeant charged the coffee shop, holding their assault rifles ready to fire as they jumped from their vehicles.

Gadgets turned and faced them as they entered the coffee shop. Glaring furiously, the six officers shoved their weapons into his face.

"You," the sergeant, a thick, grizzled veteran in his late forties, shouted, "drop your weapon and put your hands up."

Schwarz wasn't carrying one of the special identification cards Brognola sometimes issued when they were on assignments. Carefully he laid his gun on the floor under the watchful eyes of the troopers, then stood up again.

The cashier stood up from where she'd been hiding behind the counter. She pointed at Jimmy Joe. "That one was with him," she said fearfully.

The sergeant turned to the others and pointed at Masters. "Search him for any weapons, then cuff 'em both." Turning back to Schwarz, he snarled, "We should have killed you on the spot. Would have been a lesson to you damn drug pushers to stay outta Kentucky."

Drug dealers? Gadgets wondered if the two men at the other table, and the pair of thugs who'd attacked the coffee shop, were rival pushers. Just his luck to get in the middle of a narcotics war without any warning.

4

Stony Man Farm had been covered in fog for the past twelve hours. Even the naturally-carved face of Stony Man Mountain, which dominated the Shenandoah Valley, had vanished in the thick white mist.

With zero visibility the entire staff of the clandestine complex was ordered to stay inside the electronic fence that encircled the perimeter. Even the dirt jogging track that followed the inner circumference of the fence was now off-limits, as Pol Blancanales was told by one of the armed guards when he came out to use it.

Disgusted, he turned and strode toward the entrance to the gymnasium. He was full of stress from the lack of action and had to find some way to get rid of it.

Inside the large basement gym Carl Lyons kept himself busy pumping iron. Pol entered and saw the muscular ex-cop raise his thick arms and grab the metal bar above his head. There were large metal weights locked on both ends.

Lyons's old gray sweatshirt was stained with perspiration from his efforts. Sweat had even begun to stain the elastic band of the track shorts he wore. Grunting as he forced the bar up from its resting place, Lyons steadied the heavy mass of metal over his head, counting out loud as he did. "One, two, three, four, five, six, seven, eight, nine, ten."

"Hey, that's okay, Ironman. Tomorrow we start on division."

Without losing his concentration the sweating weight lifter carefully lowered the bar back into the support stand, took several deep breaths, then slid out from the contraption and glared at Blancanales. "That was a pretty stupid move," he snapped. "I could have dropped the weights."

"You wouldn't have lost much if they'd landed on your head," Pol replied sarcastically.

Lyons jumped to his feet and moved angrily toward the silver-haired Hispanic. "You wanna put your fists where your big mouth is?"

"Anytime, old buddy. Anytime," Blancanales replied, clenching his fists.

"Wrestling, boxing, karate? You name it."

"All three, plus kick boxing," Pol said.

"You're on. You set the rules."

"First man unconscious loses," Blancanales decided.

"Who starts it?"

"Me," Pol snarled, twisting his body and throwing the edge of his right toe at Lyons's head.

Ironman stepped aside quickly and avoided the move. "No holds barred?"

"None. Do your worst."

Lyons set his thick arms in front of his face and rushed the other man, stopping suddenly and ramming his left hand into Pol's side. Blancanales grunted as he felt the pain of the impact and wrapped his arms around Ironman's neck. Slipping a foot behind Lyons's leg, he attempted to throw him to the ground.

Ironman struggled with the vise-like grip on his throat, trying to ram his fists into the body behind him. In a desperate attempt to free himself, Lyons threw himself onto the wooden floor, carrying Pol with him. Rolling around the floor, Pol tightened his grip on Ironman's neck while the blond ex-cop kept kicking at the Hispanic's groin.

Almost equally matched in skill and energy, the two Able Team warriors exchanged punches, arm holds and blocks, interspersed with savage kicks. Each landed painful blows, none powerful enough to incapacitate the other. In fighting style, as in his personal life, Blancanales was a sleek racing car, dodging, twisting and parrying, while Ironman acted like an eighteen-wheeler, throwing his considerable strength into every move.

After forty-five minutes of constant combat, Blancanales began to breathe more heavily. Lyons paused in his assault. Gulping air, he asked, "Getting tired? We can quit anytime it gets too much for you, old man."

"Only after you beg me to stop," Pol gasped, and forced his body to move forward toward Ironman.

They heard a shrill whistle from behind them. "Time out!" a male voice bellowed.

Both of them turned and saw Aaron "Bear" Kurtzman leaning forward in his wheelchair and shaking his head at them. "Don't you guys know fighting isn't nice?" he cracked. Pol was about to make a comment when the burly man held up his hand to stop him. "If you say something nasty, I won't give you the news."

Blancanales calmed down. "What news?"

"Jack Grimaldi called down here to say that if you still want to ride to Washington, you better get your ass in gear. Fog's lifting, but it's going to close in again in an hour."

Pol loosened his grip on Lyons's throat. "To be continued." He struggled to his feet and wrapped an arm around Blancanales's shoulder. "You okay?"

"As okay as you can be after you've been hit by a ten-ton truck," Pol replied, smiling weakly.

"I must be slowing down. You used to say 'like a twenty-ton truck,'" Ironman laughed and looked at Blancanales. "So what are you planning to do up in Washington?"

"My favorite sport," Pol replied, grinning, as they walked out of the gymnasium. "Come to my room. I'll tell you about her while I'm changing."

LYONS SLOUCHED in the chair and watched Pol studying himself in the full-length mirror in his room as he carefully adjusted the knot on his patterned blue silk necktie. He kept manipulating the cravat until it was perfectly centered on the cream silk shirt. Finally satisfied, he straightened the thin wool beige jacket.

As Blancanales turned around to show off his newest sartorial acquisition, Lyons broke out into laughter. "For someone whose ancestors were wetbacks, you are one slick-looking dude," he said admiringly.

The olive-skinned man smiled, taking no offense at the reference to his ancestors. What Ironman had said was true. His grandfather had come to the United States as a migrant farm worker, slipping across the border illegally to earn enough money to support the large family he'd left behind in Mexico. "Humble beginnings lead to great futures. At least to the women I have honored with my company,'' he said.

"Who's the lucky girl?" Lyons asked.

"A fascinating *señorita* I met when I visited my family in Los Angeles last year. She's in Washington on business and dropped me a note about wanting to get together.''

"She got a friend?"

Ironman's question took Blancanales by surprise. Of the three of them, Lyons was usually the least interested in the opposite sex. Some tragic past experiences had made him wary of pursuing any new romantic involvements.

One thing bothered Blancanales about sharing dates with Ironman, though. Many women, especially those who had no exposure to violence, were put off by his bulk and his bluntness.

Pol decided that if Theresa could find a friend for him, he'd suggest Lyons try to act more sophisticated on the trip up to Washington. But who would someone like Theresa Morales know in Washington who could stand spending an evening with Ironman?

Theresa was an assistant professor of ancient history at USC whom Blancanales had met on his last visit to his huge family. Their meeting in the university faculty dining room over coffee had been uncomfortable at first, but Pol had slowly charmed the conservative professor into having dinner with him. The dinner extended into many dinners and, before he was summoned back to Stony Man Farm, into her bedroom for more intimate pleasures.

Now she was coming east to deliver a series of lectures at Georgetown University. The elegantly dressed man decided to describe Ironman and his manner in detail and let her decide if she wanted to call someone to join them. He wasn't about to ruin what could be a memorable evening by his desire to solve Lyons's lonely hearts problem.

"I can call and ask her," Pol said, then looked at him. "If you've got something else you can wear."

Lyons put on a hurt face and looked down at what he was wearing. His six-foot-plus frame was covered with an eye-searing Hawaiian shirt hanging loosely over a pair of baggy, worn jeans. "Planning to go someplace too fancy for this?"

"Almost anyplace except maybe a greasy spoon is too fancy for what you're wearing."

Reluctantly Lyons lifted himself out of the chair and conceded defeat. "I'll see what I've got if she can line up somebody."

"Hurry it up," Pol said. "You heard Bear about the fog."

"Movie afterward?"

"I hope something more intimate and interesting."

Lyons weighed Pol's reply. "I can live with that. Anything's better than hanging around this funeral home." He lumbered to the door. "Be back in a few minutes."

As Pol dialed the hotel where Theresa was staying, he sympathized with how Lyons felt. He was just as bored. They had been out of action for several weeks. Each day they had hung around the headquarters complex, hoping for the call from Hal Brognola that meant they were back in action.

John "Cowboy" Kissinger, the team's armorer, had taken off yesterday for a look at some experimental weapons that were being tested at the Aberdeen Proving Grounds, while Kurtzman, the resident computer genius, had buried himself in devising more efficient ways to tap into the restricted computer systems of various government agencies.

When Theresa answered the phone, Blancanales explained the situation. Even with his brutally honest description of Ironman, Theresa thought she knew one woman—a friend from her college days in California—who might enjoy an evening with him.

"She's what you might call a survivalist fanatic. She's got some kind of job with one of the government agencies, and she seems to prefer the strong, silent type."

"Line her up if she's free," Pol said, hoping she wasn't a bodybuilding freak with bulging muscles. Still, even a weight lifter might be more interesting to Ironman than spending another night killing time in the complex's gym.

"I happen to know she's available," Theresa said. "She called me a few minutes ago to see if I wanted to spend the evening with her."

POL LOOKED impressed as he glanced at Ironman's ensemble. Lyons had found a dark suit, a blue shirt and a relatively conservative tie. Blancanales walked around him, checking out the outfit. Lyons's massive frame was well hidden inside the loose-fitting clothes.

"Did your friend know anyone who was free?"

Pol forced a smile onto his face. "In fact, she did, amigo. Her name's Susan Phelan, and she's arranging to have her meet us at the hotel." He was tempted to warn Lyons that she might not be a raving beauty, but then decided to let Ironman find out for himself.

Lyons looked down at what he was wearing. "Think this will be okay?"

"Not bad," Blancanales said, "except for the bulge." He tapped the left side of Lyons's jacket and felt the bulky outline of the Colt Python .357 Magnum holstered under his left arm. "Expecting your date to give you a hard time?"

Ironman gave him a dirty look but said nothing.

"What happens if she invites you to her place for the night?" Blancanales asked.

"I'll deal with that when it happens." Lyons studied Pol. "You mean you're not carrying anything?"

Blancanales looked indignant. "Of course not."

Lyons moved behind Pol and quickly reached under his jacket. He whipped out a Colt automatic Blancanales had hidden inside a rear waistband holster.

Pol smiled sheepishly. "Even steven." He pulled out the holster and dropped it onto a chair. "Tell you what. Let's gamble and leave both of them behind."

Lyons looked as if he was ready to reject the suggestion, then reconsidered and slipped off his jacket. Unstrapping his holstered Python, he dropped it onto Pol's bed. "I'll never talk to you again," he warned, "if some drug-crazy punks shoot us dead."

Pol grinned and checked his watch. "Time to go if we want to make dinner with the girls, amigo."

"Let's say good-night to Bear and wish him happy snooping with his computer," Ironman suggested.

They found the computer wizard leaning forward in his wheelchair and staring at a bank of monitors that lined the wall in front of him. A series of arcane symbols paraded across the screens.

"If the chief calls, we're up in Washington for the night," Ironman said.

Without taking his eyes off the screen Bear asked, "Both of you got your communicators with you?"

"Yes, Papa Bear," Pol said in a resigned tone.

Brognola insisted that when any of them left the complex they carry the compact lithium-battery communication devices that Bear and Gadgets had developed so that they could be reached wherever they were.

"Just don't contact me after midnight in case she says yes," Blancanales pleaded.

"Only if it's urgent," Kurtzman replied.

"Have a heart," Pol said, remembering when he'd been in the middle of a passionate liaison with an anxious bedroom companion only to have the communicator signal that he was to call in immediately. "Can't you remember when somebody interrupted you at exactly the wrong moment?"

Kurtzman looked down at his immobile legs and smiled sadly. "Yeah. Only it was with a bullet, not a call."

Lyons changed the subject as he stared at the strange symbols on the monitors. "Can you actually read those things, Bear?"

"Of course."

"Yeah?" Lyons looked skeptical. He pointed at the monitor on the far right. "Tell me what those say."

Kurtzman turned his wheelchair slightly and glanced at the screen. "That's the FBI security system. It's a current-situation report. Somebody broke into a government warehouse a few hours ago and stole cases of weapons and ammunition. They killed two guards and a supervisor during the robbery. The state police have asked the FBI for assistance since it's a federal warehouse."

"Sounds like a typical B and E," Lyons commented.

"Except they got more than they bargained for. They bagged the revised prototype of that new laser rocket-launcher system that was being sent to Aberdeen for retesting." Bear smiled. "Poor Cowboy."

Pol joined in. "What about Kissinger?"

"That's why he flew to Aberdeen."

Ironman was suddenly interested. "Anything for us?"

"Not yet. The FBI thinks they know who's responsible."

"Yeah? Who?"

"You never came up against them directly. A white-supremacy biker gang called the White Knights. They operate in Arkansas and Mississippi."

"How come they're so sure?" Lyons asked.

Bear studied the symbols on the screen again before he answered. "The Bureau's got an undercover agent planted in the gang."

"Damn," Ironman muttered bitterly.

"Stop feeling sorry for yourself," Pol told him. "We've got to let the FBI get in some practice every now and then."

Jack Grimaldi, the dark-haired Stony Man pilot, poked his head into the computer center. "Anybody going up to Washington?"

Pol tapped Ironman on the shoulder. "Let's not keep the ladies waiting."

Lyons surrendered. "I guess you're right, Pol. We can't hog all the fun."

As they reached the door, Pol turned to Kurtzman. "If Gadgets calls in, tell him he missed a chance at a hot date."

Ironman let Pol walk out of the room ahead of him. Then he looked at Bear, who smiled at him. "Page me at any hour if it turns out they need our help," Lyons said.

5

Gadgets relaxed his right hand and let the grim-looking woman roll his fingers, one at a time, across the inked pad, then press them on the white fingerprint card. He looked down at the handcuffs attached to his wrists, then glanced at the nameplate pinned to her uniform shirt. Trooper Honey Winters.

Schwarz decided to stay calm. He'd been given his one telephone call and had contacted Aaron Kurtzman at Stony Man Farm. Bear had promised he'd reach Brognola and let him know.

Meantime there was nothing Gadgets could do except wait. He glanced around the large, sterile room. The walls were painted in drab gray. The sparse furnishings were made of metal, secured to the walls or floors to prevent prisoners from lifting them and using them as weapons. Each of the six windows was covered with thick meshed wire to prevent escape. There were two doors. One was barred, a reminder that this was a police station. The other door was made of wood and stained mahogany. There was a name on it, painted in dull gold letters—Lieutenant Harlan Golden.

From inside he could hear a deep male voice shouting questions, and the voice of Jimmy Joe Masters yelling back denials. Gadgets knew the routine well.

There was no one more expert at interrogation than his own chief, Hal Brognola.

Gadgets looked at the female trooper who was gripping his fingers. "You hold them any tighter and I'll consider us engaged."

She stared at him coldly, then continued rolling his inked fingertips on the card.

She looked no more than in her mid-twenties. "Bet you're a new recruit," Gadgets commented.

She snorted at him. "Just keep your mouth shut and wait for the lieutenant to haul your ass into his office," she growled.

"Well, you've got the attitude right," Gadgets observed. "How good's your shooting?"

Trooper Honey Winters started to snap an answer back, then caught herself and remained silent. There was something about the small man that bothered her. He just didn't seem like the typical killer they hauled into the station. And she had to admit he could handle a gun. He'd wiped out four professional hit men and had come out of it with only a few scratches. It was a shame, she reminded herself, that he was just another criminal. After suffering snide cracks from the male troopers about how tight her uniform fitted her shapely form, he was the kind of man she'd be interested in.

From a nearby room Gadgets could hear Jimmy Joe Masters shouting that he wanted to call his friend, Sheriff Judd Bushnell.

"Your partner isn't taking all of this so calm," the female officer said. "You won't be, either, once the lieutenant gets done with you."

One of the doors opened and a tall gray-haired man, followed by the sergeant, walked into the room. He signaled the woman to step aside. Turning to the other man, he snapped, "Take them cuffs off."

Gadgets rubbed his wrists to relieve the chafed feeling in them. The shapely woman stared in surprise at the senior officer.

Ignoring her, the gray-haired lieutenant glared at Schwarz. "Just who in hell are you, mister?"

Schwarz shrugged. Able Team was under strict orders never to reveal the existence of the counterterrorist group no matter what the circumstances.

The lieutenant waited for Gadgets to speak, but he remained silent and looked calmly back at him. "Out of the blue I get this call from the governor who tells me to let you go." He turned to the sergeant. "I argued with him. You can bet your ass I argued."

The sergeant and Officer Winters nodded. Lieutenant Golden made his displeasure known to everybody in sight.

"You know what he says to me?" He glared at the other two state troopers, who shook their heads. "'The President himself called me,' that's what he says." He spun around and studied Schwarz. "You some kind of government agent?"

"I can't tell you," Gadgets said, breaking the silence.

"Four men are dead, all shot by you, according to our lab, and you can't tell me?" The senior officer was on the verge of losing his temper.

The Able Team warrior tried to change the direction of the conversation. "Who were those four punks?"

The lieutenant exploded. "You mean you don't know?" He glared at the woman and the sergeant. "He says he doesn't know. Both of you heard him!"

He waited until he felt he was under control, then pointed at the sergeant. "You tell him, Max. I'm getting too old to deal with this!"

"The two punks at the table worked for the Configlio gang," the grizzled officer explained.

"Never heard of them," Gadgets replied.

"You would have if you lived around here. Configlio's a drug dealer who's been pushing his poison in Fort Campbell."

"How about the other two who came at us?"

The sergeant scratched his head. "That's the part that doesn't make sense. They're also part of the Configlio family." He shook his head and shrugged. "If you're not involved, all I can figure is maybe the two guys in the coffee shop were planning to double-cross Configlio and somehow he got wind of it."

"I guess that could be the explanation," Gadgets agreed. The sergeant was right. It didn't make sense. Somehow Schwarz was certain there was something else behind the sudden attack. The trouble was, he couldn't figure out what it might be. It was time to leave. "Okay if we go?"

The lieutenant nodded wearily. "Sure. Just don't come back this way if you can help it. We've got enough bodies to last us a lifetime."

Gadgets understood. For some reason, wherever he went, dead bodies suddenly appeared. Then he remembered something. "We had a truck parked at the coffee shop."

The sergeant pointed a thumb toward the window. "I had one of my men pick it up and bring it here."

"There are two more things," Schwarz said quietly.

The lieutenant looked as if he was ready to forget he'd gotten a call from the governor. "Yeah, what?"

"My gun."

Golden turned to the sergeant. "Give him his gun, Max."

The sergeant disappeared from the room to retrieve the weapon from the laboratory.

"What else?" Golden asked.

Gadgets pointed at the fingerprint card. "Any reason you want to keep that?"

"It would be interesting to see what the FBI had on file."

"Nothing," Gadgets assured him. Brognola had made certain there were no records of any of the three Able Team Commandos in any government file.

The lieutenant studied him. "I'll bet you're right." He picked up the card and tore it into little pieces. "Whoever you are, mister, I guess I'm glad you're on our side."

"Thanks," Schwarz said, smiling. "That goes both ways."

The sergeant returned with Gadgets's automatic. He handed it to the lieutenant, who studied it for a moment, then passed it along to Schwarz.

"One more thing," the lieutenant added. "Could you do us a favor and do whatever it is you do someplace else from now on?"

THE SMALL ITALIAN restaurant in Georgetown where they were eating was only half-full, so Ironman and Politician had a chance to talk to their dates without having to shout. As an added bonus, the place was air-conditioned, a great relief from the energy-draining August humidity that hung over Washington, D.C.

Lyons was impressed with the striking Hispanic beauty Blancanales had brought. She was almost as tall as Pol, and she was bright and animated. From the little he could detect, she was hypnotized by his Able Team partner.

Pol had that effect on women. There was an aura about him that warned women he was more than just another good-looking, well-dressed man, an attitude that made even the coldest woman vulnerable to his charms.

Lyons wasn't jealous. Pol and he were different people. Although each would have given his life for the other, he understood that their needs were different.

Pol enjoyed being wanted by women—especially beautiful, successful women. But he had no desire to find one woman and build as much of a relationship with her as his commitment to Able Team would allow.

Lyons thought of Gadgets and wondered if any woman could ever take the place of the electronic devices that consumed his interest. There had been several, but none for more than a fleeting moment.

Ironman looked at Susan Phelan, the young woman Theresa Morales had brought along as his date. She was attractive and well dressed, but she seemed too young—probably in her early twenties—and too sweet to be someone who could really interest him. He had never been on a date with someone as tiny as her. He guessed she was, at most, five foot two.

Susan and Theresa had listened quietly as Pol dominated the dinner conversation with carefully edited tales of his travels. Then Theresa turned to her friend.

"Rosario's work takes him to many interesting places around the world."

Susan looked wide-eyed at him. "Theresa never told me what you did for a living."

Pol turned to Ironman with a silent plea for help. Lyons smiled back at him. "Tell the ladies exactly how you earn your money, Rosario."

Pol glared at him. "My partner and I advise on security matters," he said awkwardly.

"Advise who, Rosario?" Lyons pressed.

Blancanales cast the blond warrior a malignant scowl. "Of course, our clients expect us to keep their identities confidential," he finally replied. He glared at Lyons. "Why don't you tell the ladies what you do for a living?"

Ironman locked his fingers behind his head and looked completely relaxed. He'd been waiting for Pol to make him squirm. "But you could have told them yourself," he said quietly. Lyons turned to the two women. "I'm a security consultant to Rosario and his business partner, Hermann Schwarz."

Pol acknowledged they were even with a glance.

"Someday I'd like to meet this partner of yours," Theresa told Blancanales.

"Perhaps someday you will. He's been traveling lately."

"Looking for pigs," Lyons added.

Theresa looked at him coldly. "I beg your pardon?"

"What Carl means is that my partner is hunting wild boars in Arkansas this weekend," Pol explained smoothly.

The small, sweet-faced young woman Pol's friend had brought along looked at Lyons. "You have a way with words."

"Never been my strong suit," he admitted gruffly.

"Obviously."

Judging by the expression on her face, Lyons was certain he'd be spending the rest of the night watching a late movie on television in whatever motel he decided to stay.

Pol turned to Theresa. "How long have you two lovely women known each other?"

"Since she was in one of my first classes at USC." Theresa thought about it for a moment. "Probably ten years ago."

"That's impossible," Blancanales said smoothly, "since neither of you can be more than twenty-one."

Ironman looked at the pleased expressions on the faces of the two women and shook his head in amazement. "If we weren't in polite company," he told Pol, "I'd suggest we pay the check and get out of this stable before the smell kills us."

The two women turned and glared at him.

"I'd say you just put your foot in it," Pol observed with a grin.

Glancing at the cold stares from the women, Lyons nodded sheepishly and reached for the check.

6

They strolled down Massachusetts Avenue for several blocks, saying nothing, stopping to study the variety of unique items on display at the many boutiques that lined both sides of the street. Lyons looked at Blancanales. There was a sad expression on his face as if he'd just remembered a temporarily forgotten agony.

Pol looked up and noticed Ironman watching him. He smiled weakly and turned to his date. "Would you mind if I made a brief stop?"

She looked confused, but shook her head.

Pol turned to say good-night to Lyons and his date. Ironman saw the expression on his partner's face and knew where Blancanales was heading. "We'll go with you," he said quietly.

The cab dropped them at the corner of Twenty-first Street and Constitution Avenue. The four of them seemed so tiny standing between the darkened stone giants that housed the National Academy of Science and the Federal Reserve Board.

Silently Blancanales led the quartet across the broad avenue and down a wide path that meandered through constitution Gardens. The tall Hispanic woman turned to him and asked, "Where are you going, Rosario?"

Pol didn't respond, so Lyons answered for him. "To visit a few of his friends," he said, holding Susan Phelan's hand.

They reached a long black wall engraved with the names of men long dead. Except for the dying flames of candles left by mourning families and friends, there was no light. A cloud had temporarily covered the moon.

Blancanales walked along the wall, saying nothing, stopping every dozen feet to seek out a name. He ran his fingers gently across the letters, mumbled something to himself, then moved on to another name.

Lyons watched him, hypnotized by the ritual his fellow commando performed. He wasn't sure that Susan had pulled her hand from his until he saw her moving along the black wall, ahead of Pol, looking for something. When she found it, she stopped.

Theresa and Ironman watched her move closer to the wall and kiss the letters as silent tears ran down her cheeks. Even Pol, having finished the visit he never forgot to make if there was time, watched as she whispered something to the name, smiled and returned to Ironman's side. He said nothing as she gripped his hand tightly.

Pol joined Theresa and put his arm around her waist. "Now we can go."

Susan nodded and turned to the wall once again. "Good night, Peter," she said quietly, then looked at Lyons. "My brother," she explained.

They walked back down the quiet path, past a small tent that had been erected by Vietnam veterans who had pledged to maintain a constant vigil at the memorial. The two men who sat in front of the tent nodded to them.

Pol hailed an empty cab that was cruising along Constitution Avenue seeking weary tourists. He held the door open and let Theresa Morales get in, then turned to Ironman. "Can we drop you two?"

Lyons looked at Susan to see her reaction. "Maybe at the corner of Calvert and Twenty-fourth," she said. "I live a few blocks from there."

A little while later, as Lyons and his date got out of the cab, Blancanales stuck his head out the window. "Don't forget. Jack's picking us up at eleven."

Lyons noted that, as usual, Pol had diplomatically left out the "a.m." after the hour. "Maybe the electronics wonder kid," Lyons commented, referring to Gadgets, "will have had his fill of hunting wild pigs by then and come home."

Theresa got out of the cab and hugged Susan. "I'll call you in the morning before my lecture." She studied Lyons, then turned to the small brunette. "Will you be all right getting home?"

Susan glanced at the tall man next to her. "I'm sure I'm in good hands."

Pol and his date got back into the cab, waved to Ironman and Susan, then signaled the cabbie to drive.

As he stood there, watching the cab disappear into the evening traffic, Lyons searched for something to say.

Susan smiled at him. "Would you like to take a walk?"

Lyons was in no hurry to find a motel in which he could spend the night. "Sure. Where?"

The streets were filled with youths carrying ghetto blasters that pierced the air with the latest in rap and heavy metal.

"Rocky Creek Park is a lot quieter," she suggested.

From what he'd heard Rocky Creek Park was much like New York's Central Park. Days in the park were meant for strolling; the nights belonged to gangs and drug pushers. He regretted listening to Pol about leaving his weapon back at Stony Man Farm.

"Sure, if you think it's safe." He knew he could handle one or two punks without a gun. It was the possibility of running into a drug-crazed gang that concerned him. "You know what the parks turn into at night."

She didn't seem worried. "It'll be fine."

They crossed the street and walked to the stone pillars that marked the park entrance. A uniformed policeman stared at them curiously as they walked down the paved pathway and wandered the tree-covered walkways.

"You haven't said who you work for," he said.

"The Federal Bureau of Investigation."

He showed his surprise. She didn't look tough enough to be one of their agents. "Doing what?"

"I started out as an instructor."

Lyons decided she had probably trained new secretaries and had probably been promoted to some internal staff position. Her conservative high-necked dress seemed exactly right for a career civil-service employee.

Still, there was something disturbing about the way she'd stared at him. Her gray-green eyes seemed to examine him carefully. He decided to change the subject. "Do you like sports?"

"Some," she said noncommittally.

He led up to his favorite sport—football. Not only had he played it in college until a leg injury destroyed any hopes he'd had for a professional career, but he was an avid fan of the Los Angeles Rams. "Football one of them?"

"I'm not much of a football fan. Too much brutality," she commented.

For Ironman that was the final statement that closed the door on any thoughts he might have had about ever calling her again. "How do you like working for the FBI?" he asked, trying to make conversation.

"It's a job."

"Is there anything you'd rather be doing?"

"I love aerobics and physical fitness," she answered.

"Then why don't you get a job doing that?"

Susan started to reply when they saw three shadows emerge from behind the trees and become three tall teenagers. Each kid wore a black T-shirt with the face of a demon boldly silk-screened in gaudy yellow.

Lyons gripped Susan's hand and continued walking. He'd have to see what the three punks had in mind before he acted.

"Nice-looking dude," one of them said loudly to the others.

"Yeah, she's a hot-looking piece, too," a second commented.

"Bet he's loaded," the third added.

"So's she," the first replied.

Lyons stopped walking and turned to face them. He could see the leers on their faces. Releasing Susan's hand, he stared back.

The leader started laughing. "Oh-oh, look. We got him mad."

"This is a big park," Ironman said, trying to control his temper. He looked at one of the teenagers. "Why don't you find someplace else to have your fun?"

"We intend to, dude. There's a little field over there." He pointed at the grassy area. "We thought your girlfriend would like to have a picnic with us."

"Wrong," Ironman growled.

The second punk joined the conversation. "You planning on stopping us?"

Lyons turned to Susan and whispered. "They're high on something. When I give you the signal, run for the entrance."

She nodded.

"Ain't that sweet, guys? They're telling each other little secrets," the tallest of the three, obviously the leader, snickered. "Maybe she'll do the same for us when we get her turned on." He nudged the young punk nearest him. "These two are your initiation, dude."

Gently Ironman moved toward the trio.

"Look at him. Now he's gonna give us a lecture on manners," the leader cracked as he gestured to the other two to encircle the couple.

One of the youths, a chunky, muscular nineteen-year-old, grinned as he danced around Lyons. "Try it, dude. Take your best shot."

Ironman moved closer, then suddenly spun around and faced away from the bobbing teenagers. Surprised at the unexpected move, the young man rushed Lyons. As he reached out to grab him, Ironman rammed his foot behind the teenager's knee.

Howling with pain, he went down on the knee and lashed out. Lyons stiffened his hand and slammed it into the guy's collarbone. The breaking of the thick bone echoed in the darkness of the park as the other two youths stared in astonishment.

The enraged youth jumped up despite the searing pain in his leg and threw himself at Lyons. Ironman easily stepped out of the punk's reach, then grabbed the guy's wrist and threw him over his shoulder. He crashed into the pavement and was suddenly still.

The leader reached under his T-shirt and pulled out an automatic. Lyons recognized it immediately—a Government Model Colt .45, the kind of weapon Able Team favored. "You get the girl," the tall punk yelled at the third youth.

Ironman was torn between stopping the teenager who was racing toward Susan, and the loudmouthed punk who was charging at him with the Colt.

There was no time to weigh the options. He'd get to Susan after he disarmed the gun-toting teenager. He waited until the furious kid stopped and pointed his gun at him, then threw himself at the young thug and grabbed his gun hand.

Lyons flipped the attacker over his shoulder, then kicked the side of the punk's head. The gun fell to the ground as blood trickled from the fallen youth's mouth.

Lyons scooped up the Colt, then moved back and waited for the kid to move. Like his companion a few feet away, though, he was unconscious.

Ironman turned to assist Susan, and was shocked to see the third youth lying on the ground, moaning in agony and grabbing at his crotch with both hands. The kid tried to grab one of the brunette's ankles. Dancing a few inches to one side, she kicked the pointed front edge of her shoe into the fallen youth's ear.

Screaming at the sudden pain, he rolled onto his face and started weeping.

Lyons stared at the petite woman. She didn't appear winded or upset. If anything, she almost seemed serene, as if nothing of consequence had taken place. Before he could ask her how she'd overcome the teenager who lay moaning at her feet, Ironman saw a handful of shadows emerge from the dark. In the dim light of the lampposts Lyons could see that the shadows had become six more angry teenagers. Each wore the same black-and-yellow T-shirt as the fallen trio. And each carried an AK-47.

Susan dipped into her open purse and pulled out a Smith & Wesson .38. Dropping her handbag onto the ground, she quickly spread her legs and steadied the weapon in the cup of her left hand as she pointed it at the emerging figures. She stared icily at the young thugs moving slowly toward her. "I figure I can get two or three of you before you can pull a trigger. Who wants the first round in their gut?"

The six stopped moving and watched as Susan carefully sighted her weapon on the closest of the group. Lyons watched them ease their fingers on their assault weapons.

Ironman raised the weapon in his hand. With any luck he should be able to kill at least two of them before they could fire their first shot. That would only leave one or two. The element of surprise might paralyze them enough to allow him to disarm them.

Nervously one of the smaller teenagers made the mistake of pointing his weapon at Lyons. Quickly Ironman squeezed off two shots, tearing two holes in the punk's right side. Screaming, the thug fell to the ground.

The others in the gang tensed as they looked at one another. One of the older thugs snarled, "Let's get 'em!"

Susan aimed carefully at the one who had given the orders and tore away two of his fingers with well-placed shots. Dropping his assault rifle, the teenager screamed, "Get them!"

Suddenly the remaining four punks stared past Lyons and Susan. Without warning they started running back into the shadows.

Ironman turned and saw four uniformed policemen running toward them. Three of the officers pursued the fleeing youths, waving flashlights to keep them in view.

The fourth, a bulky black sergeant, glanced at the fallen thugs, then angrily pointed his revolver at Lyons and Susan. "Drop those guns!"

Susan dropped her Smith & Wesson onto the ground. Lyons hesitated, and the sergeant shoved his gun into Ironman's face. "You, too!" Reluctantly Lyons released the Colt.

The sergeant quickly stared at Ironman and Susan. "You both better have some damn good explanations why you're carrying guns," he said coldly.

Before Lyons could answer, Susan reached down for her purse. While the police officer watched her carefully, she took out a leather folder and showed it to him. His expression softened as he acknowledged her status.

"Book them for attempted robbery, assault and rape. I'll stop by in the morning and sign the complaint," she told him briskly.

The officer nodded, then pushed the button on his chest-mounted transceiver. He reported his location.

"I need some backup, a patrol wagon and a couple of ambulances."

One of the teenagers tried to sit up. The sergeant pointed his .38 at him, and the youth fell back onto the ground.

From a distance they could hear the sound of gunfire. The sergeant listened carefully. Lyons looked at the cop. "Need a hand?"

They could hear the sound of a police vehicle coming closer. "Naw," the officer said, sounding disgusted. "For the moment we've got it under control." He shook his head. "Too bad we don't have the creeps who sold them the guns."

Lyons nodded. He understood how the sergeant felt. He'd felt the exact same way when he'd been with the LAPD.

"I guess I better go give my men a hand," the huge cop said. He smiled at the couple. "Enjoy the rest of the evening. And stay out of Rocky Creek Park."

Ironman led Susan back toward the park entrance. As they came close to the streetlights, she turned on him. "Sorry our walk got interrupted."

Still amazed, Ironman asked. "Where'd you learn how to do all that?"

"From the same kind of person you did."

Lyons was surprised at the reply. "You should be teaching martial arts instead of what you teach."

Her face was filled with innocence as she replied. "That's what I did when I joined the Bureau."

As they walked up the path back to the street, Lyons changed his opinion of Susan Phelan. She was a lot brighter and tougher than he'd thought. Perhaps he could make up for his indifferent attitude the next time, if she'd give him her number.

"So I guess this is good-night," he said as they reached the sidewalk. "I'll get you a cab."

"Where are you spending the night?"

Lyons tried to sound casual. "I'll find a hotel room. I'd like to call you the next time I'm planning to be in Washington."

She looked at him appraisingly. "Let me give you my number when we get to my place," she said, leading him to the line of cabs waiting at the curb. "I think we've got a lot to talk about."

"Just talk?"

She smiled enigmatically. "We'll see."

7

Hal Brognola watched as the tall gray-haired man got up from behind his desk and silently walked to the full-length windows. He stared out at the darkness and shook his head, then turned to look at the big Fed who sat patiently in a leather chair chewing on a long cigar. He waved the sheet of paper he held in his hand. "This has got to stop, Hal."

Brognola wasn't sure what was on the page the President was waving at him. He waited for the weary-looking man to explain.

"Another shipment of military weapons has been stolen." He glanced out the window. "And out there children are buying them to kill one another." He walked back to his desk and sat down. "Fifteen hijackings this month alone. What's the point of banning the sale of assault weapons? Anyone with the price can buy them on the street like a bag of drugs."

Now Hal understood why the President had summoned him to the White House. The demand for powerful assault weapons had quadrupled in less than a year. And with the increased demand had come an increase in the number of attacks on military supply depots.

"This time they've gone too far. They also stole four of our new laser rocket-launching system prototypes."

"I thought the Daniel Boone still wasn't working," Brognola commented.

"According to the Secretary of Defense, the engineers think they've got the bugs out of it." He held up a hand before the Stony Man operations chief could comment. "That's not the point. We're sure the Russians know exactly how it works. The real issue is how do we stop criminals from stealing our weapons, Hal?"

Brognola weighed the question for a long time before answering. "Make it too expensive for them," he finally suggested.

"How?"

"Don't waste time arresting them so some fast-talking lawyer can get them out on bail."

"What's the alternative?"

Brognola's reply was emotionless. He took the cigar out of his mouth, then said, "Death."

"The bleeding hearts are already crying about police brutality. The FBI's hands are tied."

"Ours aren't."

The gray-haired man loosened his tie and stared into space. Finally he turned, looked at Brognola and smiled. "I like that." He paced the length of the room before he spoke again. "The FBI's already involved in catching the hijackers on this one, so you're going to have to work with them and other agencies this time, Hal."

The expression on Brognola's face made it plain he wasn't thrilled with the prospect. "What other agencies?"

"The Treasury's Alcohol, Firearms and Tobacco unit, possibly the DEA. There may be others." The tall gray-haired man understood how the Stony Many operations chief felt about exposing his men to inter-agency rivalries. "I want you to coordinate the project. It'll be up to you to decide how closely your men will be working with the others."

Brognola stood. "Then I better get started."

"You know that if your people are caught, we'll deny you have any affiliation with the government."

"As always, Mr. President."

The President stood and held out his hand. Brognola walked to the desk and shook it. "What a thankless job you have, Hal."

"There are compensations."

The President looked at him curiously. "I can't think of one."

Brognola smiled. "Dead rats." He rammed the cigar between his teeth and walked out of the Oval Office.

LIGHTLY GRIPPING the wheel of the aluminum-bodied truck, the bearded biker kept humming an old Grateful Dead song. "Any friend of the devil is a friend of mine," Snake sang off-key.

He glanced at the side mirror. A long line of White Knights rode alongside the truck. He knew an equally long group was riding on the other side.

Snake hoped Steen would decide to get back onto asphalt. He was getting tired of bouncing around the dirt roads and was positive the rest of the gang felt the same way.

They'd been driving for hours, moving from Karnack, Texas, where the arsenal was located, then cutting across a corner of northwest Louisiana and into Arkansas, skirting large towns and cities by traveling on ungraded roads that existed on only the most detailed maps. They were heading for a national wildlife refuge in south-central Arkansas where they were supposed to meet their customer.

Forty miles into Arkansas Steen called for a short break in a small clearing before they moved onto a two-lane county road. Two dozen bikers parked their Harley-Davidsons around the truck. Beefy, bearded men swathed in black leather dismounted. The leather-jacketed women who had been riding behind them got off and rapidly disappeared into the woods.

"Tell your old ladies they got ten minutes to piss," Steen warned his men.

Dirtbag, the olive-skinned enforcer of the gang, sidled over to Steen. "Enough time for a drink?"

"Save it till after we dump this load. Then we'll have us a real party."

Bagman joined them. "How much longer before we get there, big man?"

This was Bagman's first robbery. Steen could see the excitement in the kid's eyes. "Soon, kid. Less than an hour. Just you make sure you got enough stuff to keep us happy for a couple of days."

Bagman grinned. "All I gotta do is make a couple of calls."

"It'll have to wait until we get to a pay phone."

Bagman nodded happily. "I can't wait to make that call."

Fifteen minutes later the White Knights were on the move again. The county road was deserted. As the gang members roared on, they flashed by the many poverty-stricken farms strewn along the road. Even in the dark they could see the huge outcroppings of rocks that made farming a mostly impossible task.

Inside the truck cab Snake started humming the Grateful Dead song again. "Any friend of the devil is a friend of mine."

"Keep your eyes on the road," Steen growled. "I don't wanna have to pay the devil a visit any sooner than necessary."

He picked up the CB microphone and pushed in the button. He knew that each of his bikers had a CB transceiver constantly tuned to the same channel. "Anyone who falls behind is on his own. So keep your minds on the road and save thinking about partying for later," he warned.

Glancing out his window, he saw the young blond girl who rode behind Bagman kissing his neck.

"Bagman, tell that bitch to save turning you on for when we get there," Steen shouted angrily into the microphone.

Bagman slowed his bike and waved an acknowledgment when he was alongside the passenger door of the truck.

"That goes for the bitches on the rest of the bikes," Steen shouted over the radio. He turned and glared at the redhead and blonde who were sitting on the floor with their backs against the two choppers parked behind the front seats. He caught them hugging each other. "Hey, bitch," he snapped at the redhead, "you and the blonde stop trying to get it on till we get there. Then I'll show you how we party."

Snake grinned at Steen's promise. The girls behind them were young, and new to the gang. But Snake had been with Steen for the past five years. He could remember some parties that had gotten too wild even for him. And none of the girls with them were as young and as full of energy as these two.

He glanced around the well-appointed interior. "Guy who we stole this truck from sure liked his luxury," Snake said sarcastically.

They had found the truck driver on the shoulder of an isolated road where he had parked to catch a short nap. Dirtbag had cut the man's throat before he could open his eyes, then lifted a nearby sewer cover and shoved the body down the wide pipe to give the rats below a fresh feast.

Snake glanced at Steen. "You gonna call the Badge Man and let him know we're on our way?"

"He ain't that far away. We'll be there in half an hour."

"How much you think we'll get for this load?"

"The Badge Man and I will have to haggle. We should get a nice bonus for those experimental weapons we got."

"Did he say how much he'd pay?"

"I haven't even told him I've got 'em yet."

Snake glanced quickly over his shoulder at the cases of experimental weapons stacked behind the girls. "What do you think they do?"

Steen gave it some thought. "Don't exactly know. Before we turn them over to that sheriff, we'll try out a couple of them."

Steen grinned at the girls in the back, making it clear he had something special in mind when they finally got to where they could relax. He turned to Snake. "I'll try them out on you if you don't keep your mind on the road," he warned.

Snake stopped talking. As well as he knew Steen, he was never certain when the big man was kidding or serious. Snake was careful not to upset Steen. He'd seen some of the more arrogant gang members who had angered the gang leader and ended up dead on the side of a deserted road for their trouble. So he changed the subject. "Hey, what do you think is up ahead there?"

There was a peculiar flickering glow just over the hill. Steen turned and stared through the windshield as they began the climb.

"I don't know. Kind of strange. Been on this road a hundred times and never seen it before." He kept staring at the glow as they reached the crest of the hill. Suddenly he muttered a curse. He pushed the horn button on the steering wheel and blasted out the pre-arranged warning to the rest of the gang to grab their weapons and scatter. "Goddamn it! It's a fuckin' road block!"

The bikers pulled their motorcycles off the road, yelled at the girls they were carrying to run for cover and yanked out their weapons. Ahead of them a solid phalanx of police vehicles, their lights flashing, blockaded the road. Steen shouted to Snake. "Pull this fuckin' rig off the road, asshole!"

Snake reacted instantly. The rig bounced as he left the asphalt and rumbled onto the uneven dirt.

"Keep driving!" Steen yelled, climbing over the seat to the back of the truck.

The two young girls cowered in terror. They'd come along for the drugs and party Steen had promised them. Neither had been warned that they might be facing bullets from police guns. They started scream-ing when they heard the whining slugs of 12-gauge shotgun shells bang against the truck body. From somewhere outside they heard the sound of machine-gun fire.

"Jam on the brakes!" Steen shouted.

Snake rammed his foot on the brakes, slamming the two bikes and the still-screaming teenagers against the far truck wall.

"Get a gun!" Steen ordered, grabbing an Uzi from the floor of the cab.

Snake reached down and picked up a MAC-10. He snapped off the safety and threw open the driver's door. Rolling to the ground, he turned and let loose a burst of searing lead at the three men leading the assault on foot. Each wore a jacket that identified him as an FBI agent. Flanking Snake were two guys wearing U.S. Treasury jackets, followed by a half-dozen state and county officers.

The White Knights responded with a rain of fire. They stood their ground, spraying the oncoming men with waves of 9 mm and .45-caliber slugs. Each biker fought back desperately, knowing that to be caught could mean the death penalty for previous killings or, even worse, punishment at the hands of Dirtbag and Steen.

Like the others, Snake locked his finger on the trigger of his MAC-10, panning it slowly from left to right at the uniformed officers moving toward him. For a moment it looked as if the earth were spewing cops from every direction.

Behind him he could sense Steen jumping from the now-opened rear of the truck. "Drop down!" Steen yelled.

Snake knew better than to ask why. He threw himself to the ground.

Steen placed a grenade launcher on his shoulder, aimed it quickly and fired an incendiary grenade at a rapidly approaching trio of state troopers. The grenade exploded with a loud whoosh as it slammed into the officer who led the attack. A shower of flames turned his body into a torch as he fell to the ground, screaming in pain. The other two cops made the mistake of stopping to help him.

Steen aimed his weapon at them and launched a second incendiary grenade. In the distance he could hear the sound of gunfire being exchanged. There was no way of knowing who was winning. "Get me that tube from the back," he ordered.

Snake dropped his gun and rushed into the truck. He came out with a long, tubelike device. Steen handed him the grenade launcher and peered inside. A sleek gray rocket was already in place. Steen balanced the weapon on his shoulder.

A hundred yards in front of them were the police and federal law-enforcement vehicles that had blocked their journey. Hidden behind them, Steen knew, was a small army of hidden cops. He could see some of them getting into cars, ready to launch a massive attack on his men.

If he could stop their assault, he and the others would have time to get away before reinforcements could be summoned. He hated wasting something as hard to come by as a heat-seeking missile on cops. He had been hoping to find a buyer for it. But sometimes financial sacrifices had to be made. This was one of those times.

"Prop up the rear end on your shoulder while I get this damn thing aimed," he ordered.

Snake braced the rear of the tube on his left shoulder.

"And keep your damn face out of the way," Steen warned. The bike-gang leader peered into the sighting device mounted on top of the tube, ignoring the line of heavily armed police vehicles heading toward him.

The two teenage girls had left the truck. They cowered behind Snake, holding on to each other for safety.

Unaware of their presence, the bearded biker watched as Steen started counting under his breath. "Five, four, three, two, one." The gang leader squeezed the triggerlike device, and both he and Snake shook as the small missile raced toward the parked vehicles. Behind them they could hear the screams of the young girls.

Snake turned quickly and saw that the girls had been hit by stray gunfire. Steen ignored the fresh corpses and watched with fascination as the missile made contact with the vehicles. This was even better than the tests they'd made with rusting cars hauled into a quarry from a junkyard.

The force of the missile bored through the vehicles and exploded, spraying glowing bits of metal and glass in every direction for thirty yards. The shouts and screams of the men and women caught in the conflagration died away as quickly as they had started.

Steen barely glanced at the dead girls behind him as he watched Snake get to his feet. "Load that thing in back and let's get our asses out of here before the cops get their shit together," he said as he climbed into the truck.

Snake rushed to obey him. He slammed the rear doors shut, sidestepping the bodies of the two girls, then jumped into the cab of the truck and turned on the engine. Steen leaned over and hit the car horn with the prearranged signal that meant they were moving out.

Leading the way, the truck raced forward, twisting and pitching as Snake struggled with the steering wheel. Behind them the still-functioning bikes twisted and turned over the uneven terrain, desperately trying to keep up with him.

Steen glanced at his side mirror. No cars seemed to be following them. "Head back to the road," he rasped.

One by one the six remaining members of the gang responded to his CB radio call. Most of them had been injured or wounded, but not so seriously that they couldn't travel.

Eighteen members of the gang didn't answer Steen's call. One by one Steen called out their names again and asked if anyone knew what had happened to them or their women. Each had been killed in the battle, someone told him.

"Dirtbag here," a voice reported. "Paul the Pig got hit in the stomach, but I got him slung across the back of my bike."

"Think he's gonna make it?"

"Not a chance in hell."

"Dump him," the furious gang leader spit into the microphone. "I suppose the cops got Bagman."

"No, I trashed him," Dirtbag reported. "I caught him using a flashlight to signal the cops. Son of a bitch was a snitch."

"Shit!" Steen muttered. "Now we gotta find somebody else to get us dope." He hung up the microphone and turned to Snake. "I better call the

Badge Man and have him meet us halfway with the loot."

Snake agreed. "The sooner he takes his stuff and we get our money, the happier I'll be. I just wanna get the hell out of here and get shit-faced for a week."

"Too bad about those two chicks we brought."

"Pain in the ass," Steen muttered, annoyed. "Now we're gonna have to get us some new mamas." He peered into the night. "Stop at the next closed gas station you see that has a pay phone. I gotta call the customer and make arrangements for him to meet us."

8

Their lovemaking in the darkened hotel bedroom had been slow and passionate. Theresa let her academic reserve melt away under the heat of Blancanales's sensual movements. Soon she became obsessed with fulfilling the urgent needs of her body.

Again and again they moved together, rushing headlong to completion. With a loud scream of relief she shivered in his arms, holding on to Pol until her trembling began to fade. Then, wet with perspiration, she reached up and pulled him down to her.

An irritating buzzing noise reached their ears. Pol tried to pretend he hadn't heard, but it kept buzzing, summoning him to make the inevitable phone call. Sliding off Theresa, he sat up and reached into the pants on the floor. Under his breath he muttered, "Damn *El Jefe!*"

Theresa moved behind him and wrapped her hands around his hairy chest. "Is something wrong, Rosario?"

"An emergency, Theresa. I've got to make a call." He turned and kissed her gently, then reached for the phone and started to punch out the sequence of numbers that would connect him with Stony Man Farm.

CARL WAS DOZING when he heard the communicator in his pant pocket buzzing. He looked at the brunette sleeping next to him and thought about waking her. She still had to get her things packed. Then he remembered the several hours they'd spent together. They had explored each other, testing, dueling, surrendering, separating, then coming back together to repeat the sequence. Each move, each emotion was a new discovery in conflict and pleasure. He hoped she'd been as satisfied as he was.

Ironman looked at the gentle smile on her face and knew she was. He decided to let her sleep until just before he left.

Lyons could see the street outside the bedroom window. It was still night. Only the streetlights provided illumination. Feeling for his pants in the dark, he found the communicator. He snapped off the buzzer and lifted the receiver gently so that he wouldn't wake Susan. He punched out the series of numbers that would put him in touch with Stony Man Farm. Bear answered the phone.

"What's up?" Ironman whispered into the receiver.

"The chief wants to meet with you pronto."

"Back at Stony Man?"

"No. He's in D.C."

"You contact Pol and Gadgets?"

"Gadgets is still on leave. But I just talked to Pol. He'll meet you in the lobby of the Sheraton."

Lyons grinned at the thought of Blancanales being interrupted in his favorite activity. "How did Pol sound when he called in?"

"Ticked off, like you probably are."

Ironman glanced at the sleeping woman and smiled happily. "I'm not ticked off," he answered, and knew he meant it.

After he finished dressing, he slipped into the living room and started to write Susan a note. As he struggled with the words, he felt her arms slide around him.

"No notes. No promises. Whatever happens to either one of us, just remember tonight was ours." She kissed him, then moved back into the bedroom and closed the door behind her.

THE INTERSTATE TELETYPE outside Judd Bushnell's office started printing a lengthy message. Stanley Ruddle, the chief deputy, glanced at the message and whistled loudly.

Bushnell turned and yelled, "What's up?"

Ruddle tore off the message and brought it into Bushnell's office. It was an all-points bulletin for all law-enforcement agencies to keep on the lookout for the remnants of a bike gang that had killed a number of law-enforcement officers.

Bushnell looked up from the bulletin. "Think it's Steen?"

"Sounds like something that maniac might pull."

Bushnell was furious. First that psychopath Masters had called him about the attack. He couldn't imagine what had gone wrong. Now he'd have to come up with a new way to get rid of him.

And that Vietnam friend he was bringing. Just what he needed, Bushnell groaned. Someone else he'd have to get rid of before the buyer arrived.

Now the Teletype report on Steen. When Frank Matthews called him, he'd assured him he had more than enough inventory to fill his client's needs. He even hinted there was a new secret weapon Matthews might be interested in acquiring—for the right price.

They had flown in from out of the country to see him. From what Matthews had hinted about them, Bushnell didn't want to disappoint them. There was too much money at stake.

The phone in the outer office rang.

"For you," Burley, one of the deputies, called out to Bushnell.

The fat sheriff was positive Steen was behind the killings. What he didn't need now was some influential local citizen calling to complain about teenagers making too much noise or somebody trespassing on their property. Reluctantly he picked up the phone.

In a cold, hard voice he snapped, "Sheriff Bushnell."

"It's me. Steen," the voice replied.

Bushnell was livid. "Are you crazier than I thought you were, man?"

"They tried to trap us."

"You killed a lot of cops!"

"Those butchers killed most of my men, plus a lot of their old ladies," Steen shouted back. "I'm out for blood!"

"So you turned tail and left the goods behind," Bushnell snarled.

"You think I'm crazy? I got it right here with me."

Bushnell felt a little better. "You get much?"

"I didn't count. But there's a whole mess of CAR-15s. And lots of ammo."

Judd thought about the size of Matthews's order. There should be more than enough guns to fill it.

"And that ain't all," Steen added.

The psycho biker had come up with some unusual goodies in the past—grenade launchers, portable missile launchers, infrared sighting systems. Bushnell wondered what he'd run into this time.

"What'd you get?"

"Not exactly sure. But it must be something special. The cases are marked experimental and have top-secret markings all over them."

Bushnell hid his excitement. There was always someone who asked if he'd gotten hold of anything new. It was rare, but the few times he had were extremely profitable. "Don't know if I can use them."

"We can talk it about when we get together. Right now we gotta make tracks fast, so you're gonna have to meet me with a truck." He paused and added, "And money."

"How much you looking for?"

They haggled over price without coming to an agreement.

"I'll bring money," Bushnell said, "and assuming they're in good condition, we'll work out something we can both live with."

"Don't forget to bring something extra for the experimental stuff."

Bushnell became wary. "I'll make a few calls to see if anyone might be interested. Too bad you don't know what it does." Bushnell knew he had the upper hand. He turned to Ruddle, who'd been sitting nearby and listening, and winked. "I might be able to take it off your hands if you aren't greedy."

Steen's voice became hard and cold. "And because the law would just love finding out that the Rosette County sheriff dealt in stolen guns."

Bushnell thought fast. There was always a chance that Steen and his men would be stopped before they could meet. "We'll work out something for the whole load. It's gonna take me some time to line up transportation and get to you. You're gonna have to find a place to hide out. Where you at?"

Steen told him.

Bushnell turned to Henry Gruber, a sour-faced deputy with thinning gray hair. "Anyplace near where he is that he can take cover?"

"Pretty deserted stretch," Gruber said. "Only place near him is the Mitford farm."

Bushnell didn't recognize the name.

Ruddle joined the conversation. "You know Old Man Mitford. They got that big-bosomed sixteen-year-old who's gonna marry Tommy Rae Brown next month."

Bushnell grinned as he remembered the girl. He'd watched her ripen into a full-grown woman. "And never been touched yet."

Gruber grinned suggestively. "Ain't entirely true, Judd."

Bushnell laughed. "You sly fox." He gave Steen directions on how to get to the farm. "Just make sure nobody can identify us when we get there." Bushnell hung up and turned to Ruddle. "Round up the rest of the boys. Tell Herbert to bring his big produce truck. We're gonna go get us some inventory."

"What about the White Knights?"

Bushnell winked. "I think we're about to get us some medals for wiping out a menace to society."

THEY SKIRTED Nashville and headed west on U.S. 40, driving along the edge of Memphis. Soon the exit sign ahead announced that Little Rock was thirty miles farther on. Just north of Little Rock Gadgets realized he hadn't talked to Hal Brognola himself about the attack. But why hadn't the chief signaled him?

He took his communicator out of his pocket to check it. By accident the switch had been turned off. He snapped it to the On position, and the faint red light indicated the unit was functioning. What if Stony Man had tried to reach him? "I've got to make a call," he told Jimmy Joe Masters.

His friend was concentrating on keeping the pickup on the road. The corn whiskey had made his eyes blurry. "Can't be that urgent. You can call from my place."

"No, this is important," Gadgets insisted.

Masters glanced at the device in Gadgets's hand. "What in hell's that?"

Schwarz searched for a believable answer. "A new kind of pocket pager."

In fact, Schwarz had developed the unit with help from Aaron Kurtzman and several of the engineers based at Stony Man Farm. Now the devices had become essential gear, which meant that the Able Team warriors had to take them along no matter where they went.

During the current slump, Gadgets and Kurtzman had made several improvements in the device. The most important was that any of the Able Team hell-raisers could now send a signal back to Stony Man. The Stony Man transmitter operator could trace the signal along a maplike screen until he pinpointed its location. The second feature was the ability to lower the volume of the signal so that only the person carrying the unit could hear it.

Jimmy Joe wasn't particularly interested in technical equipment. Besides, he was getting hungry. And, now that his flask was empty, he'd developed a powerful thirst. "How about buying us dinner?" he asked Gadgets.

Schwarz was glad to get off the subject of the communicator. And restaurants had pay phones. He could call in to Stony Man Farm. "You pick the spot," he said, suddenly enthusiastic.

On the outskirts of Little Rock Jimmy Joe pulled his pickup into a crowded parking lot. Gadgets looked at the one-story wooden building. The small, peeling sign over the entrance read Sparky's Home Cooking. He looked around the parking lot. There were trucks, pickups and cars crammed into every available space. As he got out of the truck, Schwarz wondered what made so many people stop to eat there. Truckers had a reputation for being choosy about food.

As he ate, Gadgets could understand why Sparky's was so popular—he hadn't eaten as well or as much in a very long time. Every time he thought he couldn't eat anything else, Jimmy Joe ordered himself a drink and another dish for Gadgets to try. He'd ordered country ham with sawmill gravy on the side, sweet potatoes and grits. Jimmy Joe insisted he also taste the country greens, consisting of a blend of turnip greens and whites, chowder peas and mustard greens. Then his friend asked the waitress to bring Gadgets a soup bowl and spooned some of the catfish stew he had ordered into the bowl.

After Gadgets sopped up his gravy with three buttermilk biscuits, Jimmy Joe served him some of the boiled freshwater crayfish he'd ordered for himself as a side dish.

"Can't eat another bite," Gadgets insisted, loosening his belt.

"Gotta try a couple of crawdaddies. Just break 'em open and suck out that sweet meat."

Acting as if he were hypnotized, Gadgets followed Jimmy Joe's instructions mechanically, breaking the bright red miniature crustaceans apart and digging out the bits of sweet meat inside. When he finally pushed his dishes away, he looked across the table at Masters and groaned, "No more. Just coffee."

"Just a little taste of dessert," Jimmy Joe said, smiling. Before Schwarz could stop him the waitress brought a fresh peach cobbler, swimming in heavy cream.

Masters waited for Schwarz to taste the dish, then asked, "Ready to go, ol' buddy?"

"Right after I go to the bathroom." He had a call to make.

Jimmy Joe signaled the waitress. "Maybe another cobbler for me while my buddy hits the john."

Dialing the complex sequence of numbers that connected him to Stony Man, Gadgets was glad to hear Bear's voice. He asked if Brognola was around.

"He's up in D.C. I can patch you through."

Before Schwarz could tell Kurtzman not to bother he heard the Able Team operations chief's voice. "Thanks for pulling the right strings," he said gratefully.

Brognola growled his reply. "Can't any of you go on vacation without taking out a few public enemies?"

"Hey, I was minding my own business," Schwarz replied.

"No injuries?"

"No new ones."

"How's the side healing?"

"Good as new," he assured Brognola. "What are Pol and Ironman up to?"

"I'm meeting with them later."

"I can be up there in a couple of hours."

"You're on leave," the deep voice snapped, "until the Walter Reed Hospital types say you're ready to go back to work. I'll contact you if you're needed. And stay out of trouble!"

There was an abrupt banging on the other end of the line. Brognola had the lousiest telephone manners, Schwarz reminded himself.

Gadgets felt abandoned. As he returned to the table, he could picture Ironman and Pol in the middle of action while he trudged through the woods looking for a big pig to shoot. He glared at the man who smiled at him from the table. It wasn't fair that the other two would be having fun while he was stuck going hunting.

"We're ready to roll," Jimmy Joe announced.

Gadgets made a face at him.

Masters handed him the check. "Soon as you pay the bill."

9

Frank Matthews looked around the Miami airport to make sure nobody was watching him. Then he found a pay phone, dialed the operator and asked her to place a call for him.

To anyone who bothered glancing at him the gray-haired man in the three-piece suit looked like one of the numerous successful businessmen who flew into Miami to negotiate a business deal, then flew back to their safe homes someplace up north.

"We just landed in Miami," the tall, slender man in the conservative pin-striped suit reported. "I've got the client and some of his men with me. Is everything set for our visit?"

"They will be by the time you get here," the Southern voice on the other end promised. "You gonna be here tomorrow like you planned?"

"We're flying into Texarkana in the morning to pick up our vehicles. The client wants to take care of some business while he's here. We should be there by to-morrow afternoon. Just make sure you've got enough of everything he wants on hand. He wants to leave before anybody finds out he's been here."

"No sweat. We're ready for you. In fact, I may have something else you'll be interested in."

Matthews became alert. Bushnell had come up with some unique items in the past. Rocket launchers. Several crates filled with heating-seeking missiles. Once he'd even offered a small truck filled with antitank missiles.

"What did you come up with?"

There was a moment of hesitancy, then the voice on the other end spoke. "Ain't sure yet. But the cases are marked Top Secret."

Matthews tried to hide his interest. "I might be interested, depending on what you got your hands on."

"We can talk about it when you get here."

"I don't want any problems, like people showing up who shouldn't be there," Matthews reminded him.

"You'll have most of the Sheriff's Department keeping strangers away," Bushnell promised.

Matthews hung up. The two of them had done business before. Their meetings had always been brief, businesslike and profitable for both of them.

Matthews dialed another number to make sure arrangements for transportation were still operative. After he hung up, he looked around to be sure he hadn't been spotted by a cop. There was one more call he had to make.

He dialed a number, let it ring three times, hung up and dialed the number again. He recognized the harsh voice that answered. "Matthews," he said quietly. "You've got the manpower lined up?"

"Best mercs in the business," the raspy voice bragged. "Eight of them. Each of them's got at least ten years of field experience. They'll meet you with the cars and truck in Texarkana."

"They'll be carrying heavy-duty equipment, won't they?"

"To these boys, carrying anything less than an M-16 is walking around naked."

Matthews grunted with satisfaction before he hung up. He glanced around the terminal again. No one was looking his way. He smoothed down his carefully styled long gray hair and moved quickly down the corridor to one of the exit doors.

He knew he wasn't just being psychotic. He had lived a very long time being careful.

Fortunately, thanks to his planning, the whole trip should be over in less than three days. Then he could fly back to Colombia, collect his fee from the head of the group who'd retained him and disappear from sight for a while.

The only thing that bothered him was the spoiled brat the head of the Medellín cartel had sent along to protect the group's investment. Matthews had dealt with all kinds of egos in his career. But Carlos Vargas thought he walked on water. Worse then that, he'd convinced his father, who headed the drug syndicate, that because he had an MBA from an Ivy League school he knew all the answers.

That didn't bother Matthews as much as the fact that the bastard had spent the entire flight from Colombia complaining about the sex-filled evening he was missing because of the business trip. He wished he could find a solution to the whining that wouldn't get him in trouble with Carlos Vargas's father.

Matthews started to walk out into the evening, then thought of a way to keep Vargas happy. He returned to the pay phones. If he found him an acceptable female substitute, perhaps he'd stop griping.

He knew somebody in Miami who would have access to a willing young woman. Searching through the telephone book, he found the guy's name—Chico Hernandez.

Hernandez and he went back a long time. Ever since the Cuban had resigned from the CIA to go private.

The last time Matthews had called the ex-CIA agent was two years ago when he was looking for a contact with the State Department. He had needed someone who could tell one of his Middle Eastern clients what confidential information on him existed in their files.

Hernandez had been helpful, for a fee. A large fee, as Matthews remembered. At the time Hernandez had asked if he'd like a girl for the night. But Matthews had been anxious to leave the United States before anyone found out he was there, so he had declined the offer.

Now that he'd thought of a way to keep the son of the Medellín chieftain out of his hair, he dialed Hernandez's number. Luckily the guy was home. He told him what he wanted without saying who the client was.

"No problem. Does this guy want her small and slender or tall with a big bust?"

Vargas was barely five foot seven, with an inflated ego. Matthews was sure he'd prefer someone tiny. "Small," he said. "About five foot two or three."

"I got the perfect girl," Hernandez replied. "A real beauty. Maybe five foot two. But hot. And a real pro. She comes well recommended. And she doesn't ask questions."

"Sounds good. Is she available?"

"I'm pretty sure she is. But she's expensive."

Matthews knew Hernandez would get a piece of the action. "How expensive?"

"How long you want her?"

"Two or three days at most."

"In Miami?"

Matthews was reluctant to reveal their destination, but he was sure Hernandez wouldn't cooperate without knowing. "She'll have to meet us in Texarkana no later than tomorrow morning." Then he decided to add, "If she doesn't charge an arm and a leg."

"Can your client stand a thousand a day plus expenses?"

The ex-CIA man was about to bargain, then decided he could tack her fee onto his expense account. "You got a deal."

"She gets her bread up front," Hernandez reminded him.

"I've dealt with whores before," Matthews replied, annoyed at the advance payment reminder. "I know the rules."

"She'll be there. Where should she meet you?"

Matthews thought quickly. "I'll have someone meet her."

"I'll get her to you. I know a guy who's flying out some stuff to that area. So have your guy look for her where the private planes land." He paused. "I was just thinking. The kid might earn herself one hell of a tip from guys who've got that kind of bread to spend." He was quiet for another moment. "I guess there's no way I can get her to fork over a share of it to me."

Matthews wanted to end the conversation. "I've got to get going. What's this high-class hooker's name?"

"Ginny. No last name. Just Ginny."

"How'll we recognize her?"

"She's a brunette. Look for a first-class beauty who looks like butter wouldn't melt in her mouth. It gets them all the time. She looks all innocence until they get her into the bedroom. Your client will want to take her back home with him."

Matthews silently hoped Hernandez was wrong. He wasn't sure how Vargas's old man would react to his precious son bringing home a whore. He wrapped up the conversation and hung up the phone, pleased with how simple it was to solve the problem of the spoiled young man's complaining.

Matthews had survived a long time by being careful. This time was no exception. He called the recruiter who'd lined up the mercenaries. "Me again," he said. "I need two or three men to take care of a personal problem I've got here in Miami. Can you handle it?"

He waited for the positive response. "Good. His name's Chico Hernandez." He picked up the phone book and read the address to the other man. "Take care of it sometime later tomorrow morning, not before." He paused. "Usual fee," he added before he hung up the phone.

Pleased with how prudent he'd been, he stepped out of the terminal. He was grateful the sky was clouded. There was no bright moon overhead to make him more visible. A hundred feet away from him a uniformed airport police officer was lecturing a hapless cabbie about parking at the curb. The jowly officer glanced at Matthews.

The well-dressed man slipped his hand under his jacket to his waistband and gripped the Heckler & Koch P-7 9 mm parabellum he had concealed in it. For a compact weapon the H&K had superior aiming characteristics and was extremely easy to fire. He could fire it without worrying that it would jam on him.

The policeman turned back to continue chastising the driver. Matthews relaxed his hand and looked around.

There was a handful of other people standing around outside, apparently waiting for transportation. Carefully he studied each of them. None of them seemed particularly interested in him. But then, Matthews reminded himself, a good agent never did.

Matthews signaled a cab. One pulled over, and the gray-haired man climbed in. "Take me to the Charter Building."

The irritated black driver turned and glared at him. "Hey, I've been waiting for a fare for almost an hour. That's no ride."

Matthews handed him a ten-dollar bill. "Just shut up and drive." Mollified, the driver turned around and took off.

CHICO HERNANDEZ DRESSED like a typical small-time gangster. He had on a pair of loud plaid pants and a multicolored Cuban shirt that he wore over his pants. His long black hair was glued to his head with greasy hair dressing.

Hernandez always looked as if he needed a shave. Most times he did. Even the women he sold disliked him. He claimed he was just over thirty, but he looked at least forty. In fact, he was closer to fifty.

Hernandez looked around his living room to make sure he was alone. Even though he had his place swept once a week he had the uncomfortable feeling that someone was eavesdropping on him.

He picked up the phone and dialed a local number. "Chico," he said to the person who answered. "A Frank Matthews called me from Miami airport. I think he came up with a group from Medellín. I don't know how much they're carrying, but they're heading for Texarkana. One of them's a big shot. He wanted me to get him a girl. Someone who's around five foot two and brunette. You know, the innocent-looking type. I told him her name was Ginny. Can you handle it?''

He waited until the voice came back on the line.

''Don't we have one of our own available? I didn't think we did joint ventures with them.''

The voice gave him further instructions.

''Okay. I'll hang around and wait for her daily call, then contact you. If I have to go out, I got an answering machine.'' He still had the uneasy feeling someone else was listening to the conversation. ''I gotta tell you, I'm not happy having outsiders know my connection with you.''

CARLOS VARGAS PACED back and forth inside the small waiting area for Frank Matthews to return. He kept waving the Colt Elite 10 mm automatic at the twelve expressionless men who kept watching him.

''Put it away, Carlos,'' the largest man said.

He glared at the speaker, then stopped and shouted at the others. ''What the hell are you staring at, you monkeys?''

Although he was eight inches shorter than the smallest of the men, they cowered when he snapped at them. Dressed in an immaculate white suit and spotless white loafers, he looked like a Miami pimp. Short, oily-skinned, with long black hair frozen in place by thick styling gel, Vargas viewed himself as the ultimate Latin lover.

The women who accepted his invitations to spend an evening with him catered to his inflated self-image. They never revealed to him that their services had been paid for by his father.

The man who had spoken before, a large, brutish-looking man in his forties, shook his head. "Nobody's glaring at you, Carlos."

Annoyed, the young man turned and stared coldly at him. "Why couldn't he make a call from here, Marco?"

Marco Lopez pointed at the Out of Order signs on the three pay phones. "They're not working, Carlos."

"That's what's wrong with this country. Nothing works." He looked concerned. "You don't think he sold out to those maniacs from Cali?"

"If he did, Carlos, he won't live to collect the money," the man promised. He pantomimed cutting Matthews's throat, then pulling out the windpipe and tongue so that the result looked like a gruesome cravat. "He'll wear a Colombian necktie." He looked at the eleven men he'd brought from Colombia and repeated what he'd said in Spanish. They all nodded in agreement. "See? We're all committed to killing him if he sells us out."

Vargas continued to pace back and forth as he spouted his complaints. "Tonight I was supposed to meet a charming lady from Paris who'd flown in to spend a week with me. But, no, Papa and Uncle Fernando decided they need more weapons to fight those ingrates in Bogotá. So they made me call up the gringo to find more weapons pronto."

"There'll be other weeks and other ladies," Lopez reminded him. He didn't add that he was sure Vargas's father would make sure there was a steady supply of women. "But you've got to try not to get so excited when you're with them."

Of all of Pedro Vargas's aides, only Marco Lopez knew that Carlos often got so excited when he was in bed with a woman that he strangled them. Lopez had spirited the bodies of a number of imported young women off the estate where Carlos and his father lived.

Vargas didn't respond to Lopez's comments. Instead he wagged a manicured finger. "I don't want to talk about women right now, Marco. I want to talk about what we're doing here. This is no way to do business. They send me to a good business school in the United States to learn how to run our business, but do they let me run it? No! Two billion dollars a year and they run the business as if it was still a small candy store."

"Your papa and uncle were brought up in the old ways," Lopez reminded him.

"Kill, kill, kill! That's all they know. I could be home right now with that hot French girl. Instead I'm sent here. For what? Guns. Buy us guns. Buy us anything to keep the police and military away. I keep telling them don't kill them. Pay them off. They pretend to listen to me until they get nervous and go back to the old ways."

Vargas's father had ordered Lopez to make sure his son didn't lose his nerve. He could sense the tall, well-dressed young man was getting frightened. "It'll all be over soon when the gringo comes back."

"It won't be over soon," Vargas insisted. "First we have to get there. Then we have to inspect the weapons to make sure they work. Then we have to get pilots to fly them back to Medellín. All before the police find out we're in the country." He pointed at Lopez. "It's all well and good for Papa to say make sure everything goes smoothly when he doesn't have to be here to make the arrangements."

"That's what this Matthews is for," Lopez said.

"I don't like his accent."

"It's only the way people in his country speak."

"It sounds so phony," the younger man snapped. "Besides, I don't trust him. He's a mercenary."

"So what? When we're done with him, I'll give him one of my presents, and poof! That'll be that."

The group of men heard the sound of the front door opening and reached for their hidden weapons. Lopez held up his hand to stop them. Matthews had returned, smiling and looking pleased with himself.

"Everything's set," he announced. "The vehicles and the extra men will meet us right after we land."

Vargas turned to Lopez and smiled. "Soon we can all go home." He turned to the conservatively dressed man. "Good work. My papa will reward you well." He turned and glanced at the thick enforcer who stood at his side. So will Marco after we're done here, he added silently.

10

Pol met Ironman in the lobby of the hotel. One look at his face and Lyons knew he was furious. "How could Bear interrupt me at exactly the wrong moment!"

Lyons tried to refrain from grinning. Of the three Able Team warriors, Blancanales was the one with the most girlfriends. "Bad timing?"

"Bad? The worst! Theresa and I made love several times and were lying very close to each other. We were exploring each other's body with our hands. She started purring. She started to move her hand down my body, and I began to shiver. The closer she got the more I shivered. She was just about to reach home plate when the communicator went off. *¡Dios!* She jumped back and asked me what I had hidden there. I excused myself and used the hotel phone to call in. And Bear told me the chief wanted us to report pronto. Pronto! Not even time to let things cool down slowly. Just pull on my pants, say good-night and rush to get here." Pol shook his head.

They got on the elevator. Pol pushed the button for the floor of the room where they were supposed to rendezvous. As the doors slid shut, he began to calm down.

When they knocked on the room door, Brognola let them in. Lyons and Blancanales nodded at Cowboy Kissinger, who sat in an easy chair. And there were other people in the room. Both commandos recognized the conservatively dressed woman.

Blancanales smiled at her. "How goes it, Sandy?"

"It goes like it goes, *compadre*," she replied with a twinkle in her eye. She seemed disappointed. "Schwarz due here?"

"He's on sick leave," Brognola snapped.

Ironman detected the hint of worry on the blonde's face. "He's all in one piece," he told her.

Pol and Ironman had worked with DEA agent Sandy Meissner on a drug-related mission in Florida, where Gadgets and she had become more than good friends for a brief time.

"Enough socializing," the Able Team operations chief growled. "Since you three playboys naturally know the lady in the room, shake hands with John McGovern of the FBI."

The raven-haired man had Ireland stamped on every feature of his face. He stood and held out his hand. The two Able Team warriors took turns in shaking it.

Lyons studied him before asking, "Field or headquarters?"

"Both," the agent replied. "Headquarters on this one, I'm afraid."

"Both of you find a seat," Brognola said. "And don't get comfortable. This is going to be a short meeting." He looked at Kissinger and pointed at the folder he was holding. "Is that the information I told you to bring?"

Able Team's armorer nodded. "Bear put together a complete report."

The big Fed pointed his cigar at Kissinger. "You're on."

Cowboy leaned back and opened the folder he was holding. "What we've got here is the theft of military weapons," he said, studying the page in front of him.

Lyons looked at McGovern. "Like the one the FBI's handling?"

The federal operative looked surprised. "You know about that?"

Lyons turned to Brognola. "We stopped by to say good-night to Bear. He was just monitoring a report on it."

"He said the Bureau people know who did it," Blancanales added.

"We did." McGovern's smile vanished. "Unfortunately the gang broke through a roadblock." He shook his head. "They got away."

"Not all of them," Kissinger reminded him.

"It was a joint operation of the FBI, Alcohol, Firearms and Tobacco people and the Arkansas State Police. We killed eighteen of the gang plus a number of women who were riding with them."

Brognola picked up the narrative. "Our side lost sixteen men and women, everyone of them a decent cop." They could hear the bitterness in his voice.

Lyons's LAPD cop instincts returned instantly when he heard that law-enforcement men and women had been killed. "Let's go after them, Chief. We'll burn their asses good."

Sandy Meissner shook her head. "You keep forgetting there are laws."

"There's only one law that works with roaches like that," Ironman growled angrily. "Grind them into the ground!" He glared at her. "Besides, what the hell's the DEA doing here? This isn't a drug case." He spun around and stared at the Able Team chief. "Or is it?"

Brognola held up a hand to stop Ironman. "Just shut up and listen."

Lyons clenched his fists to control his anger.

"We all feel the same way," Brognola said, "but the man on Pennsylvania Avenue wants us to work together and stop the hijacking of military weapons."

Blancanales looked at the still-furious expression on his partner's face and took over the conversation. "What kind of goodies did they grab?"

"In addition to a large quantity of CAR-15s they also grabbed four prototypes of the Daniel Boone, complete with everything needed to operate it," Cowboy said.

Lyons looked skeptical. "I thought it wasn't working."

"According to the designers, they got the bugs out of it. If they did, the Boone will be the most accurate targeting system ever developed. It can pinpoint targets within five thousand yards—even at night—with accuracies of less than a half inch. And you don't have to be an engineer to operate it. If you've got eyes to look through the sighting tube and fingers to adjust the dials, you suddenly become a one-man army. Imagine what you could do with a nuclear warhead."

Pol jumped in. "Are you saying they grabbed some nuclear warheads, as well?"

"No," Cowboy reassured him. "But changing the payload is easy, even for someone with only rudimentary knowledge of rockets. Put this in the hands of a country with well-trained engineers—"

"Like Russia?" Lyons interjected.

Brognola joined him. "Or one of the nutcases in the Middle East with more money than conscience, or some of the drug kings in Latin America who are fighting to stay in business. The list is endless. We're not as worried about the Russians right now as we are about someone selling it to some power-hungry bunch that would try to market the system to every terrorist group with money."

"First they've got to find somebody who can make copies of it," Ironman said.

"They're not hard to find," the Cowboy replied glumly. "There are hundreds of small-arms manufacturers that are struggling to stay in business. Offer almost any of them enough money and they'll copy anything short of a nuclear device."

"We don't know if the damn thing even works," Pol commented.

Cowboy leaned forward and stared at Blancanales. "Are you willing to take the one-in-a-thousand risk that it does, than not try to get it back?"

"It's needle-in-a-haystack time, Chief," Ironman warned.

Pol looked worried. "What if we can't find it?"

"Find the people who bought the stolen guns from the bikers and you'll find the Daniel Boone," Brognola said. "Just make sure they can't sell it."

The Able Team warriors understood the orders. Seek and destroy. Pure and simple.

Pol looked at the other two men. "All we have to do is find someplace to start."

"Read the newspapers," Brognola growled.

Pol and Ironman exchanged glances. What was the big Fed trying to tell them?

"It might be some domestic gang," Brognola said. "But gangs don't tend to go for weapons they haven't used yet. Of course, it could be a bunch of foreign terrorists." He twirled his cigar between his fingers and stared at it. "My money's on the Colombians. The Medellín cartel has been training their own army and arming them with the latest weapons, which you would know if you read more than the comic strips."

"You sound pretty sure of yourself," Pol said.

"That's where the DEA comes into the mission. They just got word that a group of Colombians arrived in Miami today by private jet from Venezuela."

Ironman stood. "It could be a coincidence."

The stocky man chomped on his cigar. "Not with Frank Matthews accompanying them."

Blancanales looked puzzled. "Who the hell's Frank Matthews?"

"A slime," Brognola replied. "He used to be one of ours—CIA until his superiors figured out that somebody in the Agency was feeding confidential information to the bad guys. Before they could play pin-the-tail on Matthews he resigned and left the country. Since then he's been acting as a consultant to a lot of not-so-nice people, like some Syrian-based terrorists, the Japanese Red Army and some of the larger Latin American drug cartels."

Ironman whistled. "Did the FBI or DEA pick him up?"

"No. They came up with a better idea," Brognola said, smiling. He turned to Sandy Meissner. "Tell him."

"One of our undercover agents in Miami got a call from Matthews, saying he was looking for female company for a friend. He wanted someone who was available immediately.''

Pol looked disgusted. ''The DEA's using pimps as sources?''

''Get off your high horse,'' Brognola snapped. ''First of all, he isn't a pimp. Or a drug dealer. That's his cover. Second, there are a lot of people who would call us even nastier names.''

Brognola looked at McGovern. ''Normally the President would let the FBI handle this one, except for one thing. If Matthews is involved in hijacking the new rocket-launching system, he wants to use him as a warning to other would-be hijackers.'' He turned to his two warriors. ''Do I make myself clear?''

Pol and Ironman looked at each other. Brognola didn't have to spell it out. They knew the objective—eliminate Matthews.

Lyons turned to the big Fed. ''You want us to work directly with the FBI and DEA?''

Sandy jumped into the conversation. ''Our interest is in finding out what new tricks the Medellín monsters have come up with to smuggle their shit into this country. We think one of the men with Matthews is the son of one of their top leaders. The only reason we can think of for his being here is to make some deals with smugglers.''

Brognola tapped his cigar on an ashtray. ''Miss Meissner has arranged for you to meet with the DEA contact and have him brief you on what he knows.''

Lyons turned to the woman. ''What's the name of that terrific seafood place on the beach that serves those great stone crabs?''

Before she could answer Blancanales jumped in with a suggestion. ''You haven't tasted heaven until you try

Cuban black bean soup with sherry at one of those cafés in Little Havana.''

''Before you tourists plan any gourmet meals I've got bad news for you. Right after you meet with the contact you get your tails back to the plane. Grimaldi will be waiting to fly you to Texarkana.''

''Texarkana?'' Pol looked disgusted. ''What's there?''

''That's where Matthews wanted the girl to meet him early tomorrow morning.''

''One more question.'' Kissinger looked at Brognola. ''The girl Matthews hired. Is she a civilian?''

''No,'' McGovern said, ''She's one of ours. Undercover. So try not to shoot her.''

''You better get your butts on the road if you want to see the sun rise on the Miami beach,'' Brognola said, standing up.

Blancanales turned to Sandy. ''You coming along?''

''Only to Miami to introduce you to our man. But the minute drugs come into the picture, we jump in with both feet,'' she warned them.

Kissinger gathered up his file and walked to the door with the other two. Before they left Pol asked, ''You gonna send Gadgets down to meet us?''

''If you need him. I'll let him continue resting until you signal for a backup.''

''Be sure to give him my regards,'' the DEA representative said as she gathered up her papers and stood.

Brognola controlled his smile. He knew all about their brief romance.

''One more problem, Chief,'' Lyons said. ''Dapper Dan and I haven't got our weapons with us, or any clothes.'' Grinning at Blancanales, he added, ''You know how our fashion plate can't survive without his wardrobe.''

Brognola allowed himself to smile slightly. "I had Cowboy pack a couple of goodie bags for you before he flew up here. I think you'll find everything you need—and something extra. Cowboy's going with you. He'll act as a stand-in for Gadgets and liaise between you and the civilized world." He checked his watch. "Get going. Grimaldi's waiting for you at Mitchell Air Force Base, and I'm not planning to pay overtime."

"Stay hard," Ironman told his superior as he followed the others out of the suite. He looked at the stern expression on Brognola's face. "Sorry. I keep forgetting you don't need to be reminded."

Brognola waited until Lyons closed the door before he let himself shake his head and grin.

11

Steen found the Mitford farm exactly where Judd Bushnell had told him it would be. None of the lights were on in the dilapidated two-story wooden structure. But there was a barn long enough to hide the truck, as the sheriff had promised.

The hulking gang leader instructed Snake to take most of the men with him and hide the truck inside the huge storage building. Then he gestured for Dirtbag to come with him.

Together they walked to the front door. Dirtbag took out a 9 mm Browning Hi-Power automatic from his waistband as Steen pounded on the wooden door. They waited until they saw a light go on upstairs and heard the sound of footsteps coming down a creaky flight of stairs.

An elderly male voice called out from inside, "Who's there?"

"Got a message for you from Sheriff Bushnell," Steen shouted.

Slowly the front door swung open. The short, wiry man inside stared into the dark, trying to make out the faces of the two men who were standing on the porch. "Who're you two?" he growled suspiciously.

Steen grinned as he rammed his knife into the man's plaid robe, aiming for the belly. "The men who just killed you, old man," he said, laughing as he twisted the knife. Gurgling mumbled words, the man fell to the floor in a pool of his own blood.

From the top of the stairs they heard another voice—a woman's. "Who's there, Pa?"

They waited until she came into the light of the upper stairwell. It was a short, heavyset woman in her forties. She stared at the bleeding body and started to scream.

Dirtbag pointed his automatic at her and began to fire. Three of his five shots tore into her, piercing her neck and chest. Still screaming, she collapsed at the edge of the top step and started rolling down, stopping only when her body hit the bottom step.

The unwashed biker placed his automatic against her ear and pulled the trigger again. The explosion echoed throughout the house. He looked at Steen. "Just making sure."

From upstairs they heard the screams of a young girl. Dirtbag ran up the stairs, jumping over the body of the woman, and disappeared into an upstairs room. The screams continued for a few moments, then suddenly he reappeared, dragging a young girl in a shapeless nightgown with him. She had a large bruise on her face. "Look here, Steen," he called out. "See what I found us."

The dark-haired girl stared in horror at the bodies of her parents, too numb with fear to continue screaming.

Steen looked pleased as he examined her with lust-filled eyes. "Nice bonus. It'll give us something to do until that damn sheriff gets here with the money."

THE USUALLY BRIGHT August moon was blocked by a blanket of clouds. The official-looking car moved slowly along the deserted back-country road until it reached the Mitford farm.

Behind the wheel Bushnell was grateful for the lack of moonlight. It made it possible for him to check out the situation before he announced his presence. He could see the shaded lights inside the ramshackle house, and he heard rock music blaring.

He stopped his car at the side of the road and checked his watch while he waited for the other car and truck to catch up with him. It was 3:00 a.m. He hoped he could get this business done quickly and get the inventory back to the warehouse. The buyer was arriving in less than twelve hours.

Stanley Ruddle pulled his car up next to him. "They all inside?"

Bushnell wasn't sure. "Take a couple of men and check the barn. Let's make sure the cases are still in it."

He waited while Ruddle and the other two deputies in his car walked quietly up the dirt road to the barn. Moments later they emerged and walked back toward him. "It's all in there. Cases of guns and ammunition. A couple of cases marked Experimental. And five of those damn Harleys."

"Good. How many men has Henry got in the truck with him?"

"Three."

"With the help of Steen's men we should be able to load up our truck in an hour." He opened his car door and got out. "Tell Henry to wait here until we signal him." He looked at Ruddle and the other two. "You three come with me."

He started to walk away from his car, then remembered something. He opened the trunk and took out an aluminum attaché case and a stubby Uzi. He checked the side arms the men who were with him wore in their leather holsters. "Everyone got their guns on cock-and-lock?"

The three men nodded. The fat sheriff led the way up the broken slate path to the front door.

As they approached, Bushnell turned to Ruddle and whispered his final instructions. Showing no reaction, the chief deputy nodded.

INSIDE, the White Knights were celebrating their survival. One of the bearded bikers tried to pull his redheaded girlfriend's T-shirt over her head.

"Not here," she complained. "Let's take it up to one of the bedrooms."

"Hey, babe, I'm proud of those jugs of yours. I want everybody to see what I own."

Tired of fighting him off, she gave up and let him start to undress her while the others near them cheered.

Steen glanced at the action across the room, smiled and passed the mason jar he was holding to Dirtbag. "Best homemade corn whiskey I've tasted in a long time," he commented, smacking his lips. He looked around the living room. The remaining members of the gang and their women were sprawled on the couch and floor, listening to rock music on the radio.

"Where did you dump the old man and his wife?"

"In an old storeroom back of the house."

"Hope you closed the door so they don't smell up the rest of the place."

"Yup. I also dumped some kerosene on them. So when we leave we can torch 'em."

"You shouldn't have done that yet," Steen said, chastising him. "Just warn the guys not to smoke when they go to the john back there." He watched as Dirtbag continued to swallow the corn liquor. "And make sure the rest of the guys get some of that stuff."

Dirtbag nodded, took another swallow and passed the liquor to a barrel-chested, bearded man in black leather who was necking with a buxom, bleached blonde on the floor.

Steen sat up in the easy chair he occupied. "Listen up," he shouted. The rest of the gang looked at him. "Soon as we get our money we take off and head back to our place. We'll divvy the money up, pack our things and take a long vacation. So start thinking where you'd like to go."

The members of the gang cheered at the news. One of them asked, "Where you planning to go, Steen?"

"Dunno," the gang leader replied, rubbing his bearded face. "Maybe I'll head down to Mexico for a while and find me some horny *señoritas* to keep me busy."

"Sounds good to me," Dirtbag commented. "Want company?"

"Sure. But only if you find your own women."

Everyone laughed at Steen's reply. It was obvious he was in a better mood than he'd been since the blockade.

Steen looked around the room, then turned to Dirtbag. "Where's Dum Dum?"

Suddenly there were the sounds of a young girl screaming from a room upstairs.

"Never mind. I know," Steen said, laughing. He winked at Dirtbag. "She was mighty fine. Young and all ready to be turned on by somebody who knew what they were doing."

"Yeah," Dirtbag replied. "Before all her yelling and begging I think she wanted me to keep going."

Steen thought about it. "Maybe when we're finished here I'll take her with me. She's got a lot of miles left in her before I dump her."

The knock at the front door interrupted the gang leader's plans for the Mitford girl.

JUDD AND STEEN sat inside a circle of gang members and deputies, haggling over how much Steen wanted for the shipment.

"Thirty thousand for the whole load," the sheriff said.

"Hey, this cost me a lot of men plus their old ladies," Steen complained.

"That's the risk you take in business," Bushnell replied nonchalantly.

"Them bikes we lost were worth twice that amount," Dirtbag added.

Steen turned his head and glared at his man. "Shut up, asshole. This is between me and him. So you butt out."

Dirtbag saw the flash of anger in Steen's eyes and moved behind another bearded biker.

"Seventy-five thousand," Steen countered.

"I wouldn't break even, even if I found a desperate buyer."

Steen changed tactics. "How much for them experimental weapons?"

"I think I agreed to three thousand over the phone."

Steen tapped his fingers on the coffee table. "My final offer. Fifty thousand for the load, including the experimental stuff."

Bushnell studied the gang leader's face. He had pushed him down as much as he would go. "How many pieces you got?"

"We double-checked after we got here. We got about sixteen hundred CAR-15s and sixty cases of ammo."

Bushnell held out his hand. "A deal."

They shook on it.

"Let's get the stuff loaded into my truck," Bushnell said. He tapped the aluminum case. "Then you get this."

"Let's see what you got inside," Steen said, his voice filled with suspicion.

Bushnell opened the case. There were stacks of neatly wrapped hundred-dollar bills. "There's exactly fifty thousand in here."

Steen started to laugh. "You sure you weren't a horse trader before you became a sheriff?"

"I'm still a horse trader." He looked around the room. "We're gonna need help transferring the cases."

"No sweat," the bike gang chief assured him. "We stole a forklift, so it should go pretty fast."

Bushnell heard screaming from upstairs. "What's that?"

"That juicy kid who lives here. One of my boys is just having some fun with her."

A tall, thin, bearded man appeared at the top of the stairs. "Hey, Steen, the bitch—" He stopped when he saw the uniformed officers. "Never mind. Tell you later."

Steen waved for him to join them. "It's okay. What'd she do, Dum Dum?"

"The little bitch up and died on me just as I was about to slam into her again," he muttered angrily. "What do you want me to do with her body?"

"Dump her in the back storeroom with her folks." He looked at the sheriff. "They were giving us a hard time about waiting here for you."

"Shame about that girl. Good-looking boy over in Gobbler Station gonna miss her something awful. They were supposed to get married next month."

"He'll get over her. There's a lot more where she came from." He gloated at the open case filled with crisp bills. Then he reached out to touch the green paper.

Bushnell pushed his hand away and closed the case. "After we get the stuff moved to our truck."

Steen shrugged. "Let's get going. I need a change of scenery."

For almost an hour the bikers and Bushnell's men worked as a team, lugging case after case into the long produce truck. Steen and Bushnell watched the teams of men transfer the military hardware.

"Why the hell don't you put that Uzi away?" Steen asked. "Makes me nervous."

"Just in case somebody who shouldn't be here shows up. Where's your piece?"

The head biker lifted his black T-shirt to reveal a Desert Eagle.

"Reliable gun," the sheriff said approvingly.

"We picked them up in that raid six months ago. The one on that importer's warehouse."

The sheriff remembered. He'd purchased the bulk of the guns and ammunition to resell to his clients. But Bushnell was getting impatient with the time it was taking to transfer the merchandise. "How close to finished are we?"

Steen walked over to the truck the White Knights had stolen and peered inside. "Almost done," he announced to the sheriff.

"After we're loaded up, let's torch the barn and house," Bushnell suggested. "Make it harder for anybody to figure out what happened."

"Good idea. There's a barrel of kerosene inside we could use," the gang leader said. He signaled Dum Dum to spread the volatile liquid around the lower level of the farmhouse and bring the barrel back to the barn. Then he turned to the rest of his men. "Let's get a move on. We've got a big party to get started back home, and the bread to pay for it."

The women cheered louder at Steen's announcement that they were going to have a party. The gang leader's parties always involved lots of liquor and drugs.

"Don't forget to pull your bikes down the driveway away from the barn," Bushnell said.

The gang leader turned and saw Dirtbag standing on the rear end of the forklift. "Get some of the guys busy moving our bikes closer to the road so we can blow this pop stand."

Dirtbag looked around, then turned to the women standing nearby. "Hey, you bitches, start earning your keep. Get them hogs moved."

Struggling with the heavyweight motorcycles, the women wheeled them slowly down the dirt road. One of the bikes toppled over as a small bleached blonde tried to roll it back onto its kickstand.

"One more dumb move like that," Dirtbag yelled, "and you walk all the way home!"

The blonde bent down quickly and righted the bike, grunting with the effort.

Dum Dum returned, dragging the half-empty kerosene barrel with him. "Got it all wetted down inside," he announced to Steen.

Dirtbag checked the insides of both trucks. "Everything's been moved. I left the forklift in your truck, so you can use it to unload," he shouted.

He jumped down from the rear end of the stolen truck and walked over to where Steen and the sheriff were standing. He looked at the gang chief. "What next?"

Steen looked at Bushnell.

"First I get Henry to move our truck away. Then your men splash kerosene in and around the other truck."

The head biker gestured for Dirtbag and Dum Dum to follow Bushnell's instruction. The sheriff walked over to the cab of the produce truck and stuck his head inside. Henry Gruber was behind the wheel. "The back's closed. So get this buggy out on the road, leave the engine running and come back here," Bushnell told him. He turned to Ruddle, who was sitting in the passenger seat, and lowered his voice. "Tell the boys to leave their engines running and follow you two. Then wait for my signal. We're just about ready to leave."

Gruber started the engine and slowly pulled the long vehicle down the dirt path and onto the country road. Setting the brakes, Gruber and Ruddle got out. They stopped to whisper Bushnell's instructions to the others waiting in the car.

The driver of the second car started the engine, then got out and joined Ruddle and Gruber. The others in the car fell in line behind them as they walked back to the barn.

Bushnell looked down the driveway as the men walked toward him. It was all falling into place, just as he knew it would. They'd be on their way home soon, with more than enough time to get ready for the buyer.

Dum Dum and Dirtbag returned to where Steen and the sheriff were standing. They nodded at the gang leader.

"I'll take the money now," Steen said, reaching for the aluminum case the sheriff had set on the ground.

Bushnell whistled, then raised his Uzi and began to spray hot lead at the three men facing him. Behind him he could hear the rapid drumroll of gunfire. Every shocked scream was proof his men were successful.

He looked down at the three men on the ground, prodding each in turn. The one the head biker had called Dum Dum was motionless. So was the one named Dirtbag. Just to make sure, Bushnell sprayed their bodies with several more rounds.

He turned to Steen. The head biker was still alive. In his eyes Bushnell could see the disbelief.

"Why?" the dying man gasped.

"You became a liability when you wiped out all them cops," Bushnell explained patiently. Then he fired several bursts of burning lead into Steen's face. When he was finished, he turned and looked down the driveway. "You all finished down there?"

"We checked each of them out," Ruddle said. "They're gone."

The sheriff was pleased. He shouted back, "Got some matches, Stanley?"

"Yeah, sure. Why?"

"Torch the house," he ordered, then reached into his pocket and took out a book of matches. He looked at the words on the cover—Sparky's Home Cooking. He remembered the place—run-down, but some of the best country cooking in the state. He reminded himself that he should drop in the next time he had to be up in Little Rock on official business.

Bushnell moved back from the barn and struck a match. It sputtered, then bust into flame. The sheriff stared at it, hypnotized, for a moment, then tossed it into the dark pool on the ground.

The kerosene burst into a river of fire, moving rapidly toward the wooden barn. Bushnell threw the book of matches into the fire and ran down the driveway to where the vehicles were parked.

Behind him he heard the rumbling explosion as the flames came into contact with the truck's gas tank. To his right he could feel the heat of the burning farmhouse. He turned and saw Ruddle running down the pathway.

As quickly as he could move his squat body, Bushnell joined Ruddle and the others. They watched the burning buildings light up the sky. Then Bushnell turned to Gruber. "Take another man and hightail it back to the warehouse. Start moving the cases. We'll join you as fast as we can."

The sheriff waited until the truck was no longer in view, then turned to Ruddle. "I guess it's time we called in and announced we caught up with the rest of the bike gang and wiped them out." As he walked back to his car to use the shortwave radio, he looked at Ruddle. "Only bad thing about this is now we gotta find ourselves a new supplier."

He didn't dwell on the thought. He was sure there were more gangs like the White Knights out there, waiting for someone to channel their activities.

12

The flight south was smooth and monotonous. Grimaldi kept the cassette player at his finger blasting away country music. Outside, a slow-moving cluster of clouds concealed the moon.

In the cabin Sandy Meissner kept pumping John Kissinger for details on how Gadgets had gotten injured.

Cowboy grinned at her. "You got some official reason for knowing?"

"Stop being an asshole, John. I'm just curious."

"You never were that curious about me when we worked together," he replied with a hint of jealousy.

"I didn't have to be. Most of the time we were working the same assignment, so I was right there if you got hit," Sandy answered patiently.

Sitting behind them, Rosario Blancanales leaned back in his seat, eyes closed, and tried to doze. The sound of their voices kept him from falling asleep. Finally he sat up and leaned forward. "Some of us need our beauty nap," he complained softly. "So keep it down, will you?"

Cowboy glanced over his shoulder at the casually dressed warrior and crooked a finger in the direction of the DEA agent. "Tell her."

"All I wanted was a simple answer to my question," Sandy grumbled. "This oversize teenager has to go and complicate things."

"Don't fight, children," Pol suggested wearily.

Sitting across the narrow aisle from Blancanales, Lyons had been concentrating on the view past his tiny window. He turned to Pol and, totally oblivious to the conversation between Sandy and the two men, commented, "From up here it doesn't look like there's anything alive down there."

"Just what we need," Sandy commented sarcastically, "a philosopher."

Lyons stared at her angrily. "What's that supposed to mean?"

"Don't jump all over me," Sandy snapped. "All I want to know is how Schwarz got wounded, and this big ape won't give me a straight answer."

"Oh, that." Ironman weighed her question for a moment, then replied. "It's simple. He got shot."

The DEA agent threw up her hands in disgust. Then she pulled herself out of her chair and glared at Lyons. "Great! That certainly explains it."

"He didn't get shot in any part that might interest you," Ironman added.

Kissinger smiled at her. "That should ease your mind."

She made a face at the three men and stomped back toward the small bathroom at the rear of the private jet. She stopped when Grimaldi's voice came over the speaker system.

"A message from Stony Man," he announced. "We're making a detour." The speakers went dead for a moment, then Grimaldi's voice resumed. "Some local sheriff wiped out the rest of the biker gang that hijacked the guns. The chief wants us to check it out. So sit back and relax. I'll have you there in twenty minutes.''

Blancanales sighed as he fastened his seat belt. ''There goes the black bean soup.''

GADGETS HAD OFFERED to take a turn at the wheel, but Masters turned him down. He knew all the shortcuts, he explained, and suggested that Schwarz get a nap.

Several hours later the Able Team warrior stretched and felt the stiffness in his arms. Yawning, he opened his eyes. He was still in the pickup truck. As he raised his head, he realized his neck muscles were knotted. Outside, there was nothing but blackness.

The nap hadn't been restful. He kept trying to figure out why the four thugs had tried to kill him. It still didn't make sense. He turned and looked at Jimmy Joe. The gaunt man was concentrating on driving. ''Where are we?''

Jimmy Joe smiled. ''Not too far from Gobbler Station. You been snoring your head off, ol' buddy.''

Gadgets could feel the massive quantities of food in his stomach. He looked down to see if his belly was still distended.

Jimmy Joe looked at him. ''Hungry for some breakfast?''

Schwarz shook his head. ''I don't think I'll be able to eat for days. How soon until we get to your place?''

''We're about ten miles from town. Sure could use a cup of coffee. How about you?''

Gadgets shivered due to the night air seeping in through the edges of the windows. ''Anything open at this hour?''

"We can grab a cup at the sheriff's office. They keep a pot going twenty-four hours a day."

Schwarz was amused at the idea of a small-town sheriff letting local citizens drop in for coffee. "Sure he won't mind?"

"Judd Bushnell? Hell, no. Judd's as sweet a man as you ever wanna meet."

Ahead of the two-lane road they were traveling, Gadgets could see the dim outlines of a metal sign. As they passed it, he could read the words—Gobbler Station. Population 195.

"Big town," he said, needling Masters.

"Actually, that sign's not accurate. Couple of people have died since they changed it last year. Population's just 192."

"How did it get its name?"

"Down these parts we call turkeys gobblers. Used to be a railhead here where the drovers prodded their flocks into boxcars for shipment to packers. At least that's what I was told by my kin."

"This the county seat?"

"Hell, no. County seat's sixteen miles away in Ashton."

Schwarz was puzzled. "So why is the sheriff's office here?"

"Judd's a local boy. He made himself a deal with the county officials to keep a branch of the sheriff's office here. Got himself another office, complete with a bunch of cells, over in the county building. But most of the time he hangs out here."

The few stores that lined both sides of the road were dark. The six streetlamps provided the only illumination in town, except for the light in the window of a one-story wooden frame building up ahead.

Jimmy Joe pulled the truck over to the curb, turned off the engine and got out. Gadgets stretched again, trying to ease the ache in his muscles. Still feeling stiff, he got out and joined Masters on the narrow sidewalk.

Jimmy Joe led the way to the lighted building. "A couple of cups of coffee will straighten both of us out."

They entered the sheriff's office. The young deputy on duty was sitting behind a desk, studying the sports section of a newspaper. He looked up when the two men entered. Staring coldly at Gadgets, he asked, "How's it going, Jimmy Joe?"

Schwarz had the feeling the young deputy was checking him out against a file of criminals he kept in his head.

"Goin' fine, Billy." He crooked a finger at Schwarz. "This is my friend Gadgets. Come down to pay me a visit. Thought we'd stop by on the way home to catch us a cup of mud."

The young deputy pointed at the aluminum pot sitting on a hot plate. "Help yourself."

The gaunt man walked over to the pot, fished around, found two chipped mugs and poured the thick, pungent brew into each of them. Handing one to Gadgets, he looked at the deputy. "Judd around?"

"Nope. Ain't you heard the news?"

"Nope. Something happen?"

The deputy shook his head. "You're something else, Jimmy Joe. Biggest story to hit this part of Arkansas in fifty years and you ain't even heard. Don't you ever listen to the radio?"

"Car radio's been busted for a month. Stop jawin' and start talkin', Billy."

"A gang of bikers stole themselves a mess of military weapons. State and federal cops set up a roadblock and trashed most of them. But a handful got away with the guns. Sheriff took himself a bunch of deputies and found them bastards up at the Mitford place." He looked unhappy. "Naturally I got stuck here."

Jimmy Joe wondered if the bike gang had been planning to bring the guns to the warehouse Bushnell had built. "What happened to them?"

"There was a fight."

"Anyone get hurt?"

"Them bastards killed old man Mitford and his wife. Raped and killed the Mitford girl. But then ol' Judd showed up and they got theirs. He and the boys cut every last one of them down, including a bunch of hard-nosed whores who was traveling with them."

"What about the guns they stole? What happened to them?"

"There was a big fire at the Mitford place. Still too hot to go digging around. Judd thinks they got burned up in the fire."

Bushnell had mentioned something about having a visitor from out of town coming in to buy some guns. Jimmy Joe wasn't clear on how all this fitted together, but somehow he knew it did.

He looked at Gadgets, who was busy drinking his coffee. "Hell of a thing, ain't it? Never thought Judd would ever have to wipe out a whole gang by himself."

"From what the deputy said he did have some help," Gadgets reminded him.

Jimmy Joe shook his head in wonder. "'Course he did. But think of it, Judd Bushnell a big-time hero."

He turned to the deputy. "Wonder if they're gonna have a parade for him over in Ashton?"

The deputy shrugged. "Dunno. He called here a while back and said he had to hang around the Mitford place until some federal agents showed up. Then he was heading for the county seat to fill out a report. As soon as he's done, he's goin' home and get himself some sleep."

Masters turned to Schwarz. "Time we got ourselves some sleep, too. Gotta be on your toes if you wanna be the one who gets the razorback and not the one the razorback gets." He began to laugh at his own joke as he led Gadgets out of the sheriff's office.

ONLY THE LIGHTS inside the prefabricated warehouse were on. For several hours the men had been moving cases from the back of the produce truck into the metal building.

"Place is almost filled up," one of the deputies told Ruddle. "Better tell Judd not to buy anything more till we move this lot."

The chief deputy nodded.

One of the men moving the heavy cases cursed as he tripped on something. "Damn, Stanley. Gotta give us more light."

"No can do, Louis. Can't risk somebody noticing us."

"Who the hell's gonna see us out here in the woods?"

"Maybe one of them rangers over in the wildlife refuge. Maybe somebody else. You just never know." Ruddle was getting annoyed at all the arguing. "Now you just get your ass in gear and keep moving them boxes inside," he snapped angrily. "We gotta be ready before them buyers show up here tomorrow afternoon.''

One of the deputies paused and asked, ''Where's Judd?''

''He's stuck up at the Mitford place, talking to some government big shots from Washington, D.C.''

''Be a tough day for him tomorrow,'' Gruber commented. ''Probably be a lot of them television and newspaper people swarming all over him in the morning.''

''He knows that,'' Ruddle said. ''Soon as he can, he's goin' home and get some rest.''

BUSHNELL WAITED alongside his car for the state-trooper vehicles he was told to expect. Paramedics from several nearby communities had already hauled the bodies away while fire fighters struggled to contain the raging blaze.

He glanced at where the barn had once stood. Only the charred frame of the structure was standing. The Mitford farmhouse was only a steaming pile of blackened wood.

He kept looking down the empty road, hoping the police vehicles would arrive. He was feeling bone-tired, and he still had official reports to complete.

All in all, it had been a good day's work. He'd retrieved the money he'd given Steen, so the proceeds from tomorrow's sale would be all profit. It was a nice way to do business.

There would be questions asked about the missing weapons, but as long as he played the role of the dumb county sheriff, he was safe. He'd have to remember to keep that facade going for the press, too.

He smiled as he thought of the reporters who had already called him on his shortwave radio. A hero, they called him. He smiled at the word. It felt good being a hero. He'd spent years being a nobody, and now he was suddenly somebody important.

It would feel even better after tomorrow when he had enough money to do whatever he wanted. Of course, he'd have to share some of it with Ruddle and the others. But if he handled the negotiations and collections by himself, he could claim he'd gotten a lot less money for the inventory.

Bushnell opened the car door and got in. He sat behind the wheel, trying to get up enough energy to push the key into the ignition and start the car.

Of course he'd have to find some new suppliers. But he didn't think he'd have much trouble. There were lots of groups like the White Knights around.

He was satisfied with the way the day had gone. Except for those incompetent punks who'd screwed up with Jimmy Joe. And the news that Masters had brought a Vietnam buddy back with him wasn't good, either. He'd have to do something about both of them. But tonight all he wanted to do was get some sleep.

The buyers were coming in tomorrow. And, according to Masters, so was his sister, Martha. She didn't worry him as much as Jimmy Joe and his friend did. She wasn't the wandering type, and she hated hunting.

He grinned as he remembered how she'd looked as a teenager. She sure was a tasty morsel. He sat for a moment and tried to re-create that first time with her. She'd fought like a wildcat, but in the end she'd given in.

He sighed as he looked out the windshield. It was time to stop daydreaming and get some sleep. As he started the car and slowly moved it down the dirt road, he thought again about the aluminum case filled with money. Suddenly he felt reinvigorated. Thinking about all that money, he decided, was a definite upper.

Then he saw the distant glow of headlights. A convoy of vehicles approached him. He recognized their Arkansas State Police markings.

Bushnell stopped his car, got out and walked down the road to meet the cars as they pulled up. He recognized the uniformed captain who got out of the lead car. He commanded the regional barracks of state troopers just north of Rosette County. There were four civilians with him—three men and a woman. Bushnell wondered if these were the federal agents.

"Hear you had some excitement, Sheriff," the captain said, shaking Bushnell's hand.

"We handled it," Bushnell replied, expressionless.

The senior state trooper looked around. "Just the handful of you?"

Bushnell smiled. "Sent the rest back with the bodies. Still got local duties to perform."

He stared at the four civilians. The captain turned and introduced them. "These four agents are from Washington to lend whatever help they can to recover the stolen guns."

Bushnell stepped forward and grabbed the hand of the tall blond man. "Sheriff Judd Bushnell."

"Carl Lyons," the unsmiling man replied. He turned and introduced the others. "Rosario Blancanales."

Pol smiled broadly as he shook the sheriff's hand.

"John Kissinger," Lyons continued.

Bushnell was impressed by the physique of the man whose hand he shook.

"And Miss Meissner," Lyons concluded.

Bushnell examined the honey-blonde. It was hard for him to believe that this attractive young woman was a federal agent. She was more like somebody he'd like to take home with him. "Pleased to meet you, ma'am," he said, exaggerating his accent. "They sure have improved the quality of federal agents."

"Thanks for the compliment." Sandy turned and glanced at the three men with her. "Nice to have somebody notice."

Lyons looked annoyed. "Get a chance to search for the stolen guns?"

The beefy sheriff pointed at the sodden remains of the barn. "Ain't cool enough to do a thorough search yet."

Kissinger joined in. "Hear any explosions?"

Bushnell wasn't sure what these guys wanted to hear. "Aside from the guns we were shooting?" He became silent as he sought a safe answer. "We were kind of busy, so if I did, I didn't notice." He hesitated, then added, "The fire was really big."

"You'd have noticed the kind of explosion I'm talking about," Cowboy replied. He signaled Ironman, Pol and Sandy to join him. Speaking in a low voice, he said, "The missiles in the shipment—"

"What missiles?" Sandy interrupted. "I thought they stole assault rifles and ammunition."

Kissinger ignored her and continued. "No way the missiles could have survived a fire of that size without exploding." He looked at the others. "Ever hear what a missile sounds like when it hits?"

Pol and Lyons nodded. "Not something you might forget," Lyons commented.

"Exactly," Cowboy agreed. "I think we can agree the missiles aren't here."

"Which means," Blancanales added, "that the CAR-15s aren't here, either."

"The question is," Pol said, glancing quickly at the sheriff, who was chatting with the state trooper, "where are they?"

Lyons turned and stared at the fat sheriff. "And who's got them?"

Bushnell pretended not to notice the four civilians looking at him. If they were like most federal agents he'd heard about, they'd hang around, make official-sounding noises and then skedaddle back to Washington, D.C. With any luck they'd be gone before the buyers showed up tomorrow.

If not? Bushnell thought that between the men the buyer was bringing and his own deputies, the four agents wouldn't be that big a problem.

13

Jimmy Joe pulled his pickup off the country road and onto a hard-packed dirt road. As the vehicle bounced on the uneven path, he turned to Schwarz and said, "Almost there, ol' buddy."

Gadgets could make out the dark outline of a two-story wooden house a hundred yards in front of him. "That your house?"

"Technically it belongs to both Martha and me. Only she don't spend much time here anymore. So I guess you could say it's mine."

Schwarz wasn't interested in Masters's long-winded explanations. All his body and brain craved right now was a bed and lots of sleep.

Jimmy Joe saw Gadgets staring aimlessly out his window. "Pretty nice country. Man can really be alone with his thoughts out here."

Gadgets saw some lights flickering through the trees. He tapped Jimmy Joe's arm and pointed. Masters stopped the truck and pretended he was bewildered. Damn that Judd. He knew better than to show lights at night. What if this had been a mess of state or federal cops? Suddenly the lights vanished.

"Probably some hunters trying to hypnotize deer with lights. Happens all the time. A couple of hunters sneak onto someone's property, carrying big flashlights and rifles. They find a buck and shine the light in his eyes. While he's standing still, scared out of his skull at the thing shining in his eyes, one of them takes a shot and kills him." He hoped his explanation would satisfy his guest.

"Pretty dirty way to hunt."

"It is. But the farmers know how to handle them. Every year the sheriff's called to haul away some dead hunters who tried to pull that stunt on private land."

Gadgets thought of something else. "I didn't hear a gun."

"Something probably spooked the deer before the hunters could fire." He started the truck moving again.

"I'm happy for the buck." Schwarz had been searching for signs of life since they'd left the darkened farm town. "Got any neighbors?"

"Sam Young and his woman live over there," Jimmy Joe said, pointing out the window, "just about three miles away." He pointed at Gadgets's window. "Over on your right, about two miles away, is the national wildlife refuge. Couple of rangers and their families live there year-round. Down this way that's a lot of neighbors."

Gadgets didn't have much time to dwell on the remoteness of his friend's home. The communicator in his pocket started buzzing. Something was up. Stony Man wanted him.

AS THE SMALL JET continued its journey to Miami, Kissinger turned around and looked at Ironman and Pol. "What do you think?"

Lyons was studying the sports section of a newspaper he'd found at the small airport they'd flown out of. He looked up from the columns of baseball statistics. "About what?"

"The missing guns."

"They're gone," Lyons replied, letting his eyes drift back to the numbers on the page.

Cowboy turned to Blancanales, who was staring out the small window. "Who do you think's got them?"

"That's a good question," Pol said without taking his eyes from the darkness outside.

Frustrated, the Stony Man armorer got up from his seat and moved back to the row of seats where Sandy Meissner had stretched out. Her eyes were closed. "Frustrating, isn't it?"

She opened her eyes. "What is?"

"The hijacked shipment disappearing."

"It won't be the last time you're frustrated," she observed.

He started to reply, then changed his mind and moved back to where Pol and Ironman were sitting. "I can't understand why the chief told us to drop it and go on to Miami. That fat sheriff, I think he had something to do with the guns disappearing."

Lyons looked up at him. "Probably." He turned to Blancanales, who nodded.

"Why didn't you two tell Brognola you wanted to check out the sheriff?"

Lyons folded the newspaper and dropped it onto the floor. "For one thing, we don't know the sheriff's involved. The shipment could have been diverted before he and his deputies caught up with the gang. For another, Brognola's contacting Gadgets, who happens to be hunting in the same county this Sheriff..." He struggled to remember the name.

"Bushnell," Pol supplied.

"This Sheriff Bushnell operates in. Hermann will let us know if he spots anything fishy." He reached down and picked up the newspaper. "So why don't you get back in your seat and let me find out if the Dodgers have a snowman's chance in hell of making it to the playoffs."

14

The dirt-spattered, dented Ford Mustang pulled up to the front of the crumbling building that served as a terminal of the semideserted airport. The young brunette who climbed out of the passenger door waved to the driver.

"Thanks, Harry. That was one wild ride," she said brightly, reaching in and grabbing a small canvas overnight bag.

The driver pulled away and drove the vehicle toward an ancient C-46 of World War II vintage, which was parked near a dilapidated hangar. Usually the workhorse cargo plane was parked inside, but the hangar was occupied by the Lockheed Lodestar the clients were flying.

Looking through the large window in the small waiting area, Frank Matthews watched the brunette coming toward him. So this was the lady Hernandez had sent. She walked with the swagger of a veteran hooker.

He studied the clothes she wore—jeans and a halter that revealed her stomach. They were a little too tight, a little too revealing. Matthews wanted her to look more innocent so that Vargas's son would believe he'd charmed her into his bed.

Still, she was pretty in a cheap way. And, as Chico had promised, could look innocent if she did something about her clothes and makeup.

He'd sent Harry Countryman, the charter pilot who'd fly the armament cases across the border, to pick her up at the Texarkana Municipal Airport, located at the opposite end of the city. Countryman had complained about playing chauffeur until Matthews had promised he could stop and buy himself a fifth of bourbon to keep him happy until they got back.

Matthews opened the door and walked toward the hooker. "Ginny?"

She nodded.

"I'm Frank."

She examined him carefully with a bold stare. "Yeah, Chico said to keep my eye out for you. You got the money?"

He was uncomfortable with her bluntness. Reaching into an inner pocket, he took out an envelope and handed it to her. She started to open it. "It's all there," he said quickly. "Put it in your purse. You can check it later."

"Three thousand?"

"To the penny."

"For three days," she said as if confirming the agreement.

"Yes." Matthews changed the subject. "Everything go all right on your trip here?"

"Yeah. Chico talked some friend of his into giving me a lift."

She had called the Miami DEA contact from the Texarkana airport to tell him she'd arrived, and to check if there were any further instructions. He had reminded her that if she called and couldn't speak, she could tap the message on the receiver in Morse code. If he wasn't in, the answering machine would take the message.

"There's something important we need to talk about," Matthews said, interrupting her. He was anxious to get to the reason for her trip. "Inside there's a young man named Carlos. I want you to keep him so busy he won't get in my hair while I conduct our business."

From the way she moved her jaws, he was positive she was chewing gum. "What kind of business are you doing, not that it's any of mine."

"Exactly," the well-dressed, gray-haired man replied bluntly. "I've come up with a cover story to explain your presence to Carlos."

He went over it with her. He was a business associate of her father. A young man she was in love with had run off with another girl. To keep her from doing something self-destructive her father had asked him to take her on one of his trips and keep her so busy that she didn't have time to think about the man who'd left.

"Sounds like bullshit to me," she commented. "Think this Carlos is dumb enough to buy it?"

Matthews wasn't sure.

She thought about it. "Yeah. Why not tell him you asked me to come along so we could spend time together? You've been trying to get into my pants for a long time. You thought taking me on a trip might give you the opportunity. If this Carlos is any kind of a man, he'll try to beat you out. Then leave the rest up to me."

Matthews decided her approach was more plausible than his. He had one more question to ask. "If

Carlos asks me what you do for a living, what do you want me to tell him?''

She smiled. ''Tell him I'm an actress and that Chico's my agent.'' She squeezed Matthews's arm. ''It ain't that far from the truth if you've ever seen me in action.''

Vargas had been glaring at the woman with Matthews ever since she'd arrived. Inside, he was seething with anger. It was bad enough that his father had made him sacrifice his evenings with the woman from Paris. But to watch this Matthews have such a beautiful girl join him was the final insult.

He forced a large, happy smile as the two of them entered the building. Walking to the young girl, he stared at her and commented, ''*Señorita,* I have never seen someone as magnificent as you anywhere.''

The young woman turned to Matthews. ''Frank, you have the nicest friends.''

The gray-haired man patted Vargas's arm. ''Carlos, this is my friend Ginny. She's an actress. Since she's between plays, I invited her to come along for the ride.''

He glanced at Lopez. The older man looked as if he was about to explode. Matthews turned to Vargas and the hooker. ''Would you two excuse me?''

Frank Matthews knew the leader of the Medellín cartel's enforcement team distrusted him. All the brutish man understood was force. He was uncomfortable with people who used their brains instead of guns or a knife. Except for Pedro Vargas, of course. But he was the head of the cartel. Besides, he had earned Lopez's respect years earlier when he personally removed the tongue and windpipe of the man who was his predecessor.

Matthews took Lopez's arm and led him across the small room. The ugly man's features twisted into rage. "I should kill you now gringo! Are you crazy, bringing a *puta* with us? This trip to Arkansas is serious business."

Both men were so busy arguing they didn't notice that the woman had heard Lopez's angry words.

"Before you have a fit, hear me out, Lopez," Matthews said. He explained that with Vargas's resentment about being dragged away from his girlfriend, it was obvious his attitude could prejudice the trip. "This way the girl keeps him busy and happy, and you and I make the buy, pack up the guns and get them on their way to Colombia. Makes sense, doesn't it?"

Lopez's sour expression began to fade as he weighed the American's words. He, too, had been concerned about Vargas's preoccupation with the French woman he'd imported. He had to admit the American made sense. "Okay," he replied grudgingly. "How'd you find her?"

"Remember Chico Hernandez?"

"The pusher in Miami?"

Matthews grinned. "He's got a side business."

Lopez had met Hernandez on previous trips. The expatriate Cuban had seemed all right.

"Just make sure she's so busy with Carlos that she doesn't know where we're going or what we're buying. If she asks too many questions, we'll have to take care of her," he warned.

"Naturally." Matthews didn't want any last-minute problems. Not when he was so close to closing the deal and collecting his fee.

Lopez remembered how overexcited the younger Vargas got when he took a woman to bed. "Has this *puta* got a family who would miss her?"

"Who cares? After all, she's only a well-paid whore."

By the time the two men returned, Ginny and Vargas were sitting in a corner by themselves, exchanging smiles and laughter. Vargas looked over at Lopez. "Hey, when are the cars coming? I promised Ginny she could ride with me in the back of my limousine." He winked at her, then turned back to Lopez. "Alone. *¿Comprende?*"

Without showing any reaction the older man nodded and grumbled, "The limousines and truck should be here soon."

He turned to the American for confirmation, and Matthews nodded. "Whatever you want, Carlos. I'll make sure you and the...young woman are alone. Except for us up front, of course."

Ginny excused herself and went into the bathroom, shutting the door behind her. She was relieved. She'd passed the first inspection. She decided to take off the Beretta Jetfire she had worn strapped to her inner thigh.

It was obvious the young Colombian expected to have free range of her body during the trip. It wouldn't do for him to find her weapon. She opened her overnight bag and slid the holstered Beretta into a pocket next to the four-inch stiletto.

She checked the bag one more time to make sure she hadn't accidentally left anything in it that might reveal her real name was Susan Phelan. After a thorough search, she was satisfied.

She checked her makeup in the small, cracked mirror over the dirt-encrusted sink. She'd applied it just thick enough to look cheap. She smiled as she wondered what Carl Lyons would think of her if he saw her like this. She hoped he never would. She liked him too much.

There was one more thing she had to do before they left. She closed her bag and straightened her clothes, then flushed the toilet for effect and came out.

Harry Countryman was entering the building. Susan took one look at him and walked over to where Vargas was waiting for her. "Carlos, do you think there's a phone in this place?"

A flash of suspicion crossed the young man's face. "Who do you want to call?"

She smiled at him affectionately. "My agent. I just wanted to tell him not to book me in anything for at least a week."

The suspicion faded. He led her into a small, shabbily furnished room that served as the office. There was a phone on the desk.

It was obvious that Vargas wasn't going to leave her alone in the room. She dialed Chico Hernandez's number. Luckily he was there. She hoped he could figure out her code.

"Ginny," she said into the phone. "Just wanted you to know that your crazy pilot friend got me here in one piece."

There were things he wanted to know—where they were going and how many in the group.

She started tapping out the number two, then the number twelve again and again as she continued to talk. She hoped he'd understand she was signaling how many guns Matthews and Vargas had with them.

"One more thing. We'll be truckin' out of here in a little while and heading for Noah's Ark. So don't book anything until I call you." She hung up and smiled at Vargas.

"This Noah's Ark you mentioned. What does it mean?"

"Don't you remember? Everybody got paired off, just like us." She tucked her arm under his and let him escort her out.

Lopez saw Countryman look around the shabby waiting room and then approach them. The Colombian turned his back on him and walked away to where the rest of his men were standing.

In his mid-sixties, Countryman exhibited the ravages of an alcoholic life-style. His eyes were bloodshot and his hands shook.

Matthews forced a smile. "Everything go okay?"

"She was waiting when I got there. Didn't have any trouble finding her. Great-looking piece of ass."

"It took you long enough to get back," Matthews admonished him.

"Had to stop and pick up my bottle of medicine. You owe me ten bucks." He held out the brown paper bag with the bottle of bourbon in it.

Matthews wished Countryman wasn't standing so close. The stale whiskey on the pilot's breath was nauseating. "I wouldn't wave that around if I were you. The Colombians don't feel real comfortable doing business with people who drink," he warned in a low voice as he took out a ten-dollar bill and handed it to the other man.

"Cheaper than using the stuff they sell," Countryman retorted. Suddenly he grinned. "You know, this'll be the first time in years I've smuggled something out of the country instead of into it."

"By tomorrow morning you should have your plane in Mexico to make the transfer to the jet they've got waiting there. Just stay sober enough so you can fly under the radar across the Gulf."

"Hey, I've flown more'n thirty missions from there to here without getting spotted. And I was pretty polluted on a lot of them."

"Meantime, you and the men we're leaving behind make sure no snoopers see the jet in the hangar. We want this one to go quick and clean."

Countryman opened his jacket and exposed the Walther P-38 in a side holster. "Anybody who comes around and asks too many questions—bang, bang!"

Matthews wasn't sure the pilot could see clearly enough to hit the side of the building. Luckily Lopez and he were leaving six of their men behind as a precaution. He had seen the AK-47s Lopez's men were carrying. His own men were equally well-armed. They carried TEC-9 assault pistols, each holding 36-round clips.

He was about to suggest that Countryman let the men they were leaving behind handle intruders when the honking of car horns outside stopped him. He turned and saw a limousine, two luxury-size cars and a long truck pull into the parking area.

Lopez sidled up to him. "The men behind the wheels—they're trustworthy?"

Matthews had used a recruiter of mercenaries to find them. He'd successfully employed the same recruiter in the past. "Each one's a professional. And they don't care who you tell them to shoot as long as they get paid."

Just like the other men the recruiter had hired for him to get rid of Chico Hernandez. Not that he had anything against his former CIA friend. It was simply a matter of making sure that nobody, even by accident, knew he was in the country.

"Good," Lopez said. "But, just in case, my men will ride with them."

Matthews understood how Lopez felt. He checked his watch. "Time to go." He led the group outside. "The cargo plane parked back there will be waiting to take off when we get back," he whispered to Lopez. "Everything's falling right into place."

"Let us hope nothing goes wrong," Lopez replied coldly.

Matthews slapped the Colombian on the back. "You worry too much, *compadre*."

"I'm not your *compadre, señor*." The icy stare he gave the American made it clear he didn't trust him. "Just remember it is your job to make sure nothing goes wrong, and mine to do something about it if it does."

15

The area of Miami known as Little Havana was filled with run-down apartment houses and small private homes. Most of the inhabitants were hard-working expatriates from Cuba, struggling to provide a decent life for their families.

What prevented them from being successful was a lack of decent jobs and housing. Some of them had surrendered to the hopeless despair of their existence by trying to blank it out with drugs.

Overflowing cans of garbage lined every alley. The oppressive heat had fermented their contents. The only moving creatures were rats scurrying through the rotting garbage.

Everywhere in Little Havana there were drug pushers. Often they were small children or teenagers selling crack. But supplying them were the dealers, the vermin who imported the narcotics and parceled them out to be sold.

It was exactly these men that Chico Hernandez was working hard to catch. Knowing their names wasn't enough. The law insisted they had to be caught in the act of handling or selling drugs.

As a CIA agent, Chico had observed firsthand how well-intended laws could be twisted to accomplish the most immoral goals. Many a dictator had used existing laws to propel themselves into perpetual power.

Now that he was with the DEA, Hernandez was determined to destroy the drug barons with the same vigor he had eradicated dictators and terrorists in his CIA days. The people who were being destroyed were his own people, Cubans who had escaped to the United States to find freedom and opportunity.

If his latest mission was successful, he'd make a major dent in the clandestine distribution network that smuggled narcotics into the U.S. It wasn't Matthews he wanted, but the men who had accompanied him.

Matthews was a mercenary. He sold his soul to the highest bidder. The leader of the other men was obviously high up in the ranks of the Colombian drug world. Maybe it was even Pedro Vargas, who was reputed to be the head of the Medellín cartel, or a member of his immediate family.

That would be a coup, but not one he could admit to publicly, not if he wanted to keep his undercover status and his life.

To the people with whom he did business he was a small-time pimp and drug dealer. In fact, he had successfully maintained both guises while feeding information to his superior in Washington. He didn't want to risk exposing himself, even to assist the FBI in capturing Matthews and this weapons hijacking they were investigating. He had agreed reluctantly to act as their undercover-agent's contact. But it made him uncomfortable. There were too many opportunities for his cover to be blown.

The three men who were coming for a visit worried him. All his Washington superior could tell him was that their authority came directly from the President.

He hoped they weren't a bunch of three-suiters who smelled of government bureaucracy. Even if he could explain to anyone who saw them here that they had come to investigate him, it might make him less trustworthy in the eyes of the people with whom he did business.

THE LIGHT-GRAY LINCOLN moved slowly along the empty street. The driver, a thickset man with scars across his left cheek, called out, "What was that address again?"

The large man sitting next to him, who looked more like a sumo wrestler than a hired killer, checked the piece of paper in his hand. He looked out the window. "It should be in the next block."

"Let's get it over with in a hurry. I haven't had breakfast," the bald man sitting in the rear complained.

"For Christ's sake, Al. You got a gut big enough for two people already. Stop bitching," the driver snapped.

"Anybody know anything about this guy?"

"Yeah," the extremely fat man in the front passenger seat replied. "His name's Chico Hernandez."

The man in the rear seat shook his head in disgust. "That's it?"

The driver looked into his mirror at the man in the back. "What else is there to know?"

The other man shrugged. "I guess nothing. Except when do we get paid?"

"Before lunch," the driver said, "so let's get there and get it over with before you starve to death."

IRONMAN AND POL had left Cowboy behind at the small military air base south of Miami to check out their weapons while Grimaldi refueled their sleek black Sabreliner. Driving a rented car, the two Able Team warriors and Sandy Meissner drove directly from the airport to Little Havana and their meeting with her undercover agent.

Blancanales was wearing a white linen jacket, and a long-sleeved dark brown silk sport shirt tucked into a pair of tan slacks. He looked over at the costume Lyons, the driver, was wearing. The multicolored Hawaiian sport shirt he wore over a pair of baggy jeans was the brightest Pol had seen on his sidekick. He reached into his jacket pocket and took out a pair of sunglasses. Slipping them on, he said, "Now I can look at you."

Without taking his eyes from the road, Ironman growled, "What's that supposed to mean?"

"Your shirt. How much did they pay you to take it off their hands?"

"So happens it set me back thirty bucks."

"You need a woman in your life, amigo. She would never let you get away with a shirt like that."

"Then she wouldn't be in my life," Lyons snapped. "I can't stand a pushy woman."

Sandy, sitting in the back, leaned forward. "Hey, don't you two ever agree on anything?"

Blancanales turned and smiled at her. "Only that you're much too lovely to work in such a dirty business."

She waved her hand in front of her nose. "Whew, I think I'll open a window before the barnyard smell kills me!"

Ironman started laughing. "Okay, homeboy. Try getting out of that one," he chortled.

Sandy moved over and sat behind Lyons. She leaned over the seat. "I take it this Susan Phelan wasn't pushy."

There was a threatening growl in Ironman's tone. "What's that supposed to mean?"

"Nothing. Except you managed to bring up her name at least four times on the flight down."

"So she wasn't a dunderhead. That doesn't mean I'm head over heels about her."

Pol knew when to back away. This was one of those times. He jumped in. "But she was a nice person. Agreed?"

Lyons calmed down. "A nice person." He was silent for a moment. "I just don't think she should be doing what she's doing."

"Which is?"

Ironman diverted his eyes from the road momentarily to glare at Pol, then turned again. "If you must, she works undercover for the FBI. Damn stupid thing for a person to do for a living."

"Believe me," Sandy said, "I'm on your side. Especially when it's me who's gone undercover. But what would she say about what you do?"

Lyons was quiet for a moment. Then, in a soft voice, he answered, "That's different."

Pol knew better than to pursue the subject. He scratched at his shirt. Under it he wore a Kevlar vest, standard garb for Able Team when they were on assignment. "It's good I used deodorant before I put on the vest."

Ironman stopped for a red light and took the opportunity to rub his chest. "Yeah. Either they've got to start making ventilated versions or send us to cooler climates.''

From the back seat Sandy snapped, "What are you two characters griping about?"

The Able Team warriors turned and looked at the well-built woman. She was tugging at the body armor she wore under a loose-fitting blouse.

"Talk about male chauvinists," she growled. "What did the characters who designed these things think I was going to do with my breasts?"

The two men looked at each other and silently agreed not to reply. They were in trouble no matter what they said.

Fortunately the traffic light turned green. Lyons called out over his shoulder, "How much farther to this guy's house?"

HERNANDEZ HAD JUST finished calling in the report from the FBI undercover agent. He started straightening up the living room of his small house. There were newspapers and empty fast-food bags everywhere.

He carried the garbage from the kitchen, opened the front door and dumped it in an open can outside. He started to go back inside when he saw the gray Lincoln moving slowing in his direction.

For a moment he thought the government types had arrived. Then he looked at the faces inside. They weren't government employees. Only one kind of person looked like them—hit men.

Hernandez ducked back inside and slammed the door behind him. He had a Detonics Combat Master in his desk drawer. He grabbed the gun and shoved it into his waistband. There were three men in the car.

Perhaps if he slipped out through a bedroom window, he could make it to his car and get away before they discovered he was gone.

The thing that bothered him the most was who had sent them. He couldn't remember slipping up at any time. Had they been tapping his phone? No, he'd swept it regularly to make sure. Even if they had been, he'd worded his messages in such a way that to anyone listening he was either pushing drugs or a girl.

It didn't make sense. But Hernandez was a practical man, and he didn't want to waste time trying to decipher the identity of the person who'd hired them.

He rushed into the bedroom and pushed up the window. Poking his head outside, he checked in both directions. Nobody. He climbed out and ran down the alley to where he'd parked his car.

The front-seat passenger in the gray Lincoln spotted Hernandez running. "Son of a bitch's trying to get away," he said, hitting the driver's arm to urge him to move faster.

The driver stamped on the gas pedal and chased after the man fleeing on foot. "Get ready to take him out," he yelled to the other two men as he turned into the alley.

IRONMAN SAW the Lincoln race into the alley. He looked at Pol. "For us?"

"Let's check."

Lyons twisted the steering wheel and spun into the alley on his two left wheels. Blancanales grabbed the Colt Government Model automatic he had tucked into his waist holster and rolled down his window. Sandy shoved her hand into her large purse and pulled out the compact Glock 9 mm automatic that had become standard equipment for so many law-enforcement agencies. With its 16-round capacity the European weapon could deliver a full clip of hollowpoints in less than five seconds.

There was a man running in front of the gray car. Two of the men in the luxury-size vehicle were leaning out of their windows, their hands gripping MAC-10s.

"Let's even the odds," Blancanales yelled. He aimed for the front passenger, who was leaning out of the right-hand window, spraying bursts of lead at the man on foot.

Pol squeezed off a pair of shots. The gunman squealed and dropped his weapon. He made the mistake of sticking his head out of the window to see who had shot at him.

Blancanales had been waiting for the move. Carefully he pulled off two more shots. Both drilled into the point of the man's neck where the head and spine met. A shower of blood spurted out of the gaping wound as he slumped over the door.

The man on foot stopped and turned to face the oncoming car. He held his Detonics Combat Master out in front of him and kept squeezing the trigger, creating a spiderweb of fracturing glass on the windshield.

The driver and the man in the rear threw open their doors and jumped out. The man on foot tried to dive out of the way of the car hurtling toward him. The impact threw him four feet into the air. The car continued to careen until it ran into a brick wall and stopped.

Lyons stopped his car. He and Pol jumped out, with Sandy right behind them.

"See what you can do for him," Lyons shouted at her. As he pursued the terrified thug, Ironman tore his beloved Python from its underarm holster. Cowboy had modified the weapon to give it more weight and balance when Ironman insisted it was the only handgun he truly trusted. Featuring .357 Magnum hollowpoints, the gun's ammo made a powerful statement of death when it was on target.

The bulky gunman raced into another alley. Ironman ran to the entrance, then stopped and moved to one side. There was a row of metal garbage cans near him. He grabbed the lid of one and tossed it into the alley.

A burst of 9 mm rounds tore holes into the spinning cover. Lyons turned the corner and belly flopped as he pushed his gun out in front of him. The gunman heard the noise and spun around to face him.

"Die, you son of a bitch!" he yelled.

Calmly Ironman plowed three rounds into the man's sternum and carotid. A shower of red fluid spurted out of the huge holes.

Pol's prey had rushed into the kitchen of one of the small run-down houses in the alley. Peering in from the edge of a window, Blancanales could see his quarry had pushed the snout of his MAC-10 against the face of a terrified gray-haired Cuban woman.

The woman babbled hysterically in Spanish, "Please don't kill me. I have a husband and children and grandchildren. Please don't hurt me."

Rage threatened to choke Pol. He could feel himself getting flushed with anger. Nobody had a right to terrify an innocent old lady.

He was thinking of how he could separate the gunman from the woman when he sensed someone behind him. He turned and rammed his gun into the stomach of whoever was there.

It was Ironman. Pol lowered the gun and pointed at the window. Ironman stood and cautiously looked inside. "Looks like a standoff," he whispered. "If he gets it, so does she."

"Unless," Pol whispered back, "it's a perfect shot."

He stepped behind Lyons and rested the Colt on Ironman's shoulder. Taking careful aim, he squeezed off two rounds—one into the gun hand of the thug, the other into his brain.

"End of story," Pol said through clenched teeth.

"There's still the man they were chasing."

Both of them rushed back into the alley and found Sandy standing over the body of the dead gunman, her gun clenched in her hand. "He made the mistake of trying to reach for his weapon," she said matter-of-factly.

Pol glanced at the second body. "What about the other guy?"

She shook her head. "He's gone."

They knelt beside Hernandez's body. The thin Hispanic stared up at them. Blancanales reached over and gently shut the dead man's eyes. He looked at the other two. "What now?"

"Let's go check out Hernandez's place," the DEA agent suggested. "He was supposed to record all of the incoming calls."

Two police cars, their overhead lights flashing, screeched to a halt in the alley. Sandy Meissner stood and walked over to the first officer to get out of his car and showed him her identification. She spoke in a low voice. The policeman nodded and signaled the other uniformed policemen to follow him.

As the Miami police took over, Lyons and Blancanales stood and glanced at the dead undercover agent.

"Every day, amigo," Blancanales said bitterly, "good people like this one are murdered and the evil ones live."

"With any luck they won't be alive for long," Ironman replied.

Sandy looked at the two men. She wasn't sure if Ironman was talking to them or to the dead man.

16

"What are Judd's deputies doing on our land?" The dark-haired young woman asked furiously.

"Now don't get yourself in an uproar, Martha."

"Whatever Judd Bushnell wants, he won't find here." Bitterness punctuated her words.

Jimmy Joe wished she would tell him why she hated Judd. But after her reaction to the question in the past, he knew better than to ask again. "They're just checking out something." He tried to change the subject. "You heard about Judd killing all them hijackers?"

"It was on the news. What's that got to do with his being on our land?"

"I think some of them might have gotten away. He wanted to make sure they weren't here."

"Sounds like Judd's bull to me."

Jimmy Joe still couldn't understand her attitude. Bushnell had always been a good friend to both of them. "You don't like him, do you?"

Her voice was filled with venom. "I want him off our land now."

"Okay. I'll go tell him. But what about my idea?"

"Is Judd Bushnell involved in your scheme?"

Jimmy Joe swallowed the piece of gum he was chewing. "No. Not at all, Martha," he lied.

"You go tell him to get his men out of here and we'll talk about it."

Gadgets heard the arguing from the front of the house. He could make out Masters's voice. He wasn't sure who the other person was. He looked around at the plainly furnished spare room where he'd been sleeping. Long spidery cracks covered every wall. The twin bed set against one wall was sheetless. Jimmy Joe had handed him a blanket before he'd turned off the lights.

There was a dark wooden bureau against one wall. The shade was pulled down to prevent sunlight from pouring through the single window in the room. The floor was bare and painted dark brown. A single, un-shaded ceiling light provided the only illumination.

Gadgets forced himself to get up. He was still tired. He'd waited until Masters had finished drinking and staggered off to bed before responding to the signal from Stony Man Farm.

The instructions had been brief. A quick recap of the hijacking and what the thieves had stolen. And orders to keep an eye on the local sheriff. Somehow Gadgets hadn't been surprised when Judd Bushnell's name was mentioned. Without meeting the man he'd had a gut feeling that he was too good to be true. The dilemma was to find transportation without arousing Masters's suspicion.

He was still smarting from Brognola's last order. "This is an observe-only assignment," the big Fed had growled through the telephone. "You call for backup if there's a need for action. Just remember, you're technically on sick leave!"

Annoyed at how the Stony Man operations chief tended to baby his field operatives if they got so much as a scratch, he yanked the shade and watched it roll up with an angry snap. Looking out the window, he saw a yard filled with rusting cars and farm implements. An old wheelbarrow leaned against another building, which he assumed was the barn. He could see the tops of tall trees behind the other building, but there was only dark gray dirt on the ground nearby.

Reaching into his overnight bag, Schwarz found a box of .45 hollowpoints for his Government Model automatic. He carefully reloaded the three clips he found in the bag, then dug out his weapon and rammed one of them into the gun.

Gadgets decided he might see things differently after he was more awake. Right now he needed something to start him on that process. There was time enough to shower and change clothes after he had a cup of coffee.

He pulled on his jeans. Then, barefoot and shirtless, he opened the door and staggered down the hall into the living room, which was a hodgepodge of sagging furniture. The only distinctive feature in it was the gun cabinet. Jimmy Joe had a collection of shotguns, hunting rifles and assault weapons.

There was a painted wooden door at the far end of the room. He assumed it led to the kitchen. He pulled it open and discovered he was right.

A table, covered with a plastic tablecloth, sat against one of the walls, surrounded on three sides by straight-backed chairs. Against the opposite wall was an antique stove and a noisy refrigerator with a cooling coil exposed on top. Even the faucets on the sink looked like something out of a Great Depression movie. They were made of iron and encrusted with fifty years of dirt. There was someone in the kitchen. A woman. She was staring out the window over the sink.

When she turned around, he recognized her immediately as Martha, Jimmy Joe's sister. Even in the Army fatigues she was wearing she was attractive. She seemed taller than her picture, but Gadgets realized she was standing stiff and erect as she turned around and stared at him. In the picture her jet-black hair was long. Now it was cut short, almost as short as a man's, and her hazel eyes examined him coldly. "Who are you?"

He stopped in the doorway. "Hermann Schwarz, a friend of your brother." He started to smile but decided against it.

"Oh, yes, the man he served with in Vietnam. He mentioned you were here for the weekend. I'm his sister, Captain Martha Masters."

She didn't have to identify her rank. She wore the double bars of a captain on her fatigues.

He looked around the kitchen. "Is there any coffee?"

She pointed at the coffee pot on the stove. "He made some. Help yourself. I don't drink coffee."

She was definitely an ice princess, Schwarz decided as he found himself a cup and poured out the steaming brew.

"You might want to put on some shoes and a shirt," she added.

So, Gadgets thought, the almost naked body of a man did something to her. He turned around. "Bother you?"

She shrugged. "I couldn't care less, but you might. The mosquitoes this time of year are ferocious, and

Jimmy Joe doesn't always remember to sweep up all the broken pieces of bottles he drops on the floor.''

Definitely an ice princess. She would be a challenge some other time. Not today. ''Where's Jimmy Joe?''

''I sent him out to take care of some business. He should be back soon.''

Gadgets swallowed the rest of the coffee. ''I guess I'll take a shower and get dressed while I'm waiting.''

She ignored his comment as she turned and stared out the kitchen window.

RUDDLE WAS busy moving the last of the cases into the warehouse when he saw Jimmy Joe walking toward him. Gesturing to the other two men to move the cases inside, he turned and waited for the gaunt man to reach him.

''Where's Judd? I gotta talk to him.''

''He's over in Ashton meeting with newspaper and television people. He'll be in touch as soon as he gets rid of them.''

''This is important,'' Masters said.

''We ain't got time for your nonsense right now, Jimmy Joe. We got some people coming in. Anything I can help with?''

''No. Only Judd would know how to handle this. Maybe I should drive over to Ashton and talk to him.''

''I wouldn't do that. Too many people around to talk openly.'' Ruddle walked over and put his arm around Masters's shoulders. ''What's going on?''

''Martha's here.''

''I know. And that ol' buddy from Vietnam. So all you have to do is keep them busy until the buyers leave.''

"She saw all of you driving to the warehouse on her way in."

The deputy's eyes narrowed. "She saw the warehouse?"

"No, not the warehouse." He studied the structure in amazement. "You sure got it finished in a hurry."

"It cost us extra. So all she saw was us driving down the dirt road?"

"I told her you were making sure none of the gang you wiped out got away and was hiding on our land."

Ruddle smiled. "Hey, now that's good thinking."

"She still wants you out of here."

"What's she got against the law?"

"It's not the law. It's Judd. She's got some hate thing about him, but I can't figure what."

Ruddle smiled. He knew exactly why she hated Judd. He'd seen them in the woods that day, years ago, when Judd caught her running away from him. He'd watched through the bushes as the sheriff had ripped away her skirt and torn off her underpants. It had been one of the holds he'd had on Bushnell all these years. As he kept reminding him, it wouldn't look good for the sheriff to be exposed as a rapist of fifteen-year-old girls.

"Judd affects some people that way. I wouldn't worry about it none. You go back and tell her you saw us leaving." The two other deputies came out of the warehouse and he turned to them. "Let's lock it up and get going." He turned back to Jimmy Joe. "See? We're leaving, anyway."

Masters looked relieved. "Thanks, Stanley. For a minute I wasn't sure what I could tell her."

The chief deputy patted him on the back. "Now you can tell her the truth. I'll tell Judd what you said when I hear from him."

He watched Masters walk away and kept staring at him as he disappeared into the thick brush. There were other truths coming up for Jimmy Joe and his sister. Like their deaths. But that was after the buyers had paid for their guns and left with them. Meantime, he thought he'd better page Bushnell and warn him about Martha's attitude.

JACK GRIMALDI STUDIED the pattern of runways faintly visible in the morning haze. "Texarkana coming up in twenty minutes, gentlemen," he announced over the speaker system of the Sabreliner he was piloting.

"There are no gentlemen back here," Pol commented, sticking his head into the pilot's compartment.

"You can say that again, Pol," the Able Team pilot said, laughing. "Tell them to get ready to fasten their seat belts."

Before Blancanales could snap back a crack, Grimaldi had picked up the microphone and was asking the tower for landing instructions.

Back in the cabin Ironman was still trying to figure out why the undercover agent had been killed. He kept staring at the tape Sandy Meissner had taken from the dead man's answering machine. There hadn't been time to listen to it before they'd left Miami.

Pol returned and sat across the aisle from him. "Still trying to figure it out?"

Lyons shook his head. "I wish we would have had enough time to listen to this thing. There may be a clue there."

"Sandy said she'd let us know if she came up with anything," Pol commented. The DEA agent had remained behind in Miami to try to repair the damage Chico Hernandez's death had done to the agency's carefully built network of informants.

Kissinger, who'd been sitting in front of them, his attention focused on an article on new developments in military armament, turned his head. "You looking for something to play that tape?"

Pol groaned. "What do you think we've been talking about since we left Miami?"

"Sorry. I was wrapped up in this article."

"Obviously," Lyons said sarcastically.

"Jack's got a cassette player up front," Kissinger said.

Pol was surprised. "He does?"

"Sure. He always carries one so he can play his favorite lady's country and western albums."

Lyons started to get up.

"I'll get it," Blancanales said, and walked toward the front of the plane. A minute later he returned with a pocket-size cassette player. "He wasn't happy giving it up."

"He'll live," Ironman said as he snapped the cassette into the unit. He slipped the small headphones on and pushed the Play button.

There were a series of guarded messages, mostly from men, referring to package deliveries or wanting to meet a female friend. Chico Hernandez must have worked hard to keep up his cover.

A female voice started talking. Someone who called herself Ginny. The undercover FBI agent. Her voice sounded familiar, but he couldn't place it.

He heard her reference to "trucking" and the sequence of clicking sounds. She kept repeating the sequence. Finally he understood. She was talking in Morse code. He racked his brain to remember what the signals meant. Finally he realized she was tapping out numbers.

Then she started talking about Noah's Ark. The familiar voice distracted him. He rewound the tape and played her message again. What was special about Noah's Ark?

He listened to the message again. There it was— Noah's Ark. Why did she put so much emphasis on the word *ark?* He stopped the machine and took off the headphones. Pol and Cowboy were watching him. "What does the word *ark* mean to you?"

"Boat. A story from the Bible," Kissinger answered.

"Didn't Noah's Ark land on a mountain someplace in the Middle East?" Pol said.

"Yeah. But that's not it. Why did she emphasize the word *ark?*"

"Maybe they're heading out to sea," Blancanales said. "On a boat."

"Maybe," Lyons muttered. "But somehow I don't think that's it." He thought about it for a moment. "Maybe it's the name of a place. There an atlas on this bird?"

Kissinger walked forward and returned with a regional map. "I borrowed this from Grimaldi. I told him to keep circling the field."

Ironman spread the map out on the floor and knelt to study it. There were lots of places. Rosette, Pine Bluff, Little Rock, Texarkana, El Dorado, New Houston. He studied the map for twenty minutes, then gave up. "We've searched through Texas and Arkansas," he said in disgust. "Nothing." He started to fold up the map. Discouraged, he handed it to Cowboy to return to the pilot.

"Tell you what," Kissinger said. "We'll stop and get some Tex-Mex food when we land in Texarkana. You'll feel better."

Ironman stared at him. "Say that again."

"I said we'll get us some Tex-Mex—"

"That's it. Tex. Short for Texas. Ark is short for Arkansas. That's where they're heading—into Arkansas!"

Kissinger returned in time to hear Lyons's enthusiastic outburst. "That's great, Ironman. Only problem is we still don't know where in Arkansas."

Lyons nodded glumly. He had just recognized whose voice he'd been listening to for the past half hour. Susan Phelan's. And she was alone with a bunch of killers.

17

The convoy had been traveling on U.S. 82 for an hour. Matthews smiled as he studied the symbols of civilization on both sides of the road. Billboards, fast-food shops, motels, gas stations. He was certain no one knew he was back in the United States. Not since he'd had Chico Hernandez silenced.

They pulled off the highway and stopped at a gas station near Magnolia to permit everyone to go the bathroom. This would be the last time they stopped until they got to Gobbler Station.

Matthews and Lopez took turns standing guard to make sure no one was watching them. In the distance they could see the sleepy campus of Southern Arkansas University just outside Magnolia.

Cars and vans filled with returning college students kept driving past, honking their horns as a car filled with teenagers passed another vehicle equally crowded with sloppily costumed teenagers.

"Disgusting," Lopez said angrily as he watched the endless parade of students racing cars along the road. "They go no place. They have too much money to waste. No wonder they buy what we ship."

"We'll be out of here soon enough," Matthews promised. He was as anxious to meet with the sheriff, conclude their business and leave as the huge man next to him. Although he didn't think the American government could prove he'd been involved in marketing government secrets when he was with the National Security Council, he was afraid of the unforgiving memory of the CIA. There had been several attempts to kill him in the past few years. He was positive the CIA was behind them.

What had Sheriff Bushnell promised on the telephone? He remembered. A look at some experimental weapon they'd captured. Probably worthless, Matthews decided. On the other hand, it might be something one of his clients would pay him extra to own.

This was the first time he'd actually see where the sheriff stored his arms. Before this Bushnell had always had his men deliver them to an agreed-upon location outside his native county.

According to the directions he'd been given, they had another forty or so miles to go before they turned onto State Highway 15 and worked their way over small country roads to where Bushnell had his warehouse.

Matthews studied his detailed map. He'd be glad when they loaded the cases onto Countryman's cargo plane so the pilot could fly them to the small airport on Mexico's Yucatán Peninsula where a private Colombian jet would pick them up for their final trip home.

Vargas, Lopez and he would fly back to Colombia on the jet so that he could start training the Colombians on how to use the weapons. Then his contract would be completed, he could collect his fee and fly back to his small villa on the Mediterranean coast.

He glanced in the back of the limousine where Vargas was having a field day running his hands over the hooker's body. She was doing a good job of keeping young Carlos occupied.

Matthews realized he had to use the rest room. "Keep an eye on things," he told Lopez. "I'll be right back."

He dropped the map onto the front passenger seat of the limousine and walked around the corner of the gas station to where the rest rooms were located.

In the rear of the limousine Susan could feel the young Colombian's lust building rapidly.

"I can't wait any longer," he breathed heavily.

He reached into his pocket and took out a silver box. Inside there were a number of folded glassine papers. He opened one and inhaled the white powder. Susan could see his eyes glisten as the cocaine started working in his system. He offered the box to her.

At first she refused, then Vargas took out his gun. "Did you see what I got for a birthday present? I really didn't want it, but my papa said it was rude not to accept presents." He put the automatic back into his pocket and offered her the box again.

Susan took one of the folded papers. Vargas smiled at her, then leaned back and closed his eyes. She opened the glassine and rubbed some of the cocaine around the edges of her nose, then palmed the rest.

"We could close the windows and do it right here. Nobody can see in," he said after he opened his eyes and grabbed her.

She realized she had no choice. "Sure," she said, pretending to feel passion for the man with her. "But I have to go to the bathroom first." She wanted a quick look at the map Matthews had dropped onto the front seat, so she needed Vargas out of the way for a minute or two. "Could you get my bag out of the trunk? There's something in it I need to take with me."

As he reached for the door handle, she let her handbag fall onto the front seat. He smiled knowingly. She was one of those modern American girls who used a device to prevent pregnancy, unlike the young women in his own country.

"Of course." He opened the door and stepped aside to let her get out, then walked to the rear of the long black vehicle.

She opened the front passenger door and reached in for her purse. Quickly she glanced at the map. Matthews had marked their route with a wide red line. The words were tiny. She barely made out their destination. Someplace called Gobbler Station.

She heard the deep, accented voice behind her spitting out a question. "What are you looking at?"

Susan grabbed her purse and turned to face him. It was Lopez. "Nothing," she said nervously. "I was just getting my purse. It fell onto the front seat."

He glared at her, then reached into the limousine and turned the map over. Vargas came up to them, smiling. "Your bag, Ginny," he said, handing her the case she'd brought with her.

She hoped he hadn't looked inside. Even though they were hidden, it wouldn't have taken a Sherlock Holmes to find the gun and stiletto. The FBI agent took the bag and kissed Vargas on the lips. "I'll only be a minute," she whispered, running her hand down the outside of his pants.

Vargas flinched at the suddenness of her touch. She winked at him, then opened the bag and took out a plastic oval case.

Lopez grabbed it. "What's that?"

She froze. Then, realizing there was nothing in the case to reveal her true identity, she relaxed. Vargas took the case from the other man and placed it back in her hands. "Something intelligent women wear to prevent having unwanted children."

The ugly man showed his shock. "Unnatural. Against the will of God." He walked away, muttering to himself.

"Lopez is very old-fashioned," Vargas apologized, laughing at the older man's discomfort.

The small woman zipped up her case and handed it to the young man. "Be a love and put this back in the trunk."

There had to be a pay phone she could use. Now that she knew their destination she needed to pass it on to the contact. She kept her eyes open for a pay phone as she sauntered around the building to the rest rooms.

WHILE GRIMALDI FOUND a place to park the jet, the pair of Able Team hell-raisers and Kissinger wandered over to the counter of an air taxi service. An attractive dark-haired woman was busy talking on the phone. She looked up and saw the three men at the counter, said goodbye to her caller and walked over to them.

Staring at Blancanales with unveiled admiration, she spoke with a soft twang. "Looking to fly someplace? Great time of year to get in some hunting or fishing."

Pol smiled, showing his white teeth. "Maybe later if you're the pilot. But right now we'd like some information about the airports around Texarkana."

"I am one of the pilots," she said.

"And I'm impressed that someone as lovely as you is also so gifted."

The praise stripped away the woman's business manner. "I've lived here all my life. What kind of information are you looking for?"

"One of our associates may be flying in on a small jet to meet us in a day or two. Where could he land?"

She looked surprised. "Why, right here, of course."

"But this is a busy airport," Blancanales said.

"Well, there are two or three private fields that can handle a small jet." She thought about it. "But they're pretty busy, too."

Kissinger joined in. "I think he'd want something more private."

She turned and looked at the ex-football player suspiciously. "You mean, so people wouldn't know he was here?"

Kissinger smiled. "Exactly."

"Sorry, I can't help you," she snapped coldly, and turned back to her desk.

Ironman was getting annoyed. "Lady, we're not running drugs, if that's what you're thinking." If he had his way, they would have shoved the stubborn woman into a back room and sweated the information out of her. While everybody was pussyfooting around, Susan Phelan was holed up with a bunch of killers.

Several people passing the counter turned and stared at him. The woman behind the counter stopped and turned around. "Then why are you so interested in an out-of-the-way place to land?"

Blancanales leaned over the counter. "Please keep this confidential," he said quietly. The woman moved closer and he lowered <u>his</u> voice. "I believe I can trust you. The man is our employer. If our reports are favorable, he's planning to fly in and make an offer to acquire enough land to construct a major business complex downtown. Naturally if word got out that he was here, a lot of speculators would rush out and buy land, then try to sell it to him at greatly inflated prices." Pol saw the glint of greed in her eyes. "Now you know why it's important that his arrival remain undetected."

She relaxed. "Sure, I understand. Hell, some of these real-estate characters around Texarkana would steal food from a starving widow for a profit." Like her boyfriend, she added silently. "I can keep my mouth shut."

"So," Kissinger asked, "what other places can he land?"

She rubbed her face, then brightened. "There's a character ten miles south of Texarkana named Harry Countryman. An old rummy who runs a sometimes cargo service. Some kind of World War II hero if you believe his tall tales. He owns a run-down field. Nobody uses it anymore. He doesn't even have fuel facilities. Just a landing strip, a broken-down hangar, a World War II cargo plane and a beat-up building with a dingy waiting room and office."

Kissinger looked at Ironman. "What do you think?"

"Sounds like something we ought to check out," Lyons said.

"Let's call home and tell them what we're up to," Cowboy suggested.

Lyons nodded. Pol turned and took the hand of the young woman. Bending over, he kissed it gently.

"Someone with your charm and talent is wasted in a place like this."

Ironman was disgusted. Politician had the magic to turn almost any woman on at will. It was a skill Lyons lacked. But then he remembered Susan Phelan and smiled. Except when it was somebody important. "Let's get going," he said quietly.

"One more thing," the woman said as they started to turn away. "This Harry Countryman, there have been some rumors—no hard facts, of course—that he's occasionally gotten involved in running drugs."

Blancanales, Lyons and Kissinger exchanged glances as they walked away from the counter.

"Make your call to the chief," Ironman said. "I think it's time for us to rent a car and unload the cargo from Grimaldi's bird. I'm ready to do some hunting."

18

Gadgets came back into the kitchen, showered and fully clothed. He wore his windbreaker over a T-shirt to conceal the automatic he wore in his waistband holster.

Jimmy Joe and his sister were sitting at the Formica-topped kitchen table, talking. Neither of them noticed Schwarz entering.

He studied them. The angry expression began to fade from the woman's face as Masters spoke. Through the large window behind them he could see a new Chrysler Sundance parked near the door that led outside. He assumed it was the car Martha Masters had driven to get here.

"So I told ol' Stanley to get himself and the other deputies the hell off our property," Jimmy Joe said. "And he apologized and said he would."

Gadgets coughed gently to announce his presence. Both of them turned and looked at him. "If this is private, I don't mind going for a walk in the woods by myself." He turned and walked toward the door that led outside.

Jimmy Joe jumped to his feet and got between Gadgets and the door. "Hell, no! I promised you a hog hunt and you're gonna get yourself a hog hunt." He turned to his sister. "You two met yet, Martha?"

She nodded. "A little earlier while you were out."

"I thought maybe the three of us could go sniffin' around for a razorback this morning." He looked at Schwarz. "Martha here used to do the best damn hog barbecue you ever did sink your teeth into."

"I think I'll pass," Martha said. "I'm going to lie down and try to catch up on some sleep." She stood and walked to the door, then stopped and turned to look at Gadgets. "Jimmy Joe tell you about his business idea?"

Gadgets nodded. "A little bit."

"What do you think of it?"

Schwarz wasn't going to get caught up in a family disagreement. "I'm no expert on things like hunting preserves," he said noncommittally. He was tempted to add that his specialty was hunting vermin—at least the human kind—but he decided that was information he didn't need to share.

"Well, I'm not convinced it's a decent thing to do," the woman said.

"We can talk about it when we get back," Jimmy Joe said hurriedly.

His sister shrugged and left the room. Masters sighed. "Sometimes she sounds exactly like them mean bastards we had for officers over in Nam."

Gadgets kept silent and showed no expression on his face.

"But underneath it she's still my kid sister."

"Doesn't sound like she's too high on your friend Sheriff Bushnell," the Able Team warrior commented.

"Causes me to wonder why she doesn't care for ol' Judd. He's been a friend of ours since we were knee-high to grasshoppers."

"Maybe something happened between them a long time ago."

"Between Judd and Martha?" Jimmy Joe laughed at the thought. "Ol' Judd's one of the nicest men you ever want to meet."

Gadgets thought back to his conversation with Hal Brognola the night before. "I don't know what you're going to face with that sheriff," the chief had said, "but according to Ironman, Pol and Cowboy, he plays country bumpkin a little too perfectly. So keep your eyes open and your weapon loaded."

Schwarz smiled. "Maybe someday she'll tell you why she feels the way she does about the sheriff. Meantime, what do we need to hunt these ferocious pigs of yours?"

JUDD BUSHNELL was furious. Ruddle had interrupted his interviews with the television and newspaper people to alert him to Martha's demands that he be kept off the property she and Jimmy Joe owned jointly. He had cut the interviews short on the pretext of having urgent police business elsewhere. As one of the television reporters commented, it made a nice conclusion to the feature piece they were planning to do on how he and his small band of deputies had wiped out a dangerous gang.

He rammed down hard on the accelerator. Something had to be done about Martha Masters before she messed up his business plans with her personal hatred of him. The two of them would have it out before she could cause problems. If Jimmy Joe objected, he'd be taken care of, too. The same went for the Vietnam War friend Masters had brought home with him.

As he sped down the dirt road that led to Masters's driveway, he spotted Martha's car parked outside. He walked around the outside of the house, looking for Jimmy Joe's pickup. It was gone.

Good, Bushnell thought. Now there would only be Martha and him. He wasn't sure just what he would say or do when he confronted her. But he was glad there was no one else around to witness their meeting.

He got out of his car and knocked on the front door. There was no answer. He knew Jimmy Joe never locked the door, so he turned the knob and stepped into the kitchen.

Near the sink he could see signs that three people had been here recently. Three rinsed coffee cups were neatly stacked on the drain board. He decided to make sure that only Martha and he were there. He called out, "Jimmy Joe?" Nobody answered.

Judd went through the door and into the living room. Masters's gun cabinet was open. Two of the rifles he'd given to the psychotic veteran were missing.

Bushnell was pleased. Masters must have driven his friend deep into the woods to hunt for razorbacks. They would be gone for hours, more than enough time to knock some sense into Martha.

Carefully he climbed the stairs to the second floor of the old farmhouse. He listened for signs of life. There were none. Peering into Jimmy Joe's bedroom, he saw the unmade bed and bits of clothing strewn around the floor.

As he passed the open bathroom door, he looked inside. Hanging over the shower curtain rod were two pair of sheer panties. Judd smiled, remembering the last time Martha and he had been together. At least these panties weren't torn to shreds.

The door to the second upstairs bedroom was closed. Taking out his Smith & Wesson .38 from his holster, Bushnell gently turned the doorknob and pushed open the door.

Martha was stretched out on top of the sheets, facedown and sound asleep. She wore nothing but a pair of thin panties. Judd admired how much woman she had become.

Smiling, he walked to the edge of the bed and called out, "How's it goin', Martha?"

She turned over and stared at him, fury flashing in her eyes. As he stared appreciatively at her substantial breasts, she spit out, "Get the hell out of here, Judd!" and grabbed for her robe.

Bushnell stepped between the cotton wrapper and the young woman. "Now don't go doing anything to spoil my view," he snickered, leering at her.

She pulled the sheet over her body and stared at the revolver. "What do you want?"

"I came looking for Jimmy Joe."

"He's out hunting with that Army buddy of his."

"Well, then I guess we're all alone. It's time the two of us had a little talk," he said, sitting down on the bed close to her.

She glared at him. "About what?"

"About why you don't appreciate what I done for you."

She looked stunned. "You dirty son of a bitch! What you did for me was to screw me up."

Judd grinned. "I heard you prefer women these days. What a waste of a good lady."

"You heard that right. So get the hell out of here."

"I was going to knock some sense into your head about this little business deal Jimmy Joe and I cooked up."

She sneered at him. "I knew you had to be behind it. Jimmy Joe couldn't have come up with anything that crazy without help."

"Actually, it was all my idea." He kept staring at her body, now hidden under the hastily grabbed sheet. "But that can wait for a bit. Right now I think I might be performing the world a good turn by showing you how to enjoy a man again."

She shuddered as he stood up. As he started to take off his clothes, he kept his revolver pointed at her.

"Now you just lie there and get ready to have as much fun as I plan to have."

The horrified young woman watched the obese man drop his trousers onto the floor, then suddenly turned away and threw up all over the bed.

19

Susan Phelan was talking into the pay phone mounted on the side of the gas station when Matthews came out of the men's room and saw her.

"Gobbler Sta—" she started to say when his hand pushed down on the receiver cradle. She turned and stared at him, her eyes filled with concern about what he'd overheard.

He smiled pleasantly as he asked, "Who are you calling?"

"I just wanted Chico to do me a favor," she said, forcing a grin. "Y'know, I've got a couple of steady guys who are gonna wonder what happened to me if I'm not there when they get their weekly 'hornies.' So I wanted him to call them and—"

Matthews took the receiver from her hand and replaced it. "I don't think Mr. Hernandez will be able to hear you anymore," he said. "Shall we go back and keep our friend Carlos happy?"

Trying to hide the concern she felt, Susan let Matthews lead her back to the limousine.

THE FADED SIGN over the building read Countryman Aviation Services. Except for two cars parked in front of it, the place looked as if it had been deserted for years.

Ironman stopped the rented van at the side of the road. He stared through the windows into the small waiting room. "See anybody?"

"No. But that doesn't mean nobody's there."

Ironman eased the Python from its shoulder holster. He saw the modified Colt Government Model that appeared almost magically in Blancanales's hand.

"We may need something heavier," Pol suggested. Lyons agreed. Pol and he got out and walked around to the back. They opened the rear doors.

Kissinger was sitting on a heavy metal case. There was another case like it next to him. "Are we here?"

Ironman nodded. Kissinger jumped out and helped the others pull the cases to the rear lip of the vehicle. He opened one of the cases. "Take your pick, gentlemen. Courtesy of Stony Man Equipment Rentals."

Lyons and Blancanales peered into the case. Cowboy had filled the metal box with a pair of M-16s as well as a Mossberg 12-gauge slug gun and a pair of MAC-10s. Neatly stacked at one end were filled clips for the automatic weapons and boxes of shells.

Ironman selected an M-16. He loaded the weapon, then jacked a round into the chamber. Grabbing three 30-round clips, he shoved them into his waistband.

Blancanales studied the contents, then looked at Kissinger. "What's in the box you're sitting on?"

"A grenade launcher and an assortment of grenades as well as some handguns we might need."

Pol thought about it and selected one of the MAC-10s. He searched through the case and found several loaded clips. He glanced at Cowboy. "Teflon coated?"

"Better. Glasser rounds. They'll cut through anything that isn't an inch of cold steel," the Able Team armorer promised.

Blancanales looked pleased. "Feel like joining the party?"

"Wouldn't miss it for a minute," Kissing replied.

He shoved a clip of hollowpoints into the other MAC-10 and hung it on his shoulder by its leather strap.

"You might want to bring the grenade launcher along just in case," Ironman suggested.

Cowboy opened the second case and shoved several grenades into his pocket, then picked up the launcher.

"Ready when you are," he announced.

"Then let's do it," Lyons said.

They held a quick strategy meeting. Ironman would move in on the rear of the building while Pol and Cowboy got into position to cover the front.

"Listen for my whistle or shots before you rush in," Lyons said in a low voice.

The three warriors separated.

IRONMAN MOVED to the front of the building and peered into the waiting room. It was empty. From the dilapidated hangar across the unkempt field he saw a beat-up Ford Mustang racing toward him.

Lyons dropped behind a stack of empty crates piled high near the rear of the building. The car came to a stop near him. The front door opened and an overweight man in his sixties staggered out. He was carrying an empty ice chest.

Lyons wondered if they'd come to the wrong place. Despite the automatic he wore in a belt holster, the man looked more like a drunk than a hired gun.

He watched as the man struggled to open a rear door, then staggered inside and disappeared into a room. Lyons whistled and moved through the rear door. Through the front windows of the small building he could see Pol and Cowboy, their weapons ready to fire, peering inside. He waved for them to join him.

Led by Ironman, the Able Team trio moved to the inner door. The stout man was sitting behind a chipped wooden desk, taking swigs from an almost-empty bottle of bourbon.

Pointing the M-16 at the man behind the desk, Lyons stepped into the room, followed by Blancanales and Kissinger. Stunned at their sudden appearance, Countryman dropped the bottle and raised his hands. Stammering, he asked, "Is this...this a...a robbery?"

"Nothing that nice," Lyons snapped. "Take out that side arm slowly, put it on the floor and kick it toward me."

Shaking with fear, the old man leaned down and put the Walther on the linoleum floor, then shoved it toward Ironman with his foot. Lyons bent down and scooped it up.

Still quaking, the man stammered, "What...what do you want?"

"Information," Ironman growled. "Where are the men who hired you?"

"They've gone to—" Countryman started to say, then stopped. "What men?"

"If you want to keep living, you'll get right to the point," Cowboy said. "Understand?"

The bleary-eyed man stared at the huge figure hovering over him and bobbed his head. "Y-yes. They went on a trip. They won't be back for a few days."

Pol joined in. "Where did they go?"

"I don't know."

Blancanales pushed his Colt automatic against the man's chest. "Try to remember."

"Arkansas," Countryman screeched. "That's where they went."

Lyons sat on the edge of the desk near the terrified man. "Where in Arkansas?"

"I don't know." He turned quickly to the other two armed intruders. "Honest, I don't know. Some rural section."

"Yes, you do," Blancanales told him coldly.

"All I know is that it was only about three hours from here, because they said they'd be back before dark," Countryman answered nervously.

Lyons picked up the questioning. "What were they going for?"

The pilot started to say he didn't know, but looking at the deadly expression on Ironman's face made him change his mind. "Guns. A lot of guns."

"How were they planning to get them out of the country?"

Terror had begun to sober up Countryman. He was sure he would be killed if he lied. "I was supposed to fly them out."

"In what?"

He had given up trying to bluff his way out. "I have a C-46 parked behind the hangar across the field."

Kissinger looked at him, then asked, "And they left you here alone to guard the plane?"

Countryman thought of what the six men in the hangar would do to him if he revealed their presence. "Yes," he replied, gulping.

"Whose cars are parked out in front?"

"They . . . they left them here. They all got into a truck."

Lyons turned and stared across the field. He could make out the tip of the C-46's left wing peeking from behind the old hangar. "Why isn't your plane inside?"

"It's . . . it's old. I never think of using the hangar."

Lyons shook his head. "I don't believe you. What's inside the hangar?"

Countryman sighed. "Their jet. The one they came in. I'm supposed to have it ready for them when they get back."

Pol pushed his face against the pilot's. "How many of them were there?"

"I don't know exactly," the half-sober man said, trying hard not to whimper. "Ten or twelve." He remembered something. "They had a girl with them. I think she's a hooker."

Blancanales glanced at Ironman. Lyons hadn't reacted to the news that Susan Phelan might be with them. Pol understood. They were on a mission, and personal feelings weren't permitted until their job was completed.

Pol continued the questioning. "Is there anyone else here?"

"No!" Countryman shouted. "No, I'm here all alone!"

Blancanales turned to Lyons. "Think he's telling the truth?"

"Let's go back to the hangar and find out. I'm curious to see this jet they've got hidden back there." He stared at the frightened men. "If we find out you weren't lying, we might let you live to face a judge. On the other hand, if you're holding back, the only judge you're going to face is down in hell."

20

Jimmy Joe led the way as they crawled through the tall prairie grass heading for a swampy area a hundred yards away. Gadgets was close behind him, wondering why he was so willing to let the sharp blades of grass cut at his face when he could be back at Stony Man, comfortable and dry.

They had left the pickup at the edge of the large field. Both of them were armed with large-bore hunting weapons provided by Masters. Jimmy Joe was carrying a Harrington & Richardson Model 308 semi-automatic rifle. Gadgets had a Winchester 1300 Police 12-gauge shotgun.

Masters gestured for Schwarz to stop, then crawled back to him and whispered. "Hear that scraping and banging ahead?"

Gadgets had wondered what was making the noise, and he nodded.

"A pair of razorbacks fighting. Probably over a harem of sows." Masters grinned. "Just like a couple of horny men."

Gadgets whispered, "What do we do?"

"If there'd been time, I would've borrowed a pair of Sam Young's dogs. Best hunting hounds in the county. I guess we just crawl up as close as we can and shoot the damn hogs." He started to turn away, then stopped. "Be sure you aim for the head. We don't wanna spoil the meat. And be careful. They're even meaner when they're hit."

He crawled ahead and gestured for Gadgets to follow. Just past the edge of the prairie grass Schwarz saw the two razorbacks slashing at each other with their curved tusks. In the background he saw a harem of mud-covered sows waiting to see which of the two wild boars would be the victor.

Jimmy Joe pointed at one of the hogs. "You take that one," he whispered. The gaunt man rose from the grass and pointed his H&R at the nearest of the two hogs. At that moment his scent reached the battling boars, and they suddenly pulled away from each other as Masters fired.

The two hogs vanished into the thick brush. Jimmy Joe pulled himself to his feet and cursed loudly, then turned to where the harem of sows had been. They, too, had vanished. "Damn, I forgot I was in front of the wind," he muttered.

Schwarz stood and joined him. "What do we do now, Coach?"

"Ain't gonna be a hog hanging around for a mile. Only thing we can do is go borrow a pair of Sam Young's dogs to find them."

Schwarz was growing tired of Jimmy Joe's company. He had dominated the entire morning with more tales of gory nostalgia interspersed with stories of how his family had spent their lives outsmarting the law. "Why don't I wait here until you get back?"

Masters looked as if he was about to argue, then shrugged. "Why would you want to do that?"

"I don't get much of a chance to get out in the woods and smell the fresh air," Gadgets said. He wasn't exaggerating. Much of his life since joining Able Team had been spent in battles with very little time to get away from killing and death.

"Okay," Jimmy Joe agreed reluctantly. "But you stay put. Don't go wandering off by yourself. Never know what you'll run in to. Lots of cottonmouths swimming around with their families in these swampy areas, and there's rattlers nesting all around you as well as some real ornery wild hogs who'd rather slash you than let you walk away in peace."

Gadgets smiled at the feeble attempt to frighten him. He watched as the emaciated ex-soldier walked back through the woods toward his pickup.

As he heard the distant rumblings of the old truck fade into the woods, Gadgets walked to a rise of dry land and sat down with his back against a tall oak tree. It was peaceful here. He could hear birds whistling their messages to one another. A slight breeze rustled the leaves over his head. He rested his shotgun against the tree and put his hands behind his head.

He hadn't met Sheriff Bushnell yet. He'd ask Jimmy Joe to introduce him later today. He wondered why Brognola wanted him to keep an eye on the country law officer. From everything he'd heard the sheriff sounded like a typical county police official.

The only person he'd met who seemed to dislike the sheriff was Masters's sister. But then she seemed to have a personal dislike for men of any sort. He wondered if that attitude was the result of being an officer in the military or from something more personal. Not that it mattered. As attractive as she was, Gadgets wasn't available to start a relationship with a woman, not as long as he was part of Able Team.

He closed his eyes and inhaled the perfume of the woods. Stony Man Farm seemed so far away now. Gadgets could barely remember ever feeling so relaxed.

The sense of peace he felt was rudely interrupted by a series of snorts to his right. Opening his eyes, Gadgets saw a huge black form charging him at full speed. A pair of curved tusks protruding from either side of the angry head were aimed right at him.

Rolling to one side, he saw the wild boar crash into the thick trunk of the oak, then pull away and turn to resume its assault. There was no time to grab the shotgun Jimmy Joe had lent him. This was no human foe who could be tricked or outmaneuvered. This was hundreds of pounds of animal fury intent on impaling him.

Grabbing the Colt Government Model from his waistband holster, Gadgets released the safety and pointed the automatic at the head of the oncoming beast. He pulled the trigger again and again until metal clicked on metal. Quickly releasing the empty magazine, Schwarz rammed a fresh clip into the gun, jacked a round into the chamber and continued firing until the magazine was empty.

He had been so engrossed in defending himself that he hadn't dared to take the time to see what effect his hollowpoints had had on the wild hog. He saw the body of the huge creature lying on the ground a mere fifteen feet away. Blood was streaming through the series of gaping holes in its skull and face.

Gadgets dug out the remaining full magazine he was carrying in his windbreaker and replaced the empty magazine with it. Carefully he moved closer to the huge carcass, watching for any signs of life. Like many of the human foes he'd shot in the past, he wanted to be sure this one was really dead before he came too close.

A minute passed and there were still no signs of life in the still creature. Schwarz moved even closer and studied the wild hog. It was truly a magnificent animal, as noble and defiant-looking in death as it had been when it was alive.

There was no point in standing there and staring at the bleeding carcass. Gadgets retrieved his shotgun and decided to wander through the woods until he heard the sound of Jimmy Joe's pickup returning.

The hardwoods and conifers competed with the soft pine for space in the untouched wooded area. Working his way through the trees and bushes, Schwarz saw a long snake slither quickly through the leaves, trying to escape him. He waited until the snake had vanished, then continued wandering.

Noisy birds resumed their chattering in the higher branches of the trees. A red squirrel chattered angrily at him as Gadgets inadvertently stepped on its hidden cache of nuts.

Smiling at the annoyed animal, Schwarz moved through the woods to the edge of a small hill. Parting the brush with his hand, he was surprised to see a large corrugated structure standing in a freshly cleared area.

Was this the old still Jimmy Joe had mentioned? Gadgets dismissed the thought. This building was brand-new. For a moment he wondered if he'd crossed from Masters's property to the national wildlife refuge next door.

No, he could see the strands of rusty barbed wire that marked the property line at the far end of the cleared area. He wondered what the building contained.

Checking that no one else was around, Gadgets climbed down the slight incline and circled the structure. There were no windows, just a pair of wide doors, like those on a warehouse loading dock, and a huge padlock sealing the doors.

He saw a yellow forklift parked near the building. What could be inside that was so heavy that it required a forklift to move it?

He examined the rubber-tired machine. There were some words stenciled on the control panel, partially covered with mud. Gadgets scraped the dirt away with his nails and studied the stenciled letters. Property of U.S. Army Arsenal. Karnack, Texas. There was an inventory number stenciled next to the words.

He'd found the missing shipment of hijacked guns, or at least a forklift from the same arsenal. He had to get to Masters's house and call Stony Man.

Jimmy Joe wouldn't be home. Gadgets was glad. He wouldn't have believed that his onetime Nam buddy could have gotten involved in stealing guns and killing law-enforcement officers. But it had been twenty years, and Schwarz realized even old friends could change.

Both saddened and elated by the discovery, Gadgets started to walk back toward the hill when he heard a vehicle approach behind him. Quickly he raced around to the rear of the building. There was a door there. He tried to open it, but it was locked.

As Schwarz watched, a police vehicle stopped at the front of the structure. Three uniformed deputies got out and looked around. Gadgets was about to come out and announce his discovery when he heard the tallest of them give orders to the others. "Let's open it up and get them guns ready for the buyers. Judd'll be here soon."

The tall deputy took a key from his pocket and unlocked the padlock. He slid the doors open.

Gadgets needed to contact Stony Man and let them know he'd discovered the location of the hijacked weapons. He decided to slip away when the three deputies were inside. Then he heard the sound of a second vehicle.

He saw another official car pull up alongside the first one. Three more deputies got out. The tall deputy who had led the first group walked over to them. "You three stand guard while we get things ready inside," he ordered.

Gadgets wondered how he could escape. He only had the one magazine of hollowpoints in his automatic, and three shells filled with slugs in the shotgun Jimmy Joe had lent him.

He squatted and searched through his pockets. The communicator was in his hip pocket. At least he could alert Brognola that there was a problem here.

He set the buttons for an emergency signal. He knew the signal would hitchhike along telephone and power lines until it reached the communications center in the Shenandoah Valley.

The small red diode on the unit kept flickering. He had to hide the communicator so that, in case he was captured, it wouldn't be found. Quickly he scooped a shallow trench in the dirt and buried the small metal transmitter.

He was going to try to talk his way out of this situation. Standing, he checked the shotgun to make sure there was a round in the chamber, then started walking slowly toward the front of the warehouse.

KISSINGER PULLED their van alongside the hangar. They could see the C-46 parked behind it as the three of them got out. Harry Countryman remained inside the van, seemingly frozen to his seat.

Pol gestured for him to get out. The now-fully sober man refused to move. Blancanales reached in and dragged him out. He stared at him suspiciously. "You afraid of something?"

"I don't want to go inside, that's all."

Pol turned to his two partners. "You hear that? He doesn't want to go inside." He turned back to the frightened pilot. "Why?"

"I just don't."

The Able Team commandos traded looks and gripped their weapons. Lyons studied the building, then turned to their captive. "How many entrances are there?"

Too terrified to refuse to answer he blurted out, "Three. The hangar doors, one around the corner and the one in front of us."

Ironman, Pol and Cowboy held a quick conference. "I'll take this entrance."

"Leave the hangar doors to me," Cowboy offered.

"That leaves the door around the corner for me." Pol grinned. "Aren't I the lucky one?"

Lyons checked his watch. "I'll wait three minutes, then barge in. Okay?"

The other two nodded.

"And stay hard," Ironman reminded them.

"You do the same, homeboy," Blancanales replied, then took off with Kissinger for the other entrances.

Lyons gripped Countryman's arm tightly as he watched the hands of the watch move. Finally it was time. "Let's go and see what's inside," he said, pushing the old pilot ahead of him toward the side door. Checking his watch again, he counted to ten, then threw open the door and shoved Countryman into the hangar.

The pilot panicked. Running toward the six men sitting around the table, he shouted, "Look out! It's a raid!"

The six men grabbed their weapons and dived away from the table. One of them unleashed his TEC-9 and tore the terrified pilot in two as a reward for his warning.

Lyons fell to the ground and rolled away from the path of the rounds being poured at him. With no time to aim he pumped rounds in a sweeping pattern, alternating between firing high and low.

Two of his shots punched a hole in the chest of one of the thugs. The hot slugs knocked the squat man backward until he crashed into the side of the jet. Screeching in Spanish, the dying man cursed Ironman before he stopped functioning.

Pol and Cowboy moved quickly to pocket the remaining thugs between the waves of slugs they sprayed. Two more men exploded into bloody masses before they could fire back.

The remaining three hired guns pushed the card table over and used it as a shield.

"The launcher," Lyons shouted at Cowboy.

Dropping his MAC-10, Kissinger aimed the grenade launcher and fired it at the overturned table. A wash of flaming chemicals covered the screaming men who had taken refuge there.

"The jet! Get inside!" one of them shouted.

The three thugs ran for the stairs. Lyons reduced the number to two when he fired two 3-shot sequences and severed the spine of the last thug to try to rush into the plane.

The two hoodlums inside the jet punched out windows and started to lay down a steady stream of hot lead in all directions. Lyons knew it was too dangerous to try to rush them. He turned to Cowboy. "Pump some of those grenades into the fuel tanks and let's get the hell out of here."

Kissinger waved his understanding and backed away toward the door from which he'd entered. Pol and Ironman followed his lead. With his back to the open door Cowboy pumped four grenades at the jet's fuel tanks, then dived outside. So did the two Able Team warriors.

They moved rapidly away from the hangar and crouched low. Suddenly they heard the rumbling explosion ripping through the inside of the hangar. As they watched, the corrugated roof of the structure lifted a few feet, then crashed down inside the walls of the building.

They waited until the debris had settled before they checked out the thugs in the jet. What had once been savage killers were now just charred bodies. Kissinger retrieved his MAC-10 as they walked back toward the van.

Kissinger drove the van back to the small building. "What now?"

"We call Stony Man and tell them," Lyons said.

"Yeah," Blancanales said in disgust. "We tell them we still don't have a clue where the guns are hidden."

Ironman would have added, "Or where they took Susan Phelan," but he resisted. Whatever they had started back in Washington would have to wait until this mission was completed.

21

Aaron Kurtzman reluctantly interrupted Brognola's nap. He knew the Able Team operations chief had been up all night monitoring the new mission. "Sorry to wake you, but I thought you'd want to see this."

The big Fed had been dozing on the couch in his office. Rubbing his eyes, he stretched and pulled himself into a sitting position. He grabbed the unlit Honduran cigar from the ashtray and shoved it into his mouth. Finally he took the page from Bear and studied it. "When did this come in?"

"We started getting this signal about fifteen minutes ago."

"Where's it coming from?"

Kurtzman handed him a detailed map. "As best we can figure, it's coming from this area."

Brognola studied the map. "South-central Arkansas?"

"Exactly. Near Gobbler Station."

"Only man with a communicator down there is Gadgets Schwarz."

Bear nodded. "I know."

"I told him to keep his eyes open and stay out of trouble," Brognola growled.

"You know how the three of them are," Bear replied sympathetically.

"I want to talk to Lyons or Blancanales the minute they call in," the Justice man snapped, suddenly wide-awake.

BUSHNELL LOOKED at the body of the woman. He hadn't meant to shoot her, but she'd kept scratching his face with her nails until he'd been forced to do something to stop her. He sighed as he got dressed and consoled himself with the thought that he would have had to kill her sooner or later, anyway.

From outside he heard the sound of a vehicle stopping in front of the farmhouse. He glanced out the window and saw Jimmy Joe getting out of his truck.

Bushnell locked the door to the bedroom and hustled down the stairs. He reached the kitchen just as Masters entered. Jimmy Joe looked surprised to see the sheriff. "I thought you were over in Ashton getting your picture took," the gaunt man said.

"Had to come back to take care of some unfinished business."

Masters looked suspicious. "What're you doin' here?"

Bushnell smiled broadly. "Decided it was time for Martha and I to patch up our differences. We had us a long confab and got everything straightened out."

Jimmy Joe sounded relieved. "I'm glad that's out of the way." He looked around. "Where is she?"

"Said she had to run over to Ashton to pick up some things," Bushnell said, sounding nonchalant. "Told me to tell you she'd be back in a couple of hours. Told me to give you a present."

"What's that?"

Bushnell grinned as he pulled out his .38. "Say goodbye, Jimmy Joe. You're goin' on a real long trip."

The sheriff pulled the trigger and drilled the surprised Vietnam veteran in the face.

SCHWARZ STARED back at the tall, thin man. His hair was thinning on top. Like the other two, he wore the uniform of a sheriff's deputy. "I was invited here by Jimmy Joe Masters," Gadgets said.

"Ain't you that guy he was in Vietnam with?" The tall man stared at him. "You don't look like you could have been much of a hero. What are you doin' here?"

"We were out hunting. Jimmy Joe went back to get some dogs and I decided to go for a walk."

"That was your first mistake, mister," the deputy commented.

One of the other deputies walked over to them. "What do you want to do with this one, Stanley?"

The man called Stanley shook his head. "Dunno yet. We'll wait for Judd to come and decide." He thought of something and called out to one of the men inside the building. "Gruber, come on out here."

A short man in uniform responded to the call. He glanced at Gadgets, then turned to the other man. "You want something, Stanley?"

"You stayed behind with Judd at the Mitford place. Was this one of them federal agents who came by to nose around?"

The man called Gruber turned and studied Schwarz carefully, then turned to Stanley and shook his head. "No, he wasn't one of the three men, and he sure wasn't that pretty lady agent."

Gadgets barely heard the conversation. He kept wondering if the communications center at Stony Man Farm had picked up his emergency signal.

"Well, that gets you a little longer to live," Ruddle told him, interrupting his thoughts.

"This is all a mistake," Schwarz said.

"And you made it, mister, nosing around here."

The other two men inside the building came out to see what the commotion was.

Gadgets glanced at the building. "What is this place? One of Jimmy Joe's businesses?"

"None of your business, mister," the tall deputy snapped. "It's private and you're trespassing."

Gadgets tried to brazen it out. "Isn't this Jimmy Joe's land?"

"Yeah, but this ain't his business." He saw the five uniformed men staring at the manacled stranger. "This ain't no time for dawdlin'. Y'all get back to work before I tell Judd on you. We got customers coming this afternoon!" He prodded Gadgets with his weapon. "You get inside. I'll find a safe place to store you until Judd gets here and decides what to do with you."

FRANK MATTHEWS NUDGED Lopez and tilted his head toward the back of the long black limousine. The ugly Colombian glanced over his shoulder.

Young Vargas had practically undressed the woman with him. They were kissing furiously while his hands explored her body. The son of the Medellín cartel leader looked up and grinned when he saw Lopez watching him. "She's good, Lopez. Much better than that French girl." He returned to his lustful exploration of Susan Phelan.

Lopez turned to Matthews. "You were right. He's happy." He glanced out the window. "When do we arrive?"

Matthews consulted the map. "It should be no more than thirty minutes." He studied the rural landscape outside. "There's a county road not too far ahead. We should turn right there."

Lopez nodded. "This sheriff, is he reliable?"

"That sample shipment of TEC-9s came from him. Did they work?"

"They worked fine. But there weren't enough of them and he charged so much. *El Jefe* was unhappy at the price."

"You can't walk into a store and buy a large quantity of assault rifles without somebody asking questions. Naturally he charges a lot."

"These new guns, they better be as good as you say they are. *El Jefe* will be very disappointed if they're not."

The CIA turncoat understood the warning. The South African mercenary Pedro Vargas had used to train his men before Matthews was hired had talked him into acquiring Chinese-made AK-47s that constantly jammed in action. The lifeless body of the mercenary had been found on a lonely Colombian highway with his jugular vein torn from his neck.

"They're the latest U.S. military issue. You've heard of the Green Berets?"

The thickest man nodded, keeping his eyes on the road.

"They swear by them," Matthews said.

"It all sounds good, *señor,* but the final test will be when our men use them."

A small sign ahead read Hope. Matthews pointed to it. "We turn there."

Lopez twisted the wheel and drove onto a narrow gravel road. As the limousine bounced over the loose gravel, the Colombian shook his head. "I thought Americans had the best roads in the world."

"The sheriff wanted us to take this side road to avoid being seen. We'll only be on this for about fifteen miles."

Behind them the second car and the truck bounced. Lopez swore in Spanish, then turned to Matthews. "I think maybe we should have taken a big helicopter instead of cars."

"And have everybody notice us?"

The Colombian sighed. "The things I do for *El Jefe*." From the back seat he heard shrieks of laughter.

"Hey, Marco," Vargas called out happily, "this is even better than one of those water beds!"

Matthews saw the disgusted expression on Lopez's face. Lowering his voice, he said, "Look at it this way. At least he won't be telling you what you're doing wrong."

"If only he wasn't Pedro Vargas's son," the Colombian muttered. "Still, it's my responsibility to be sure he doesn't get into trouble."

THE HELICOPTER LANDED in a small field on the edge of town. There were two state-trooper vehicles and a van waiting. A call from Stony Man Farm to the governor had brought quick results.

Two uniformed troopers rushed over to the Bell to help haul the two metal cases into the van. A lieutenant got out of the second car and joined them.

"Lieutenant Schrieber of the Arkansas State Police," he said, introducing himself. Lyons introduced himself and the other two hell-raisers. "I was told to meet you men here with a van. What's up?"

"In a minute, Lieutenant," Lyons said. He turned to Grimaldi. "We'll signal you when we want you back. Where are you planning to put down?"

"I'll be waiting for your call at the Little Rock Air Force Base," the dark-haired pilot said. "Checking out the local supply of good-looking women."

"Just be ready to take off on a moment's notice," Ironman warned.

"Hey, they don't call me a minute man for nothing."

Pol smiled and withheld the crack he was about to make. "You can take longer than a minute, Jack."

Grimaldi grinned and lifted the Bell up into the air.

The Arkansas State Police official studied the three Stony Man hell-raisers. "Where'd you men come in from?"

"Texarkana," Kissinger replied.

"I hear they had some excitement down there. Found the bodies of a bunch of foreigners and professional hit men buried under a collapsed airport hangar. Know anything about that?"

"They're history," Lyons said coldly. "What were you told about our mission, Lieutenant?"

"Not much. Only that three federal agents on a special assignment would be arriving. And that we were to cooperate fully with them."

"For now all we need is some information," Lyons said. "Do you know a town called Gobbler Station?"

"Sure. It's on the other side of the county about fifteen miles from here."

"Know a farmer named Jimmy Joe Masters?"

The lieutenant shook his head. "I can find out for you." He walked over to his car and picked up his police microphone. After a few minutes of conversation, he replaced the microphone and walked back to Ironman. "Jimmy Joe Masters lives about ten miles out of Gobbler Station. I can show you how to get there on a map."

"That'll be fine."

"Anything else you need from us?"

"For now we'll take it from here. But if you don't mind, would you alert your people that we might have to call on you for help."

"There's a police band two-way radio in the van. What kind of help will you need?"

"Tactical Squad kind of help," Lyons said grimly.

The lieutenant studied Ironman carefully, then smiled. There was something very familiar about the blond visitor. "Didn't realize the federal government was finally getting smart and hiring ex-cops," the state trooper said.

Lyons nodded. "What's that old expression? You can take the man from the police department, but you can't take the police department from the man."

The lieutenant borrowed a felt-tipped pen and marked the route to Gobbler Station and Masters's property on a map. He handed the map to Ironman. "I'm curious about one thing," he said, staring at the two metal cases Pol and Cowboy were loading into the back of the borrowed van. "What have you got in those cases?"

Lyons looked at Blancanales. Pol was better at smooth conversation. "The fixings for a hot meal," the silver-haired charmer said.

"I don't think I want to know who you're planning to cook," the senior state trooper said, and signaled his men to move out.

22

Bushnell blew his top when Ruddle told him about capturing a stranger and handcuffing him to a pipe inside the warehouse. "Why the hell didn't you just blast him?"

"You know how you get if we do something like that without you knowing," Ruddle said nervously. He tried to change the subject. "I had two of the boys hide the bodies."

"Where?"

"There wasn't enough time to bury them, so they shoved Jimmy Joe and his sister into an upstairs bedroom closet."

"Sometimes you don't use your head. As soon as this is over, you take some men and get rid of the two of them." He shook his head. "As far as this buddy of Jimmy Joe's is concerned, let's get rid of him now before the—"

The sound of vehicles interrupted him. He looked up and saw the long black limousine leading another luxury-size vehicle and a truck. The convoy pulled around the building and stopped.

Bushnell turned to Ruddle. "We'll get rid of him as soon as they leave," he muttered, then walked over to greet the visitors.

INSIDE THE WAREHOUSE Gadgets struggled with the handcuffs. There was no way he could open them without a key. The men outside might be rogue cops, he decided, but they knew how to manacle prisoners. If he could only get hold of one of the handcuff keys. They were usually interchangeable.

He stopped struggling and looked around the large space. Dozens of open wooden crates were stacked everywhere. He could smell the sour aroma of the oil-saturated packing material that lined the weapon boxes.

Most of the crates were clearly marked as property of the military, with the name of the arsenal or munitions warehouse where they had been inventoried. Gadgets found the stacks of crates marked Karnack Munitions Depot. These were the weapons Brognola had told him had been hijacked.

Stacked right next to him were a number of cases stenciled Experimental. Top Secret.

Gadgets knew that these were also part of the shipment Brognola had been seeking. Smiling to himself, Schwarz decided that no matter what happened he had at least completed his assignment to help find the hijacked weapons.

He wondered if the pipe could be sawed through with the edge of the handcuffs. He began to rub his manacled wrists up and down the metal pipe, tearing the skin around his wrists each time he moved. Biting his lip to keep from yelling, he continued to work the manacles against the pipe.

A deputy wandered into the building and looked around. The scraping noises from where the stranger was handcuffed caught his ear. He walked over and watched Gadgets's desperate efforts. "Ain't gonna do you one damn bit of good, feller," he said, sneering.

"Watch me," Gadgets said as he continued to move his wrists against the pipe, trying to ignore the searing pain from the bleeding cuts.

"Ain't got time," the deputy answered. Then, without warning, he lifted the wooden stock of his M-16 and smashed it against the side of Schwarz's head. Blood seeped slowly from the gash as Gadgets slumped to the ground, unconscious.

"Never could stand somebody who liked to make noise," the deputy said to no one in particular, humming to himself as he turned around and walked out of the building.

OUTSIDE, BUSHNELL was chatting with Matthews and Lopez while their men watched from a distance. The noise from inside the limousine reached Bushnell's ears. He started to lean over to look inside when Matthews stopped him.

"One of our associates is getting acquainted with a young lady," he said, pulling the sheriff away.

Bushnell grinned. "Hell of a time to get horny. But from what I hear, these Latin types do it anytime of the day or night."

Lopez leaned over and whispered in Matthews's ear. The well-dressed man nodded in agreement and turned to the sheriff. "Would there be a place nearby where our associate could...uh, entertain his lady friend privately?"

The sheriff's grin widened. "I know the perfect place." Bushnell thought of Jimmy Joe's and Martha's bodies stuffed in a closet. "And I'm sure nobody will mind."

Matthews looked in the back-seat window and gestured for Vargas to roll it down. When the Colombian did so, he whispered some words to the young man, who nodded enthusiastically. Leering at Susan, Matthews grinned. "Now you two young people can be more comfortable."

Bushnell turned to his chief deputy. "Would you mind running the limousine up to Jimmy Joe's place, Stanley?" His grin became a leer as he added, "And I don't think you'll have to wait around. You can pick up the folks after we've finished with our business." As Ruddle drove the limousine away, Bushnell turned to Matthews and Lopez. "Now let's have a look at what I've got for you."

The sheriff was about to lead the group into the warehouse when Gruber leaned over and whispered in his ear, "Don't forget we got that stranger inside."

Bushnell had forgotten. Quickly he made a decision. "You and some of the other men haul out a case of them guns and a case of ammunition."

"We can inspect them inside just as easily," Matthews suggested.

"You'll wanna test them, too, so we might as well do it all out here," the sheriff said glibly.

Lopez looked around the area. "And nobody will hear the shots?"

"Naw," Bushnell replied. "Ain't nobody around for miles."

Gruber drove the yellow forklift out of the warehouse. He had opened two cases loaded on it. Bushnell reached into the top case, pulled out a CAR-15 and handed it to Matthews. "Best weapon the U.S. Army's ever produced. Relatively light, damn accurate and can empty a 30-round clip in seconds. Not only that, it doesn't jam like some of them cheap foreign-made guns.''

Matthews studied the assault rifle, then handed it to Lopez. The Colombian balanced the weapon in his right hand, then looked at the fat sheriff. ''You say it's accurate?''

''One of the most accurate at fifty yards.'' He pointed at an oak tree in the distance. ''That there tree's just about fifty yards away. Try it yourself.'' He reached into the case of ammunition and grabbed a handful of rounds. ''We got clips for them inside, but you can single-load them for testing.''

The Colombian gestured for one of his men to join him. He handed the assault rifle to the slender, grim-looking man and pointed at the tree. The gunman took the rounds from Bushnell and slipped one into the firing chamber. Aiming carefully, he squeezed the trigger. The bullet chopped away a large wedge of wood from the tree trunk.

Bushnell told one of his men to get a handful of clips and fill them. Then he turned to Lopez and Matthews. ''Why don't you have all of your men try them?''

The gray-haired man glanced at Lopez. ''Why not?''

They waited while two of the deputies filled two dozen clips with ammunition.

With a nod of approval from Lopez and Matthews, the men each grabbed a rifle and loaded it. At first they were satisfied to shoot at the tree. Then one of the Colombians challenged a mercenary to a sharpshooting contest.

The mercenary walked over to Bushnell. ''Got any paper targets?''

The sheriff shook his head. Gruber leaned over and whispered, "How about that guy we got chained up inside?"

Bushnell's eyes lighted up for a moment as he considered the idea, then became dim again. He wasn't sure how the customers would feel about using a human target. "We'll take care of him later. Go inside and bring out a bunch of those crate covers. And find something to paint circles on them."

LYONS DROVE the borrowed van while Blancanales and Kissinger reloaded their ammunition clips. "Be sure to reload the grenade launcher just in case we need it," he called out.

Cowboy grunted his agreement as he concentrated on pushing rounds into the MAC-10 clips.

Pol looked at Lyons. "Could you keep this thing steady? I feel like I'm dancing the rumba sitting down."

"Tell it to the gravel road," Lyons replied. He glanced at the map the lieutenant had given him. "Better hurry up and get finished. We turn onto a dirt road three miles from here."

The three men became silent as they concentrated on what they were doing. Ironman tried hard to keep Susan Phelan out of his thoughts.

Blancanales helped in that respect. "What kind of trouble do you think Gadgets is in?"

"We'll find out soon." Lyons glanced over his shoulder at Kissinger. "Almost finished, Cowboy?"

"Keep this boat from rocking for another minute or two and we're home free," the Stony Man armorer said.

Lyons glanced at the deserted road. Except for the squirrel that had risked its neck to cross in front of him, he had seen no signs of life. If the low-hanging branches of trees that scraped the roof of the van hadn't been there, he would have sworn nothing living existed here.

Lyons slowed the van down as he saw the dirt road marked on his map. "Ready or not here we go," he announced.

Kissinger grunted as he rushed to complete the reloading. "Ready," he announced.

Ironman turned the van onto the narrow dirt road. The vehicle rolled and bucked as it bounced on the loose dirt. The trees and bushes scraped the sides of the van as well as the roof. Overhead, Lyons heard chattering noises. He glanced at Blancanales. "What the hell was that?"

"Birds of some kind," Pol said. "They're talking to one another."

Lyons looked around him. This was no fairy-tale forest. This was wild, unpleasant-looking woods, the kind a killer could successfully hide in until his unsuspecting prey was close enough to ambush.

There was a dilapidated farmhouse just past a stand of hardwood trees. To Lyons it looked just as forbidding as the rest of the landscape. "Something up ahead," he announced. "We stop here and check it out."

Jumping out of the van, the three Stony Man soldiers grabbed their weapons and moved closer to the building. A brand-new Sundance was parked outside next to an ancient pickup. Two hound dogs were in the back of the truck, tied to the body with thick ropes.

The dogs jumped up when the three armed men approached.

Pol tried to quiet the dogs. He reached over to try to pet one of them, but the dog growled and tried to bite his hand. Quickly Blancanales pulled his hand away.

"You got a way with animals," Lyons commented in a low voice with a faint smile. He looked at the house. "Let's check it out." He gestured for Cowboy to move around to the rear of the building. "Just make sure whoever's inside isn't armed." Then he signaled Pol to follow him as he started for the front door.

The two Able Team commandos started to enter the house when they heard the sounds of gunfire in the distance. They stopped and stared in the direction of the sound. Kissinger came back around and joined them. He looked at Ironman. "What was that?"

"Trouble. It may involve Gadgets," Lyons snapped. He turned to Cowboy. "Grab a pair of binoculars and let's go."

INSIDE THE FARMHOUSE Vargas had led Susan up to one of the bedrooms. They were sprawled on the bed, still fully clothed and kissing. He could feel the excitement building inside as he began to caress her neck. He wanted to close his fingers around her soft throat and slowly squeeze. He was sure this one would last longer than the others.

Susan froze as he continued to rub her neck. The Bureau's files were filled with undocumented reports of Carlos Vargas's psychotic behavior with women in bed. Never before had she been forced to go farther than hinting at intimacy. This time she knew she couldn't prevent it.

His caresses were interrupted by the sudden sound of gunfire. Susan sat up quickly and asked, "Did you hear that?"

Vargas smiled at her. "It was nothing. Probably just some of my men having fun."

He started to pull her back down on the bed, but she stopped him. "They have a nutty idea of what fun is."

"But I don't, my sweet Ginny."

She jumped off the bed and grabbed her overnight bag. Vargas stared at her suspiciously. "Where are you going?"

"Into the bathroom for a moment. I want to be as fresh and sweet as a passion flower for you."

His eyes glistened at her words. "Don't take too long."

"I'll be back in a second," she promised as she walked into the hallway and entered the bathroom.

Closing the door, she slipped out of her clothes and checked herself in the mirror. As tiny as she was, she knew she was all woman. She felt nauseated at the thought of having intercourse with the crazy creature in the bedroom. Still, she was committed to doing anything she had to do to bring Vargas and his cohorts to justice.

She reached into the bag and took out a large fur mitten, making a face as she examined it. One of the streetwalkers the Bureau had hired to instruct her had suggested buying it, explaining that special "tricks" gave bigger tips when a mitten was used to arouse them.

Susan had another use for it. There was nothing in the oath she'd taken when she joined the FBI that demanded she give her life unnecessarily.

She took out the Beretta Jetfire from where she'd hidden it in her bag, made sure the clip was full and that there was a round in the chamber, then set the weapon in the cock-and-lock position. She slipped it inside the fur handpiece. Checking herself again in the mirror, she knew she couldn't delay coming out any longer, so she walked back into the bedroom.

Vargas had taken off his clothes. He was sitting on the bed, inhaling white powder from an unfolded piece of glassine paper.

Susan moved to the window, letting the sunlight shine on her from behind. She glanced out the window and was stunned to see Carl Lyons and two other men directly beneath her. There was no way she could signal the Able Team warrior that she was here without arousing Vargas's suspicion.

The Colombian, high on the cocaine he'd snorted, opened his eyes and looked at her. He was overwhelmed by the almost-perfect body framed by the sun pouring in through the window. "¡Dios! You are fantastic." He held out his hand. "Come join me. I have so much of this wonderful powder."

She glanced once more out the window. Lyons and the other two men were running in the direction of the gunfire. Reluctantly she turned from the window and slithered across the room to the bed. "I don't need anything more than you to get me high," she whispered as she pressed against him.

Vargas's eyes narrowed as he saw the fur mitten on her right hand. He became suspicious. "What's that for?"

"I'll massage every inch of your body into an ecstasy you've never experienced before," Susan promised, faking passion in her tone of voice. "Lean back, close your eyes and be prepared to get higher than you've ever been before."

Vargas fell back onto the bed, smiling as he let his eyelids droop. Quickly Susan slipped the small Beretta out of the glove and under a pillow.

"I'm ready," Vargas said, sounding desperate.

"So am I," Susan replied as she began to run the fur mitten lightly over his body.

23

The testing of the CAR-15s had turned into a shooting party. Lopez's eight men kept throwing money onto a pile as they bet Matthews's five mercenaries they could outshoot them.

In a mixture of Spanish, English and several other languages the professional gunmen tried to outbrag the others. Pairing off into teams, the first two Colombians stood behind the line drawn in the dirt and fired three rounds at a painted crate cover.

One of Bushnell's deputies acted as both range officer and judge. "Two hits on the edge of the outer circle," he yelled.

One of the Colombians gave the rest of Lopez's men a thumb's-up gesture as he stepped away from the firing line.

Two of Matthews's mercenaries were next. Standing a few feet apart, they aimed the assault rifles and fired a pair of shots, then stepped back. The uniformed deputy walked over and examined the wooden target. "One inside the outer ring. The other's a bull's-eye," he shouted.

The two mercs slapped palms and walked away.

Until now Lopez and Matthews had kept in the background, content to watch their men testing the new weapons. As the competition between the mercenaries and the Colombians grew more hostile, they began to edge closer to the firing line. Before long the two leaders were egging their men on to achieve greater accuracy.

"A bonus of five hundred dollars for every bull's-eye you get," Matthews announced to the mercenaries.

Lopez stared at him, then turned to his men and, in Spanish, offered double that each time the center of the target was hit. Matthews smiled at him. In a sarcastic tone of voice he asked, "You don't really believe your men could beat a professional soldier in a shooting contest?"

"These are men I've personally picked. They would die for me. Your men are like *putas*. They kill for whoever pays them. Loyalty will always win in the end."

"Willing to put your money where your mouth is?"

"As much as you care to lose," the angry Colombian snarled.

"Let's make it a friendly bet," Matthews said, sounding confident. "You name the amount."

"Five thousand American, if you're not afraid to lose that much," Lopez growled.

"You're on." Matthews held out his hand. The Colombian stared at it, then turned and walked to where his men were getting ready to take their turns at shooting.

Watching them, Bushnell turned to Ruddle. "Sooner or later we're gonna have to make them stop before we run outta ammunition." He grinned. "I think we might be able to up the price a bit, seein' how they like them guns so much."

"Don't forget about them top-secret cases."

"I almost did," Bushnell admitted. "Why don't you go inside and open a couple of 'em? Let's see what we got."

The tall deputy turned and walked into the warehouse.

GADGETS HAD PAUSED in his efforts to saw through the metal pipe to listen to the gunshots outside the warehouse. He looked at his wrists. They had become swollen from the constant rubbing, and the dried blood that filled his open wounds felt like sandpaper every time he moved his hands.

He could hear the footsteps of someone approaching him. Was this his executioner? Schwarz made up his mind he wasn't going to die without one last fight.

He allowed himself to slide down to the ground. If whoever it was came close enough, perhaps he could trip him.

Then what? Gadgets wasn't sure. Kick him in the head? Perhaps. He'd have to let his martial-arts instincts take over.

Breathing deeply, the Able Team soldier let his body relax. He could feel his mind release the fear and anger he'd stored since his capture. He could almost sense the presence of Chan Lao.

He opened his eyes and glanced at the tall, uniformed man walking in his direction. It was the same deputy who had captured him. Closing his eyes, Schwarz let his mind take over.

Ruddle glanced at the chained figure slumped on the floor. Gruber had told him he'd knocked the prisoner out because he was making too much noise.

The cases he was looking for were stacked just behind the unconscious man. Ruddle started to step over the fallen figure when he felt himself losing balance.

Gadgets had locked his legs around the right knee of the deputy and twisted them quickly. As the rogue officer tried to struggle to his feet, Schwarz threw the tip of his left foot into the man's crotch.

Grunting with pain, the deputy reached for the weapon he wore in a side holster. The Able Team warrior stomped on the man's hand and heard bone crack.

Gadgets knew the man would start shouting for help. He had to silence him immediately. As the deputy grabbed his broken wrist with his other hand, Schwarz locked his feet around the man's neck and began to squeeze.

He lifted his head and watched the tall man's face flush as his feet crushed his windpipe. The deputy tried to tear Gadgets's viselike feet from his throat, ignoring the nauseating pain in his broken wrist as he fought for survival.

The warrior's feet were like tentacles on an octopus. Nothing could force them to release the throat they were clamping. Gadgets saw the man's face become purplish.

If this were just a martial-arts demonstration, he would have unlocked his feet by now. But this was no practice session. This was a battle.

The other man squirmed and twisted in an effort to escape the killing power of Gadgets's legs. No matter how he struggled, they refused to let go of his throat. Years of training had turned them into powerful weapons.

Suddenly the man gave up the struggle and let his head slump. Gadgets wondered if he was faking. As reluctant as he was to use the next move, it was necessary if he wanted to live. With a sudden twist of his legs he snapped the other man's neck. Exhausted, Gadgets let himself fall backward and rested for a moment.

A voice from outside shouted into the warehouse, "Hey, Stanley, move your ass and get them weapons out here."

Using his feet to pull the body of the dead man closer, Schwarz twisted his own body so that he could use his manacled hands to search through the deputy's pockets. He found a key chain in one of the rear pockets. Scooping it closer with a foot, Gadgets picked it up and searched through the various keys until he found the one he knew would open his handcuffs. Twisting his arms, he carefully inserted the key into the handcuff opening and tried to push it in.

The set of keys fell to the ground. Frustrated, he tried again, this time twisting his hands to make it easier to reach the handcuffs' keyhole. He forced himself to ignore the excruciating pain of the raw wounds around his wrists as he again inserted the key.

Twisting it carefully, he felt the subtle click that meant he was free. Quickly he opened the other cuff, stood and examined his wrists. He'd have to have somebody look at them. But that was later, after he took care of a more immediate problem.

He searched the area around him for a weapon. Reaching down, he took the holstered Beretta 92-F automatic from the dead deputy and shoved it into his waistband.

He needed something more powerful. He looked into an open crate and grabbed one of the CAR-15s. Searching around, he found three empty clips and a case of ammunition.

Somebody would be coming to look for the fallen deputy. But he knew he had to take the time to fill the clips if he wanted to survive.

One by one he pushed the rounds down on the spring inside each clip until all three of them were fully loaded. He pushed one clip into the firing chamber and shoved the rest into one of his windbreaker pockets.

Now he was ready. He wasn't sure how many men there were outside, or if Brognola had received his signal and was sending reinforcements to assist him. For now he was alone, facing what he suspected was a large number of professional killers. Smiling grimly, he moved out of the warehouse.

IRONMAN SQUATTED and studied the area below them through the binoculars Cowboy had brought. There were twenty-one men, all armed, milling around in front of a corrugated structure. Thirteen of them seemed to be firing at makeshift targets. Lyons studied the weapons they were using, then lowered the binoculars and turned to Blancanales and Kissinger, who stood next to him. "I think we found the hijacked guns," he whispered.

Cowboy stared at the scene below them. "Any sign of the Daniel Boone crates?"

"If I had to guess, they're inside the building," Lyons replied.

Pol looked down at Lyons. "So what's our next move?"

Ironman thought for a minute. "We're going to need some help." He turned to Kissinger. "Leave the grenade launcher and some loads and get back to the van. Call that Lieutenant Schrieber. Tell him what's going on and ask him to send every available man."

Cowboy nodded and vanished in the direction of the farmhouse where they'd left their van. Lyons resumed studying the area below through the binoculars.

Pol knelt next to him. "What do we do in the meantime?"

"Wait." Lyons panned the glasses across the field. There was a movement just inside the warehouse that puzzled him. He adjusted the focusing ring until he could see more clearly. It was Gadgets, kneeling just inside the front doors of the building, holding an assault rifle.

"Shit," Ironman muttered. "Gadgets is planning to take on the whole bunch by himself."

He handed the glasses to Pol, who studied the warehouse and whistled. "Loco," he replied. "But we can't just stay here and let him grab the brass ring by himself."

Lyons shook his head in disgust. "No, we can't. Let's give him a hand." He picked up the grenade launcher and checked the load. Cowboy had loaded the weapon with both fragmentation and incendiary grenades. The next round was a fragmentation grenade.

He aimed the launcher at where the thirteen men were involved in a shooting competition and squeezed the trigger. The two Able Team hell-raisers watched as the grenade twisted a path toward the cluster of men.

It landed just before them, spattering bits of fury-driven metal in every direction.

Two men, a Colombian and a mercenary, fell to the ground as slivers of metal sliced through their skulls and into their brains. Three more armed men, two of them Colombians, screamed with pain as shards of metal tore into their stomachs and chests. Clutching their wounds, the men fell to the ground, still screaming.

Panic took over among the competing riflemen. The eight who hadn't been killed or seriously wounded kept twisting and turning to see where the grenade had come from. They didn't have to wait long. Lyons released another round, aiming this time at where the vehicles were parked.

The incendiary grenade spewed a spray of chemical flame in every direction when it hit the top of the long black limousine. Two of the sheriff's cars began to burn. So did the interior of the truck's cab.

Ironman checked the launcher. The next round was another incendiary grenade. "We move in after this one," he told Blancanales.

The grenade landed between a police vehicle and a luxury car. Its chemical flame covered both vehicles. As Ironman and Pol watched, they could see that all of the vehicles below were on fire. The only escape for the gunmen would be on foot.

"Let's spread out and move in," Lyons said, moving down the incline.

Blancanales worked his way around the top of the incline until he was fifty yards away, then he climbed down toward the large building.

GADGETS WATCHED with stunned amazement as grenades exploded and men fell. He saw the two incendiary grenades set the vehicles afire. It was a familiar tactic, one the Able Team warriors had used many times before to start an assault.

His partners were out there somewhere. He hoped they had spotted him and wouldn't mistake him for one of the other men. That was a chance he'd have to take. Life itself was a daily risk, he reminded himself as he moved out into the open, spraying deadly 3-shot bursts at the men in front of him.

Two deputies fell before they could turn their weapons on him. He glanced at them. One was motionless, cut almost in two by the lead spray. The other glared up at him as he clutched his stomach to keep his intestines from spilling onto the ground. He reached for the weapon he wore in his side holster. Gadgets stopped him with another 3-round burst.

Marco Lopez turned and saw the Able Team warrior coming toward him. He held his Smith & Wesson .44 Magnum in his huge right hand. Furious at the death all around him, the Colombian fired two shots at the oncoming Stony Man soldier.

Schwarz twisted to get out of the path of the bullets, but one of them cut through the fleshy part of his upper arm. He reeled for a moment from the pain, then forced himself to ignore it and fired back at the thickset Hispanic.

Two of his rounds shattered the other man's collarbone. Staggered from the wound, the Colombian turned and ran behind the warehouse before Gadgets could fire another burst.

Schwarz paused momentarily to check his wound and see if he needed to tie a temporary tourniquet around it. Blood was flowing slowly. He decided he could wait until the battle was over to tend to the wound—if he lived.

24

Matthews glanced around at the confusion and decided to leave before whoever was firing grenades caught him, as well. He ran to where the vehicles were parked.

The fire in the rear seat of the lead sheriff's vehicle had demolished the vinyl upholstery and burnt itself out. He looked in the front seat window. Keys were in the ignition.

Tearing the door open, Matthews jumped into the driver's seat and turned on the ignition. The engine coughed but refused to start. He kept trying again and again until finally he heard an explosion and the engine was running.

The stench of burnt plastic permeated the vehicle. He rolled down the window and put the car into reverse. All he could think about was getting away from the wholesale mayhem around him. He'd worry about where to go and what to do after he got on the highway. He hadn't survived all these years to die in some wretched wilderness in Arkansas.

A tall, husky man stood in his path as he turned the car around and raced for the dirt road. It was the Egyptian, Faisel, he had employed before. The man held up a hand to stop him. Matthews pressed down on the accelerator and tried to get around him.

Faisel moved to the right to stop him. He grabbed the door handle, and Matthews gunned the car and dragged the man along. He could hear the Egyptian hammering on the metal door. Then, suddenly, there was no more hammering.

Matthews looked out the rearview mirror. The large Egyptian lay in the middle of the dirt road. Matthews looked down at the road and saw a blond guy standing in his way. This time he didn't recognize his impediment.

There was an assault rifle in the man's hands. A MAC-10, as far as Matthews could make out. But nobody was going to stop him. He aimed the car at the blond giant.

Ironman braced the assault rifle against his shoulder and squeezed the trigger. He focused on the front windshield, knowing it would take more than one or two rounds to penetrate the safety glass. Round followed round, each coming within a fraction of an inch of the prior round.

The windshield finally shattered under the pressure of the lead slugs. Matthews swerved the car as he pulled his head out of the path of the flying glass shards.

The police car went out of control as the terrified man in the driver's seat tried to regain control. His foot seemed frozen on the accelerator as he twisted the steering wheel.

The side wall of the corrugated warehouse loomed directly in front of him. Panicked, he tore open the driver's door and dived out of the car just before it crashed into the building.

Stunned, he pulled himself to his feet. His H&K P-7 had fallen to the ground. He stooped and picked it up, only to hear a voice call out to him, "Drop it."

He looked up. The blond stranger was pointing the MAC-10 at him.

Matthews thought quickly. He opened his hand as he clicked off the safety on the automatic, then twisted it up and fired at the ominous intruder.

Ironman fanned a burst of shots at the well-dressed mercenary, almost severing the guy's right hand before the man could complete his trigger action. Matthews was shocked as he looked at his hand hanging loose and the blood dripping onto the ground from a ruptured artery. He tried to grab his automatic in his other hand, but Lyons fired a second burst that punctured a neat pattern across the man's midsection. Matthews fell forward, collapsing in a pool of his own blood.

Lyons wasted no time in examining the body. There were other fires to put out.

POL FACED the two Colombians who pointed their CAR-15s at him. Before they could fire he sprayed them with a pattern of hot lead. Shocked at the suddenness of his action, the two thugs stared at him for almost a full minute before they fell forward.

He turned and surveyed the killing field. Gadgets was in a duel with the last of the still-standing gunmen. Dancing out of the path of a burst of shots, Schwarz turned back and released a wave of lead vertically, almost cutting the other man in two.

He saw Pol and waved to him before turning to check on the status of the other gunmen. From a distance he could hear the sound of oncoming police vehicles. His face became hard until Pol called out, "Cowboy called the state police."

Gadgets smiled and nodded. He winced as his weapon accidentally touched the gaping hole in his upper arm. Then he moved to Blancanales's side. "There's two of them missing. The sheriff and another guy."

Pol looked around. He didn't see anyone in a sheriff's uniform. "Was the other man built like an ox?"

Gadgets thought about it. "Kind of."

Pol led him behind the warehouse. Marco Lopez was leaning against the rear of the building, his eyes staring blankly into space. "He called my mother a dirty name in Spanish," Blancanales said, "so I decided to teach him a lesson."

Most of the dead man's chest was missing. What was clearly visible was the torn muscles, tissues and severed arteries from which droplets of blood still ran.

Gadgets looked around. "Where's Ironman?"

"Mopping up."

JUDD BUSHNELL HAD only one thought in mind—to get as far away from this place as he could. Martha Masters's car was still parked at the farmhouse. He could drive to his office, get whatever money he had hidden there and take off.

He had no specific destination in mind, only to escape from here. Later he'd decide what to do next.

He kept running through the woods, clenching his Colt .38 in his hand and looking over his shoulder to make sure no one was following him. In the distance he could still hear the sound of gunfire. Good. Whoever had attacked was busy battling with the others.

Who were these men? Government agents? He didn't think so. The few he had met lived by the rules. These were hunters. They had fought as if they were in a deadly battle with some hated enemy.

He decided it didn't matter who they were. He was glad he had made the decision early to get away.

He could feel the sharp spines of the bushes tearing at his clothes and body. It didn't matter. He could take care of the scratches later.

There was a large black form hidden under the brush. Bushnell didn't notice it as he raced by it, but his left foot accidentally kicked the shape.

He glanced behind him to see what he'd encountered. The form rose up and became five hundred pounds of black fury. The curved tusks that protruded from the wild boar's maw easily measured eight inches.

The fat sheriff paused and fired his puny .38 at the charging beast. The bullets penetrated the thick skin beneath the creature's skull. As if it had been barely scratched, the enraged animal pursued Bushnell around trees and through the brush.

Desperate to escape its deadly tusks, the sheriff jumped up at the lowest branch of a nearby oak tree. He tried to pull his weight up as the huge boar pierced his legs with its tusks.

Screaming at the searing pain, Bushnell let go and fell to the ground. The boar turned and charged again, slamming into his stomach with the now-bloody points of its curved weapons.

Three shots from the rifle Lyons held stopped the beast. It turned to glare at Ironman, then fell over on its side.

The sheriff looked up at the stranger. "Thanks."

"Don't bother. They can't send dead men to prison," Ironman replied icily.

"Yeah, I never thought of that," the sheriff gasped.

The stranger stared down at him. "Where's the lady?"

"What lady?"

"The one who came with the group."

Bushnell winced with pain. He could feel a numbness creep through his body. Despite the agony he smiled. "Would you believe she and her boyfriend are up at the farmhouse screwing right this moment." He laughed, then gagged on some blood in his mouth. "If they only knew they had two people watching them."

Lyons was puzzled. "What two people?"

"Jimmy Joe and his sister," Bushnell said in a harsh whisper. "We shoved their bodies into the bedroom closet." He tried to laugh but began to choke again. "I guess they'll change the charge from hijacking to murder." Bushnell stared at the unforgiving expression on the stranger's face. He looked more like an executioner than anyone he had ever seen before.

Bushnell thought about spending the rest of his life behind bars even if he pleaded unpremeditated murder. It didn't make much sense. He hated giving his hard-earned money away to lawyers. He glanced at his right hand. In it he still held the .38.

For a moment he thought of shooting the stranger. But what was the point? He couldn't make it out of the woods, not with the holes in him. There was only one practical solution. The sheriff shoved the revolver into his mouth and pulled the trigger before Lyons could stop him.

SUSAN HAD BROUGHT Vargas to fulfillment twice. He lay on his back, his eyes closed, and moaned gently as she continued to arouse him with her fur mitten. Finally the Colombian reached out a hand and stopped her. "Enough, my love. Now it's time for you and me together."

Reluctantly she put the mitten down. She had hoped she could escape without going any farther. Faking enthusiasm, she snuggled up to him.

Vargas turned his face toward her. "You have given me much pleasure. Now I'll do the same for you." He kissed her as he began to caress her throat. "Such a perfect neck," he murmured as he began to close his long fingers around it.

Susan could feel the strength of his fingers. She tried to pull away, but the Colombian continued to squeeze tighter. She wanted to scream at him to stop, but she knew it would do no good. For some insane reason he believed he was giving a woman pleasure by strangling her.

"This is the ultimate thrill," he whispered as he began to force her throat between his hands.

Susan panicked. As strong as she was, she couldn't tear his hands away. She remembered the pillow and forced her right hand under it. "Let go of my throat," she gasped.

"Not yet, my love," Vargas said almost lovingly. "But very soon I will."

Her fingers searched under the pillow. Finally she felt the cold metal of the small Beretta. Frantically moving her fingers, she pulled the weapon closer until she could get her right hand around the grip.

"Please, Carlos, don't do this," she whispered.

"Tell me how much you enjoy it," he said, his voice becoming hysterical. "Tell me you love it!"

She released the safety and twisted her body so that she was on her side.

"Don't fight me," Vargas shouted.

She was rapidly losing consciousness. Quickly she lifted the small weapon and shoved it against the Colombian's left eye. She pulled the trigger twice.

A fountain of blood spattered into her face. Vargas's head slumped to one side and the blood ran from behind his eye onto the bedclothes.

Sickened at the gory sight, Susan crawled from the bed and dragged herself into the bathroom. She climbed into the antiquated shower and turned on the water. As she felt the water wash away the lifeblood of the dead man, she began to relax. The tepid water felt good on her bruised neck.

Through the sound of running water she heard another noise. Somebody was running up the steps. She reached out of the shower and grabbed the Beretta. It wasn't accurate at anything but close range, but it might stop the intruder temporarily. She heard the footfalls go into the bedroom, then come out again and stop at the bathroom door.

"Susan!" a voice called out.

She recognized it immediately.

The door opened. Lyons rushed in and saw her standing under the shower. He stared at Susan as she handed him the Beretta.

She smiled at him. "What kept you?"

Lyons shrugged. "I got busy."

EPILOGUE

Hal Brognola presided over the meeting in the Stony Man conference room. Blancanales, Kissinger, Kurtzman and Schwarz were in attendance. Only Carl Lyons was missing.

The big Fed looked at the sling Gadgets was wearing. "How's the arm healing?"

"Medics say it'll be as good as new in a few weeks."

Brognola grunted to hide his concern. There had been some worry by the doctors about whether Gadgets would keep the arm. "You're to do nothing active until the doctors give you the high sign."

Gadgets thought of his date with Sandy Meissner over the coming weekend. "Does that include women?"

"Aggressive women."

Gadgets tried to hide his pout. Pol glanced at him and broke into laughter. "Just tell her to be gentle," he suggested.

Gadgets glared at him. "Did you ever try telling a woman that?"

"I don't have to," Blancanales bragged. "They always expect me to be the aggressive one."

"Calm down, you pair of lovesick birds," Brognola snapped. "Here's the wrap-up on the last mission." He shuffled through the papers in front of him.

"We recaptured most of the hijacked shipment of CAR-15s—except the ones you destroyed. And we got the Daniel Boone prototypes back."

Gadgets turned to Kissinger. "They ever get around to testing them again?"

Cowboy nodded. "They're still malfunctioning."

"Maybe we should have let this Matthews sell them to the Colombians," Pol suggested.

"That's not our decision," Brognola reminded him. "Back to the report." He glanced at the papers again. "The Arkansas State Police captured three of the group Matthews brought with him. The rest were all dead." He looked up to see the expression on their faces.

Pol and Gadgets looked pleased.

"In the farmhouse we found the bodies of the two people who owned the property. And the body of one Carlos Vargas, who happens to be the heir apparent to Pedro Vargas, one of the heads of the Medellín cartel."

Pol raised his hand. "What did we do with the body?"

"Shipped it back to his family. Why?"

"We should have given it a Colombian necktie," Blancanales said.

"We're not savages," the big Fed reminded him.

"Sometimes it's not such a bad thing," Pol suggested.

"I'll forget you said that. Besides, our people down there tell me the old man is so devastated over his son's death that he's withdrawn from active participation in the cartel."

"That's good news," Cowboy commented.

"The bad news," Brognola replied, "is that someone has taken his place. So that war goes on."

Pol looked at the head of the table. "Anything else?"

"I think that wraps it up for now. All of you who want it have next week off."

The group started to stand. Brognola turned to Pol and Gadgets. "Have either of you heard from Lyons since he left for Washington?"

Gadgets grinned. "He called in this morning to leave a message for Bear." Schwarz turned to the wheelchair-bound genius. "If you need to reach him for the next few days, don't waste your time trying to use the communicator. He's shut it down."

Kurtzman started to protest. Brognola cut him off with a smile. "Like I keep telling all of you, a little cooperation with some of the other federal agencies can go a long way."

"Especially," Pol added, "when they're named Susan."

SURVIVAL RUN

by
Gar Wilson

A Phoenix Force novel

PROLOGUE

The four men remained hidden until full darkness had fallen, waiting patiently in the shadows. Although anxious to carry out their task, they lay motionless, watching the house and the five American Secret Service agents who guarded it. Their task was to remove the Secret Service men who were protecting their objective.

They knew the layout of the house and its grounds. Each man had a specific part in the operation. Once the moment arrived the team would move to preappointed positions, perform the required task, then move to the next phase. If everything went as planned, the whole operation would be over in a matter of minutes.

The leader glanced at his watch, then turned and nodded sharply. Without a word they slipped silently out of concealment, moving swiftly across the deserted road to the wall that surrounded the house. They progressed to the east corner, where they had located a blind spot in the security. Helped by their partners, two of the men climbed the thick wall, then dropped unseen to the ground on the other side.

Each man was equipped with a modern crossbow. The weapons were powerful, accurate and completely silent. The quivers on their belts held short, stubby bolts with red feathers, indicating that the bolts contained cyanide in the fiberglass shafts. Once injected into a body the cyanide would bring almost instant death.

The two-man assassination team had used their crossbows before. Concealed in the darkness at the base of the thick wall, they readied their weapons. The crossbows were set and loaded. Each bow was equipped with a powerful night-sight scope.

When both were ready, the assassins slipped deeper into the cultivated garden that fronted the house. Neither man spoke. There was no need. They knew exactly what they had to do, and they were ready to do it.

They parted, taking separate paths. The taller of the two was the first to locate a target. Hiding behind a carved marble figure, he watched the bulky figure of one of the American Secret Service men cross a marbled patio and skirt the edge of an ornamental pool.

The American, dressed in light clothing and carrying an Uzi 9 mm submachine gun, made an easy target. The tall assassin raised his crossbow, snugging the wooden stock against his shoulder. His fingers curled around the cool metal of the weapon. He pressed one eye to the rubber cup of the scope, quickly clicking the focus wheel to bring the American into sharp relief. The pale moonlight provided enough illumination for the sensitive scope to throw the figure into startling clarity.

The assassin waited until the American reached the limit of his patrol area. Here the Secret Service man paused and carefully checked the garden. He was about to turn around when the assassin gently squeezed the trigger.

The bolt left the cradle in a flash. It made a soft, gentle hiss as it streaked toward its target, striking the American in the side of the neck just below the right ear. The terrific force behind the bolt took it through the neck so that the steel tip emerged from the far side.

The stunning impact was enough to render the target speechless. With the added flood of cyanide from the fiberglass shaft coursing through his flesh, the American agent had no chance. The Uzi slipped from his fingers. His left hand jerked up toward the rigid object that had penetrated his neck, quivering fingers barely brushing the red feathers before his whole body stiffened in a terrible spasm. Moments later he crumpled to the ground, squirming in silent agony, then became still.

By this time the assassin had moved on, further penetrating the grounds. His second target stood framed by the light from a window of the house. A tall, balding man in his early thirties, he also carried an Uzi suspended from his right shoulder. The assassin fired a bolt into the man's chest, and he went down instantly, making no sound.

Loading his third bolt, the tall assassin stalked his next target around the side of the house by the garage. Parked on the gravel driveway was a gleaming white Rolls-Royce Corniche. On a silver rod fixed to a front fender was a small American flag. The Secret Service agent walked by the car, unable to resist a glance at the automobile. It was the last thing he saw. Moments later the assassin's deadly cyanide bolt drilled into his back, directly between his shoulder blades.

The agent fell forward against the Rolls. As he slithered to the ground, the muzzle of the Uzi traced a long, jagged scratch on the gleaming car body.

The tall assassin looked at his watch, a smile softening the taut line of his mouth beneath the folds of the keffiyeh that covered his face and head, leaving only his eyes exposed. The operation was running well. If his comrade had carried out his part with as much ease, the rest would go equally as well.

Like clockwork, the other man returned. He crouched beside his partner, holding up a hand with two fingers extended.

The tall man's eyes glittered. That left only the chief Secret Service man inside the house, plus the three members of the household staff.

Moving at a faster pace now, the assassins ran for the house, skirting the front and slipping like shadows along the side. At the open kitchen door they paused, peering inside.

In the spacious modern kitchen the three members of the domestic staff were busy. The cook was preparing a light salad supper. His assistant was at the stove, making coffee. Arranging cutlery on a silver tray by the table was the house servant. The door leading from the kitchen to the main part of the house was closed.

With crossbows at the ready the two assassins slipped through the doorway. The twin hum of fired bolts disturbed the tranquil kitchen. The cook and his assistant slumped to the floor. The only noise came from a spoon dropped by the cook's assistant.

The house servant stared in horror at the assassins. His eyes widened with shock as he realized his own delicate position. He had little opportunity to react. The tall assassin reached him in swift strides, holding a knife that glittered with merciless brightness. As the steel bit into soft flesh, brilliant red flowers blossomed on the servant's white robe. The flowers grew and expanded, then redness spotted the floor, the drops becoming a pool that flowed out from the crumpled body of the servant.

The tall assassin put away his knife and signaled to his partner. The man left and returned in less than a minute with the other members of the team. They moved through the doorway to the rest of the house, spreading out as they moved along the wide passage that opened out onto the spacious lounge.

It was a large room, richly decorated and furnished. The floor was strewn with priceless rugs. The walls were hung with works of art. The light fixtures alone were worth a small fortune. The whole room reeked of limitless wealth.

As the group fanned out across the room, they located the two men who occupied it. One was the chief of the Secret Service team. He was a tall, broad-shouldered American with a brown, strong-featured face. He had pale blue eyes and light receding hair that was cut short.

The Secret Service agent faced the four intruders, realizing instantly that their presence meant his own men were dead. The realization did nothing to stop the agent from attempting to carry out his job, which was to protect the man seated just a few yards from him.

As he drew the automatic pistol under his left arm, the American was aware he was a dead man. It made little difference. His assignment was to protect the man in his charge. He could do little else except die trying.

The American's weapon had barely left its holster when the tall assassin fired his crossbow. The steel-tipped bolt struck the American in the left eye, driving deep into the socket. The agent screamed in agony, clamping a hand to the hard shaft jutting from his eye. He stumbled back, tripped over a low table, and fell, crashing down on the table and bouncing awkwardly to the floor. His legs kicked frantically as the bolt expelled its dose of cyanide into his system.

The leader of the strike team crossed the room and stood before the seated American. The man was staring with shock and revulsion at the motionless form on the floor.

"Take a good look," the strike team leader said. "Look and remember how easy it is for a man to die. The memory may serve to restrain you if you consider trying to escape from us. You are going to die, anyway, but we would prefer you do so at the time and place we have chosen."

The American glared into the sharp, glittering eyes of the speaker. "Why don't you take off that damn hood and face me like a man? Or don't you have the guts to show your damn faces? You say you want to kill me? At least let me know who you are!"

The leader tore aside the folds of the keffiyeh.

"You wish to know who we are? I will tell you. We are your judges. We are your jury. And we are also your executioners. Does that satisfy you? Does that make you feel better?" The leader smiled. "Now you will come with us, Mr. U.S. Secretary of State, because your transport is waiting. We have a long trip ahead of us. For you it is only one way. This time you do not go home!''

1

"There are times when I get tired of having to say this," Hal Brognola remarked. "But as I can't find any other way of expressing it, here goes. We have a problem."

"*We* as in nation, or just as in Phoenix Force?" Gary Manning asked.

Brognola settled into his comfortable chair. "Both. The Administration has a problem, and you guys are going to have problems solving it."

The Fed looked and sounded tired. Brognola spent his life on the move, trying to coordinate the activities of Phoenix Force, Able Team and often Mack Bolan. In between he also ran Stony Man and its complex organization, fitting in meetings and conferences. He liaised with the White House and security agencies. Brognola had enough problems to handle. The last thing he had wanted, or expected, was a hectic flight by jet to the U.S. air base at Zaragoza, Spain, so that he could hand out a mission to Phoenix Force. The Stony Man commandos had recently completed a mission in Spain.

"I wouldn't ask you to undertake another mission so soon if it wasn't special," Brognola said.

"But you're still going to, anyway," McCarter suggested.

The Fed glanced at the tall Briton, aware of his weakness for sarcasm and downright rudeness. He had come to accept it as part of the cockney's character.

"I know you guys are tired. It isn't hard to figure you'd all rather hit the sack than sit here listening to me."

"No kidding!" McCarter muttered with all the grace of a grizzly bear woken from its winter slumbers.

"I agree with David," Calvin James remarked.

"All I can say is sorry, guys, but this one is important—and urgent."

"Go ahead, Hal," Yakov Katzenelenbogen, the Phoenix Force commander, said. "There won't be any more interruptions."

The Israeli glanced around the room at the Force, his face stern. McCarter, sitting opposite Katz, fiddled with the tab on a can of Coke Classic, pointedly ignoring him.

Katzenelenbogen's almost benign appearance, heightened by his gray hair and blue eyes, had fooled many into believing that the middle-aged Israeli was harmless. The fact that he wore a prosthesis on his right arm only added to the deception. Katz happened to be one of the world's top practitioners in the art of warfare and espionage. He had battled the Nazi hordes during the Second World War and the British and the Arabs during Israel's War of Independence. During the later Six Day War, Katz lost his arm and also his only son.

The son of Russian Jews, Katz had learned to fight at an early age. Life was a battle, he had found. During periods of calm, he had learned to master English, French, German and Russian. As he grew, he expanded his knowledge, fired by a natural curiosity and a love for the finer things in life. All these things were absorbed during his military career, followed by a move into espionage and intelligence, where he became a top agent in the Mossad, coming into contact with agents of the CIA, British MI6, the French Sûreté and other covert intelligence outfits.

Katz had been eager to accept the offer to join Phoenix Force at its conception. The secret commando force had been established to combat terrorism in all its many and varied forms. Katz had been the natural choice for commander of the group. He had taken the position with his usual modesty, quickly earning the respect and loyalty of the other members of Phoenix Force.

"Two hours before I took off from Washington to meet you guys," Brognola explained, "the President received a letter from a terrorist group that has kidnapped the secretary of state."

"The secretary kidnapped?" Katz repeated.

"Two nights ago," Brognola said. "As you might have heard, the secretary of state was on an extensive goodwill tour of Arab nations. The current climate deems it important for the U.S. to make at least a gesture toward stabilizing relations with Middle Eastern countries. The seven-day tour kept him pretty busy. His last two days were spent in Saudi Arabia. The Saudi government placed a house at his disposal so he could at least have a little time to relax. The house was outside Riyadh. During the evening, the house was hit by a well-organized force. They took out the five Secret Service men guarding the grounds with crossbows. The shafts of the bolts contained cyanide. Once inside, the attack force murdered the three Saudi nationals employed as domestics. They also killed the section chief in charge of the Secret Service team. When they left, they took the secretary with them.''

"What are their demands?" Rafael Encizo asked.

Brognola took out a copy of a letter from his file. "There are no demands," he explained. "The guys already have what they want."

"The secretary?" McCarter asked.

"Yes," Brognola answered. "He was their target—in more ways than one."

"Sounds ominous," Katz said.

"This terrorist group—they call themselves the Hammer of Allah—intend to execute, their word, the secretary of state as a punishment for the crimes the U.S. has perpetrated against Islam."

"What do they interpret as crimes against Islam?" Katz asked.

"From the way these guys are talking, the very fact that America exists is a crime. We're corrupt. We worship money and possessions. Our foreign policies are directed toward causing dissension among the true believers of Islam. We covet their land and their oil. We defile their women. The list is long and detailed."

"Sounds to me like the Great Satan syndrome," Manning remarked.

"The Hammer of Allah follows the strict fundamentalism of the late Ayatollah. They're Shiite Muslims. Totally dedicated and fanatical in their chosen crusade."

"Their crusade being directed at the United States," James said.

"You got it," Brognola agreed. "There isn't anything really new about their policies. Only their methods. They appear to go for direct action. As far as the Hammer of Allah is concerned the secretary of state is a representative of the U.S. government, so he's going to pay for the crimes of the nation."

"Has there been any attempt at negotiation?" James asked.

"All the normal channels have been tried, without result. The Iranian government can't or won't help. They say the Hammer of Allah is a separatist group with no government contact, consisting of Muslims from a number of countries. They see no reason why they should interfere with something that has been decreed by the will of people acting on truly religious convictions. The U.S. should cast off its evil ways, renounce its war against Islam and ask forgiveness."

"Bloody gobbledygook," David McCarter snorted. "We're dealing with a bunch of fanatics who figure they're on a crusade." The Briton swallowed half the contents of his can of Coke. "These people are so caught up in their beliefs you can't even talk to them. How do you reason with that kind of thinking?"

With his usual candor the cockney rebel had put into words what everyone else was thinking. McCarter never worried about being blunt or outspoken. He always spoke his mind, sometimes too freely, and tended to upset people. Not that doing so ever bothered the East End tough. McCarter had always lived his life on the edge. He was an adventurer and a man of physical action. Born to fight, he hated to waste time and energy on nonessentials. He preferred direct action. That was why he had joined the SAS, serving in worldwide hot spots that allowed him the opportunity to exercise his talents for combat. Phoenix Force with the challenges it offered, might have been created with David McCarter in mind.

"I haven't told you the worst part," Brognola interrupted. "The Hammer of Allah intends to show the whole of the so-called trial and the execution on television. It'll broadcast to the Arab nations live, then distributed on tape to other Islamic communities."

"That's sick," Manning said, his revulsion showing.

The Canadian was no wimp. In fact, his rugged build concealed a sharp brain that had allowed him to become a civil engineer, concentrating on heavy explosives, and when he joined Phoenix Force, he found his skills in constant demand.

Manning had little or no military training. He ran his own firm of security consultants whose clients included major corporations, provincial and city governments in Canada, the United States and Europe.

"It's the kind of act that could inflame a lot of Muslims to do copycat kidnappings," Encizo said. "The hard line leaders will use this to stoke up anti-American feelings. Just the way the Ayatollah Khomeini used to. Mass hysteria. Big speeches, big lies. Just like Hitler did at the rallies. The way Castro goes on about the U.S. It might look and sound crude to an outsider, but it gets results."

Encizo knew what he was talking about from personal experience. Having disagreed with Castro's takeover of Cuba, he had been forced to flee the country. Although volatile by nature, he was capable of great restraint in the face of extreme provocation. It depended on the circumstances. When it came to the crunch Encizo was never to be found at the back of the queue. He was a hard fighter, something he'd learned during the Castro takeover, and especially during his return to Cuba as part of the Bay of Pigs invasion force when he was captured. In the dreaded El Principe political prison he had resisted brutal attempts to indoctrinate him. True to his character, he had escaped, returning to the U.S. and becoming an American citizen. He had worked in a number of professions. Despite his unease with the intelligence community, he undertook assignments for American law-enforcement agencies from time to time. The offer to join Phoenix Force came like a breath of fresh air. Encizo liked the freedom the Force gave him, and also the opportunity to work with honest men.

"I'm beginning to see where we come in," Katz said. "No way to get the secretary back by negotiation or any other official means?"

Brognola shook is head. "This is a no-win situation if we try talking to these people. They've made that clear."

"So if we want the secretary back we have to go in and get him ourselves?" Manning asked.

"That's about it, guys. And it doesn't get any better. For starters, we don't have a clue where he's being held. Or when this trial takes place. For all we know it could be tomorrow. I wish I could give you more to go on. But more we just don't have.''

"How did the terrorists get the secretary out of Saudi Arabia?" McCarter asked. "If they've quit the country, that is."

Brognola shrugged. "Sorry to be so unhelpful, guys, but we don't have any info on that."

"Somebody must know something," Katz protested. "Even terrorists need information, especially when it comes to breaching the security of the secretary of state. From what you've told us, they obviously knew the place and time, and how much protection there would be. You don't just drop in and figure out that kind of thing without prior knowledge. There had to be some kind of information leak. If we can find that, maybe we can get a fix on where these terrorists might be."

"It's a long shot," Brognola said.

"What else do we have?" McCarter snapped. "It's better than bugger all, Hal."

"David, shut up a minute," James said. "I've been thinking about something."

"Save me from educated people," McCarter grumbled. "He'll be counting on his fingers next."

Since joining the Force, the former cop and Navy SEAL had learned to ignore McCarter's sarcasm. The youngest member of the Stony Man team, the tall, lean black man, coming as he did from Chicago's toughest area, was well equipped to handle McCarter. "You admit we don't know when these terrorists plan to carry out their execution. This is a pure guess, but I think it might be five days from now."

"Why five?" Encizo asked.

"Because that brings us to the Fourth of July," the Chicago badass said.

"It's sound reasoning," Katz said. "Executing the secretary of state on American Independence Day would certainly ram the point home."

"Well, since we don't have much else, let's go on that," Brognola said.

"Unless we come up with anything to the contrary, our assumption is that we have five days," the Israeli said. "Five days to locate the secretary and launch a rescue attempt."

"The President has sanctioned this mission," Brognola said. "He's aware of the difficulties you'll face, but he's been around long enough now to realize if anyone can do it, you're the ones. We'll back you. I hate saying this, but if you get into a jam, we might not be able to do anything. Remember, we're dealing with people who just won't talk to us."

"We understand the rules, Hal," Katz said. "They apply to most missions we carry out, so don't worry."

"Anything you need?"

"A few items," Katz said. "Plus Jack Grimaldi and Dragon Slayer. We might need some fast extraction on this. I'd rather have Jack standing by than have to depend on local help or chance finding our own transport."

"Make your list," Brognola said. "I can get most of what you need from the base here. Anything else can be shipped in with Jack."

"Can you fix it for us to get into Saudi Arabia without too much fuss?"

"That's already been arranged," Brognola told the Israeli. "The Saudis are feeling a little embarrassed over what happened to the secretary while he was their guest. You'll get all the cooperation you need. An Air Force plane will fly you to Riyadh where you'll be met by Captain Maji of the Saudi National Guard.''

"Do we have anyone from home as backup in the area?''

"No,'' Brognola said. "Considering the circumstances of this mission, the less interference you have the better. The President agrees with me. Of course, he had resistance from other agencies. They all considered it was their baby, but the President made it clear he doesn't want other people involved. Of course, we'll be using all the information departments of the agencies to keep us up-to-date with any incoming intelligence reports. There won't be any second chances with this mission. You get one shot and that's it. As far as I'm concerned, you're the only team capable of pulling this off. So don't let me down, guys.''

Katz led the Force from the office, leaving Brognola alone. The Stony Man head troubleshooter allowed himself a few moments of relaxation. He couldn't spare any more than that. There was a jet waiting to whisk him back to the U.S. and the inevitable pressures of the current crisis.

Brognola straightened, feeling ashamed. What did he really have to grumble about? His was an enclosed, reasonably secure world, not like the savage place Phoenix Force had to operate in. They were forced to work in the shadows, ankle-deep in the debris of humanity's frailty. Evil, violence and deceit shadowed the Phoenix warriors, ever ready to strike without warning. The Phoenix commandos were engaged in an unceasing struggle with these antisocial misfits.

That was Phoenix Force's lot. They fought in solitude, without recognition. Their war was one devoid of medals and decorations, not that they would have wanted it any other way. Their reward was achieving a victory against the dark forces, no matter how short-lived. Phoenix Force waged the classic struggle of good against evil. In the end that was what mattered.

2

Abu Niad entered the room, conscious of the eyes on him. The lithe, tall Arab crossed the room, then turned to face the waiting group. He studied them for a time, aware of their need for him to speak. Their eyes burned with the fervor of their devotion. Each and every one of them would obey his commands. They would risk anything for him. Indeed, they would die for him.

Niad surveyed the faithful warriors of the Hammer of Allah. As of this moment, they were unaware of the importance the group would achieve. When Niad's great plan was put into action, the whole world would know about them, would cower in the shadows as the power of Allah's legion stepped forth.

The mere thought of what he would achieve in the months to come sent a quiver of excitement through Abu Niad's body. He felt again the rush of blood, the pounding that filled his skull. Aroused by his inner feelings, he turned his gaze upon his faithful followers, raising his hands toward them.

"My brothers!" he intoned, his powerful voice reaching out to envelope them. "We have achieved our goal. Even now the American secretary of state is our captive. During the next few days, he will have the opportunity to consider the crimes of his nation. When the day of atonement is reached, he will pay the penalty for the insults and deceits the United States has hurled into the face of Allah. The whole of Islam will be able to see that the wrath of Muhammad can strike the posturing infidels of America. The just execution of this man will be the signal that the greatest jihad in the history of Islam has commenced. No longer will we sit back and allow the Americans to dominate our world. We must bring Islam into the light and make our face known. Soon our followers will take the jihad to the United States itself, where we will strike at the very heart of the Great Satan. For Islam. For Allah. For our beloved and mourned Khomeini, who gave us the wisdom and the strength to devote our lives to the glory of Allah.''

Responding to Niad's words, the assembled followers' voices filled the room. The Arab leader listened with pride as his followers chanted their loyalty to Islam.

''We dedicate ourselves to Allah. *Allahu Akbar!* God is great! Allah grant victory to the jihad, the holy war in the defense of God's will. May the followers of the Hammer of Allah march to paradise through death! Only in death will we really become alive. We are ready to lay down our lives in the service of the one great and supreme God!''

Abu Niad waited as his supporters expressed their feelings. Finally he raised his arms, palms outstretched, calming the surging crowd of men. Only when their chanting had receded did he speak.

''From this day forward we will make the United States aware of our growing strength and the spreading of our faith. The Americans have no faith. Theirs is a nation of depravity and evil. They seek to force their will upon a world that no longer accepts their way. America is weak. It is soft and falling apart. Even their government is corrupt, with the sickness of capitalism eating away at its very heart. The American continent is awash with drugs that create violence and crime. Cities are no longer safe for Americans, yet they try to impose their will on others.

"The United States is guilty of many crimes against Islam. The Ayatollah Khomeini saw this and decreed that America was the offender against Islam. Too many times the Americans have insulted our religion and our heritage, condemning us as nothing more than heathens. They thought their vast wealth could buy our friendship as well as our oil, but they did not allow for the way of Islam. Now they must be made to see the errors they have committed.

"This man of their government, who was delivered into our hands by the will of Allah, shall be the first. His punishment will be our beacon. His death will open the path. His blood will feed our wrath. His execution will be a just and timely omen. And the Hammer of Allah shall be the front line of the offensive against Islam's greatest, most evil enemy!"

The tumultuous roar that climaxed Abu Niad's speech was heard beyond the walls of the room. It echoed and reverberated throughout the building so that everyone present heard it, though some received it with less enthusiasm than others.

SITTING IN quiet resignation on the edge of the bed in the room he regarded as his prison cell, the secretary

of state raised his head as the distant roar reached his
ears. He was unable to make out any words, aware in
any event that they would be in Arabic. Still, he recognized the chilling tone in the voices. He had heard
the sound before. Sometimes on news broadcasts. A
couple of times in his presence.

It was the sound of fanaticism, a mindless, baying
chant, howling from the throats of men who had been
roused to fever pitch by some gifted orator. There were
men capable of doing that to their followers. Clever,
manipulative men who could reach into the heart of a
cause and rip out its very core. They could hold that
bleeding, pulsing core aloft and use it to hypnotize
their captive audience. Their words were often simple, the very words the crowd carried in their own
hearts but were unable to express until the orator became the catalyst. Once the two came together the
chemical reaction was set in motion, culminating in a
single, cohesive organism that thought and acted as
one. Emotions, prejudices, hatreds were tumbled together in the melting pot of hysteria. Once generated,
such power was difficult to stop.

The secretary realized he was in the hands of fanatics and understood that he was in a precarious position as far as his life was concerned. The man named
Abu Niad had made it patently clear that negotiation
wasn't being considered. He had explained, very
clearly, that the secretary wouldn't be used as a pawn
in a game of exchange. Exchange had nothing to do
with the exercise. The American's presence was necessary for one thing only—an execution. The fact that

the secretary was going to die was ordained, and the mechanics of the act had already been arranged.

The secretary was hoping for an opportunity to escape. He was dammed if he was going to sit back and allow these fanatics to murder him in cold blood. Whether or not Washington mounted some kind of rescue, he wasn't going under quietly. The sons of bitches would have to nail him to a damn plank if they wanted him still and silent so that they could kill him.

The secretary had been in the Marines in his younger years. He had served in Korea during the war and knew the fear and excitement of combat. It was something that never left a man. If it became necessary, he was prepared to fight for his freedom. He might have left the active service of the Marines, but the training and the discipline never faded. He'd been proud to wear the uniform and carry his nation's trust. That was still as strong as it had ever been. Marine training left its mark on a man.

He regretted being unable to tell his wife he was alive and comparatively unharmed. Other than that, he was prepared to accept whatever happened to him. It always seemed unfair that others had to suffer, as well. Those who were closest to a kidnap victim often experienced deep personal emotions, partly brought on due to their ignorance of the victim's condition, whether he was dead or alive or was being hurt or tortured. Those were the kinds of hurts that left the deepest scars, and they were beyond his power to control.

As he listened to the incessant baying of Abu Niad's followers, the secretary of state promised himself that if an opportunity arose, he would personally pull the trigger on the terrorist leader. Abu Niad might consider himself a disciple of Allah, but that wouldn't save him if the secretary had his way.

3

Phoenix Force arrived at Riyadh airport at midday. They stepped from the cool interior of the U.S. Air Force transport into the solid, pressing heat of the Saudi Arabian climate. Above the clean lines of the airport buildings could be seen the unbroken curve of the hard blue sky.

Calvin James, his flight bag swinging from his fist, fell in beside Gary Manning as the Force crossed the concrete apron, heading for the terminal building.

"Man, this is *hot,*" the black warrior said.

"Too hot for me," the Canadian grumbled. "I'd prefer some snow."

"You must be joking," James remarked. "I would have thought you would have had your fill of snow after that time you and Encizo were stranded out in the wilds of Finland."

Manning smiled wryly as he recalled the event. The Force had been combating a KGB plot in Finland. During the mission, he and Encizo had been flying across the country when a bomb planted in their plane had exploded. Crash-landing in the snowy wilderness, the Phoenix pair had been forced to combat hungry wolves as well as the severe winter weather.

"I wasn't thinking about Finland when I mentioned snow," Manning said. "I was thinking about Canada."

"Right now a Chicago winter wouldn't seem too bad," James reflected.

"A right pair of bloody old women you pair are," came David McCarter's voice from behind Manning and James. "Always complaining. Too hot, too cold. Raining. Windy. God help us all. Anyway, this isn't hot for this part of the world. Now, when I was in Oman, *that* was hot. You could fry an egg on the bonnet of a Land Rover."

Calvin James stopped and turned to the Briton. "Why would anyone want to do a crazy thing like frying an egg on the hood of a Land Rover?" he asked.

McCarter frowned as his agile mind sought an answer. "Was stupid, wasn't it?" he said brightly. "I never could understand it myself. Especially when you could boil them perfectly well in the radiator." Looking very pleased with himself, the Briton stepped around James and continued walking.

The black commando shook his head and glanced at Manning, who was smiling. "Yeah, I know," James said. "Only got myself to blame. I should have known better than to try to outtalk that dude."

The Force entered the terminal building. The spacious building was packed with a mix of people dressed in Western style clothing and traditional Arab garb. Suits vied with spotless white robes. The contrasting styles were in keeping with Saudi Arabia's blend of Arab culture and Western technology.

"I think this guy's looking for us," Encizo said, drawing Katz's attention.

The Israeli turned. Coming toward them was a young Saudi dressed in an impeccable suit.

"Ask him for the name of his tailor, David," Manning suggested.

McCarter wasn't known for his sartorial elegance. He wasn't happy unless his clothes took on the appearance of garments that had been slept in. McCarter called them comfortable; everyone else called them disgusting.

"Mr. Mertz?" the approaching man in the suit asked.

Katz responded to his cover name. "Yes."

The young man held out his hand. "I am Amar Hussein. If you would like to follow me, all customs formalities have been waived for you."

Hussein led them to a gap in the customs desk. Standing beside the desk was a handsome Saudi dressed in an immaculate tan suit. His dark hair was cut short and brushed back from his face. He waited patiently, his hands clasped together in front of him.

"Gentlemen, may I introduce Captain Ibrim Maji, Central Intelligence Department of the Saudi National Guard."

"Welcome to Saudi Arabia," Captain Maji greeted Phoenix Force. He bowed his head while touching the palm of his right hand to his forehead, the traditional Muslim salutation. *"As salaam alaykum."*

"Wa alaykum as salaam, Captain Maji," Katz replied, giving the correct response. "May I introduce my colleagues?"

The Israeli gave the current Phoenix Force cover names. McCarter was Marsh, James was Fuller, Manning was Scott and Encizo was Ruiz.

"My name is Mertz," Katz concluded.

"I have a car waiting outside," Maji informed the Force. "Please follow me, gentlemen. Your luggage will be collected and brought to our destination."

The Stony Man commandos followed the Saudi CID officer from the terminal building. A long, low white Mercedes was waiting at the curb. As soon as everyone was inside, Maji leaned forward to tap on the glass partition that separated the passengers from Amar Hussein, who had slipped behind the wheel. The Mercedes slid away from the terminal without a sound. The ride was smooth and silent, the only sound inside the car being the low hum of the air-conditioning unit.

Through the tinted windows the sprawling city lay on either side of the highway. Shortly after leaving the airport, the Mercedes rolled by the University of Riyadh, a large complex that would have put many Western universities to shame. It was possible to see a number of tall buildings thrusting their way into the desert sky.

"Did you enjoy your flight?" Maji asked.

"We slept," Katz told him. "We've had a busy time just lately."

"We have placed a comfortable house at your disposal," the Saudi CID man explained. "Under the circumstances, it was considered best to maintain your privacy. Please make full use of the house and its amenities."

The Mercedes wound its way through the busy streets, leaving the main thoroughfare to negotiate narrower streets that hadn't been designed for modern traffic. It finally turned into a quiet courtyard and drew up before high, scrolled iron gates. Hussein got out and opened the gates. Returning to his seat, he drove through the gateway beneath a stone arch that brought them into an inner courtyard surrounded by high white walls. The courtyard was like a set from a Hollywood movie. There were softly bubbling fountains spilling water into stone pools. Hanging baskets of flowers added bright color to the restful scene. Across the courtyard was the main house.

"All we need now is Howard Keel singing 'The Desert Song,'" Gary Manning whispered.

A smile crossed Maji's dark face as he caught the Canadian's words.

"I believe I preferred him as Clayton Farlow in *Dallas*," he confided.

McCarter chuckled as he followed the Saudi policeman from the car.

Maji led the way into the house. Inside it was shaded and cool. There was a mix of traditional Saudi design, blended with modern accessories. The tiled floor was broken up with scattered rugs. Thick, comfortable cushions rested on the low armchairs. In one alcove of the low-ceilinged lounge was an expensive stereo combination, equipped with tape decks and compact disc players. A large-screen television set dominated one corner of the room, with a VCR unit next to it. There was a collection of videotapes on a shelf over the VCR.

"The kitchen has a freezer of food and drinks," Maji said. "Please help yourselves."

"Can we talk a little business?" Katz asked as he sat down.

"I am at your disposal, Mr. Mertz," the Saudi said. He sat down across from Katz. "Please ask your questions."

"Have you been briefed about the kidnappers' terms?"

Maji nodded. "There are no demands of any kind from these terrorists. Just a statement that they intend to execute the secretary of state for the *crimes* of the United States."

"We believe—only a theory—that the execution will take place within the next few days," Katz explained. "And the secretary will be killed on the Fourth of July."

"American Independence Day." Maji pondered the fact. "That gives you only four days to locate the secretary."

"As you can realize," Katz pointed out, "we have little time for the niceties of life. In plain and simple terms we need to move damn fast. So without wanting to appear rude or inhospitable, we need everything you have on the kidnapping. Right now we don't have a thing to go on."

"In anticipation of such a request," Maji said, "I have arranged for all the evidence to be brought here for you to examine. There is very little, I'm afraid. The bolts from the crossbows that killed the Secret Service men, some written reports on the scene of the crime, the officers who were the first to attend the scene. If I may use the telephone, I will arrange for these matters to be put into action.''

The Saudi rose and moved to a telephone close by. The conversation was swift and in Arabic. Replacing the receiver, he returned to Phoenix Force. ''I have made all the arrangements. You will have the evidence here within the hour.''

''Thank you, Captain,'' Katz said. ''In the meantime, is there anything you can tell us?''

Maji sat down, smoothing the material of his pants across his knees as he considered his words. ''I would like to explain something first. May I?''

''Please,'' Katz replied.

''There is, in the outside world, a great misunderstanding of the Muslim religion, inasmuch as the mass is judged by the actions of a few. A Muslim is faithful to his religion, of that there is no argument. The vast majority of Muslims carry out their daily tasks, content that they are in the hands of Allah and that he will protect and guide them. They follow the rules of their religion and devote themselves to the prayers and rituals. To a Muslim the Koran is sacred and its word is law.

''As with any religion, however, there can be more than one interpretation of the Holy Book. There are those who read the Koran and who see its commands differently. They devote themselves to that interpretation and become so bound up in their devotion that it becomes an obsession. In itself there is nothing wrong with that. It has happened with believers of the Christian faith. They understand in a different way and practice their religion to those standards. Unfortunately, if their way deviates too far from the common view of their religion, they may find themselves isolated, pushed away from the main body.

"The Shiite fundamentalists, in certain cases, have gone beyond what the moderates consider permissible. Outright acts of aggression will do none of us any good in the long term. We must all learn to exist together in some kind of harmony. But only a small band of extremists is needed to create a great deal of trouble. I am telling you this so that you may accept that not all Muslims are like these Shiite fanatics. We of the Sunni Muslim faith can only apologize for these agitators."

"Don't blame yourself for the acts of others," Katz said.

"So," Maji said, "how may I advise you?"

"This Hammer of Allah group," Katz said. "What do you know about it?"

"Very little, I'm afraid," Maji admitted. "It has been in existence for over a year, I believe. Very secretive. We have gained very little knowledge about it, except to establish that its adherents follow the strict fundamentalist teachings and doctrine of Iran's Ayatollah Khomeini. The membership appears to be made up of Shiites from several Muslim countries. The sect has kept itself out of the public eye, although we suspect it is responsible for a number of murders and some bombings. From time to time it has released information to the press, declaring its policy and its intent.

"On that score the Hammer of Allah has been extremely forthright. From the start it has declared itself totally opposed to any dealings with the Western nations, and America especially. It has promised to mount an eternal campaign against the U.S. and all its allies. The Hammer of Allah has declared itself the savior of Islam. It is prepared to go to any lengths to destroy the power and influence of the United States. To rid the world of imperialist rule by the capitalist American infidels. Their propaganda becomes very tiresome after a while, but I am sure you have heard this kind of doggerel before."

Katz nodded. "From all kinds of groups, in any number of languages, and supporting many causes."

"Has the Hammer of Allah threatened anyone else?" Manning asked.

"Yes. They are not only interested in America," Maji said. "They have warned other countries they may come under the Hammer of Allah's scrutiny. For example a British oil company. Also a French oil group. The Hammer of Allah wants a pure Islam. They want all ties with Western nations severed as they consider them all to be evil. It is as simple as that, gentlemen."

"What we need is an opening," Katz mused. "Something that might point us in the direction of this group."

"Don't you have any street talk in this town?" James asked.

"I do not understand," Maji said.

"He means do we have informers, local gossip, underworld information."

Phoenix Force and Maji turned toward the sound of the voice. It belonged to Hussein. The young Saudi had entered the room silently. As all eyes focused on him, the young man smiled with embarrassment. "I did not mean to intrude," he apologized.

Maji beckoned Hussein. "Come in, Amar. I should have explained that Hussein is with my department. He has the makings of a first-rate investigator, if only he can overcome a certain timidity. Now explain to these gentlemen how you are able to understand their words better than I."

"I spent a number of years in England, studying language and economics," Hussein said.

"London?" McCarter asked.

Hussein nodded. "Yes. You know it?"

"My hometown," the Briton said.

"I lived in Bayswater," Hussein said, smiling suddenly. "I enjoyed it very much. I was sad to leave. I had many friends. London is a very nice place."

"You said it, chum," McCarter agreed.

"May we continue?" Katz asked. "To return to what Fuller asked, is there any talk about the Hammer of Allah?"

"Nothing we have heard," Hussein replied. "But we could certainly ask around. There are individuals who sometimes have access to information they might be willing to part with for a price."

"It's the same wherever you go," Encizo said. "The country might change, but people don't."

"Do you think it would help to seek out these informers?" Maji asked.

"It's worth a try," Katz said.

"Hussein could accompany you," Maji suggested. "He could be your interpreter and local guide."

Katz nodded. "We have to start somewhere." The Israeli turned to McCarter and Encizo. "You go with Hussein. See if you can come up with anything."

McCarter stood. "We'll need our luggage first."

"That has arrived," Hussein said. "It's in the front hall."

"Part of our luggage consists of weapons cases," Katz explained to Maji. "Do you have any objections to us being armed?"

Maji shook his head. "After what happened to your secretary and his people, I would be surprised if you wished to leave this house unarmed. Do not worry about carrying weapons, gentlemen. I will take full responsibility."

4

Amar Hussein led McCarter and Encizo through the house, which was larger than it seemed from the front. Emerging at the rear onto a paved area with a double garage, the Saudi swung open the garage door. Parked inside were two vehicles.

One was a dusty American Chrysler, the other an equally dusty Range Rover. Hussein opened the driver's door of the Range Rover and climbed in. The Phoenix pair followed, Encizo sinking into the rear seat while McCarter sat up front with Hussein. Starting the engine, the Saudi eased the powerful vehicle from the garage. Swinging around the garage, he drove to a high wooden gate. Then, reaching under the dash, he produced a black plastic remote unit, which he aimed at the gate. When he pressed a button, the gate swung open, allowing Hussein to drive out. Once clear of the gate the Saudi leaned out his window and triggered the remote again, this time causing the gate to close.

"I love that gadget," he said cheerfully. "It's really jolly good."

"You didn't learn that kind of talk in Bayswater," McCarter remarked as the Saudi gunned the Ranger Rover into motion along the narrow back road.

Hussein grinned, white teeth contrasting with dark skin. "Of course not," he admitted. "The trouble is, the kind of language I did learn wouldn't go down too well over here."

McCarter laughed. "That sounds more like it."

At the end of the road Hussein turned left. Now they were on a slightly wider road, running behind a row of houses.

"Where are we going?" Encizo asked.

"To the old part of the city," Hussein replied. "If you want to find out anything unofficially, that's the place to be."

"I suppose with the right amount of money you can get anything?" McCarter said.

"Yes," Hussein replied. "Buy, sell, barter, whatever you want, you'll find it there. Pirated tapes of the latest Western pop music, videotapes, clothes, gold and jewelry. Go to the souk and you will find it."

They drove through the bustling city, its roads packed with vehicles and people. The Phoenix warriors were able to observe the indifference of the Saudi mentality to change. Partly constructed buildings stood deserted and forgotten. Roadways gave out suddenly, construction having ceased for some reason or other, probably long forgotten. Piles of building materials were piled haphazardly on empty lots. Abandoned cars were common. In the poorer areas dilapidated old buildings housed the less fortunate.

Hussein drove to the edge of the souk, parking the Range Rover at the side of a crumbling building. Switching off the engine, the Saudi opened the glove compartment and took out a folded *ghutra,* the red-and-white-checked headdress worn by the National

Guard. Amar donned the garment, fixing it in place with its double head cord, the *aghal*. When everyone climbed out, the Saudi locked the vehicle and beckoned to a young boy clad a long shirtlike robe. He spoke to him in Arabic, and the boy nodded and went to squat beside the vehicle.

"It will be safe," Hussein said. "He's the leader of a gang of young street thieves. He also knows who I am, and that I'm aware of his business. So we've struck a deal. He watches the Range Rover and I forget his indiscretions."

"This place gets more like Miami every minute," Encizo said with a smile.

"Come," Hussein said. "A warning. There are many pickpockets around here, so if you have anything of value, keep your hand on it." He led the way into the souk.

The buildings were close together, pushing in on each other. The narrow streets, some cobbled, some dusty underfoot, wound in and out, crisscrossing. Merchandise spilled out from open shop fronts, dangled from the walls and from overhead wires. It was a warren, shadowy in some areas, sunny in others. And it was noisy. Raised voices, and the racket of many radios all blared out at once.

Before McCarter and Encizo had gone many yards their ears were aching. They were constantly being harangued by traders wanting to attract the attention of the Phoenix pair. They were offered watches, gold, precious spices, perfumes, rolls of silk and carpets. McCarter had a Japanese camera thrust at him. There was anything and everything up for sale. On top of the noise and bustle and color were the mingled smells of the place: a blending of food and spices, rich Arabic coffee and tea, the tang of overripe fruit, smoke and steam and sweat.

Hussein strode through it all with indifference, McCarter and Encizo following, alert for signs of potential danger. They were both fully aware that here, in this seething place, violence could strike from any number of places. They were exposed and unprotected.

Occasionally Hussein stopped to ask questions. These were usually answered by swift head shaking and waving of hands. A couple of the men he spoke to reacted with visible alarm. Undaunted, the young Saudi moved on.

Hussein paused before a shop displaying electrical goods and beckoned to McCarter and Encizo. "We may be lucky here. This man, an Egyptian named Faroun, is said to know more about illicit dealings than anyone else in Riyadh. He's never been in trouble with the CID, but he bears watching, I think."

"Can you trust him?" Encizo asked. "Men of his type aren't the most trustworthy."

"Don't worry," Hussein said.

"When people tell me not to worry," McCarter observed, "that's when I *start* to worry."

"I must remember that," Hussein said.

"You want us to come in with you?" Encizo asked.

"Better you wait out here," Hussein suggested. "Faroun could be alarmed by too many strange faces. It could silence his tongue."

"Yeah, you win," McCarter said. "Just make it snappy, Amar."

The Saudi slipped inside the shop, leaving the Phoenix pair waiting restlessly outside.

The minutes dragged by.

With each passing second McCarter became more and more agitated. Encizo could understand why. He wasn't too pleased with the situation himself. Too much was stacked against the Phoenix warriors in this strange place. There were far too many variables, and neither McCarter nor Encizo were in control, which meant too many things could go wrong.

From deep inside the shop came the unmistakable sound of gunfire—a single shot followed in rapid succession by three more.

"Bloody great!" McCarter snapped. "That's all we need." He plunged into the shop, Encizo on his heels, both drawing holstered handguns.

McCarter brandished the 9 mm Browning Hi-Power autoloader that he had refused to swap for the Walther P-88s carried by the rest of Phoenix Force. Nothing could persuade the fiery Briton to give up his Browning. He had been using it for so long that to lose it would have been akin to having a hand removed. Since accepting the new weapon, Encizo, like the other Force members, had come to terms with the P-88. The Cuban found the Walther an easy pistol to handle and had no qualms about it.

The shop was lined with shelves of radios, tape recorders, VCR units, TV sets and other electrical goods. The plaintive wailing of Arabic singers issued from a radio.

McCarter crossed the narrow shop, seeking a way through to the rear. Then he spotted a beaded curtain. The Briton waved for Encizo to slow down as he approached.

An instant after McCarter's warning the curtain was thrust aside. A wild-eyed Arab, clad in a light tan shirt and pants, burst into view. He was brandishing an Uzi. The moment he set eyes on McCarter the gunman opened fire, recklessly sending a stream of 9 mm parabellums through the air.

McCarter dodged the volley of slugs, which passed within inches. He slammed into a stack of cardboard boxes, losing his balance.

Halfway into the shop, Encizo halted, raising the Walther swiftly with two hands. He sighted along the barrel for an instant before triggering. Three slugs tore into the stranger's head and neck, slamming him against the doorframe. Entangled in the bead curtain, he slithered loosely to the floor, tearing it free from the top of the door.

Regaining his feet, McCarter ducked and went through the doorway with Encizo close behind. They emerged in a large storeroom cluttered with boxes and packing cases. A naked bulb, suspended on a plaited cord, was the only illumination. It provided enough light for the Phoenix pair to see that a corpse was stretched out on the floor.

An autoweapon opened up from across the storeroom. Streams of bullets whacked into boxes, chipping splinters of wood from packing cases.

McCarter and Encizo dived for cover. The Cuban spotted the muzzle-flash of the enemy weapon and returned fire, driving the would-be assassin to cover.

McCarter worked around a stack of boxes and peered around the edge, seeking the gunman. He saw a flicker of movement as the man attempted to gain a better firing position. McCarter gave the gunman time to move farther into view, then flipped up the barrel of the Browning, sighted and stroked the trigger. The Hi-Power crackled twice. The gunman gave a choking grunt as two bullets caught him in the right side, caving in his ribs as they cored into his body. The guy flopped onto his back, his weapon spilling from his dying fingers.

"Try to find Amar," McCarter said, springing to his feet and racing across the storeroom.

The Briton sensed there were probably more gunmen around. He reached a pair of high wooden doors and a smaller access door nearby that was ajar. Kicking aside the Uzi the dead man had dropped, he heard a shout from outside and flattened against the wall. Out of the corner of his eye he saw Encizo across the storeroom. Using the barrel of his Browning, McCarter eased the small door open.

He looked out on a dusty back street, across which was a bleached, uneven wall. McCarter peered left and right.

A car engine burst into life. McCarter saw two armed men hustling Amar Hussein into the rear of a dented, dusty old Dodge sedan.

"He's here!" the cockney yelled to Encizo as he barreled through the door.

The shout drew the attention of one of the gunmen. Bringing up his Uzi, the Arab turned toward the Briton while his partner continued shoving Amar into the car. As the Saudi CID man fell across the rear seat, his captor piled in alongside and the gunman with the Uzi pulled the trigger. A stream of slugs ripped into the doorframe just over McCarter's head. Powdery wooden splinters filled the air.

Seeing the Uzi tracking in on him, McCarter had launched himself in a full-length dive, landing on his left shoulder and rolling desperately. The ex-SAS man was no novice when it came to handling unfriendly gunfire. He had been in too many firefights to play the fool at such a time.

The Briton rolled over twice, then came up, leveling the Browning. With the enemy dead in his sights, he stroked the hair trigger. The weapon cracked twice, hitting the Arab high in the chest and slamming him against the Dodge's open rear door.

His partner grabbed the fallen man by the shirt and dragged him into the Dodge as it began to move. It took off with a high roar, tires skidding and dust billowing as it accelerated along the street. The vehicle slithered back and forth until the driver managed to bring it under control.

McCarter scrambled to his feet as Encizo burst through the door in time to see the Dodge skid out of sight around the end of the block.

"Bloody hell!" the cockney ranted. "Damn it all to bloody hell! The buggers have got away, and they've taken Amar with them!"

5

The Phoenix Force commandos were together again at the safe house, discussing the events of the day. For the moment they were without their Saudi hosts. Captain Maji and his people had excused themselves to pray.

"You have to hand it to these people," Calvin James remarked once they were alone. "They're really dedicated to their belief."

"Muslims don't take their religion lightly," Katz confirmed. "It takes total dedication to follow their way."

"Dedication or not," McCarter said, "we need some hard action around here. Without trying to sound disrespectful, I hope they get a move on. We have too much riding on this mission."

Katz picked up a cup of hot, rich coffee and took a sip. "Any more to add to the attack in the souk?" he asked.

McCarter and Encizo glanced at each other, shaking their heads.

"We've detailed everything that happened," the Cuban said. "There's nothing else we can add. Since we waited outside, we didn't know what Amar walked into. By the time we got inside, the main event had taken place. The guy called Faroun was on the floor with a couple of bullets through his chest, and David saw Amar being hustled into a car. We took out the two Arabs who opened up on us. David put a couple of shots into one of the Arabs who snatched Amar, but he was dragged inside the car as it left. It happened so fast that we didn't have time to ask questions.''

''Maybe Faroun will be able to answer some questions if he pulls through,'' Manning suggested.

''Our problem is, we don't have the time to wait,'' Katz said.

''Perhaps we'll get something from the fingerprints on the weapons we picked up at Faroun's place,'' McCarter suggested.

Katz nodded. ''And off the crossbow bolts that were taken from the Secret Service men. Captain Maji was embarrassed when I asked if that had been done. None of his people had even thought about it. He might look polite and gentle, but he really tore a strip off his men. I think he was more angry because I'd pointed this out and his people hadn't even considered it.''

''Let's hope it stirs them into action,'' McCarter said.

''So the Saudis haven't come up with anything from the scene of the kidnapping?'' Encizo asked.

James patted the file on the coffee table. ''This is their report on the investigation. To put it plainly, they have nothing. No ideas. No suspects.''

''Hell, it must have crossed their minds that somebody leaked information,'' Encizo said. ''The operation was too smooth not to have been planned beforehand. Those Hammer of Allah terrorists didn't ride up on a bus and do it on the spur of the moment."

"Agreed," Katz said. "But how do you pick out a Hammer of Allah sympathizer in a place like this?"

The door opened and Captain Maji entered the room. He crossed to the table holding the drinks and helped himself to a cup of black coffee. "So, gentlemen," he began, as if he hadn't even been out of the room, "where were we?"

"We've been going over what we have," Katz explained politely. "Which doesn't help us too much."

Maji sat down, his face holding an expression of regret. "I only wish we could have presented you with more information. Truly, though, it is all we were able to discover."

"What about Faroun?" Manning asked. "Before his abduction Amar indicated to Marsh and Ruiz that he felt the man could be useful. Have you anything on Faroun?"

"Only suspicions," Maji admitted. "He was known as a dealer—in many things, from what we have learned. A man who knew many people and who traded with many. It has been said that he would negotiate business deals for anyone regardless of their religious or political persuasions. However, we have never been able to come close to proving any of those things. Faroun is a very clever man."

"Not that clever," McCarter observed. "He wasn't able to dodge those bullets."

"What I would like to know is why those men shot him," Katz said. "Was it because of something he'd found out, or had he been working with them and they decided to eliminate him because they felt he wasn't trustworthy?''

''There's another possibility,'' Manning said. ''Maybe Amar walked in on Faroun and the terrorists doing a deal. They realized who he was and the shooting started. What if it was Amar who shot Faroun?''

''Good thinking, Scott,'' Katz said. ''We should add that to our findings.''

''Why didn't the terrorists just kill Amar?'' James asked. ''Why snatch him?''

''Because they felt he might know more about them,'' Manning said. ''They'd want to find out how much, keep their security tight.''

''I get the feeling we're going in circles,'' McCarter muttered.

There was a sharp tap at the door. Maji called for whoever it was to enter. A uniformed National Guard entered, handed a thick file of papers to Maji, then left.

''I believe this is what we have been waiting for,'' the Saudi said. He opened the file, laying the sheets of paper on the coffee table for everyone to see. ''Here are the fingerprints taken from the bolts used to kill your Secret Service people. This next sheet is . . . ah, yes . . . the prints taken from the Uzis left by the terrorists at Faroun's. Here we have the prints of my people who unfortunately handled the weapons. That leaves us with these fingerprints.''

Maji spread the appropriate sheets across the table for the Force to study. He removed a silver pen from his pocket and used it as a pointer as he continued. ''This set here belongs to a man named Jamal, a Kuwaiti, who has been in trouble before. He has been twice arrested during riots, but on both occasions was released through lack of evidence. His prints were found on a bolt used in the raid of the secretary's house. He was also one of the men killed at Faroun's shop."

"So that at least ties him in with both events," James said.

Maji studied the handwritten report that had come with the fingerprint identification. Then he drew out another photo-sheet. "These are Faroun's fingerprints, taken at the hospital. They match prints found on one of the crossbow bolts."

"So Faroun *was* in on the kidnapping," Katz said triumphantly. "At least we're getting something out of this mess."

"Anything else?" Encizo asked.

"One more set of prints," Maji said. "From a bolt, one of the Uzis, but not from either of the dead terrorists. However, we have identified the owner. A Saudi named Said Ziadeh."

"Known to you?" Katz asked.

Maji nodded. "A Shiite with strong convictions of the fundamentalist doctrine. He has clashed with the authorities many times, but never to the extent that it was found necessary to take the matter further. It appears we were wrong in that assumption."

"So this Ziadeh could be one of the terrorists who made it to the car," Encizo said. "Any idea where he lives?"

"There is an address here somewhere," Maji said. "Ah, here it is."

"It's all we have," Katz said. "Let's act on it."

"You wish to search for this man?" Maji asked. "Here is a photograph of him. It was taken over a year ago."

McCarter and Encizo examined the picture.

"I'm pretty certain that was one of the pair bundling Amar into the car," McCarter said.

"Do you wish to go now?" Captain Maji asked. "Or wait until morning?"

"We can't afford to wait," Katz said. "And for all we know Ziadeh might have moved on. But we have to try. Where is this place?"

"A gas station on the road beyond the city," Maji replied. "Ziadeh runs it."

"Do you have a map?" Katz asked.

Maji nodded. He beckoned to one of his men. The Saudi brought across a cardboard tube from which he extracted a thick roll of maps. He spread them out on the table, peeling away the upper charts until he reached the one Maji required. The National Guard officer traced the line of the highway running out of Riyadh, stabbing at a point.

"Here is the gas station," he explained. "It is fairly isolated. No other buildings around it, and desert on all four sides. The land is very flat in this area. You will have little cover, my friends."

"We have the night," Katz said.

6

The gas station sat in total isolation beside the asphalt road. The road itself ran in a straight line across the empty land, vanishing in the starlit darkness. The vast spread of the desert lay around Phoenix Force, wide and silent and truly mysterious. Aware of how far sound could travel in the desert night, the Force made its final preparations.

Each man was clad in a black combat suit. Faces and hands had been darkened to reduce the chance of pale flesh reflecting light. Black wool caps had been donned.

Final weapons checks were being made. The Force had come fully armed in case resistance was offered. Since they were uncertain of how many people would be in the gas station, Phoenix Force had come equipped for the worst.

Katz carried his favorite Uzi, slung by a strap from his shoulder. In a shoulder holster he carried his Walther P-88. Manning had picked the 7.62 mm FN-FAL assault rifle, while Encizo carried his Heckler & Koch MP-5. Still preferring an assault rifle to an SMG, James had brought his M-16. The 5.56 mm weapon was also fitted with an M-203 grenade launcher, and James carried a selection of rounds for the launcher on his combat harness. McCarter's Uzi machine pistol dangled from a shoulder strap. The fiery Briton had a preference for close-up work, so he preferred the Uzi's short-range capabilities. In addition to their hand weapons the Stony Man commandos carried an assortment of stun and fragmentation grenades, knives and also wore holstered automatics.

Captain Maji had provided vehicles for the journey to the station. The CID officer had brought along a squad of six armed National Guard men to provide backup. The two Land Rovers used to transport the party had been left half a mile down the road, parked behind an abandoned truck. From there the group had made its way on foot to within a few hundred yards of the gas station.

The concrete construction, once painted in bright colors, stood pale and weathered under the night sky. Exposure to the drifting, windblown sand had scoured the concrete walls of most of their decoration. The station site had a derelict appearance, with oil drums scattered around the area. A number of vehicles, in various stages of repair, stood beside the building. A row of pumps fronted the main office block. Next to this was a medium-sized garage, its roller-shutter door pulled down. Not far from the station was a partly constructed building, roofless, with scaffolding still in place around the walls.

"There was supposed to be a restaurant next to the garage," Maji explained. "But it did not get completed."

"There's a light on in the office," Encizo whispered.

"I see it," Katz acknowledged. "You ready?" he asked the Force.

It had been agreed earlier that Phoenix Force would lead the assault on the station and Captain Maji and his men would remain in reserve.

Katz gestured for Manning and Encizo to join him. "I want you around the far side in case there's a break in that direction. How long do you need to get into position?"

"Five minutes," Manning said.

"Wait for my move," Katz said.

Manning and Encizo slipped into the shadows, making a wide circle around the rear of the station. The others settled down to wait.

McCarter, who had been studying the cars parked beside the station, tapped Katz on the shoulder.

"What is it?" the Israeli asked.

"One of those cars is the Dodge that took Amar away," he said.

Katz nodded and seemed about to speak when James whispered, "Look!" Then he gestured toward the station building.

A man had emerged from a door and was pacing slowly up and down alongside the building. He wore light tan clothing and a white headdress. As he passed before one of the windows showing light, the autorifle slung from his right shoulder was illuminated briefly.

"We've hit the right place," McCarter whispered.

The man moved beyond the station. He stared out across the desert, head raised as he scanned the sky.

"Looks like they might be expecting visitors," James said.

"We're first," McCarter muttered. He was becoming restless, a sure sign that he considered action long overdue.

"That one out there could hold us up," Katz said.

"We can't have everything going our way," McCarter remarked. "You want it easy or something?"

At that moment there was a high-pitched scream from inside the station. The sound sent a chill through the Force. It was one they had heard before. Someone in terrible agony.

"I think it's time we moved," James urged. "I have a horrible feeling that was Amar."

Katz hefted his Uzi. "I'm afraid you could be right." The Israeli glanced at his watch.

"Let's move!" McCarter growled.

"The others need a couple of more minutes to get into place," Katz warned.

"That poor sod could be dead in a couple of more minutes," McCarter snapped. "You want us to sit here and listen to that sound?"

"You know better than that," Katz said.

The sound of an approaching helicopter reached their ears. There was no mistaking the distinctive thwack of the spinning rotors as the aircraft swept in out of the darkness. There were no running lights showing. The dry red dust of the desert began to swirl up as the chopper dropped to the ground, its noise sweeping across the empty land. As it landed behind the station, the man with the rifle moved out to meet it.

"We have to go *now*," McCarter insisted. "They might be bringing in reinforcements."

Katz snatched a quick look at his watch. Just over fifty-five seconds left before the deadline. He knew McCarter was right, yet he still had to consider Manning and Encizo, which put him between two arguable situations.

"All right," he said, making his decision. "We go in now!"

The three Stony Man warriors made a dash for the station.

Katz took it upon himself to watch the man who had gone out to meet the helicopter. The Israeli had a feeling about the guy, something that warned him to keep his eyes open.

Katz was right. Maybe someone in the helicopter, just touching the ground, had spotted the Phoenix trio. Or it could have been pure instinct on the part of the guy himself. Whatever it was, it made him turn around.

He spotted the dark figures running for the station, and didn't hesitate. His autorifle—an AK-47—rattled out a short, sharp burst. The slugs chopped into the ground around the Phoenix trio.

Katz slowed, turned and ran toward the man. It was an unnerving sight to have someone running at you in the face of gunfire. The effect threw the man off balance for a few seconds. During these seconds, the muzzle of his AK-47 drifted off-target. It was all the edge the Israeli needed. He crouched, his Uzi thrust forward, finger tightening on the trigger. The Uzi cracked viciously. Its volley hit the guy in the upper chest. He stumbled and went down, crashing on his face, twisting and writhing.

"Keep going," Katz instructed James and Mc-Carter.

The helicopter began to rise, retreating. From a side hatch a figure leaned out, wielding an autorifle. The chopper turned sideways to give the gunner a wider angle of fire. The weapon spit flame.

On one knee Katz aimed carefully, steadying the Uzi against his steel prosthesis, easing back on the trigger. The weapon crackled fiercely and stitched a flaming line of pain across the gunner's middle. Yelling in agony, he dropped his weapon to clutch at his bloody torso. As the helicopter swung away sharply, the wounded man fell from the hatch, hitting the ground in a slack heap.

GARY MANNING and Rafael Encizo knew the action had started the moment they heard the first crackle of gunfire.

"Let's go," the Canadian said, rising to his feet from behind the cover of the slight rise in the ground.

Keeping low, the Phoenix pair cut across the rough earth toward the station. To their left was the shell of the unfinished restaurant Captain Maji had mentioned.

From the far side of the station the gunfire increased. Manning and Encizo had seen the helicopter come in and sink out of sight. Now they heard the rising throb of the chopper's engine and saw its dark bulk rise above the roof of the station. The helicopter swung around, the flash of autofire winking from an open hatch. The fire ceased abruptly as a shape tumbled from the aircraft.

A side door of the unfinished restaurant opened and three figures clad in tan clothing, wearing head-dresses, appeared. They were armed with AK-47s. Seeing the Phoenix warriors, one yelled something in Arabic, waving his arm toward the station front, and one of the trio turned and ran that way. The others turned their weapons on Manning and Encizo.

Manning's FAL crackled. The volley tore through the lead man, shredding the tan shirt and flesh beneath it. The terrorist staggered, dropping his AK-47, slumping back against the station wall.

During this time, Encizo's MP-5 ripped off a sharp burst, catching the other terrorist in midstride. The guy slithered facedown in the red dust, swallowing a mouthful of gritty sand before darkness veiled his eyes.

The third terrorist, attempting to reach the car parked in front of the station, heard the gunfire and glanced back, seeing his fallen brothers in the dirt. A wild rage seethed in his heart. He turned, brought up his AK-47 and triggered it, but a fraction too soon. The AK-47's muzzle jerked wildly.

At the sound of the AK-47 Manning and Encizo dropped into a crouch. Each tracked his weapon in toward the terrorist, each firing. The terrorist was knocked off balance by the force of the multiple hits, flew back and crashed to the ground in a twitching heap.

"Let's go for that door," Encizo said.

Manning nodded, following Encizo. They flattened against the wall beside the outward opening door. Manning used the muzzle of his FAL to ease the door open. Encizo, having pulled the pin on a stun grenade, lobbed it through the doorway. Immediately both warriors drew back, eyes averted and hands clasped over their ears.

The grenade exploded with a loud crack and a burst of brilliant light. Smoke gushed from the open door.

Manning went in, crouching low, his rifle held ready. The Canadian moved to the left as he entered, Encizo taking the right. The room contained storage shelves and no people. Most of the shelves were empty, though some held engine parts. On the opposite side of the store was another door.

Manning and Encizo headed for the door. As they approached it, the sound of a loud explosion reached them from outside. And in the same instant the door burst open, revealing an armed figure bearing down on them.

7

Katz deftly ejected the magazine from his Uzi and replaced it with a fresh one, then joined McCarter and James along the gas station wall.

"We set?" Katz asked. He received a sharp reply from McCarter.

James, who had been busy with his M-16, glanced up. "One thing to do first," the Chicago tough guy said.

"What now?" McCarter asked, irritated.

"This," James murmured. He stepped away from the building and shouldered the M-16, swinging the muzzle up to where the dark bulk of the helicopter was hanging.

The machine was sweeping around to where the trio of Stony Man commandos stood, a second man in place of the gunner Katz had terminated.

James slid his finger around the trigger of the grenade launcher, aiming quickly, then firing. He had loaded an M-433 HEDP, a High Explosive Dual Purpose round. The M-433 had no problem with the chopper's alloy skin. It ripped its way through and exploded with a tremendous din. The helicopter blew apart in a swirling blossom of fire, scattering debris across the station's back lot.

As the explosion drowned out all other sound, Katz readied a stun grenade and indicated the door to McCarter. The British brawler drove his booted foot at the door, smashing the lock free. The door crashed inward. Katz tossed in the stun grenade, and seconds after it detonated, he followed it, breaking left, McCarter in his wake. James delayed his entry to ensure that no one was creeping up behind them.

Two men were in the office. Stunned by the concussion and blinding light, they were on their knees, their weapons on the floor where they had been dropped.

"Cuff them," Katz snapped.

McCarter pulled plastic riot cuffs from a zip pocket. He quickly secured the dazed terrorists, pulling their arms behind them and binding their wrists. When he had both men flat on the floor, he frisked them, taking away the additional weapons he found.

From the doorway James said, "All clear here."

McCarter pulled the pin on another stun grenade, nodding to Katz, who had moved to the door to the station's work area. The Israeli commando eased the door handle, then pulled it open far enough to allow McCarter to lob the grenade through. Cries of alarm came from the other side of the door, then the explosion.

"Watch yourselves in there," Katz warned. "It's a large area and some of the terrorists might have escaped the effects of the grenade."

He yanked open the door, ducked low and darted through. Close on his heels were McCarter and James.

The workshop area, lit by powerful overhead lamps, was littered with bits and pieces of car bodies and dismantled engines. There was a power lift in the center of the shop and littered workbenches along one wall.

Several men were in the workshop, some slumped on the floor, some staggering in a daze. Others, though, were upright, armed and capable of resistance.

Amar Hussein was also there. The CID man had been bound to a steel frame seat, his clothing torn from his upper body so that his tormentors could reach his flesh. Whatever had been done to Hussein had reduced his upper torso to a bloody mess.

The Phoenix Force commandos had only a fleeting glimpse of the workshop and its occupants. Then the whole place erupted into a confused mixture of noise and movement as the trapped terrorists engaged the Stony Man warriors.

Being first through the door Katz had to react swiftly. Although middle-aged, the Israeli moved with the speed and agility of a much younger man, though he admitted to himself in quieter moments that each time he exerted himself it took a greater effort. In the heat of the moment, with the adrenaline pumping through his veins, Katz was able to outmove and outthink any adversary.

Confronted by determined opponents wielding AK-47 assault rifles, Katz leveled his ever-ready Uzi, firing at the closest assailant. The volley cut across the man's chest and left shoulder, spinning him around, his AK-47 suddenly becoming a deadweight in his hands. He fell numbly to the floor, his face smeared with dirt and oil, the sound of battle rapidly fading.

Katz turned as another terrorist suddenly loomed large in his vision. This one had already triggered his

AK-47. Luckily for Katz, the terrorist had slipped on the oily floor, causing the muzzle to rise a fraction. The stream of slugs passed a scant fraction of an inch above Katz's head, tearing into the wall behind him. Needles of splintered concrete peppered Katz's neck, drawing blood.

The sting of the splinters caused an instant reaction. Katz tracked the barrel of his Uzi around, triggering a short blast that penetrated the terrorist's ribs, burning deep into his body. The guy grunted in shock and fell.

David McCarter, faced by a terrorist screaming wildly in Arabic, thrust his Uzi machine pistol forward, triggering a blast that silenced the Arab. Turning, the Briton moved deeper into the workshop, using every means of cover he could find. Despite the racket McCarter heard the rush of footsteps to his right. He turned to see a terrorist lunging at him. The guy was swinging a metal bar above his head. Blood trickled from his nostrils and ears from the concussion blast of the stun grenade.

The Briton tried to bring his Uzi to bear, but realized he wasn't going to make it. Ducking as the iron bar slashed at him, he slammed his shoulder into the terrorist's groin. The man cried out. His forward motion carried him over McCarter's shoulders, and as the cockney thrust up from floor level, he lifted the Arab bodily, tossing him clear.

The terrorist crashed to the floor on his back, breath whooshing from his lungs. He struggled to rise, still clutching the iron bar. McCarter lashed out with his boot, the hard toe cap crunching against the terror-

ist's jaw, spinning the man over on his back, unconscious before he landed.

With his M-16 braced against his hip, James
scanned the workshop, ready to assist his partners.
One of the unwritten rules of Phoenix Force was that
each member looked after the others. James, bringing up the rear, was doing just that. His eyes darted
around the workshop, picking out specific terrorists
who might yet prove to become a threat to Katz and
McCarter.

James zeroed in on a bearded individual who
scrambled onto the hood of a car that had suffered a
rear-end smash. As the terrorist leveled an AK-47 at
McCarter, James swung the muzzle of his M-16
around in a tight arc, centering his sights on the terrorist. A 3-round burst pushed the man from the car
hood into eternal darkness.

James released another trio of slugs at a second
terrorist. The guy crashed headfirst into a stack of
metal drums, his blood mingling with the oil pooling
on the floor below the drums.

Something heavy smashed into James, knocking
him to the floor. The Chicago badass rolled onto his
back, seeking the cause of his fall. A broad-shouldered
Iranian, his black hair streaming back from his angry
face, dived at the downed Phoenix warrior. In the
guy's right hand was a long, cold-looking knife. As the
terrorist dropped, James stuck out his right foot,
catching him in the stomach.

The knifeman grunted, twisted free, then slashed at
James. The terrorist's eyes had a glazed look, and
James realized he was in some kind of frenzy, proba-
bly brought on by intense prayer and concentration.

Using every ounce of muscle power, James swung the stock of his M-16 sideways into his adversary's head, producing a loud crack. The blow drove the terrorist to his knees. Blood streaming from the long gash in his face, he lashed out again, his keen blade slicing through James's left sleeve and just grazing the flesh beneath.

The ex-SEAL, pushing up off the floor, rammed his left knee into the terrorist's face. Bone crunched and blood spurted in all directions. The fanatic's head snapped back, mouth open wide to expose broken teeth. James hit him again, whacking the M-16's stock across the guy's skull. The terrorist was slammed to the floor, where he lay very still.

James, on his feet now, peered around the workshop, his M-16 held ready, finger just brushing the trigger. By then, however, all gunfire had ceased. The terrorists were offering no more resistance, and Katz and McCarter were moving among them, kicking aside discarded weapons and cuffing every man who moved.

"Fuller, see what you can do for Amar," Katz said over his shoulder.

James nodded and went to the Saudi CID man, who sat slumped in his seat.

Manning and Encizo entered from the far side of the workshop, dragging a cuffed and bloody terrorist between them.

"Late again," McCarter mocked. "What took you so long?"

"We didn't want to cramp your style, old chum," Manning mimicked in a fair cockney accent.

"Someone call Captain Maji and his people, and get them here," Katz said.

Encizo stepped outside.

With the terrorists secured, the Phoenix warriors searched the workshop. They were still doing so when Maji entered. The Saudi CID captain examined the workshop with interest. "It would appear we have chanced upon a Hammer of Allah unit. And their local base, too, by the look of it. This is an extremely important find."

"Captain, can you get an ambulance out here?" James asked. "Amar has been badly tortured. I can't do a great deal for him out here. He needs hospitalization."

Maji ordered one of his men to radio for one of the Land Rovers. Then the Saudi helped James comfort Hussein. The young Saudi had been beaten heavily around the face and body. He had also been tortured with tools from the workshop. Pincers and pliers lay on the floor at Amar's feet. The floor was spattered with blood, some of it fresh. Maji's face registered extreme revulsion when he saw what had been done to the young man.

"And these animals call themselves followers of Allah? Never in a thousand years would Muhammad condone such acts of brutality." The Saudi turned to Katz and the others. "Now you see why all Muslims are blamed for the actions of these people. If your Western press was to report this, we would all be branded as fanatical, blood-crazed monsters."

Maji was plainly upset by what he had seen. He ordered his men to round up the living terrorists and watch them closely. James did what he could for the wounded terrorists, while Katz and the other Phoenix warriors began a thorough search of the building.

"What are we looking for?" McCarter asked after a few minutes.

"I don't know," Katz answered. "Anything that might give us some indication where the Hammer of Allah is holding the secretary of state."

"Maybe Cal will get something out of the prisoners," Encizo said, referring to James and his scopolamine, or truth serum.

"Maybe," Manning replied. "No guarantees and we don't have all that much time to spare."

8

"At least we know how the information about the secretary got out," Rafael Encizo said, slumping in a chair.

The Force had just returned to the safehouse in Riyadh. Still in combat gear and carrying their weapons, the Stony Man warriors were winding down after the furious firefight at the gas station.

David McCarter emerged from the kitchen, clutching a tuna salad sandwich. He chuckled hollowly. "Ironic the bloke came from the Department of Information."

Katz glanced up from lighting a Camel. He drew in a deep breath, allowing the smoke to relax him. "He won't be passing any more."

The man they were discussing had been one of those killed at the gas station. Captain Maji had picked him out as he had examined the corpses.

The dead had been removed from the station to a morgue. The wounded had been ferried to a hospital. Three unharmed terrorists had been brought to the safehouse for questioning. They were being given a medical examination by Calvin James so that he could assess their fitness for the injection of scopolamine. Due to its composition the drug could be dangerous to anyone with a weak heart or high blood pressure. Before he would even consider giving the truth serum to anyone James always conducted a thorough medical examination.

Manning helped himself to a mug of hot coffee. The Canadian took a long gulp of the strong brew. His mind was still at the station, and he could still see the wild eyes of the terrorist who had burst through the door to confront Encizo and himself. Only the swift reflexes of the Phoenix pair had saved them.

The moment had been close, too close to forget easily, and Manning had to force the images from his mind. How many more times would the dice come up lucky for the members of Phoenix Force? Each time they went on a mission, it seemed, they were stretching their luck just that much further. One day something had to give. The burly Canadian silently observed his fellow warriors, and the question crossed his mind—who would be first?

"Hey, man, you're looking serious," James said as he passed Manning on the way to the coffeepot.

The Canadian shrugged off his somber mood. "How are your patients?"

"I injected them a couple of minutes ago," James replied, filling a mug.

"Need any help?" Katz asked.

"I know you can handle some Arabic," James said. "How about asking our friends a few questions?"

"I'm not that proficient," the Israeli admitted. "You'll need Maji for that."

"Did I hear my name mentioned?" The Saudi had come into the room.

"Fuller needs an Arabic-speaking assistant to put his questions to the prisoners," Katz explained.

"I would be delighted to help," Maji said, following James out of the room.

"At least one of us is happy in his work," Mc-Carter observed, extracting a Player's cigarette from a crumpled pack.

"I'd be happier myself if we were moving forward in this investigation," Katz said snappily. "All we seem to be doing is coming up against resistance but not gaining information."

"Tonight wasn't exactly a waste," Encizo pointed out. "We pulled Amar out of trouble and we apparently broke up the local cell of the Hammer of Allah."

"We're supposed to be pulling the secretary of state out of trouble," the Israeli said. "Time's going by and we still don't have a damn clue where he is."

"Let's keep our fingers crossed that the Hammer of Allah's finest are in a talkative mood," McCarter said as he munched his sandwich. "Hey, I wonder if anyone's missing them?"

"WHAT IS THE WORD from Riyadh?" Abu Niad asked, glancing up from the document he was studying.

The slender, dark-eyed Lebanese spread his hands. "Not good."

"Please enlighten me then," Niad said.

"There was a raid by the National Guard on the base outside Riyadh."

"The gas station owned by Said Ziadeh?"

"Yes."

"Go on."

"There was a firefight. Our people were overwhelmed. A number killed. Others wounded. Some taken prisoner. The helicopter that was to have taken away the National Guard prisoner was destroyed. We have also lost Bahar. He was among the dead."

"Bahar will be difficult to replace. His position in the Department of Information was extremely useful. It is unfortunate that his dedication to the cause demanded he become involved in direct action."

"We tried to persuade him to remain uninvolved."

"It is done. Now, has our backup team provided any further information?"

"The attack on the station appeared to have been led by a group of Westerners working in cooperation with the National Guard CID."

"Interesting. Do we know who they are?"

"From what Bahar was able to learn before his death they appear to have been carrying out an investigation into the disappearance of the secretary of state."

Abu Niad smiled. "I should have expected such a move by the American government. They must have accepted that we are not going to trade their secretary. The fact that we have promised to kill him has pushed them to making a rescue attempt. What else can they do? They have nothing to lose."

"Then these people could cause difficulties for us," the Lebanese said.

"Unlikely," Niad said. "If they had any idea where we had the secretary, they would not be blundering around in Saudi Arabia. I do not think we have much to fear from these Americans. On the other hand, it would be unwise to dismiss them too quickly. Do we know where these American assassins are based?''

The Lebanese smiled confidently. ''The backup team has located the safehouse provided by the CID.''

''Then it must be destroyed,'' Abu Niad said.

''That is already in hand, Abu Niad. There is one small complication. Three of our brothers, taken prisoner, were delivered to this house, most likely for questioning. To effect a rescue would pose great problems. It was decided, with much regret, that these three would have to be sacrificed for the good of the cause.''

''You have decided well,'' Abu Niad said. ''Allah will reward our brothers for their sacrifice. It will not be in vain. For every one of us who dies in this jihad, so shall a hundred Americans and their allies. Tell me,'' he continued, ''when will this destruction of the safehouse and the American assassins take place?''

The Lebanese studied his watch for a moment. ''It is happening, Abu Niad. It is happening right now.''

9

The M-72 rocket launcher belched flame and smoke as it expelled its 66 mm load. The rocket slammed into the front of the house, exploding and ripping a gaping hole in the wall. The air was thick with shattered masonry and broken glass.

As the rocket exploded, the Hammer of Allah terrorists rushed for the breached wall, weapons up and ready. There were nine of them in the frontal assault. At the rear seven more repeated the opening move. Their M-72 took out the rear door and the wall on either side.

Two National Guardsmen were killed by the blast. Another was wounded, his left arm practically torn from its socket. Despite his injury the Saudi managed to draw his side arm and put a bullet through the head of the first terrorist through the rear wall. Moments later the CID man was riddled with terrorist bullets, his bloodied body crashing facedown across the rubble.

Gary Manning dropped his mug of coffee and grabbed his FAL, turning toward the door. Close behind was Encizo.

"I thought things were getting too quiet," McCarter said, snatching up his Uzi.

The Briton raced after Manning and Encizo. Snapping a fresh magazine into his Uzi, Katz followed.

Smoke from the explosion was rolling along the passage. Dark figures, hooded and armed, burst through the hole in the front wall, fanning out on either side.

"Tut-tut," McCarter said. "Bad manners. They didn't knock."

Several terrorists turned toward the Phoenix commandos. With rising yells they began firing. Bullets from their AK-47s lashed the walls, knocking out chunks of plaster.

McCarter and Encizo dropped to kneeling positions, their weapons snapping to their shoulders. They returned fire, and their bullets tore into the enemy raiders, knocking two terrorists from their feet.

Hearing noise from the rear of the house, Katz signaled for Manning to follow him. They backtracked along the passage, meeting Captain Maji as he came down the stairs.

"What is happening?" the Saudi asked.

"We're under attack," Katz said over his shoulder as he and Manning continued along the passage. "Stay with Fuller."

At the end of the passage a short flight of stairs led down to the kitchen and other rooms. Katz and Manning reached the stairs just as the Hammer of Allah terrorists were approaching.

Katz hooked Manning's sleeve with his steel prosthesis, pulling him back. A second later, AK-47 slugs tore into the wall inches from his face.

"Thanks for that one," the Canadian gasped.

Just then a terrorist made a dash for the stairs, firing on the run. He made a lot of noise with his weapon, but failed to hit anyone. Manning didn't make the same mistake. He triggered FAL slugs into the reckless gunman's chest. The Shiite emitted a strangled grunt as the bullets cored deep into his body.

Katz noticed a head peering round the corner, followed by the barrel end of an AK-47. The Israeli took aim and touched the Uzi's trigger, sending a short blast into the unwary terrorist's head. Skull shattered, he crashed to the floor, blood streaming from his headdress.

A moment later someone rolled a grenade from behind the wall. The sphere of metal wobbled to the foot of the stairs and exploded, filling the area with deadly fragments.

Katz and Manning had drawn back around the corner the second they saw the grenade. Now they waited as the swirl of smoke filled the stairwell. They both knew enough to remain under cover and to allow the enemy to come to them.

The sound of scurrying feet and subdued voices told them they had assumed correctly. Men slithered across the loose debris, boots clattering on the lower steps.

Katz glanced at Manning and nodded. ''Go!'' the Israeli whispered.

Together the Phoenix pair stepped into view at the top of the stairs, weapons ready. Achieving target acquisition, they opened fire.

Three Hammer of Allah devotees were caught in the open. Manning and Katz cut them down in a few short bursts. The trio was driven down the steps in a bloody haze, bodies numbed and shattered.

Katz and Manning followed them down, stepping over their dying forms. Flattening against the wall, they ejected spent magazines and replaced them with fresh ones.

"Ready?" Katz asked.

Manning nodded.

Katz angled his Uzi around the corner and triggered a long blast. Taking his cue, Manning crouched and cleared the corner, his FAL held ready for firing.

Midway along the passage, with the smoldering wall at his back, the surviving invader from the group that had breached the rear was fumbling with the release catch on an M-72 launcher. He was on his knees in the rubble. His head rose as Manning appeared. With a muttered curse, muffled by the folds of his headdress, the terrorist dropped the M-72 and snatched the AK-47 that hung from his shoulder.

Manning leveled the FAL and triggered a single shot that thumped the Arab in the chest, knocking him into a sitting position. Still the wild-eyed fanatic tried to raise his weapon. Manning fired again, planting a bullet directly between those wild eyes.

Katz tapped Manning on the shoulder as he passed. "Let's see if there are any more outside."

The rest of the frontal group scattered as the first two terrorists went down. McCarter caught one hiding behind a heavy carved wooden chest. The Briton's Uzi crackled, emptying the remaining bullets in the magazine. Flesh punctured, the terrorist stumbled and fell. His left side felt heavy, and when he touched it, he felt the thick pulse of blood oozing from his wounds.

Three of the remaining six invaders, ignoring the risk to themselves, charged along the rubble-littered passage. AK-47s at the ready, they dashed headlong to where McCarter and Encizo were positioned.

Rising to face the trio, Encizo's MP-5 burst into life. His first volley caught the central figure, ripping into his throat. The stricken terrorist continued forward, smashing headlong into the wall and slumping in a bloody heap to the floor.

Easing the MP-5's muzzle a fraction, Encizo opened up on a second fundamentalist, driving a trio of slugs into his chest. The terrorist's AK-47 tilted upward, spraying the ceiling. He struck the wall with his left shoulder, the shock seeming to snap him back into control of his movements. Despite his heavy wounds he made an attempt at aiming his assault rifle at Encizo. The Cuban triggered again, putting down his adversary for keeps this time.

McCarter was just pushing home a fresh magazine when the surviving terrorist of the three smashed into him, sending him reeling. Recovering, McCarter eyed the fellow, seeing that he was making no attempt to fire his AK-47 and was likely out of ammunition. The terrorist confirmed McCarter's suspicions by suddenly swinging his weapon, butt first, at the Briton's head. McCarter swayed back out of harm's way, then retaliated by driving the toe of his combat boot up between the other guy's legs.

The blow lifted the terrorist off the floor. He released a pained scream and fell back against the wall. McCarter followed him, driving a heavy fist to his jaw. Ramming his knee into the guy's stomach, McCarter slammed the Uzi across the back of his skull as the Arab folded.

"Where did the others go?" McCarter demanded as he slammed a fresh mag into the Uzi.

"I think they'll be going for the rear stairs," Encizo said. "Maybe they want to free the prisoners."

"Or shut them up," McCarter said, never one to cloud the issue when it came to human behavior.

"You take the main stairs," Encizo said. "I'll take the rear ones and cover the terrorists from behind."

McCarter nodded and headed for the main stairs. He went up two at a time, meeting James at the top.

"What the hell's going on down there?" the black warrior asked.

McCarter grinned. "Visitors. The unwelcome kind. We've got three of them coming up the back stairs. Encizo's behind them."

"Oh, shit!" James muttered. "Maji went that way."

The Phoenix pair ran along the passage to the rear stairs. They were halfway down it when the crackle of gunfire echoed loudly.

James reached the far end of the passage as Maji backed into view. The Saudi was firing his handgun left-handed. His right arm hung limp and bloody at his side, his shoulder a mass of blood and pulped flesh. Maji was cursing in strong Arabic tones.

The M-16 in James's hands stuttered briefly, sending one of the Shiite terrorists plunging back downstairs, dead before he reached the bottom.

AK-47 autofire raked the walls and ceiling as the remaining terrorists returned fire. Plaster flew in all directions.

McCarter eased by Maji, who had sagged against the wall, face twisted in agony. Angling his machine pistol over the banister, the Briton triggered a sustained volley. From the bottom of the stairs Encizo opened up with his MP-5. Caught between two lines of fire, the terrorists had no chance. Riddled front and back, they rolled down the stairs, weapons clattering behind them.

"We'd better check out front," Encizo called.

"Go ahead," James said. "I'll look after things up here."

McCarter followed Encizo to the hole that had been blown in the front of the house. Covering each other, they edged across the shadowed courtyard. They found two of Maji's National Guards lying in pools of blood, their throats cut. Approaching the gate, McCarter and Encizo heard a couple of cars start up, tires screeching as they were driven away at high speed. Stepping through the gate, they searched the street.

"That's it," Encizo said. "I'd guess the cars we heard were waiting for our late callers."

McCarter grunted an unintelligible reply. He was watching lights coming on in the windows of neighboring houses. "Tell you what, chum. We aren't going to be very popular with the locals."

Encizo smiled. "So what's new, amigo?"

Katz sat in a communications room at the National Guard HQ in Riyadh. He held a Camel cigarette in the steel pincers of his prosthesis and the handset of a powerful transceiver in his left hand.

It was midmorning. Since the attack on the safe house the previous day, a great deal had happened. Medical teams and additional National Guardsmen had been rushed to the house, sealing off the area. Dead and wounded had been ferried away to hospitals. Before being taken away Captain Maji had assigned a young officer to work with Phoenix Force, instructing him to give the Stony Man team as much practical help as possible.

Once the house had been made secure Calvin James had resumed questioning the drugged Hammer of Allah prisoners. The black warrior had gained all the information he could before sedating the men and allowing them to be taken away. With that task completed the Force had abandoned the house and had been relocated at the National Guard HQ. Too tired to do anything but collapse, the battle-weary commandos had slumped onto the cots provided for them and slept. Brilliant sunlight streamed through the windows when Katz was awakened by the young Saudi CID man.

"Mr. Mertz, there is a call for you from the United States," the officer said.

Katz sat up, his body aching from the uncomfortable cot. He peered at the Saudi with bleary eyes. "Do I look as terrible as I feel?"

The Saudi, called Amad Sadak, smiled benevolently. "Yes," he answered truthfully. "You look terrible. Would you like some coffee? Perhaps food?"

"Right now coffee would be appreciated," Katz said. "Very strong and very black."

"If you will follow me, I will show you where you may speak to your superiors," Sadak said.

Katz followed. Minutes later the Israeli was alone in an office, waiting for his call to come through. Sadak had brought him a cup of coffee, then left. Finally the transceiver came to life, and Hal Brognola's voice boomed out clear and steady.

"Mertz here," Katz said.

"Glad to hear your voice," the big Fed said. "Anything to report?"

"We've had a hell of a reception," Katz stated flatly. He gave Brognola a short, sharp rundown on the events of the Force's first day in Saudi Arabia.

"Sounds like things are a little on the touchy side over there," Brognola said.

"The annoying part is that we haven't actually gained a great deal," the Israeli admitted. "The opposition is obviously doing its best to stall us, and up to now they've succeeded. I'm just hoping Fuller managed to get something useful from the prisoners he questioned last night. As soon as we finish speaking, I'm going to go over his notes with him and see if we can pick out anything helpful."

"I might have something for you," Brognola said. "How soon can you quit Saudi Arabia?"

"The way things have been going, the sooner the better," Katz replied dryly. "Why?"

"We've been going through every report we've been able to get our hands on from the CIA and the NSA, Naval Intelligence in the Gulf, whatever. All we were picking up were vague murmurs about an event liable to take place soon. It was all too flimsy to make any sense out of until we latched onto CIA reports from Israel. It seems the Mossad have got a guy who deals with Middle Eastern affairs, and he has an undercover man in the Gulf States. This undercover man passed information suggesting he was onto something, though he wasn't able to pin it down. The Mossad agent didn't get any further than being fed the basics—fingering the Shiites. Then his undercover man broke contact. I don't know whether this ties in with your mission, but I think it's worth pursuing. Agreed?"

"At this point in time I'd listen to advice from Roger Rabbit," Katz admitted. "Did the Mossad tell us where the undercover man was working from?"

"Saudi Arabia," Brognola said.

Katz fell silent, his mind sifting through recent information.

"Mertz?" Brognola's tone was sharp but anxious. "You okay?"

"Yes. A question. Did the Mossad identify the undercover man?"

"No name or description. That information is known only to the agent concerned."

"So what's our move?" Katz asked.

"You leave the same way you arrived. Your transport will fly you to Israel where you'll be met and briefed."

"Our contact?"

"Will be the Mossad agent involved. I have a feeling he could be very useful to you."

Katz smiled. He knew what that phrase meant. Cooperate with the Mossad man. "Anything else?"

"Your personal transport will be waiting in Israel."

That meant Jack Grimaldi and Dragon Slayer were operational.

"Fine. I'll be in touch."

"Once in Israel you can contact me via the U.S. embassy."

Katz broke contact. He picked up his cup of coffee and drained it. He felt ready for another. Finding his way back to the room where he and the rest of Phoenix Force had slept, the Israeli found the others just stirring.

"Listen to this, guys," Katz said. "We'll be moving on later today. First I want to have a look at Fuller's notes. Then we need to visit the hospital. I need to talk to Faroun."

"Where are we heading after that?" Manning asked.

"I'll let you know later," Katz said.

"First thing I want is a shower and a change of clothes," McCarter said.

"I think we're all agreed that would be the best thing for you," James quipped.

The Briton curled his lip. "You don't exactly look too cool yourself."

James grimaced. "You're right there, man."

"Fuller," Katz said, "you get cleaned up first. I want to get over to see Faroun as soon as possible."

Forty minutes later Katz and James were at the hospital where Captain Maji, Amar Hussein and Faroun were being attended to. Amad Sadak, who had escorted the Phoenix warriors to the medical center, cut through the protests of the doctor in charge, explaining in no uncertain terms that he was on government business. The doctor gave in, albeit reluctantly, and Katz and James were taken to the patients. James went to Amar Hussein, Katz to Faroun's room. An armed National Guardsman was stationed outside.

The Egyptian was connected to monitors and tubes but was still able to watch Katz approach his bed. Obviously, despite his serious condition, he remained alert.

"I was told you understand and speak English," Katz said. "If you prefer, we can use Arabic, though I'm not an expert with that."

There was no response.

"Two of my people were with Amar Hussein when he visited your shop. They were the ones who fought with the Shiites. The Hammer of Allah, I believe they call themselves."

A flicker of interest showed in Faroun's deep-set, dark eyes.

"My colleagues and I came to Saudi Arabia to investigate the kidnapping of the U.S. secretary of state," Katz explained. "Our mission is to rescue him if possible from the Hammer of Allah before they execute him. We believe the so-called execution is planned for the Fourth of July, which means we don't have a great deal of time in which to locate the secretary."

"You are an Israeli," Faroun stated suddenly in excellent though accented English.

"Yes, I am. Just like your contact in the Mossad."

Silence filled the room. Faroun stared at Katz. The subdued sounds of the busy hospital beyond the closed door of Faroun's room intruded on the silence.

"If this is true, then perhaps you know his name," the Egyptian said.

"*Perhaps* I'll get to know his name when I meet him. My people and I are flying to Israel later today. We're going to work with this man."

"And maybe you are lying," Faroun said flatly.

"My only answer to that is to say I'm not," Katz replied. "You'll have to decide that for yourself."

Faroun stared at the patch of blue sky beyond the window. "There are times when I truly believe my first mistake was to leave Cairo. My second was not returning there," he observed. "But that is all in the past." He glanced at Katz again.

"I am going to trust you, Israeli."

"Thank you," Katz said. "Now, can I ask who shot you?"

"It was the young Saudi—Amar Hussein."

"Why did he do it?"

Faroun managed a weak smile. "A foolish error. Such things must be expected when a man is in this business of deception. Sometimes one is misunderstood by those who are on the same side."

"Misunderstandings like that could get a man killed."

Faroun's expression was one of acceptance of his fate.

"Tell me what happened," Katz said.

"I had been gaining the confidence of the Shiites after many months of doing business with them. They had begun to trust me, to the extent of asking me to store some special weapons for them a few weeks ago. At the time I had no idea what the weapons were to be used for. There was no warning that they were planning to kidnap the secretary of state."

"Am I right in assuming the special weapons were crossbows?"

Faroun nodded. "Yes."

"And while the weapons were in your keeping you were able to examine them?"

"I did so in order to be able to inform my contact of the type of weapons the Shiites were purchasing."

"Which would explain why we found your fingerprints on one of the bolts."

"When I heard of the deaths of the American Secret Service men and the Saudi domestic staff at the house where the kidnapping occurred, I realized that I was involved with the Hammer of Allah. This is one of the terrorist groups we have been trying to infiltrate for some time."

"What is the importance of this group to the Mossad?"

"The Hammer of Allah has been instrumental in causing the deaths of a number of Mossad agents.

They have also carried out strikes against Israeli targets. These are clever people. They do not make a great show of their existence. Anonymity is part of their creed. They prefer a successful strike to worldwide publicity. The cause is all-important to them, and that cause is an ongoing jihad against the non-Islamic world.''

"So Amar walked in just as you were dealing with your contacts?"

"He could not have chosen a worse moment. He must have overheard our conversation and decided to place us under arrest. Oh, to have the impetuousness of youth."

"How did the shooting occur?"

"By chance I was handling a weapon at the time. The Shiites were anxious to arrange a consignment of these weapons for their brothers in Yemen. My part of the deal was to fix the actual delivery. When Hussein challenged us, I was the closest to him, so he decided to deal with me first. I cannot fault him for that. After he shot me, I can only assume that the Shiites overpowered him. He was lucky that your people intervened. He could just as easily have been killed on the spot."

Katz scratched his ear. "We decided the terrorists took him because they were worried he might have information about them that could weaken their security."

"Have you spoken with him yet?"

"My colleague is with him now."

Faroun fell silent for a few moments. His face was pale.

"If I'm tiring you, please tell me," Katz said.

The Egyptian raised a hand in silent protest.

"Is there anything you can tell us that might help us locate the secretary?" Katz asked.

"They are not great talkers, these Shiites," Faroun explained. "When they visited me, it was only to discuss business. I was aware of their suspicion, so I had to take great care not to pry openly into their affairs."

"Did they mention anything about the kidnapping? Surely they realized you would have connected the attack and the special weapons you had stored for them? We haven't yet been able to learn how or if they took the secretary out of the country."

"I am sure they removed him from Saudi soil," Faroun said. "The Hammer of Allah is not the kind of organization that would gather much favor in this country. They will have removed the secretary to a country that would be sympathetic to their cause."

"One of the more radical Arab nations?" Katz suggested. "Iran, Libya, Syria?"

"There is a man who operates a freight service from Dhahran on the east coast. His name is Quince. I have heard talk about him. That he will fly anyone, anywhere, for the right price. It is also rumored that frontiers and borders mean nothing to him. I know for a fact that he has been seen in both Iran and Libya. He is the kind of man no one likes, but many have a use for, if you understand what I mean."

Katz knew exactly what the Egyptian meant. The same phraseology could have been applied to Phoenix Force. Their very existence was kept secret, almost denied by those they served. But those very same people, who banished the Force to the shadows, were usually the first to call on the Stony Man team when the chips were down and drastic measures were required.

"Is he referred to as the Irishman?" Katz asked.

Faroun nodded. "You know of him?"

"Only as a name we extracted from one of the Shiite prisoners we took."

"You made them talk? What did you do to them? Skin them alive? Those Shiites are not the kind to give away information easily."

"We don't resort to torture," Katz said. "We use a drug that makes people speak the truth—scopolamine."

"Very clever."

"Do you think this Irishman, Quince, might be the sort who would accept a contract from terrorists?"

Faroun almost laughed, but checked himself against the threat of pain. "Quince would deal with the devil for the right price."

"Could be worth a trip to see him."

"Dhahran is only a couple of hours flying time away," Faroun said.

Katz stood and walked to the door. "Take care of yourself, Faroun."

"And you, Israeli."

11

Completing his prayers, Abu Niad returned to his desk and leaned back, in no hurry to return to the tasks of the day. Mentally and physically relaxed by his meditations, he felt the spirit of Allah flow through his body. As long as his faith remained strong and pure, he was sure no power on earth could harm him.

Abu Niad brought his concentration back into focus. He drew the plain-looking folder to him, opening it and reading the Arabic script on the enclosed pages.

That was his plan of action, his master plan for the operation that would take his jihad to the very shores of America itself. Abu Niad had devised and written his great scheme without help from anyone. The copy before him was the only one in existence. When the time was right, he would provide other copies for his men, but for now this was enough.

The plan was simple enough. He was going to take the war to America. His people, some already living and working there, would be joined by other Hammer of Allah soldiers. They would spread all across the country. At a given time assigned teams would plant explosive devices in government buildings, radio and television stations, police buildings, power plants, railroad establishments, airports.

America would be plunged into chaos. The most powerful nation on earth would be exposed for what it really was: a corrupt regime that was weak and incapable even of defending itself. Following the explosions, the soldiers of the Hammer of Allah would strike at chosen targets, including national and local government officials and military and police personnel.

The Hammer of Allah would lose many warriors, but it would score a great victory against the Americans. The exposure of America's inner weakness would encourage others to strike. The final outcome was impossible to foresee. It might be a great victory or simply a short-lived triumph. Either would satisfy Abu Niad. It would be the start of a long and bloody war against the United States, a terrorist war of hit-and-run, of continued resistance against American imperialism.

Abu Niad saw this as the beginning of the spread of Islam across the globe. It was the vision of the late Ayatollah Ruholla Khomeini, the man who had shaped Niad's life and made his destiny clear. There was no other path for Niad to follow. Already his plan was in motion.

The first defiant strike against America would be the rightful and just execution of the U.S. secretary of state, the man who had been spreading the blasphemy of the American government throughout the Islamic nations. He was to be held up as an example of the way America had lied and cheated the Arab world. For years the Americans had courted the nations of Islam, fawning and manipulating over them in return for the precious oil that lay beneath the sacred earth. Now they would pay the price for those years, for the deceit, the bribery, the corruption.

First the execution—for all of Islam to see.

And then the war would begin in earnest.

To the death.

He returned to his document. He had barely commenced reading again when there was a knock at the door. Abu Niad put aside the file. "Yes?"

The Lebanese entered. From the expression on his face Niad knew immediately that the man was bringing bad news.

"What is it this time?" he asked.

The Lebanese rubbed his long-fingered hands together nervously. "We have received word from Riyadh about the strike against the National Guard safe house."

"It did not go well," Abu Niad stated.

"No. Our force was defeated. Most of them killed. Others badly wounded."

"So the American force has survived again? And we have failed to rescue or silence those of our people taken prisoner?"

"It is so, Abu Niad."

The terrorist sighed. One of the misfortunes of embarking on a great crusade was the necessity of depending on others. It allowed for failure. Although by no means a total disaster, it tainted the rest of those involved and made true followers doubt that theirs was the correct path.

"How many know?"

"I intercepted the message and kept it to myself."

"Good. For now let it remain so. Give me a while to consider what our next move should be against these meddling Americans. If nothing else, they are a nuisance. A persistent nuisance, nevertheless."

DAVID MCCARTER dropped the helicopter ground-ward. Flying into Dhahran, he and the others of Phoenix Force glimpsed the hazy blue waters of the Persian Gulf to the east. Easing the chopper over desert oil fields, McCarter swept around on a heading that would have eventually brought them over Dhahran itself. Their destination, however, lay some four to five miles short of the city, where the Irishman named Quince had his freight service.

The airstrip that served Quince Airfreight was decidedly downmarket when compared to the area's vast commercial establishments. Set a half mile off the main highway, it consisted of a scattering of untidy hangars and buildings surrounded by the clutter of Saudi Arabian consumer castoffs.

"Passengers disembarking at Quince Airfreight, have your tickets ready for checking," McCarter droned in excellent mimicry of airline messages.

"Do you think they'll have a hospitality lounge?" Calvin James asked.

"Listen, chum, you'll be lucky if they even know what hospitality is," McCarter replied.

"Remember what Amad told us about this man Quince," Katz said. "He's not noted for his charm. The man is hard and lives by his wits. So be on your guard."

"Let's not forget what the CID investigation unit reported about the helicopter Cal shot down," Manning reminded everyone. "They definitely tied it in with Quince. So we *know* he's involved with the terrorists."

"Agreed," Katz said. "David, that doesn't mean you go in with all guns blazing."

"Are you trying to say I'm too impulsive," the cockney asked cheerily. "The way you blokes go on, you'd think I was a bloody Rambo clone."

"Don't you mean Rambo *clown?*" Manning asked.

"I've a good mind to stay in the helicopter," McCarter threatened. "Serve you lot right if I made you handle this all by yourselves."

"Promise?" James asked.

"Just land the helicopter, David," Katz said.

The chopper made a tight, controlled descent as McCarter brought it to a gentle landing short of the main building. "Maybe I should leave the engine running and the hand brake off," the Briton muttered.

Katz released his seat belt, opened the canopy door and climbed out. As McCarter cut the power, the others exited from the rear. The Briton climbed out and joined his teammates.

The Phoenix warriors were casually dressed in light clothing, their jackets concealing Uzi machine pistols. The weapons hung from quick-release shoulder straps. As well as the Uzis, the Stony Man commandos also packed their handguns.

The five troubleshooters stood casually by the helicopter, taking an unobtrusive look around the airfield. Quince Airfreight was obviously run on a day-to-day basis. It was far from tidy. Spare aircraft parts lay around the place. A stripped-down twin-engined plane stood to one side of the largest hangar. One landing wheel had been removed, leaving the plane supported by heavy wooden blocks. A sturdy wooden cradle held a dismantled engine. Out on the landing strip a pair of Dakota DC-6 workhorses drooped in the blazing sun.

"You don't think they're closed, do you?" McCarter asked, breaking the silence. The Briton had an uncomfortable feeling. He didn't like the unnatural quiet.

Warm wind drifting in from the desert brought misty trails of sand that rattled and hissed against the buildings. Katz approached the main building, his keen eyes searching the shadows inside the open door. He was certain he had seen movement.

"I'm looking for Quince," he called out, facing the doorway. "I need to talk to him."

Behind him the rest of the Force eased apart, each taking a different section of the airfield to watch. A thin trickle of sweat eased down the back of Katz's neck and under the collar of his shirt. The desert sun burned through his jacket and shirt. He could feel it hot on his back.

"Quince?" Katz called again, a little louder.

"Now what would you be wanting with me?" a man said from just inside the shadowed doorway.

He moved into the light and stepped outside. Quince was a tall, sandy-haired man. His broad, craggy face was burned red-brown from long years under the Saudi sun. His pale blue eyes were hard and cold and had little humanity in them.

"Well?" Quince demanded, his gaze sweeping over Katz and the rest of Phoenix Force.

The big Irishman had a powerful look. His wide shoulders were muscular, his arms long, ending in big, capable hands. He wore light tan pants and shirt, both of which were grubby and wrinkled.

"What is this? A deputation?" Quince's Irish accent became more pronounced as his temper rose. "Just who the fuck are you?"

"We need to ask some questions, Mr. Quince," Katz began, his tone moderated and almost pleasant.

"About what?" the Irishman demanded. Despite his outward antagonism Quince was almost smiling, as if he already knew what Katz's answer might be.

"I have a feeling you know the answer to that," the Israeli replied, aware now that Quince was playing a game, albeit a dangerous one.

"Maybe you'll be having to give me a clue," the flier said.

"How about unauthorized flights out of the country?" McCarter said sharply. "Aiding and abetting terrorism? Breaking the laws of the country you do business with?"

"You're crazy!" Quince yelled. "Get the hell off my airfield before I set the law on you."

"The law sent us," Katz explained. "You see, they're concerned about your activities as much as we are."

"No man is going to tell—" Quince's angry response was interrupted as Katz lunged at him.

The Israeli's move caught the Irishman off balance, and the Phoenix Force warriors off guard.

As his right shoulder thumped Quince's lean stomach, driving the cursing Irishman backward Katz called out. "Main hangar! Man with a gun!"

"Oh, shit," James said, hurling himself toward a stack of worn-out aircraft tires.

The other Stony Man commandos made similar speedy moves. In driving forward Katz had felt one of Quince's powerful fists slam down across his back. The pain only increased Katz's power. He put every ounce of energy into driving the big Irishman backward. Quince yelled as his heels caught the step of the door behind him. Unable to stay upright, he stumbled back inside the building, crashing to the floor with Katz on top of him.

From outside came the crackle of gunfire.

A wild roar exploded from the Irishman, his body twisting beneath Katz. He grabbed Katz's jacket and lifted the Israeli clear. Freeing one hand, he lashed out at Katz's face, catching the Phoenix commander across the left jaw. The force of the blow propelled Katz clear, and he thumped heavily to the floor.

Quince struggled to his feet. He swung one heavy boot at Katz's head. The Israeli, recovered, rolled out of the way. Seeing his opportunity, Katz swept his own leg around in a scything movement that knocked Quince to the floor, flat on his back, his skull pounding the pavement.

Quickly rising, Katz reached beneath his jacket for the Uzi, bent over the dazed Irishman and jammed the muzzle into the side of his face. "Can we start again, Mr. Quince? Or do I get nasty?"

THE UNSEEN WEAPONS were AK-47s. Their owners opened up without choosing a particular target. By the time the twin lines of slugs advanced across the concrete, Phoenix Force had already moved.

James took the pile of tires, followed closely by Encizo. Manning had turned about-face, vaulting over a large, shallow packing case lying a few feet away. The Canadian landed on his shoulder, breaking his fall.

McCarter was last, delayed by reaching beneath his jacket for the machine pistol. He ran to the right, cocking the Uzi and opening it up as he moved. He sent a long stream of 9 mm slugs toward the hidden gunners. The bullets chewed hungrily at the alloy frame of the hangar door and clanged noisily against the aluminum panels.

To McCarter's left Rafael Encizo opened up with his automatic weapon at the same target. The bullets dented and tore the metal. Encizo's covering fire enabled McCarter to close in on the hangar. He needed to get nearer the source of the gunfire. The Briton, acutely aware of the possibility of being hit, moved quickly. He put his back against the hangar, peering along the front of the large structure.

While the hail of bullets kept the gunmen out of sight, James made a dash for the hangar. He ran along the side of the building until he reached a door. The Chicago commando didn't hesitate. He shouldered the door open and entered.

The interior was dim and cool. There were no aircraft inside. Much space was taken up by stacks of crates and boxes. Old plane parts and other rubbish were piled against the side of the hangar.

James moved quickly through the hangar. He could see the large, sun-bright rectangle of the doorway. And just inside the door was one of the gunmen. Another guy stood a few feet away. The Phoenix badass crept up behind the pair. They were too busy firing to notice his approach.

When he was a couple of feet away, James raised his Uzi and rattled the weapon in the ears of the two gunmen. "First of you suckers to make the wrong move and this goes off," he said evenly.

Inevitably one of the gunmen decided he was faster than a bullet. He swung around, grunting, his AK-47 driving clublike at the black warrior. The blow was ill-timed. James avoided it easily. As he swayed back, James kicked out, the toe of his shoe driving up between the guy's legs. The gunman lost all interest in his original move as a burst of pain erupted in his groin. As the guy sagged forward, James smashed the side of his right elbow into the unprotected face. Bone snapped and the mashed nose spurted blood. The dazed gunman slid to the floor.

Sensing the second gunman was about to attack, James launched a brutal backfist that connected with the guy's jaw. The force snapped the guy's head around, and he cannoned into the hangar wall. Before he could recover, James rapped him sharply behind the ear with the Uzi. The gunman fell against the wall of the hangar, sliding to the ground.

James picked up the AK-47s, removed the magazines and tossed them aside. Then he moved to the hangar door. "Okay, guys, all clear!" he yelled.

"Trust you to have all the fun," McCarter grumbled as he entered the hangar.

"Not my fault if you're slowing down," James replied with a wide grin.

McCarter wagged a finger in his face. "Now you've done it," he warned. "I'm really upset." The Briton turned to the two dazed, bloody gunmen. "Up on your feet, you miserable pair of specimens!" the cockney yelled in his best sergeant major's voice.

The disarmed gunmen struggled upright, staring at McCarter with wide, terrified eyes.

"Face the wall," McCarter went on. He pulled plastic riot cuffs from his back pocket. "Hands together, boys, and be bloody smart about it." Moments later he had both men securely cuffed. "That fast enough for you?" he asked Manning and Encizo.

"Let's get over to the main building and see if Katz needs any help," the Canadian said.

Phoenix Force and the two prisoners crossed to the main building. Encizo went on ahead, checking the doorway. He waved the others on. "We needn't have worried."

Katz had the Irishman in a chair. The Israeli sat in a second chair, facing Quince.

"Sit over there," McCarter told the two prisoners. "We want to see if Quince's story matches yours."

When the Irishman saw his two men, his face darkened with rage. "What the hell have you told them? Sweet Jesus, I'm surrounded by idiots. Didn't I say to keep your damn mouths shut?"

"But we haven't said a thing," one of the gunmen mumbled through mashed lips. Despite the distortion of his voice it was still possible to recognize a strong Australian accent. "They're playin' bloody games."

Manning jabbed the muzzle of his Uzi against the guy's neck. "You're wrong, pal. Whatever else we might be doing, playing games isn't one of them. You're in this up to your grubby necks, and there's no easy way out."

"Unless you cooperate," Katz said.

"We don't know anything," Quince insisted.

"Don't insult my intelligence with remarks like that," the Israeli said. "When we first spoke, I had a feeling you weren't exactly surprised at our arrival. I'm sure you knew we might be paying you a visit. The fact that you had your thugs waiting for us only confirms my suspicions."

"Really smart, aren't we?" Quince sneered.

"Guess we must be," James remarked. "We're the ones with the guns and you're stuck between a rock and a hard place."

"Meanin'?"

The black warrior smiled at the belligerent Irishman. "Meaning, my man, that whichever way you happen to fall, you're in deep trouble. You either get it from us and the Saudi cops, or from the terrorists who employed you."

"You bastards talk like you hold the winning hand," Quince said.

"That's because we do," Encizo told him.

"You have a choice," Katz explained. "Talk to us and we leave you to work things out with the Saudi authorities on your own terms."

"And the alternative?"

"You won't like that," McCarter said with a wolfish grin.

"We hand you over directly to the National Guard CID," Encizo said. "They're not too happy about the way a number of their people have been killed. They don't like the fact that terrorists have been coming and going so easily. Anyone who has been helping those terrorists is liable to be in for a rough time. I'm sure you understand what I'm getting at.''

"You'd hand me over just like that?"

Katz nodded. "With as little conscience as you had helping the Hammer of Allah take the U.S. secretary of state out of the country."

Quince began to look troubled. It was obvious he hadn't expected to get involved so deeply. And he was realizing that he couldn't expect sympathy from Phoenix Force.

"I didn't know who their hostage was until it was too late," he said suddenly. "By the time I did, we were airborne. What the hell was I supposed to do— tell them I wanted to quit? Once I said that I was a dead man. You don't fuck with those boyos. They're real serious characters. Try to go against them and they lose their sense of humor."

"You were expecting us," Katz said. "Who warned you?"

"I got a call yesterday, from the guy who was working on the inside for the terrorists. He just said to carry on as normal but keep my eyes open. Something about an investigation going on."

"That's us, mate," McCarter announced. "We're the investigation. And what we found led us straight to you."

"Just what did you find?" Quince asked, his curiosity getting the better of him.

McCarter gave him a cold grin. "Tell me, Quince, is one of your aircraft missing? Like, say, a Sikorsky helicopter, ex-Saudi air force, one you bought at an auction of retired military hardware about a year ago? Your chopper happens to have the same engine number stamped on the casing as the machine that got shot down during a firefight at a gas station outside Riyadh. A firefight we had with a bunch of Hammer of Allah terrorists.''

"The National Guard CID tracked the number down through retained records," Manning said. "It wasn't difficult. The Saudis are deep in with computers. It didn't take them long to pull your card."

Quince shrugged. "Okay, okay, so I *did* help the mothers. They came offering me a bloody good deal. I was in no position to turn down money like that."

"All right, Quince," Katz said. "Just tell me where you took them."

"What's in it for me?" the Irishman demanded.

"How about we let you stay alive?" Encizo said.

"You bastards are as hard as those bloody Arabs."

"Tough on you, isn't it?" McCarter said. "Now just answer the man's question. Where did you drop the terrorists?"

"There's an abandoned airstrip on the Syrian coast. I airlifted them there. They got off, and I refueled and came back."

"Did anyone meet them?" Katz asked.

Quince nodded. "Some more of their people, I guess. Last I saw, the bunch were in a jeep heading west."

"Toward the coast?"

"I'd say so. Nothing else between where we landed and the Med."

Katz drew back. He wandered across the room and stood gazing out through the open doorway. He heard soft footsteps as Gary Manning joined him.

"What are you thinking, Katz?" the Canadian asked quietly.

"That our terrorist group had a rendezvous on the coast. A pickup by boat, out of Syria to some final destination."

"Lebanon?"

Katz shook his head. "I'd say no. Too much unrest in that country. Our terrorists would be looking for comparative peace and quiet. Somewhere the regime would have sympathy for their cause. Maybe even a reason to hate the U.S. as much as the Hammer of Allah does."

"Libya," Manning said. "Khaddafi's Libya!"

12

Waking from a light, disturbed afternoon sleep the American secretary of state remained stretched out on the uncomfortable bed. A jumble of thoughts, images, words raced around his head, and he fought off the impulse to abandon his earlier plan. He wasn't going to quit. The end result of just sitting back and waiting was certain death. He was totally convinced of that.

The terrorist leader, the one who called himself Abu Niad, had taken great delight in showing the secretary around the base. He had shown his captive the television cameras and the high-tech control unit housed in a small trailer.

The sight of all the communications equipment convinced the American that the threat of death was no idle one. Abu Niad fully intended to carry out his trial and execution. At the end of the so-called trial the secretary would end up slowly strangling on the end of a steel noose.

Abu Niad had shown him the wooden gallows, with a thin steel cable suspended from the cross beam. The secretary had stared at it for a long time, aware of Abu Niad's close scrutiny. He refused to allow his feelings to show on his face, but the secretary's stomach was shrinking with fear. The secretary admitted he was scared. No man could look upon the instrument of his death and not experience some kind of reaction. It was only when a man faced and admitted to the fear of death that he found the courage to resist, and to survive.

Now, alone in his cell, the lone American made his decision and prepared to act. His captors might think they had him whipped, but they were in for a damn surprise. If he was going to die, with little chance of rescue, then it was up to him to save himself. He had done it in Korea more than once when faced with seemingly insurmountable odds. He was a lot older and slower, but he was far from finished. He'd give these sons of bitches a taste of good old American fighting spirit, and it was going to be hard on anyone who got in his way.

He glanced at his watch. According to their schedule, his evening meal was due. They fed him just before dark.

He sat up on the edge of the bed, waiting. His meal arrived on time. The door of his cell was unlocked and pushed open. There were always two of them. One carried the tray holding the bowl of food and a tin mug of hot black coffee. He would have to go without his meal tonight if things went according to plan.

The secretary watched the tray-carrying terrorist approach. The other one stood just inside the cell. Both men carried AK-47 assault rifles strapped over their shoulders.

Bracing himself, the secretary waited until the man with the tray was in front of him. He inhaled deeply and stood, making to reach out for the tray. Instead he slammed his elbow into the guy's exposed throat. Choking, the terrorist dropped the tray, desperately trying to breathe through his damaged throat. The secretary snatched the shouldered AK-47 from the man.

Grasping it by the barrel, he swung the autorifle in a wide circle. The thick wooden stock cracked against the second terrorist's head as he attempted to bring his own weapon into play. The blow sent him reeling across the room, blood pouring from the deep gash in his head. The secretary slammed the AK-47 down again. The impact split the wooden stock, and the terrorist pitched facedown onto the floor, his body jerking in small spasms.

Breathing hard, the secretary picked up the second AK-47. Forcing himself to move calmly, he checked that the weapon's safety was off, then he pulled back the cocking lever. As he discarded the Kalashnikov with the shattered stock, the American removed its magazine, pushing it into the waistband of his trousers.

He moved to the door, peering up and down the corridor, seeing the door that led outside. He remembered the door from the time Abu Niad had taken him to the gallows. Reaching it would be no problem. The problems would start once he was outside.

Having been outside, the secretary knew that the base lay in a shallow basin in desolate semidesert country. From what he had seen the base had once been part of an oil camp. There were several buildings, some constructed of wood, others more permanently built of cinder blocks. A little distance from the buildings were some oil derricks, now still and abandoned. Discarded odds and ends of equipment and machinery littered the area, along with a couple of forgotten trucks.

Two helicopters sat on a concrete platform. Both were fitted with door-mounted machine guns and rocket pods. Beyond the base the desert spread in all directions, inhospitable and offering nothing but discomfort and possibly death.

The secretary eased open the door. He scanned the base. No one seemed to be around. He decided to move. There was nothing to be gained from waiting.

Stepping outside, he slid to the corner of the building. There was little between him and the empty desert, just a few piles of scrap metal and a stack of oil drums.

Gripping the AK-47 in damp hands, the secretary reached a scrap pile. He crouched, feeling very vulnerable and exposed. He peered around. There had to be guards somewhere. Terrorists, especially, had reason to feel insecure. No base would go about its business without a security setup.

The secretary remained in position for an eternity, it seemed, scanning the area, seeing nobody. He had to go on. Each passing moment brought closer the time when his escape would be detected.

He broke from cover, making for the oil drums. He had barely covered half the distance when he heard shouts. His breakout had been discovered!

Pushing himself forward, the secretary made for the oil drums. The loose sand underfoot slowed him. The harder he struggled the less he gained.

He was yards from the oil drums when an armed Arab, face covered by a headdress, appeared on the far side of the pile of drums. The terrorist raised the AK-47 he carried.

The American lifted his weapon and pulled the trigger. The AK-47 ripped out a short burst of fire. The slugs fell short, but were close enough to make the Arab jump away. The secretary fired again, following the gunman with the muzzle of the gun. A line of slugs whipped up dusty geysers in the desert sand.

Hearing the roar of an engine, the secretary twisted around as a dusty jeep bounced into view over a rise. The vehicle was crammed with armed terrorists. As the jeep roared up to the American, the terrorists spilled over the sides, fanning out around the lone fighter. More than half a dozen weapons were leveled at the secretary.

The last man out of the jeep was Abu Niad. He crossed to the secretary and took the AK-47 from his hands. "At least we will be executing a man of courage," he said. "Your gesture was foolish and wasteful. Even if you had managed to elude the perimeter guards the desert would have killed you."

"Did you expect me to accept what you intend without a fight?" The secretary faced the Arab eye to eye. "Don't be fooled into believing America will allow you to do whatever you want, either. We don't take kindly to threats or intimidation. You bomb us, kill our people, we'll fight back."

"We shall see," Abu Niad replied. "Shall we return? You may be interested to know that both men who came to your room are dead."

The American glanced at the terrorists. "Well, it can't get much worse for me, can it? I mean, what are you going to do? Hang me twice?"

13

Phoenix Force's transport landed at Israel's Ben-Gurion International Airport in the early hours of what promised to be a hot, dry day. Touching down then meant that the Stony Man team arrived during the lull that preceded the buildup of air traffic and passengers at the busy terminal.

The U.S. Air Force transport was directed to a quiet corner of the field, where the Force disembarked with their luggage and waited to be met by their Israeli contact.

"This is getting to be like one of those lightning tours of Europe," Manning said. "Ten countries in seven days."

"Trouble is, we get the economy trip," McCarter said. "Cover the Middle East in four days and get shot at in every one."

"At least there's no time to get bored," Encizo pointed out.

"Only by a bullet," James added.

"I think we have company," Katz said.

A Ford 4x4 pickup was approaching. The rugged truck, its paintwork bleached and dented, looked as if it had had a hard life. It drew up a few yards from the

Stony Man commandos. The driver left the engine idling as he climbed out.

He was a tall, lean, muscular man who moved with easy confidence. His thick hair was dark, the skin of his ruggedly handsome face a light brown. Women would have been charmed by his casual air, and there was no denying the appeal of his dark eyes. A deeper glance would have revealed the streak of ruthlessness that lay just below the surface. Even his dress emphasized the casual picture he presented. He wore a thin light blue T-shirt, a faded denim jacket and jeans. The jeans were pulled over the tops of brown leather Western-style boots.

"I'm Ben Sharon," the newcomer said by way of introduction.

Katz nodded. The name and description matched the description of the Mossad agent they were supposed to meet. "Mertz," the Stony Man warrior said, using his cover name.

"Good to meet you," Sharon replied. He glanced at the rest of Phoenix Force. "Marsh, Scott, Ruiz, Fuller."

"Cover names, of course," Katz explained. "Necessary in our particular business."

Sharon smiled. It was a slight smile, mysterious, as if he had more knowledge than he should have. "Whatever you say. You all ready to go?"

McCarter lifted his suitcase and aluminum weapons case. "When you are, chum."

"Take us about twenty minutes to reach Tel Aviv," Sharon said as he led the Force to the truck. "Jaffa really. My place is in Old Jaffa, overlooking the port."

The Force placed their luggage in the back, then climbed inside the roomy vehicle.

"Your helicopter pilot is already waiting for you at my place," Sharon said. "He arrived yesterday."

"What about the chopper?" James inquired.

"Safe and under guard," Sharon told him. "That's some machine you have there."

"One of a kind," Encizo said.

They left the airport without delay. Strings had obviously been pulled and all formalities waived. Sharon was passed through the customs exit after a cursory look by the officers on duty. Once clear of the airport Sharon picked up the main Jerusalem/Tel Aviv highway and pushed the Ford pickup to a steady fifty miles per hour.

"How's Faroun?" the Mossad agent asked, glancing across at Katz, who was sharing the front seat with Manning.

"Making a slow recovery," the Phoenix Force commander replied. "He took a couple of bullets in the chest, so he's going to be out of action for a while."

"Damn bad luck," Sharon said, obviously annoyed at having lost Faroun's intel.

"I don't think Faroun is all that tickled by it," McCarter said sharply.

"The guy nearly died," James said.

Sharon glanced in the rearview mirror, sensing the hostile stare of the Phoenix warriors. "Hey, I didn't mean it to come out like that," he explained. "I'm as worried as anyone. I've worked with Faroun for nearly three years. Been through a lot together. I don't want to lose him."

"He'll pull through," Katz said. "We had words with the Saudi authorities, and they agreed to send him back to Israel once he's fit to travel. If we hadn't, he might have ended up in prison or worse. It was lucky he was after the Hammer of Allah terrorists. The Saudis aren't too happy with the Shiites themselves, so they were open to discussion over Faroun's position."

"I appreciate that," Sharon said. "I won't forget what you did."

"Have you made progress with your investigations?" Manning asked.

"We were getting close to the Hammer of Allah," Sharon explained. "Closer than we've ever been."

"We want to get even closer," Encizo said.

Sharon grinned tightly. "From what I picked up via your people in Washington, you boys have been pretty close to our Shiite friends already."

"Those mothers play a mean game," James said.

"The cause is everything with these people," Sharon said. "Not that I have to tell you that."

"Any idea where they might be holding the secretary of state?" Katz asked.

"Possibly," Sharon answered. "I need to confirm some intelligence reports. If I'm right, we may be able to pin down the base the Hammer of Allah maintains in Libya."

"So I was right," Katz said. "They are in Libya."

"There's a good chance," Sharon admitted. "I know there's been a fair amount of activity over there. We picked up whispers about some special equipment being shipped in, though we couldn't pin it down to any one city. Two days ago I received information connecting the equipment with a small village on the Israeli coast up near the border with Lebanon. The Mossad has been trying to get something on a group we suspect of being followers of the Hammer of Allah. Up to now we haven't succeeded.''

''Do you have any idea who runs the Hammer?'' Manning asked.

Sharon nodded. ''We're certain it's an Iranian Shiite named Abu Niad. This guy was one of the Ayatollah's most fervent disciples. Hung on every word Khomeini uttered. He translated everything he heard to mean deliberate actions against the United States and her friends and allies. We're pretty sure he's responsible for several bomb attacks in Israel and the murders of several Mossad agents. Niad, from all accounts, is totally ruthless. Reports have him as meaning everything he says. The man has tunnel vision as far as his faith is concerned. No variation. No left or right. If Abu Niad is the guy in charge of the terrorists who snatched the secretary, then he'll carry out the execution threat. The only way to stop him is by putting him out of action for good.''

''Sounds reasonable,'' McCarter muttered from the back of the truck.

The streets of Tel Aviv were only just beginning to stir as Sharon drove through the city, heading toward the coast and Old Jaffa. By an intricate route Sharon brought the 4x4 into Old Jaffa, cutting back and forth through side streets and eventually parking at the side of a partially demolished building. He set the brake and switched off the engine. ''We walk the rest of the way,'' he announced cheerfully.

The Force climbed out after Sharon, shouldering their luggage. They followed him into the bustling community. Though the hour was still early, many local inhabitants were already busy. Shops were opening, and the smell of freshly baked bread and pastries drifted in the air.

Manning, walking beside Katz, noticed that the Israeli seemed to be enjoying the sights. "Something you like?" the Canadian asked.

Katz nodded. "Of course," he said. "Probably the same feeling you get each time you go home."

Manning smiled, feeling a little foolish. There was every reason for the Phoenix Force commander to be content, even if it was only for a short time. He had briefly forgotten that Israel was home to Katz.

"Here," Ben Sharon said.

At the top of a cobbled street, between a bakery and a bookshop, was a small art gallery. Stone steps ran up the side of the gallery, opening out onto a veranda that ran the length of the upper story.

Standing on the veranda, Katz gazed out over the rooftops. Just beyond was the blue water of the port. The red-and-white-striped tower of Jaffa Port Lighthouse stood framed against the morning sky. Boats bobbed on the water. Seabirds swooped and shrilled as they waited for any scraps tossed overboard by the fishing boats unloading at quayside.

"I forget how beautiful this place is," Katz said. "I could retire here and be happy."

McCarter chuckled softly. "You retire? Come off it, Mertz. You won't quit until they force you to."

The Israeli glanced across at the tall Briton. There was a distant look in Katz's eyes. "Maybe, maybe not."

"Not today, amigo," Encizo said.

Katz laughed. "Certainly not today."

They followed Sharon inside.

The apartment was bright and airy, with open shutters allowing the warm sunlight to enter the large living area. The place was inviting, friendly. Casual furniture and fittings, most of it in natural wood, stood beside green plants and flowers in clay pots. Many books were stacked on shelves. At one end of the room, on a raised section, was an artist's studio.

"Who's the artist?" Manning asked.

Sharon waved a hand. "I am. When I have the time. It's good therapy. Helps me relax."

"Everybody should have a hobby," McCarter observed with his usual sarcasm.

"Drinking Coke and smoking Player's doesn't count," Encizo said.

As the Force entered, Jack Grimaldi greeted them, a tall glass of chilled orange juice in one hand. A wide grin shone from his tanned face. He wore light, casual clothing, and looked more like a tourist than a combat pilot.

"Hi, guys," he said. "Took your time getting here. What did you do—go the pretty route?"

"Tut-tut," McCarter said. "The hired help gets more downmarket every mission."

"One more crack from you, Davey, and I won't renew your season ticket for Dragon Slayer."

"Can I have that in writing? Providing they've managed to teach you how to write, of course."

"By the way, I'm Walker this trip," Grimaldi said. He turned to McCarter. "*Mr.* Walker to you."

McCarter grinned. "Up yours, Yank."

"Okay, boys, playtime's over," Katz said. He turned to Sharon. "Is it all right if I call you Ben?"

"*Bevakasha,*" Sharon replied. "Please. Now make yourselves comfortable."

He vanished into the kitchen area, returning shortly with a tray that held drinks. There was orange juice in a large jug and cans of beer. To McCarter's relief there were also cans of Coke Classic.

"Later we can eat," Sharon said as he sat down. "Help yourselves to a drink."

Katz poured himself a glass of juice and took a long swallow. "How hard is the information on this village you mentioned?"

Sharon ran a hand through his hair. "It's ten percent information, ninety percent instinct. You know how it works. Not much on hard facts, but a certainty as far as gut instinct goes."

"We need something," Katz stated. "If there's the slightest possibility of gaining useful information, then we have to take the chance. We're working against the clock on this one. We don't have the time for dragged-out assessments of the feasibility of an operation."

Ben Sharon smiled thinly. He understood Katz's frustration, because it was the same for him. Too much red tape always seemed to hamper the day-to-day workings of frontline operations.

"I want this Hammer of Allah group out of action as much as you do," he said. "Though for different reasons. Your priority is pulling out the secretary of state. Mine is Israeli security. Saving lives, as well, I suppose, but with a broader time scale than you have. At the end of the day we both need the same thing—a location for this group and a hard strike to take them down.

"I'm not a hired assassin, my friends, but if I have to kill to secure some kind of peace for my country, I'll do it. I've done it before and I can live with it. The important fact to remember is that these Hammer of Allah terrorists are the extreme extremists. No flexibility. No compromise or time for discussions. They chose the hardest path of all to achieve their objectives. If we've learned anything from them, it's that. And the only way you deal with such hard-liners is to operate under the same rules."

"Then we go for this suspected base?" Katz asked.

"Yes," Sharon agreed. "We go for it."

"We'll get organized," Katz said.

"Can you provide maps?" Grimaldi asked.

"No problem," Sharon said.

He crossed the room. From the bottom drawer of a desk he pulled out a roll of maps. Selecting one, he showed it to Grimaldi, indicating the location of the village and the terrain between it and Tel Aviv-Jaffa.

"The village is on the coast, so there isn't much cover close by. The area is pretty flat. The closest we can get by helicopter is around here, about half a mile from the village. My only worry is the engine noise. If the wind's moving in the wrong direction, it could warn them we're coming."

"No real problem," Grimaldi said. "I can cut to silent mode for the final run in. It reduces the engine noise to a whisper. We should be able to sneak in pretty close. Enough time for me to drop you guys, then pull back until you call me in.''

"Sounds fine to me," Sharon said. "Let's get to it."

The Force opened their luggage and began to extract suitable clothing for the trip. They chose lightweight combat gear. When the weapons cases were opened, Sharon was impressed by the collective firepower the Force had brought.

"Do you guys fight full-scale wars?" he asked.

"Sometimes it feels that way," Encizo said as he checked his Uzi machine pistol and the H&K MP-5.

Sharon picked up a Walther P-88, examining the weapon with an expert eye. He checked the mechanism, working the slide, and weighed the automatic in his hand. "I've heard good things about this. You all carry one?"

"All of us except Marsh," James said. "He's old-fashioned. Still uses a Browning Hi-Power 9 mm."

"Nothing old-fashioned about the Hi-Power," McCarter protested. "It's got a proven track record, and I can hit anything that gets in my way."

"How do you feel about handguns, Ben?" Encizo asked.

Sharon smiled. "What I feel I keep to myself. Gun talk, like politics, can get emotional. So I don't get in too deep. All I'll say is I prefer the .357 Desert Eagle, and not just because it's a homegrown weapon. It suits me, and I like its delivery and accuracy."

"A man with good taste," Manning remarked. Until the recent weapons change Manning had also carried a Desert Eagle. "My own favorite," he explained.

The Force carried on with their preparations as Sharon left to get changed.

"How's the lady?" James asked Grimaldi, referring to Dragon Slayer.

"Better than ever," the Stony Man flier said. "I think the Special Projects Department guys at Stony Man have finished playing around with her. This time I think we've got the definitive Dragon Slayer."

"What have they done this time?" Manning inquired.

"Uprated the power for starters," Grimaldi said. "Twin turboshaft engines, each giving about 1,690 shaft-horsepower. There's a new missile firing system. TADS, short for Target Acquisition and Designation. Uses lasers to give instant range measurement and positions that are passed to the missile and the pilot. All locked into the IHDSS helmet the pilot wears. The rotary cannon has been replaced by a 30 mm chain gun that gives about six hundred rounds per minute. The gun is also connected to my helmet so that I can sight and fire at will. All I do is look at the target, and the slaved cannon locks in."

"Sounds like me when I'm shooting," McCarter said.

No one made any comment. It had been found that ignoring McCarter was sometimes better than becoming involved in a verbal duel with him.

"They've also added some extra armor," Grimaldi went on. "The pilot and passenger compartments are surrounded by boron. The rotors can take a fair bit of fire and still hold together. Some new kind of composite construction."

"Jesus, Jack," James said. "Whatever else you do, don't lose the damn thing. You'll be paying for it the rest of your life."

14

The flight took nearly an hour. Grimaldi kept Dragon Slayer well below cruising speed. He had taken the combat helicopter out over the Mediterranean before setting his course north. Dragon Slayer had been given flight clearance by Israeli air control, so they weren't likely to be challenged.

Their destination was an isolated village half a mile into Lebanon. The closest Israeli community was Rosh HaNikra, renowned for its white cliffs and spectacular grottos.

The Stony Man commandos, clad in camous, were fully armed and ready for any emergency. Each man carried his particular assault weapon, and a handgun in shoulder holsters. Manning also carried an Anschutz air rifle. The high-powered weapon was useful for taking out targets swiftly and silently with Thorazine hypo darts. Even Grimaldi was armed. He had a full-size Uzi in a rack beside his seat and carried a holstered SIG-Sauer P-226.

Ben Sharon, in standard Israeli Defense Force fatigues, was armed with his Desert Eagle and carried an Uzi SMG. Sheathed on his left hip was an SOG-TEC combat knife, which featured a seven-inch carbon steel blade, a brass guard and a Kraton handle.

As they approached the invisible line that separated Israel from Lebanon, Grimaldi throttled back and took Dragon Slayer to within a couple of feet of the sea. His fingers touched the chopper's instrument bank, and Dragon Slayer's powerful engines were muffled. "ETA approximately four minutes," he announced.

"We're all aware of the delicacy of this operation," Katz reminded everyone. "If we get caught on Lebanese territory, it means trouble for us all, in more ways than one. This has to be a hard and fast strike. We need to be in and out before anyone can reach us. Our main objective is information, documentation if we can find it, plus a prisoner who can furnish us with the information we need. Marsh and Ruiz, your main task is getting hold of that prisoner."

"Fine," Encizo said.

"Scott and Fuller, I want you to locate and immobilize any communications setup. This has to be done before we make the main strike. No messages are to go out once we hit them. Ben and I will provide cover for you all, as well as locating any paperwork we can lay our hands on. Since he knows this village a little better than we do, Ben will also provide intelligence backup." Katz looked to Ben Sharon.

"The village is isolated," Sharon continued. "About a half mile inland. Stone houses. Dry stone walls all over the place, dividing the village. As I mentioned before, there isn't much cover. There are a few trees in the village itself, but little natural vegetation of much use to us on the approach."

"How did you get this intel?" James asked.

"One of our border patrol planes managed a high-altitude diversion and took some aerial photographs," Sharon said. "Strictly by accident, of course."

"I love it when everyone gets sneaky," McCarter said. "Makes life more fun."

"Going in," Grimaldi announced.

Dragon Slayer skimmed the waves, cruising in toward the rocky coastline. The sandy beaches flashed beneath them, and Grimaldi boosted the combat chopper up over the rising terrain. He swung to the left, bringing Dragon Slayer in line with a deep gulley that ran parallel with the coastline. Searching for a landing place, the Stony Man flier chose one that would provide fairly deep cover. He brought the machine in beneath a swell of land that formed a curving basin that lay in partial shadow. Dragon Slayer touched down gently, and Grimaldi ran the chopper to the area of deepest shadows, then cut the engines.

"Let's move," Katz said.

Grimaldi opened the pressurized hatch, and Phoenix Force exited, Ben Sharon following.

"Just activate your tracking device when you're ready," Grimaldi said to Katz. "I'll be in to pick you up before you know it."

Katz nodded.

"Good luck, guys," Grimaldi said.

The Force fell in behind Sharon. The Mossad agent moved at a steady pace, scaling the side of the basin without a pause. Once they cleared the crest of the slope Sharon signaled for everyone to go to ground.

Ahead of them the rugged, sun-bleached terrain rose and fell in a series of low hills. As Sharon had predicted, there wasn't a great deal of natural cover. Little vegetation grew in this particular area—some coarse grasses and hardy scrub, and the occasional stunted tree, bent and gnarled by the harsh environment.

"The village is in that direction," Sharon said. "Nothing we can do about the lack of cover. All we can do is move fast and hope they don't have spotters out too far. I have a feeling these people feel pretty secure. They're on safe ground here in a sympathetic country, so they won't be too paranoid about security." The Mossad agent grinned. "Of course I could be completely wrong."

"That's what I like to hear," Manning said. "Confidence."

"What do you want?" McCarter asked. "An easy life?"

Sharon moved at a fast pace. He knew his business, keeping their line of travel low-profile. That meant taking a circuitous route, having to double back sometimes when a particular trail dead-ended. It could become frustrating, but the Force knew the penalties of careless movements in enemy territory. This was nothing new to them. Infiltration often called for slow, tedious travel. It was, however, better to arrive late than not arrive at all.

The heat and dust added to the discomfort. And there were the insects that buzzed and hovered around them, seeming to deliberately seek out exposed, vulnerable flesh. Every man in the group was beginning to sweat uncomfortably.

Sharon threw up his hand, indicating a halt. Hugging the ground, the Phoenix Force members waited in silence until Sharon beckoned Katz to join him. Together the pair edged their way to the rim of the rise below which they had halted.

"Perimeter guard," Sharon said softly. "He's off to the left, carrying an AK-47."

Katz took a careful look. He picked out the guard. The man, clad in combat gear and wearing a head-dress, lounged against a low rock. His Kalashnikov was cradled in his arms as he surveyed the surrounding terrain with eyes narrowed against the sun's hot glare.

"He's no farmer, or fisherman," Sharon observed.

"We need him out of the way," Katz said. "The village is just beyond him." They returned to the rest of Phoenix Force and explained the situation.

"I'm up," Manning said, unlimbering his An-schutz. He loaded the precision air rifle with a Thorazine hypo dart.

Sharon led him to the slope and pointed out the guard. Stretching out on the ground, Manning snugged the rifle to his shoulder and studied the guard through the scope. He also studied the village, taking note of various buildings. Finally satisfied with his observations, the Canadian returned to his main target.

The Anschutz made a gentle, coughing sound as Manning touched the trigger. Through the scope he saw the guard jerk abruptly upright, reaching for the side of his neck. The Thorazine worked quickly, and the guy slumped to the ground, curling into a ball at the base of a rock.

"All yours," Manning said as he returned to the main group.

"You spot anything interesting through the scope?" Katz asked.

"Armed men, a truck and a Ford transit van," Manning reported. "I also pinpointed what I believe will be the communications center." Manning picked up a sliver of stone and sketched in the dirt a quick outline of the buildings he had seen. "The second building, here, has an aerial fixed outside. If I'm right, and it's the communications center, it needs taking out first."

"That's your job then," Katz said to Manning and James.

The Phoenix commandos prepared to move out. Manning passed his Anschutz to McCarter, as well as the extra hypo darts. He didn't want the bulky air rifle to hamper his approach to the village.

"We'll cover you all the way in," Katz said. "Once you get well clear we'll follow at a distance."

Manning and James slipped over the rim of the slope and began their cautious, silent approach. They used the lay of the land as best they could. Every piece of cover, each depression, was utilized to its full potential. The cover was scant, yet Manning and James reached the outer stone wall of the village without detection. They lay in the shadow of the wall, giving the others time to approach. As soon as Katz and the rest had reached a reasonable distance, they took cover, weapons coming up to cover Manning and James.

A second armed guard walked along the perimeter of the village. His line of travel would eventually bring him face-to-face with Manning and James.

Seeing him, McCarter quickly loaded the Anschutz. Down on one knee, the cockney raised the rifle to his shoulder and took aim. He held his fire until the guard was in line with a building that hid him from view of the main village. Then, easing gently on the trigger, he fired, barely noticing the Anschutz's slight recoil.

The guard continued walking, and McCarter thought for a moment that he had missed. And then the guard's step faltered. He attempted to keep moving, and fell facedown into the dust.

"Close," Encizo said.

Manning drew his gaze from the unconscious guard and glanced at James. The black warrior's expression said it all.

"Let's get this over with before we have any more surprises," the burly Canadian suggested.

"I'm with you, man," James said.

Manning checked that the way was clear on the other side of the low stone wall. He scrambled over, moving quickly to the cover offered by an old animal pen. The pen hadn't been used for a long time. The split wood and weeds sprouting around the pen showed how long it had been unattended.

Moments later James vaulted agilely over the wall, crawling across to Manning's side. "That your communications building?" he asked, indicating the low stone construction that lay ahead of them.

"Yes," Manning said.

The Stony Man commandos flattened against the ground and slithered from the pen to the rear wall of the hut.

"Stun grenade in first," Manning said. "Then we follow. You see anyone trying to get a message out, stop them. If we're right and this is a Hammer of Allah base, we don't want them alerting anyone. If word gets out we're getting close, they might decide to carry out the execution earlier than planned."

James plucked a concussion grenade from his combat harness and pulled the pin. He gripped the grenade in his left hand and nodded to Manning. "I'm set."

"Let's do it, pal."

They rose to a crouch, easing to the corner of the hut, then down the side. Manning had been hoping for a window. This would have eased their problem, but there were no windows in the stone wall. That meant they would have to make a frontal assault.

Reaching the edge of the wall, Manning indicated for James to hang back while he checked the front. The stone hut faced the main street of the village. Peering round the corner, Manning saw numerous armed people moving around. There was also a man lounging against the wall of the hut beside the partly opened door.

Turning back, Manning said, "Guy on guard at the door. I'll take him out. You toss in the grenade. As soon as it detonates, we're going to have to get inside quick, because every guy in this village is going to be looking at us."

The Canadian eased round the corner and took three long strides that brought him up behind the guard. "Hey," he said to attract the guy's attention.

The guard turned, surprise crossing his face as he realized that Manning wasn't one of his comrades. Manning slammed the stock of the FAL rifle across his face, pitching him against the wall. The AK-47 slipped from the guy's fingers. Manning hit the man a second time, driving him to the ground.

James stepped around the Canadian, leaned toward the door and tossed the stun grenade inside. There was a startled yell, followed by the loud crack of the grenade as it detonated. A brilliant flash of intense light flared briefly, and smoke billowed from the door.

As the noise subsided, James and Manning ducked inside. The Canadian kicked the door shut as the crackle of AK-47 autofire filled the air. Bullets rattled against the stone walls. Some thudded into the thick wooden door but failed to penetrate it.

As he entered the hut, James faced a dazed, bloody-nosed Arab holding a Kalashnikov. The guy was suffering from the effects of the concussion grenade. Seeing an invader, he tried to bring the AK-47 into play. James crashed the butt of his M-16 between the guy's eyes. The Arab stumbled back, his legs buckling. A second buttstroke from James finally laid him out.

The smoke-filled hut was indeed a communications center. Along the back wall was a powerful transceiver, set on a sturdy wooden trestle table. Underneath were several battery packs. The transceiver's power indicator light was on, showing that the equipment was up and running. At the far end of the table was a television monitor. A second man lay on the floor by the table, an overturned chair beside him.

James pulled plastic riot cuffs from his pocket and secured both unconscious men. Checking them for weapons, he produced handguns and a knife, which he tossed onto the table. Then he dragged the men across the hut.

The black commando could hear the slap and whine of bullets striking the outside wall. He was thankful the hut was constructed from stone and not wood.

"Stay to the side of the door," Manning said. "They could figure out enough bullets will eventually penetrate."

"Partner, we're stuck like fish in a barrel," James commented. "No damn windows in this place means they can't shoot inside, but it also means we can't shoot out."

"Let's hope the others get a move on," Manning said.

THE EXPLODING CONCUSSION grenade was the signal the others had been waiting for. With Katz in the lead they rose to their feet and approached the village.

They paused briefly next to the guard McCarter had dropped with the Anschutz. The Briton glanced briefly at the unconscious Arab. The man's headdress had slipped free, exposing his face. McCarter stared at the face for a moment, then stared harder. "Well, I'll be buggered," he muttered, more to himself than anyone else.

"What is it?" Katz asked, catching the cockney's surprised comment.

"This bloke is one of the sods we clashed with at Faroun's shop in Riyadh."

"Are you certain?" Encizo asked.

"There were two of the buggers bundling Amar Hussein into a car," McCarter said eagerly. "I shot one. The other bloke was the one concentrating on Amar. This is him. No bloody doubt."

"Another connection," Katz said.

"Let's make sure he doesn't wake up and sneak away," McCarter suggested. He pulled plastic riot cuffs from a pocket and secured the Arab's wrists and ankles.

"All right," Katz said. "Let's move out."

They separated into two groups. McCarter and Encizo took the southern end, skirting the hut Manning and James had occupied. This brought them in at the extreme end of the village.

Katz and Sharon moved in the opposite direction, covering about twenty yards before they cut between two huts and emerged onto the main street of the village. Within seconds they were involved in a hectic firefight as the occupants of the village responded to the unexpected attack.

Armed men rushed out of huts to join those already on the street. There was little coordination among them. They milled around, confused, trying to determine which attacking force they should engage.

By the time McCarter and Encizo had appeared at the far end of the street, decision time was over. The only thing that mattered was who would live and who would die.

15

Katz and Sharon encountered resistance almost as soon as they reached the street, which was little more than a well-trodden path between the stone buildings.

The Phoenix Force commander stood his ground as a couple of attackers opened up with their AK-47s. He felt the breeze of a slug as it passed. The Israeli positioned his Uzi across his prosthesis, pulled the trigger and delivered a spray of 9 mm bullets to the terrorists. The hot slugs ripped them open like overripe fruit. They stumbled drunkenly, limbs giving way as they collapsed in the dust.

Sharon, close on Katz's heels, clashed with a shouting, wild-eyed Arab who came at him in a headlong rush, his AK-47 in the air. The Mossad agent didn't give the terrorist the opportunity to bring the weapon into play. He leveled his Uzi and triggered a short blast.

The Arab, incensed at the infidels, kept on coming, ignoring the bloody patch spreading across the front of his shirt. He was mere inches from Sharon when the Israeli agent fired again, this time at the guy's throat. The slugs ripped the Arab's flesh apart, and he crashed to the ground, his yelling reduced to a horrible gurgle.

Katz had spotted a number of armed guards in front of a building slightly larger than the others. He sensed that this might be the HQ building and told Sharon.

"You could be right," the Mossad agent agreed, plucking a grenade from his belt. He pulled the pin on the run, weaving from side to side as the bunched terrorists opened fire.

The terrorists began to scatter as Sharon launched the grenade into their midst. Only a couple managed to get fully clear, and Katz hosed those with bullets from his Uzi.

The grenade detonated with a loud crack, sending its deadly spray of fragments into the fleeing terrorists. Men were hurled across the ground, bodies ripped and shredded. They tumbled into the dirt, blood spurting from their lacerated flesh.

Katz and Sharon closed in on them, firing on the ones who were only marginally wounded and able to maintain resistance.

One terrorist, bloody-faced, triggered his AK-47 at Sharon and had the satisfaction of seeing his target stumble as a bullet gouged his right upper arm. Undeterred, Sharon emptied his Uzi into the terrorist, puncturing the man's heart and lungs a half-dozen times.

Reaching the building, Katz and Sharon paused to reload. Katz tossed a concussion grenade through the closest window. The explosion drowned out the startled yells inside.

Sharon booted the door open, ducking inside and angling to one side. He was closely followed by Katz.

The one big room was filled with smoke. A dark shape loomed on Katz's right. The Israeli ducked as he turned. A terrorist, staring through streaming eyes, struck out with an autopistol. Katz deflected the steel barrel of the pistol with his prosthesis. The curving hooks of the prosthesis then smashed across the terrorist's face, splitting the right cheek and breaking the bone. The terrorist slumped against the wall, immobile. Taking no chances, Katz shot him with his Uzi.

Sharon had located two terrorists on hands and knees, disoriented by the blast. Moving quickly, Sharon secured both men with plastic riot cuffs.

"Ben, go through this place with a fine-tooth comb. See what you can find," Katz said as he reloaded his Uzi.

"Where are you going?" the Mossad agent asked.

"To help my buddies," Katz replied. "We'll clear the area, then come back for you."

"Watch yourself," Sharon said.

Katz grinned. "I always do."

BEFORE MCCARTER and Encizo hit the street the Briton slipped the Anschutz from his shoulder and laid it at the foot of a stone wall. He didn't want the heavy weapon hampering his movements.

"Gary won't like it if you lose his rifle," Encizo commented.

"Hard bloody luck," the Briton replied. "I'll have to buy him another."

The rattle of autofire told the Phoenix warriors that Katz and Sharon were already in action. McCarter and Encizo swiftly rounded the hut at the end of the street and saw Katz and Sharon up at the far end, engaging the enemy.

"I don't like the odds," Encizo said. "Let's help them out."

"Sometimes you talk good sense," McCarter said, running in a crouch toward the action.

The impulsive Briton had failed to see one terrorist step from an open doorway. The guy, clad in fatigues and a headdress, snatched at the AK-47 hanging from his shoulder.

Encizo raised his MP-5 and triggered a 3-round burst. The slugs cored through the terrorist's back, splintering bone and rupturing vital organs. The terrorist fell, his weapon unfired.

The racket of the Cuban's weapon attracted other Hammer of Allah terrorists. The Briton opened fire before they were able to make eye contact. His Uzi machine pistol ripped the life from a Lebanese and an Iraqi terrorist. They were flung to the ground in agony.

Three others, smarter than their Hammer of Allah brothers, took cover behind a battered and doorless truck. One of them quickwittedly made a dash for the cab, throwing himself behind the wheel. He switched on the ignition and fired the engine into life, tromping hard on the gas pedal. As the truck engine roared, the other two jumped aboard, one onto the flatbed rear, the other on the cab step around the rear.

The truck lurched into motion, kicking up clouds of dust as it picked up speed. The driver, a big, bearded Arab, yelled instructions to the other terrorists clinging to the bouncing vehicle.

Encizo was able to avoid the truck. But McCarter found he was directly in the path of the oncoming juggernaut.

"David!" Encizo yelled, forgetting cover names and security as he called to his friend.

The agile Briton dropped to one knee. He sensed the truck's bulk growing as it bumped along the uneven street.

The terrorist hanging from the passenger door opened fire with a 9 mm Spanish Star. The pistol spit bullets into the ground around McCarter. The Briton snap-aimed his Uzi and sent a 3-round burst that ripped into the guy's throat. The Star pistol dropped from his hand, and the terrorist fell from the truck.

The driver yanked hard on the wheel, and the truck lurched directly at McCarter. The Briton threw himself flat onto the ground and the truck swept over him. For long seconds McCarter's ears were filled with the boom of the engine, and he breathed in the stench of oil and diesel fumes. Something brushed across his back, causing the cockney to swear in surprise, then the dark shape was gone and he felt the hot sun again.

Pushing to his feet, McCarter leveled his Uzi at the retreating truck. He centered the weapon on the armed terrorist who was balanced precariously on the flatbed. The terrorist raised his AK-47 at McCarter.

"No second chances in this game," McCarter muttered as he trigged the Uzi twice in rapid succession.

Thrown back, the terrorist lost his balance and rolled from the truck. His body bounced under the rear tires of the truck as it passed.

McCarter, seeing the truck halt, took temporary cover at the back of the vehicle. The driver burst into view, hanging from the cab doorframe, wielding an Uzi. He hurriedly aimed at McCarter and triggered.

As a long, erratic burst of 9 mm bullets whizzed overhead, McCarter dropped to one knee.

He fired as the driver began to step down from the cab, knocking him off the cab step. Then Encizo blasted him from behind, driving three bullets into his skull.

"You okay?" Encizo asked as he joined McCarter.

"I came close that time," the cockney said.

"That reckless streak will get you killed one day," Encizo warned him.

"Nag, nag, nag," McCarter chanted.

The rattle of autofire caught their attention. Katz was taking out the last terrorists on the street. The Israeli had caught the pair about to plant a grenade at the door of the radio hut. There was no more resistance. The area had been cleared of all the Hammer of Allah fanatics.

McCarter rapped on the door of the radio hut. "You can come out now, girls. All the nasty men have been frightened away."

The door swung open and Manning leaned out. He glanced at McCarter. "No, they haven't. You're still here."

The cockney smiled, then turned as if remembering something. He jogged down the street and returned with Manning's Anschutz. "I believe this is yours."

Manning took the weapon with thanks. "Find anything useful?" the Canadian asked.

"I left Ben up at the HQ building," Katz said. "We'll rejoin him and find out. There anything in there?" he said, indicating the radio hut.

"Only communications equipment," Manning replied. "Looks like it could be long-range stuff."

"Could it reach as far as Libya?"

Manning nodded. "There's also a television set."

"I'll bet the bastards were getting ready to watch a live special," James said bitterly.

"Well, if we don't locate the terrorist base in time," Katz said, "that special might still go on as scheduled."

"I'll fetch our prisoner," McCarter said. "We'll see if we can get him to do some talking."

Katz activated the small electronic tracking device Grimaldi had given him.

"I'll go check the bodies," James said, "and see if there are any wounded I can help."

"The rest of us will check all the huts," Katz said. "We'll pick up anything that might give us information."

As they moved through the village, Katz glanced at his watch. The date read July 2.

God help us, he thought. We only have one more full day left before they kill the secretary of state. Let's hope we can reach him in time.

16

"Radio contact with the base in Lebanon has been lost," the Lebanese terrorist said.

He watched Abu Niad closely to see if the Hammer of Allah leader exhibited any signs of concern. If he was worried, Niad didn't show it. He remained impassive.

"Is it possible that the American specialists are closer than we anticipated?" the Lebanese asked.

"Everything is possible," Abu Niad replied. "It is possible we may fail in our mission, though I doubt that very much. The possibility that I might shoot you before you leave this room is also not out of the question. Again it is unlikely. My point is that there are many things that may happen, but as instruments of Allah's will, we can see only what is before us. The future is known only to Allah, and if he chooses not to enlighten us, there is a reason."

The Lebanese considered Niad's words. He was aware of the terrorist leader's devotion to Allah. It was a devotion that had become absolute, to the degree that Niad was in danger of losing contact with the real world. It was all very well basing decisions on religious guidance. There also had to be some logic involved in making those decisions. The Lebanese terrorist was a believer and wanted the Americans and the Israelis punished for their crimes against Islam. He was also a realist, capable of separating the hard facts of life from the ethereal dogma of religion.

He couldn't fault Abu Niad's power of persuasion over the Hammer of Allah followers. The ranks of the faithful would go anywhere and do anything for Niad. His hold over them was absolute, and until now everything he had promised had come to pass. Yet he seemed deaf to the disturbing rumblings that had come out of Saudi Arabia since the arrival of the American specialists. Whoever they were, the Americans had proved their worth by defeating the Hammer of Allah group in Saudi Arabia, and by surviving the attack on their safe house.

The American team had vanished from Saudi Arabia without warning. Then the Hammer of Allah base in Lebanon had broken contact. There could be a logical explanation—a malfunction of equipment, interference by Israeli intelligence. For some time the Mossad had been tracking the Hammer of Allah, which had eliminated several Mossad agents and attacked a number of Israeli targets.

The other, more worrying possibility, was that the Americans—maybe even working with the Israelis—had found the base. That would bring them even closer to the Libyan connection. A base remained secure only if no one knew its location. Breached security left it open to attack. It was a certainty that if the Americans did locate the Libyan base, they would attack.

"Perhaps we should execute the secretary of state earlier," the Lebanese suggested. "In case this American team locates us."

Abu Niad glared at him. "That would be an admission of failure. Everyone would know we had been frightened into action because of a few American murderers. The whole of the Hammer of Allah terrified by Yankee killers! No! That will never happen.

"We are showing by this trial and execution that the Hammer of Allah is not in awe of America and its power. We have their secretary of state, and we will not negotiate nor be intimidated by threats. The great American nation is powerless against us. Let them send their team of assassins. A few minor victories in Saudi Arabia mean nothing. They will not gain victory over us. Even if they find us, do you believe they can defeat our superior numbers?"

The Lebanese didn't respond. He wished he had Abu Niad's simplistic faith. Unfortunately he had been born with a slightly jaundiced view of life and its contrary ways. Strong and abiding faith didn't always move mountains. He was a believer in the Muslim way, and he agreed with every aim of the Hammer of Allah. Yet he also saw the other side of the coin. The enemies of Allah, and they were many, had their own faiths. They, too, believed their way was right and were prepared to resist any intrusion into their lives. Shiite Muslims weren't invulnerable to their bullets and bombs.

The Lebanese terrorist met Abu Niad's stern gaze. He knew he should have answered his leader's question, even if he had lied. Yet he couldn't deny his own heart and remain true to his own ideals.

"Leave me," Abu Niad said coldly. "I must pray and ask Allah to bless us with strength to see us through what lies ahead. It might serve you well to do likewise. Redefine your loyalty to Allah. Clear your mind of thoughts of weakness. Harden your heart and *believe* we will achieve victory in everything we do."

After the Lebanese left, Abu Niad decided to increase security at the Libyan base. Then he knelt on a small prayer rug, facing Mecca, and made supplication to his deity for victory against the accused American infidels.

17

"Are they going to make it, Hal?" the President of the United States asked.

"Phoenix Force has never failed yet," Brognola answered.

The head of Stony Man sat facing the President across the large desk in the Oval Office. Even more disheveled than usual, he was in need of a shave and a good night's sleep. He knew his suit and shirt looked borrowed from a back alley derelict, but the big Fed was unconcerned. His personal appearance was of little importance when compared with the important matters he was supposed to be dealing with.

Brognola wished he was anywhere but with the President. It wasn't that he didn't like the man, just that he was up to his neck in work, which was normal for the Justice agent. Stony Man operations never ceased. The secret base for the SOG ran on a twenty-four-hour basis. There was always something happening. And it was Brognola's job to keep the whole operation running smoothly.

Even while he was away from the place, Stony Man kept on running. Brognola had a team of totally dedicated people behind him, people who had accepted the challenge Stony Man offered and who gave their best under pressure. They worked day and night, providing the backup that Mack Bolan, Able Team and Phoenix Force needed. The Executioner and his combat teams were on the front line of the war against terrorism, crime, espionage and other insidious evils. While ordinary American citizens conducted their daily business, the Stony Man warriors combated the hordes intent on destroying the world's greatest democracy.

Right now Brognola's priority was the Phoenix Force mission to rescue the kidnapped secretary of state.

"Hal," the President said, "I know your people are giving everything they have. They always do. But even you must accept that this particular mission has slightly different rules to others they've undertaken."

Brognola nodded tiredly. "The Force is usually out on its own. This time they're even more isolated."

Brognola was referring to the fact that Phoenix Force, due to the nature of the mission, was acting totally without any kind of assistance from other U.S. agencies. It had been realized at the start that Phoenix Force would handle the mission without backup.

"What's the latest update?" the President asked.

"Phoenix Force has joined up with Ben Sharon, the Mossad agent in charge of the Hammer of Allah investigation. It appears that the Egyptian, Faroun, whom the Force encountered in Saudi Arabia, is Sharon's undercover man. A number of threads are being pulled together. With luck they might lead to the secretary of state."

"Doesn't sound as if we can do much on this side."

"Except to be there if they need us," the big Fed said.

"They're in my thoughts," the President said. "And my prayers. The problem is we're running out of time."

"I know that, sir, and so does the Force. Those guys will give every damn thing they've got to pull this off. As far down the line as they need to go."

"I appreciate that, Hal," the President said. "And I won't forget what they're doing for this Administration and this country."

"Thank you, Mr. President," Brognola said.

PHOENIX FORCE and Ben Sharon demolished the Hammer of Allah base with a high-explosive rocket from one of Dragon Slayer's pods. Before the destruction the Force helped Sharon collect paperwork in the HQ building and the radio hut.

The surviving Hammer of Allah terrorists were secured in a storage shed. There was no way they could all be transported to Israel. Eager to leave Lebanon before hostile forces turned up, Phoenix Force had no time for anything very elaborate. The only totally secure way of dealing with the prisoners would have been to kill them all. That wasn't the way the Force operated. They were hardened combat specialists, not cold-blooded killers. McCarter returned with the unconscious guard he had recognized and placed him in Dragon Slayer. One other prisoner was selected and also put in the helicopter.

"Anyone find anything interesting?" Katz asked when the Force regrouped beside the combat chopper.

"A store of weapons and explosives," Sharon said. "This bunch must have been planning some outings. And I bet they would have been over the border into Israel."

"Dragon Slayer can put that out of commission, too," Katz said. "If we have everything we need, let's get out of here before we have visitors."

They climbed into Dragon Slayer, Katz taking the seat next to Grimaldi. The hatch shut with a hiss of hydraulics and the powerful war machine lifted off, Grimaldi handling the controls with ease.

The Stony Man flier swung Dragon Slayer in a tight circle and lined up on the targets below. He brought his TADS system into play and laid HE rockets down. The radio and weapons huts were flattened by explosions.

"Let's go home," Katz said.

Grimaldi took the sleek combat chopper out over the Mediterranean and turned south, streaking back toward Israel.

Settled on the padded seats behind Grimaldi, Phoenix Force and Sharon examined the papers and documents they had picked up at the Shiite base.

"The bastards," Sharon muttered suddenly, his eyes scanning a sheaf of papers.

"You found something?" Manning asked.

"The Hammer of Allah was just about ready to start a campaign of bombings and kidnapping," the Mossad agent said. "There are details here of locations and names." He thrust the papers out for anyone to see. "They were going for hospitals, supermarkets, cinemas, all places where people gather together. On the kidnap list they have members of the

Knesset and even Mossad agents. They were planning to use the hostages in bargaining for the return of terrorists held in Israel.''

Sharon slumped back in his seat. His face was taut with anger as he reviewed the list of names and locations. He glanced across the cabin at the two bound Hammer of Allah terrorists.

"Tell me something," he asked Grimaldi. "Can you open the hatch while we're in flight?"

"In an emergency," Grimaldi replied. "Why?"

"Because I'm seriously thinking of dumping some excess weight," Sharon replied, staring at the prisoners.

"Need a hand?" McCarter asked eagerly.

"Hey, cut it out, you guys," James butted in. "A joke is a joke but—"

"Who mentioned jokes?" Sharon said. "I say dump these sons of bitches."

"Who needs 'em?" McCarter asked. "Come on, get the hatch open. I don't know why we brought them along in the first place. We don't need them. What could they tell us, anyway?"

Sharon lunged from his seat and pushed his way along the cabin.

"Enough, man. We don't do things that way in this outfit," James protested.

"Maybe you would if you'd seen the kind of things these guys do—to anyone who gets in their way, women and kids included. I've seen it too many damn times. I've had it with these bastards."

The Mossad agent snatched his Desert Eagle. He dropped to his knees beside one of the captives and grabbed a handful of his tangled black hair. The

Hammer of Allah fanatic stared at the cold muzzle of the weapon as Sharon waved it under his nose. He uttered a shrill cry as the Mossad agent clicked the hammer back.

Sharon spoke rapidly in Arabic. The terrorist's eyes widened, sweat beading his face. Words began tumbling from his lips in a wild cascade. Sharon asked a couple of questions, letting the frightened prisoner rant on. The words trailed off after a time, and the terrorist slumped back against the compartment wall. His chest heaved from his exertions and his eyes remained fixed on the Desert Eagle in Sharon's fist.

The other terrorist spoke in a low, forceful voice to his companion. He was plainly angry at the other's outburst.

Sharon swiveled on his heels and thrust the Desert Eagle under the guy's nose. "Don't bet I'm fooling, Jamal," the Israeli said in English.

The terrorist was startled by the fact that Sharon knew his name. "You know me?" he asked in English.

"Yes, I know you. The Mossad has a nice thick file on you. We know everything about you—your crimes, the people you associate with, even the fact that you belong to the Hammer of Allah."

"I will not talk," Jamal said defiantly. "Not like that coward. You will never learn anything from me."

"Then we truly have no use for you," Sharon said. "Either we toss you over the side or I take you back so you can spend the rest of your miserable life in prison."

James had pulled a small leather case from a back-pack stored on a rack. He took out a gleaming syringe, holding it up to the light. "Seems a waste not to try to get him to talk," the ex-SEAL said.

Jamal's face was set as he stared at the syringe. "What is that?"

"Something that will help your fading memory, my friend," Encizo said. "It'll give us everything we need."

Jamal looked from face to face. "You can do what you want. The day will never come when I willingly help such as you."

"I'll give you some time to think about it," James said, waving the syringe in Jamal's face before returning to his seat.

Sharon also returned to his seat, slumping against the backrest.

"Pretty good performance," McCarter said in a theatrical whisper. "You had me fooled for a second, mate."

"I'm still not certain he was fooling," Manning said.

"Oh, I think Ben's little outburst was intended to create an effect, which it did," Katz said. "But at the same time his real feelings went into every word he uttered."

Sharon caught the Phoenix Commander's eye. He smiled thinly, realizing that someone had spotted the chink in his tough act. "It gets hard sometimes, trying to maintain your own values in this mess. There's so much hatred and distrust. We should be working side by side to build our lands, not spending it trying to destroy each other."

"I think I hear a guy who wants peace here," Encizo said.

"Of course I want peace," Sharon said. "I'd quit this job tomorrow if I thought it might bring a permanent peace. I've got no personal ax to grind with the Arab world. They're good people. They don't all want endless conflict and destruction."

"A few troublemakers are all it takes," Encizo said. "They can affect the lives of millions with their fanaticism. The subversive terrorist is the most difficult to pin down. He can mix with the crowd surreptitiously, plant a bomb and vanish before it explodes and kills dozens."

"This philosophical discussion is all very cozy," McCarter said, "but it isn't doing much to help our problem."

"Did you get anything from all that chatter?" Manning asked Sharon, indicating the terrorist the Mossad agent had scared into talking.

"He was too busy asking me to spare his life. Apparently he hasn't been with the Hammer of Allah very long, and the life of a terrorist isn't what he expected. That one is more of an intellectual than a dyed-in-the-wool Shiite hard-liner. His idea of resistance is ideological. He thinks we should all sit down and talk our problems over. Not a bad thought, but he's in the wrong club for that."

"So no help?" James asked.

Sharon smiled. "Well, he did let slip a couple of things. Abu Niad's name cropped up a few times. Something about him being the chosen one to lead the Hammer of Allah victory over the Great Satan and all who lived in its shadow. There will be great celebrations after the followers of Allah destroy the unbelievers. That's all the usual crap you get. The only thing that might give us a lead is his reference to Camp 12. That's where the humiliation of America begins the day after tomorrow. That came out just before he stopped talking. I have a feeling he realized he'd let too much slip.''

"Camp 12?" Katz repeated. "New to me. Any ideas, Ben?"

"It has to be where the secretary is being held," Encizo said. "Going by Fuller's reckoning, the day after tomorrow is July the Fourth. That would be the day of humiliation, when they execute the secretary."

"So all we have to do is locate this Camp 12," Manning said. "Shouldn't be too difficult to pinpoint. It's *somewhere* in Libya, is all."

"I'll do some checking when we get back," Sharon said. "I can access maps and aerial-surveillance photographs. We have a pretty extensive file on Libya, out of necessity."

"Hey, Walker, step on the gas," McCarter called to Grimaldi. "I thought you said this crate could move."

18

At the secure landing field near Jaffa, the Hammer of Allah terrorists were handed over to Israeli security agents, who took them away for questioning. As Dragon Slayer was refueled, the Force returned to Ben Sharon's home.

After cleaning up, Calvin James dealt with the bullet burn on Sharon's arm. The Force was ready for a break and some food. Sharon insisted on preparing a meal. While the Force relaxed the Mossad agent vanished into the kitchen.

Sharon emerged sometime later, spreading the pine dining table with his meal. There was salad to start, comprising humus, a mixture of ground chick-peas seasoned with tahini, sesame paste with lemon juice, garlic and cumin. And there was salad and pickled vegetables, followed by *shashlik,* grilled sliced beef with lamb fat. Sharon even provided local wines—red and white, and afterward there was fresh fruit—kiwi, persimmon and papaya.

The Stony Man commandos ate heartily. The hectic pace of the past few days had interfered with their regular eating habits, forcing them to grab quick snacks along the way.

Partway through the meal Sharon's telephone rang. The Mossad agent left the table to answer it. When he returned to the table, he had a pleased smile on his face. Sitting down, he refilled his wineglass and raised it to Phoenix Force.

"That call was from my people at HQ," he said. "They've located our Camp 12. It was the base camp for an oil field that dried up about five years back. The Libyans gave it up and just left it to rot after the oil ran out. The field was known as Number 12. The camp is located some fifty miles inland from the Mediterranean coastline of Libya."

"I think we have our target, gentlemen," Katz announced. "Let's finish our meal and get organized. The sooner we get airborne the better I'll feel. Walker, get details from Ben and work out your course. As soon as you've decided, let me know. We may need help getting there before tomorrow morning."

"Tomorrow morning?" Grimaldi asked.

"A dawn strike gives us the best chance to catch the terrorists at their weakest."

McCarter glanced around the table. He tapped his fork against the side of the wineglass. "Make the most of this, mates. Tomorrow we'll be up to our necks in dust and bullets. I have a feeling we're in for a hell of a fight." He grinned suddenly. "So dig in, mates. This might be our last supper!"

A REQUEST WENT OUT from Katz to Hal Brognola. Jack Grimaldi needed a refueling stop somewhere out on the Mediterranean. Dragon Slayer wasn't capable of making the trip from Israel to Libya without replenishing her tanks. There had been some delay in receiving the reply, but it finally came, and as usual Brognola had come up with the goods.

A British Royal Navy aircraft carrier was in Mediterranean waters. The ship was on a goodwill visit to the area. Orders from the Admiralty, who were acting on a request from the British prime minister, had caused an alteration in course for the carrier. It would be waiting for Dragon Slayer thirty miles off the Libyan coast. The combat chopper would be refueled once it touched down. To add to its fuel capacity extra tanks were to be fitted on the chopper. These would give an extra hundred miles of travel before Dragon Slayer started using its main fuel load. Once the extra tanks were used up they could be jettisoned at the flick of a switch. The British carrier would maintain its position off the Libyan coast and would provide a landing place for the Force on completion of the mission.

The arrangements were hurried and not the way Phoenix Force liked to work. However, they weren't in a position to be too fussy. Time was running short.

The flight from Israel to the rendezvous with the carrier would take the rest of the day and through the night. Luckily McCarter could fly the chopper, so he would be able to relieve Grimaldi during the trip. Even Manning had flown a few hours in Dragon Slayer and was capable of handling the combat chopper in a straight run.

The Stony Man commando force was going in fully equipped with autopistols, SMGs and rifles. In addition, each man carried an assortment of extra weaponry, including grenades, both fragmentation and concussion. Calvin James had an assortment of rounds for his M-203 grenade launcher. He was also carrying his Blackmoor Dirk, attached to the Jackass shoulder holster. Rafael Encizo still carried his Cold Steel Tanto knife. As well as his FAL, Gary Manning took his Anschutz. McCarter's KG-99 SMG shared space with a Barnett Commando crossbow and the Gerber Predator knife the British ace favored. All weapons, fully loaded, were backed up with extra magazines of mixed Hydra-Shok and NATO Match-9 ammunition.

Ben Sharon had his Desert Eagle and Uzi, plus his SOG-TEC combat knife. He also had a Franchi SPAS Model 12 combat shotgun. The formidable weapon fired a 12-gauge cartridge. Sharon had loaded the tubular magazine with heavy metal slug cartridges capable of penetrating steel sheets.

Each member of the group carried a compact walkie-talkie that would enable each man to keep in contact with the others and also Grimaldi. And, in addition to the standard weaponry, there were a number of MPG tear gas grenades. These were CN—chloracetophenone—chemical agent canisters and were to be used against the Hammer of Allah terrorists when Phoenix Force launched their attack.

The tear gas would cause enough of a diversion, it was hoped, for the Force to enter the base buildings and locate the secretary of state before the terrorists attempted to kill him. Phoenix Force and Ben Sharon carried respirators to protect them from the gas, with an extra mask for the secretary of state.

In theory the plan appeared relatively straightforward. But past experience had taught Phoenix Force never to take anything for granted. Too many things could go wrong, and it took only a minor incident to set off a chain reaction that could turn a low-key penetration probe into an all-out firefight.

The situation called for a high-risk operation. Despite the odds against them Phoenix Force accepted how it was. Professional warriors, they were aware that planning a strike was a pure gamble. No matter how you covered the permutations, there was always the unknown factor, the rogue incident that could easily throw all your plans out the window. In such cases survival usually depended on those with the quickest reflexes and the strongest desire to stay alive.

THE SAHARA DAWN was barely established. Slowly, imperceptibly, the light of the new day had begun pushing aside the final shadows of night.

For Phoenix Force the long, seemingly endless flight from Israel to the British carrier on the Mediterranean, then west into Libyan airspace and the final touchdown a mile from the terrorist base, lay behind them. They left Dragon Slayer hidden in a deep basin and trekked the dusty mile to a gritty ridge overlooking Camp 12.

Katz lowered the high-powered binoculars he was looking through. He replaced them in the carrying case before speaking. "I picked out five armed sentries. And there are two machine gun emplacements."

Manning, who had been surveying the base from a different angle, rejoined the group.

"How many did you see?" Katz asked.

"Five."

"Anything else?" Encizo inquired.

Manning nodded. "Couple of machine guns."

"Same as me," Katz affirmed.

The Israeli used the tip of his prosthesis to sketch a layout of the base in the sand. "Both machine guns are outside this large building," he explained. "They're at each front corner of the building so as to cover the front and the sides, as well. Two of the sentries are on the roof of this building. The other three form a roving patrol around the perimeter."

"Gives the impression that building is pretty important," James said.

"Right," Katz agreed. "Hazarding a guess, I'd say it's where we'll find the secretary of state."

"The problem is the bloody place is right in the center of the base," McCarter said. "It's going to be that much harder reaching the place."

Katz marked a cross on his rough outline.

"There are two helicopters right here—Bell UH-1B Hueys. Old models maybe, but they'll do the job. The roving patrol covers them, as well."

"We could put them out of commission," Encizo said. "If they get them into the air, we could be in trouble."

"Walker can deal with them," McCarter said. "They won't offer much resistance to Dragon Slayer."

"Walker's first priority is getting the secretary of state on board Dragon Slayer," Katz insisted. "The same as ours. Once we locate him the most important thing is to get him out where Walker can pick him up. We can't afford to get involved in anything liable to interfere with getting the secretary to safety."

"Perhaps I could plant explosives that we could detonate later," Manning suggested.

"I don't doubt you could do it, Scott," Katz said. "All I'm worried about is the time we're going to have once we make the hit."

"Two of us could do it," Manning suggested. "If someone can cover me, I'll rig those choppers to explode at the touch of a button."

"Mertz," Ben Sharon said.

Katz glanced at the Mossad agent.

"If Scott will have me, I'll cover him," Sharon said.

"You're on, pal," Manning answered.

"All right," Katz said. "Get organized and make your way in as soon as you're ready."

Manning and Sharon moved aside. The Mossad agent watched with interest as Manning opened his backpack and pulled out a couple of blocks of C-4 explosive. From a pocket in his combat fatigues the Canadian drew out detonators. These were capable of being set off with a remote device about the size of a pack of cigarettes. Manning removed this unit from another pocket of his backpack, checking that the battery was functioning.

"Once the C-4 is in position and the detonators are inserted, all I have to do is switch this unit on and press the button. The signal goes out to the detonators and the rest is history. When we get to the choppers, all I'll need is a couple of minutes to set the charges."

"You take all the time you need," Sharon said.

Manning placed the various components in different pockets of his fatigues, then slipped off his pack and laid it on the ground. "Don't let anyone pinch that. Got my lunch in there." To Katz he said, "We're set to go."

"Good luck, guys," James said.

"Take care," Katz told the pair.

"See you later," Encizo said.

"Hey, Scott," McCarter called, "if you don't come back, can I have your record collection?"

MANNING FLATTENED himself against the dusty earth as the armed sentry moved closer. The terrorist was no more than four feet away. His eyes, the only part of his face visible because of the keffiyeh he wore, were constantly on the move. The guy had obviously been alerted by something. He came to a dead stop directly in front of Manning. The Canadian warrior froze. If the terrorist glanced at the ground, he would have seen Manning instantly.

Behind and to the left of the sentry Manning spotted movement. Without turning his head Manning focused his gaze and recognized Ben Sharon as the Israeli rose to a crouch. Sharon moved with deliberate ease, in complete silence, and there was a look in the Mossad agent's eyes that revealed his utter dedication to the task before him.

The blade of the SOG-TEC caught the early-morning light as Sharon readied himself, then lunged up and forward. The sentry didn't know what hit him. Sharon's left hand snaked around to clamp tightly over the terrorist's mouth. His knee slammed into the sentry's lower back, and Sharon applied pressure with his left hand, drawing the terrorist back, bending him against his knee, while his right hand, gripping the SOG-TEC, swept up and round.

The razor edge of the blade touched the sentry's taut throat, then bit deep as it drew a long gash. The steel opened flesh and muscle. Instantly a surge of bright blood gushed forth, spilling down the sentry's front. His body shuddered violently against the fatal wound. His struggles were useless against Sharon's grip, and they lessened rapidly. Sharon pulled the man to the ground.

"Set your charges," he told Manning.

The Canadian raced to the helicopter pad. He slid underneath the first Huey. With practiced ease he drew the C-4 from his pocket. He placed it in position, then inserted the detonator, checking that it was functioning. He wriggled beneath the chopper to the second craft and repeated the procedure.

Sharon was waiting for Manning as the Canadian emerged from beneath the second Huey. The Israeli held his Uzi in his hands, cocked and ready.

"I'm done," Manning said.

"Let's get out of here," Sharon said.

They eased away from the helicopters, making for the shadows beneath a fuel tank set on iron legs.

Once they had gained cover Manning pulled out his walkie-talkie and activated the instrument. "Scott," he identified himself.

Katz's voice reached him a scant second later. "Receiving."

"Go when you're ready," Manning said. "Over and out."

"DAVID, I want Encizo and you to aim for the main building," Katz said. "Hit it with tear gas from the side and go in. Cal and I will take the front. We'll take out the machine gun emplacements."

McCarter unlimbered his Barnett crossbow. "I want those rooftop sentries out of action first," the cockney said. "They have too good a view over the place."

"Fine," Katz said. "Get into position, then give me the word. The moment Cal drops his first grenade you can take out those sentries."

The four Phoenix warriors parted company. Each pair made their way to the position they favored for the opening shots in the action to come.

Katz and James reached their spot quickly. They were in the favorable position of being able to launch their attack from a safe distance. Crouching behind a stack of steel pipes, apparently left over from the days when the terrorist base had been a functioning oil camp, James loaded his M-203 grenade launcher with an M-406 HE round.

The minutes ticked by with agonizing slowness as they waited for McCarter's radio call. When it finally came, the relief was tremendous.

"Ready to kick off?" James asked.

Katz simply nodded.

The black commando raised the M-16, taking careful aim. His finger brushed the M-203's trigger, and the HE canister sailed toward the first machine gun emplacement in a graceful arc. It exploded with a tremendous noise, destroying the dawn's peace instantly.

The second he had fired the round James loaded another and set his sights on the other emplacement. The pair of terrorists were startled but motionless from the sound of the first explosion. Their stunned immobility was disturbed by the arrival of James's second grenade. It landed directly between them and exploded. Their world vanished in a blinding flash of heat and noise.

MCCARTER HAD the sentry farthest away from him in his crossbow sights, following the man's progress along the edge of the roof. The crossbow was loaded with a cyanide bolt. The Briton had waited with waning patience until he heard the first grenade explode. Before the roof sentry could react McCarter's finger had eased back on the trigger, sending the stubby bolt whistling through the air. It struck the Hammer of Allah fanatic in the chest, directly over the heart. The guy dropped his autorifle and made an ineffectual grab for the shaft protruding from his body. As the cyanide coursed through his bloodstream, he stiffened and fell.

A second bolt lay on the ground next to McCarter. He recocked the crossbow and placed the bolt in position. Raising the weapon and taking aim, the Briton heard the second explosion.

The surviving roof sentry moved to the edge of the roof and peered down at the machine gun emplacements. It was a foolish move. He should have sought cover, then looked for the enemy. McCarter's bolt hissed through the air and lodged in his throat, severing his windpipe. Slumping to his knees, waving helplessly, he slowly leaned forward and fell from the roof.

"Up and at 'em, chum," McCarter said. He slung the crossbow over his shoulder and picked up his KG-99.

Together he and Encizo broke cover and legged it toward the side of the main building.

"Watch your left," Encizo warned as armed figures stumbled from one of the smaller buildings. From the way some of the terrorists moved they were evidently just waking. Others, fully dressed, had obviously been up longer.

Hosing them with short bursts from his MP-5, Encizo cut down two with his initial blast. They crashed to the ground in bloody heaps, twitching, plunging back into a sleep far deeper than any they had previously known.

The KG-99 in McCarter's capable hands began to stutter loudly. He downed one terrorist who was fumbling with his reluctant AK-47. The Briton blasted into the guy's left chest and shoulder, slamming him to the ground. As the man hit the dirt, his AK went off with a crack, shooting up the side of the building.

Three terrorists, ducking and weaving as they ran forward, triggered their weapons in unison. Anticipating their move, McCarter and Encizo dived to the ground. The bullets howled over their prone bodies. McCarter triggered a stream of slugs at the trio. The terrorist on the left caught a couple of them in his hip.

The surviving terrorists parted company. They weren't fast enough to avoid the fragmentation grenade Encizo tossed between them. Thrown by the blast, the terrorists were shredded by the deadly steel fragments.

On their feet again the Phoenix warriors closed in on the building. As they neared the outer wall, they pulled tear gas canisters from their combat harness and yanked the pins with their teeth.

Pressed against the wall, they smashed two windows with the barrels of their SMGs, then tossed in the tear gas canisters. The dull sound of the cans detonating reached their ears as they raced along the building, repeating the process at the next set of windows.

In the near distance they could hear the rattle and crack of weapons. The occasional louder explosions of detonating grenades jarred the desert air.

The door that McCarter and Enciso were approaching suddenly burst open as two terrorists spilled out. Armed with the obligatory AK-47s, the fanatics turned their weapons on the Phoenix pair, but too late. Enciso, firing from just behind McCarter, took them out of the game in a withering blast of 9 mm fire.

McCarter tossed another tear gas canister through the doorway. His Cuban partner covered him while the Briton unclipped the respirator from his belt and pulled it over his head. Reversing roles, McCarter provided cover for Enciso as he donned his respirator. Enciso tossed a second canister through the door.

As the tear gas spread, the Phoenix commandos reloaded their weapons, cocking them in anticipation of their next move. McCarter glanced at his partner, and Enciso nodded his readiness.

"Go!" McCarter snapped, and they vanished in the thick, swirling coils of white gas.

19

James's grenades shattered the calm.

"Time to set off the fireworks," Manning said.

He flicked the switch to activate the detonating device and was about to press the button when Sharon yelled a warning.

Autofire crackled and pounded against the frame below the fuel tank. Manning jerked aside to avoid the incoming bullets, his shoulder banging against an iron stanchion. The device slipped from his hand.

Before Manning could retrieve it a heavy volley of shots rang out, peppering the area with slugs that clanged against the metalwork and chipped the concrete base of the tank stand.

Sharon swung his SPAS shotgun from his shoulder, turning toward the advancing Hammer of Allah terrorists. Working the slide, he fed a shell into the breech and triggered the weapon. The SPAS bellowed with a thunderous noise, spitting a gout of flame from its muzzle. The charge of heavy shot ripped apart the lead fanatics. He chose another target and fired repeatedly, each shot removing more of the charging terrorists.

Manning snatched his FAL from his shoulder and shot an approaching attacker on his left, piercing the guy's chest. Two more terrorists broke cover from behind a stack of sheet metal. The Canadian caught one with a shot that knocked the terrorist's legs out from under him. The guy fell onto his face, blood jetting from his crushed nose. He tried to stand. Manning hit him with his rifle butt, then swung his weapon around on the second terrorist whose AK-47 was pointed at Sharon's back. The FAL's hot slugs cored deep into the enemy's skull.

The sound of a helicopter engine firing reached Manning's ears. One of the Hueys was powering up, the rotors beating the air as the pilot laid on the power. The Canadian searched for the detonator. It lay exposed beneath the fuel tank. Manning made a dive for it, risking his life. Bullets thumped the concrete around him until Sharon's SPAS eliminated the men behind the triggers. Manning grabbed the detonator.

The active Huey lifted off, the pilot apparently giving it every ounce of power. It shuddered violently, slewing to one side before the pilot righted it. He made frantic adjustments to the controls, and the Huey suddenly rose into the air, then zoomed forward and vanished between two buildings.

Gritting his teeth, Manning found the button and pressed it. The remaining Huey vanished in a ball of flame, showering the area with debris.

The pall of smoke that resulted covered the immediate vicinity around Manning and Sharon. They took the opportunity to break away from the fuel tank.

"One down, one free," Sharon said.

"Damn charge didn't go off," Manning said angrily.

"We'll worry about that later," the Israeli said.

His reasoning was sound. More Hammer of Allah terrorists were emerging from various buildings. The sound of gunfire came from all directions.

Sharon fed fresh shells into the SPAS, then put the weapon on automatic fire. Something on his right caught his attention. The Mossad agent turned and fired, the blast from the SPAS almost cutting a terrorist in half. His mangled body flopped to the ground, twitching violently.

Side by side Manning and Sharon worked across the compound. They used every piece of cover they could, weapons up and firing at the terrorists who kept sniping at them.

A window shattered close by. Sharon whirled around, seeing an armed figure leaning out. The morning sun glinted on the barrel of the AK-47 pointed at them. The Israeli didn't hesitate. He slammed into Manning's back, knocking the Canadian to his knees just as the AK crackled. The slugs passed over Manning's head. In return Sharon triggered two shots from his SPAS. The heavy metal shot ripped the terrorist's head apart.

Two Hammer of Allah fanatics emerged from the side of a building. The Canadian sharpshooter whipped the FAL to his shoulder and emptied his magazine at the pair. The terrorists crashed against the building and flopped loosely to the bloody ground.

The Canadian reloaded and tapped Sharon on the shoulder. "This place is getting hostile. Time to find cover."

Side by side they dodged down the alley between two buildings, emerging on the far side of the compound. Ahead of them stood a solid stone building.

Metal pipes emerged from one side, curving into the ground and disappearing.

"Pumping station," Sharon said.

They sought cover behind the structure. It gave them a brief moment of calm, allowing them to regain their breath and check their weapons and reserve ammunition.

Glancing across the compound, Sharon saw several terrorists moving in their direction. A volley of fire began to hammer the stonework protecting them. The Mossad agent unslung his Uzi, checking that it was ready to fire. "Here come our hosts," he remarked, triggering the SMG at the advancing terrorists.

As McCARTER BOOTED the door open, he heard the distant explosion from the helicopter pad. The door swung back and smashed against the inner wall. Coils of white tear gas swirled through the opening. The Phoenix warrior crouched close to the ground, covering the corridor with his KG-99 as Encizo dodged around him. The Cuban swung to the right, flattening against the inner wall, and covered McCarter as he entered.

An autorifle—recognizable as an AK-47—opened up down the corridor. Whoever was handling the weapon was firing blind. A series of ragged holes appeared in the wall high overhead.

Aware that the shooter's luck might easily change, Encizo, peering through his visor, caught the blurred shape moving in the corridor. He heard a man cough. The AK opened up again, filling the corridor with a deadly hail. The gunner was simply spraying the area with bullets in the hope of hitting the intruders.

The Cuban advanced, his MP-5 up and ready. Hearing the snap of a bolt being drawn back as a weapon was cocked, he dropped. A fraction later the AK rattled out its ugly sound. The wall just about where Encizo had been standing vibrated under the impact. Plaster rained down on his back.

Swinging the MP-5 around and tilting the muzzle up, Encizo triggered a short blast at the blurred shape. The torrent of lead tossed the wheezing victim back off his feet. He crashed to the floor, the AK bouncing along the corridor.

Scrambling to his feet, SMG thrust forward, Encizo advanced on the fallen man. The squirming, coughing shape took on form and color as Encizo neared. The Cuban fighter recognized fresh blood on the guy's chest. He searched the terrorist for weapons but found none.

The terrorist looked at Encizo through inflamed, tearful eyes. Yet it was as if he could clearly see Encizo's face. He began to spout a rolling, toneless stream of profanity in Arabic, interspersed with bouts of coughing.

McCarter loomed out of the dissipating gas. He glanced at the fatally wounded terrorist, then gave the thumbs-up sign to Encizo. "Let's check these rooms out," he said, his voice muffled by the respirator.

The first door opened onto an empty room. The next door had heavy bolts on the outside. McCarter slid them free. With Encizo backing him the Briton kicked the door open. It slammed back against the inside wall.

The room held only a bed. Sitting on the edge of the bed was a man dressed in creased, stained shirt and pants. He glanced up as the door crashed open, his keen eyes taking in everything about the two men who entered his room.

"Mr. Secretary, we've come to take you home," McCarter said.

The voice was distorted by the respirator, but the secretary understood every word.

"Put this on," Encizo said, handing the secretary a respirator he'd taken from his belt. "When we get outside, sir, do exactly what we tell you. Don't question anything we say. Understand?"

The secretary nodded as he put on the respirator.

"All right, sir. Let's get the hell out of here."

The moment they stepped outside the full fury of the firefight hit them.

The rattle of autofire filled the air. Armed figures darted back and forth. Yells and cries competed with the crash of gunfire.

"Go!" McCarter yelled, giving the secretary, a hearty shove. The Briton crowded close to the secretary, keeping his left hand on the man's shirt as they skirted the wall of the main building.

Encizo followed, keeping watch for them. A couple of Hammer of Allah gunmen broke cover and dashed toward them, raking the area with bullets. One put a short burst into the wall inches behind McCarter's shoulders, but the British ace kept on moving, urging more speed out of the secretary.

Seeing the bullets slap the wall, Encizo swiveled, his MP-5 snug against his hip, aimed and triggered a long burst, arcing the muzzle back and forth. The fanatics were hammered by bullets.

Passing the front corner of the main building, McCarter and the secretary skirted the machine gun emplacement James had taken out with his grenade launcher. The bodies of the Arab terrorists lay in bloody, mangled sprawls, dumped by the force of the detonating HE canister.

Seeing that the tear gas had virtually disappeared, McCarter yanked off his respirator and tossed it aside. He gulped in fresh air, sleeving the sweat from his face. "Get down!" he told the secretary. The Briton snatched his walkie-talkie from his belt and thumbed the transmit button. "The fish is on the hook. Get in here with that flying beetle, *Mr.* Walker."

Grimaldi's voice came through the soft hiss of static. "On my way."

Crouched next to McCarter, the secretary dragged off his own respirator, aware of Encizo close behind him. He wanted to express his thanks, but he remained silent. Now was not the time. They weren't out of trouble yet. Abu Niad's terrorists hadn't given up the fight.

Tossing aside his respirator Encizo quickly reloaded his MP-5, then worked the cocking mechanism. "It's getting a little hot around here."

"I just called a cab," McCarter replied.

Behind them the beat of a helicopter's rotors filled the air.

"That was quick," Encizo said.

"Not ours," the cockney replied. "One of Scott's bangers hasn't gone off."

The sandy-colored shape of a Bell UH-1B Huey rose above the roof of the main building. It hovered for a few moments, then swept forward over the compound, searching. The side hatch was open, exposing the machine gun on its sling.

"That's all we bloody need," McCarter grumbled.

"We can take cover in here," Encizo said.

Scrambling over the tumbled, shredded sandbags, Encizo caught hold of the secretary's collar and unceremoniously hauled the man into the emplacement. A fraction of a second later McCarter landed beside them.

"Heads down!" he yelled as he hit the ground.

A moment later the Huey's door-mounted M-60 opened up. A line of slugs chopped across the compound as the gunner tried to fix his target.

"Maybe this wasn't such a good idea," Encizo remarked as bullets ripped open the sandbags, cascading sand over them.

"Seemed like it at the time," McCarter replied. Under his breath he whispered, "Come on, Jack." In answer to his plea the rising howl of Dragon Slayer's turbo-powered engines broke through, and the sleek black combat chopper swept in across the compound.

It headed straight for the Huey. The gunner swung his M-60 around in a vain attempt to shoot Dragon Slayer from the sky. He had little chance. The Huey's pilot, sensing Dragon Slayer's superiority, gunned his machine up and away.

Dragon Slayer executed a tight turn and fell in on the Huey's tail. The terrorist pilot was no novice. He threw the Huey across the sky in a series of hard turns, rising and falling as he made an all-out attempt at getting Grimaldi off his tail rotor. He needed to lose Dragon Slayer in order to reverse positions, or at least get himself in a position to use his missile pods. Grimaldi knew both this and also the fact that his presence was needed to airlift the secretary to safety. With that in mind Grimaldi kept the pursuit to a minimum.

The moment both choppers had cleared the compound area Grimaldi activated his IHDSS helmet system. The Stony Man pilot found his target, locked on and opened up with the 30 mm chain gun.

The Huey seemed to shudder as the unrelenting stream of cannon fire ate away at its fuselage. Shattered pieces flew from the chopper. Without warning it slewed off course. Smoke began to stream from the engine mounting.

Dragon Slayer homed in with the dedication of a bird of prey, pouring more 30 mm fire into the crippled helicopter. The Huey blew apart in a ball of orange-red flame, dropping earthward. It struck hard and exploded in a huge ball of flame. Before the debris had settled Dragon Slayer had executed a tight turn and was headed back toward the compound.

"My God," the secretary of state breathed, "is that one of ours?"

"Well, I bloody well hope it isn't one of theirs," McCarter answered.

The secretary managed a sheepish grin. "Okay, guys, I get it. Top secret. What the hell? As long as it gets us out of here, I don't care."

Dragon Slayer plunged across the compound, scattering men and dust with equal indifference. It came to rest on the side of the compound near the secretary, McCarter and Encizo. The passenger compartment hatch opened with a low hiss.

"You any good at running, sir?" Encizo asked.

"It's been a long time since I played quarterback," the secretary admitted.

"Well, give it your best, chum," McCarter said. "Get your arse over those bags and just go."

Encizo cleared the bags first, his MP-5 sweeping the way ahead.

The secretary rolled over the emplacement, crouching beside the Cuban until McCarter joined them. "Now!" Encizo snapped.

The secretary began to run, pushing his body to the limit. The sand dragged at his feet, and within a few paces his chest began to burn. The damn helicopter didn't seem to get any closer. He could hear men yelling around him, guns firing. Somewhere a man was screaming in pain. Smoke drifted across the compound. Dust got into his eyes, stinging fiercely, and the secretary figured this was how hell must be.

Close by an SMG clattered and an Arab with wild eyes tumbled to the ground. The image was brief but shocking. A man rolling, jerking, bleeding profusely from his throat and face. Then it was gone, blurred by the sweat running into his burning eyes.

His limbs felt leaden, lungs straining. He felt sure he wouldn't make it. Then he felt something strike him between the shoulders. For a crazy second he thought he'd been shot. Then he heard the Briton yelling at him to keep moving or he'd be dead.

The open hatch was in front of him, and a dark-haired man was leaning out, a strong brown hand reaching for him. The hand grasped the secretary's, heaved, and he was tumbling inside the helicopter. He fell onto the floor, gasping for breath, aching from head to foot.

"Get him out of here," McCarter yelled as he reached Dragon Slayer. "Pick us up later."

Grimaldi began to speak. His face registered alarm, his right hand reaching for the autopistol holstered under his left arm. He didn't make it. From behind McCarter an AK crackled. Grimaldi stumbled back across the passenger compartment, blood seeping from the bullet tears in his shoulder and arm. He slumped to the floor.

"Bloody hell!" McCarter cursed. The Briton dropped to one knee, swinging round.

He was in time to see Encizo trigger a blast from his MP-5 into the chest of the terrorist who had dropped Grimaldi. The Hammer of Allah fanatic crashed to the ground, clutching at his shattered body.

"Get in there and take off!" Encizo yelled. "Just do it!"

McCarter hopped inside, went to the front and dropped into Grimaldi's seat. He swiveled the seat to its front position and reached for the controls.

Dragon Slayer's engines responded instantly as McCarter boosted the power. He grabbed the controls, feet and hands in perfect coordination as he felt the chopper move.

McCarter was an experienced flyer, having piloted everything from single-engined planes through to jet fighters. His talents as a pilot were bettered only by Jack Grimaldi. The fiery Briton, often cocky and over-confident, had spent several sessions with the Stony Man pilot handling Dragon Slayer and had flown the combat chopper solo a couple of times. He had never yet handled it in an actual combat situation.

The fact did nothing to deter McCarter. His only worry was that he hadn't been briefed on the new weapons system. McCarter was sure he could figure it out, but for that he needed time. The problem was that he was seriously short of that commodity right now. His priority was getting his Phoenix buddies out of the enemy camp.

As Dragon Slayer rose, McCarter heard Encizo say, "You handle the guys. I'll look after Walker."

McCarter grabbed the discarded helmet. He worked it over his head, then set the radio to receive. While he waited for contact he scanned Dragon Slayer's instrument banks. Most of the main panels were the same. He identified the weapons control panel and flicked the selector to manual. A red light glowed on the control stick, indicating that he had the chain gun back under his thumb.

The speaker in his helmet crackled, and Manning's voice came through. "Ready for pickup, Dragon Slayer."

Activating his throat microphone, McCarter acknowledged the Canadian's contact.

"That you, Marsh?" Manning demanded.

"Yeah, so talk to me nice or I'll let you walk home. Now where are you?"

"Out by the pumping station. Could do with some help. Lot of unfriendlies around."

"On my way."

McCarter eased the controls, letting Dragon Slayer slip to the right. He took the chopper in low, skimming the ground and picking out the low stone building that housed the water pump. There were a number of Hammer of Allah terrorists converging on the building and firing. McCarter spotted return fire from Manning and Sharon.

He banked Dragon Slayer, lining up on the advancing terrorists, and opened up with the chain gun. The cannon spewed out a deadly stream of sizzling death. The 30 mm shells walked in on the terrorists, blasting into them with terrible results. Bodies vanished in clouds of dust. Flesh and bone disintegrated under the awesome firepower of the Stony Man combat chopper.

McCarter overflew the area in a tight circle and returned from the opposite direction. He laid down another barrage of fire, scattering the remaining terrorists in a second blaze of 30 mm hell.

He lowered Dragon Slayer to within a foot of the ground, then heard Encizo yelling at Manning and Sharon to move their asses. "Go!" Encizo ordered.

Dragon Slayer rose at McCarter's bidding. Gary Manning appeared at his side, slipping into the copilot's seat. The Canadian was sweat-streaked and dirty. He had a gash on his left cheek that had left his face bloody.

"Look at you," McCarter remarked. "Have you been crawling around in the dirt again?"

"Just fly the damn thing," Manning said. He picked up a headset and slipped it on. "Come in, Mertz. Give us your location."

There was no response.

"Shit!" Manning said forcibly.

"Maybe they haven't the time to reply," McCarter said.

He swung Dragon Slayer in toward the compound. The remaining terrorists seemed to be converging on a point on the far side of the compound.

"Lot of gunfire down there," Manning said. "Go for it, David."

McCarter put Dragon Slayer into a long, swooping dive across the compound, hoping desperately that they would reach Katz and James in time.

20

Katz and James breached the main building's front door, respirators in place as they hurled primed tear gas canisters ahead of them. Thick white tear gas swirled around the room. As James went through the open door, he triggered his M-16 at the yelling terrorist who was trying to bring his AK-47 into firing position. The guy felt the deep burn of the slugs in his chest, knocking him back into the room.

Peering through the visor of his respirator, his Uzi braced across his prosthesis, Katz lunged to the right as he entered, firing at a group of armed figures. His blast hammered the two closest men and shattered the shoulder of the third. The wounded man dropped his autorifle and grabbed the handgun on his right hip. The weapon hadn't even cleared his holster when Katz fired again, driving burning slugs deep into the guy's skull.

By this time James had crossed the room. He kicked open the door. Before he could move on, a terrorist with streaming eyes sprang out of the white swirl. Weaponless, the man attacked James with unconcealed fury, his fingers clawing for the black warrior's throat. James twisted aside, feeling the terrorist's fingers brush his shoulder, and lashed out with his booted foot, catching the Hammer of Allah fanatic in the groin. The guy howled but still managed to slam into James, knocking him against the wall.

The Stony Man warrior recovered quickly. He slammed the butt of his M-16 into the terrorist's gut, making the man double over. Reversing his weapon, James smashed it down across the back of his adversary's neck. There was a snapping sound as the guy hit the floor with a solid thump, where he lay twitching gently.

Katz reached James's side. The Israeli took another tear gas canister and tossed it through the door, following it, his Uzi sweeping back and forth.

This room was empty.

Katz indicated the far door, covering James as the black commando advanced and drove his boot against the panel, smashing it open. An autoweapon opened up from the far room. A stream of bullets sizzled across the open space, chunked into the wall behind Katz and splintered plaster.

James tossed in another gas canister. The white mist rapidly spread. A man began to cough. The autorifle opened up again, ripping wood from the frame of the open door.

Flat against the wall beside the door, James rapidly reloaded his M-16. With the weapon cocked and ready he angled the barrel round the edge of the frame and triggered a long blast into the room. There was the sound of running feet. The enemy gun stopped firing.

On the other side of the door Katz crouched and peered into the room, searching the swirl of gas for the telltale shape of a human figure. Nothing appeared to move in the room.

Then Katz caught a quick shadow of movement. Leaning forward, he aimed quickly and triggered a sustained blast. He heard the sound of bullets striking flesh, the sudden gasp of surprise and pain, the thump of a falling body and the clatter of a dropped weapon.

Ducking low, they entered the room and spread to opposite sides. The downed terrorist lay on his side, blood pumping from his chest. He saw the Israeli appear. His eyes, bright and wild, began to film over as he succumbed to the overwhelming weariness that stole over him. He collapsed without warning.

Raised voices, seemingly in argument, reached the Phoenix pair from the corridor. More shooting came from the rear of the building. Katz assumed it was McCarter and Encizo.

He caught James's eye and indicated the corridor. The warriors moved quickly along the corridor. The tear gas hadn't penetrated this far. They heard the raised voices again.

An armed terrorist suddenly appeared in a doorway. Seeing Katz and James, he raised his AK and opened fire. James heard Katz gasp and twist to one side, banging into the wall.

Anger drove the Phoenix commando forward. He triggered his M-16, pumping bullets into the terrorist. It was the slender Lebanese who had earlier been advising Abu Niad of Phoenix Force's progress through Saudi Arabia. He felt his body burn as the M-16's slugs ripped into his flesh. He was pinned to the wall for a few seconds before his weight dragged him to the floor.

Still unable to attend to Katz, James strode to the open door of the room the Lebanese had exited. It was a functional office. James was amazed to see a man sitting calmly behind the desk.

Abu Niad, sensing someone watching him, scooped up the last of the papers from his desk. He stared at the mysterious figure dressed in combat fatigues and wearing a respirator.

The Hammer of Allah leader, refusing to recognize defeat, cursed the evil United States and grabbed the Uzi lying on the desk. His finger curled around the trigger as the weapon began its swing up to target acquisition.

Triggering, James emptied the last of his magazine into the Hammer of Allah headman. The force propelled Abu Niad into the wall behind him, blood and bits of flesh exiting from the ragged wounds in his head. He bounced back over the desk and fell in a bloody heap, arms outstretched across the wooden surface. The Uzi slipped from dead fingers and clattered to the floor.

James snatched the papers Abu Niad had dropped and stuffed them into his combat jacket. They might prove useful to Brognola back at Stony Man. As he passed the window he saw McCarter and Encizo escorting a civilian toward the front of the building.

Quickly he retraced his steps to where Katz was kneeling by the wall. The Israeli raised his head as James approached. There was blood streaking the Phoenix commander's face.

"Katz, you hurt?" James asked.

Straightening, the Israeli exposed his right arm. Bullets had torn into his prosthesis, mangling the metal. A stray chunk of metal had flown up to gouge Katz's face.

"I'll never play the guitar again," Katz muttered as James helped him to his feet.

"David and Rafael rescued the secretary," James informed him.

"Time we left ourselves," the Israeli said.

They retraced their steps to the main door. There was still a great deal of activity going on. Without pausing Katz and James ran from the building, cutting to their left.

Moments later they were engaged in a furious firefight as they ran headlong into a group of terrorists. For what seemed an eternity Katz and James exchanged fire with the desperate Hammer of Allah terrorists. Side by side the Phoenix heroes shot their way across the compound. When their bullets were exhausted, they had little chance to reload. Without a pause they snatched fragmentation grenades from their combat harnesses and launched them at the enemy. The twin blasts hurled the yelling terrorists in all directions.

"Go for cover," James said.

The closest available was behind a sandblasted dumper truck. Long devoid of tires, it sat in the drifting sand like a prehistoric steel dinosaur.

Katz and James threw themselves behind the metal barricade. Releasing empty magazines from their weapons, they slammed in fresh mags, cocking the weapons. As they worked, they heard the clang and whine of bullets striking the steelwork that concealed them.

Katz peered around the edge of the truck. Out over the compound Dragon Slayer was sweeping across the sky.

Reaching for his walkie-talkie, Katz found that the radio had caught a bullet. It hung from his belt shattered and useless.

"Cal, use your radio and call the Dragon in," the Israeli snapped, poking his Uzi into position. He opened up, catching the closest terrorist in the legs. The enemy soldier went down heavily, clutching at his shattered limbs.

James snatched his radio from his belt and keyed the button. The walkie-talkie remained silent. James rattled the instrument. Tried it again. Nothing.

"I don't believe this," the Chicago badass said. "The mother doesn't work."

He dropped the radio and joined Katz in holding back the gathered terrorists. With methodical precision he picked off a number of them, his M-16 cracking with deadly accuracy.

"They're starting to spread," Katz said. "Trying to get around us."

James was about to reply when he caught the familiar howl of Dragon Slayer's engines. Seconds later the black shape hurtled across the compound. The chopper's chain gun opened up with a deafening racket, spewing its 30mm cannon shells into the Hammer of Allah fanatics. Totally unprepared for such superior firepower, they scattered in panic. The thunderous roar of the cannon fire drowned out the screams of the dying as Dragon Slayer returned for a final run, taking out the surviving terrorists in a hail of red-hot death.

When James and Katz emerged from cover, the compound had fallen silent. The calm was broken a little by the distant groans of some wounded terrorists.

Dragon Slayer swooped in over the compound, settling with the soft sound of hydraulic suspension. The hatch swung open and Encizo appeared. The Cuban jumped to the ground, his weapon up and ready as he checked the compound.

"They've had it," James said.

"You guys okay?" Encizo asked.

"Fine," Katz said. "Anyone hurt in there?"

"Walker caught a couple of slugs in the shoulder and arm. He needs some attention."

"I'll handle that," James said.

"Before we leave," Katz told McCarter, "I want this place leveled, especially those gallows and the television trailer."

"That'll be my pleasure," the cockney said.

"So how's the secretary?" the Israeli asked.

"Take a look," the Cuban said.

The secretary of state was seated in the passenger compartment. He looked tired and dirty. Apart from that he looked well enough.

"Any problems, Mr. Secretary?" Katz asked.

The secretary shook his head. "Not anymore," he answered. "And while I have the opportunity, thanks, guys. You did one hell of a job."

"You're welcome," Manning said.

"Glad we could be of service," Sharon added.

Katz caught the Mossad agent's eye. "Thanks for all your help, Ben."

Sharon grinned. "Anytime. You ever need help, just call."

"Anything *I* can do for you guys?" the secretary asked. "I owe you one."

"Have a word with the President," McCarter suggested. "See if he can get our boss to give us a vacation. I'm ready for one if nobody else is. This mission has bloody shattered me."

"For once," Katz said, "I entirely agree with you, Marsh. We deserve a break. And I intend to start mine the minute we get back to Israel. In Jaffa, to be exact. A nice, long break."

ZEBRA CUBE
by
Robert Baxter

A Vietnam: Ground Zero novel

For ex-LAPD street coppers Larry Winn and George Currie, who took a chance on one cop-turned-writer and gave him a "real job."

1

TAN CHAU VILLAGE
CAMBODIAN BORDER

They had already sent him to the armpit of the world—no place could be more punishment than Vietnam's Mekong Delta during a hundred-degree monsoon—but something about this mission smelled like a week-old corpse.

His outline just a blurred image, Master Sergeant Joe Dillon leaned back from the Garand scope's eyepiece and slowly wiped at the crawling layer of gnats and mosquitoes pressing against his brow. He blinked hard several times, softly cursed the shifting sheets of rain pounding down on their position, then resumed eyeballing the assemblage of black and olive drab umbrellas bobbing on the middle of the bridge barely a hundred yards downslope from the ledge where his team had been lying low for forty-eight hours.

Prisoner exchanges were nothing new—the armchair commandoes at Saigon's Disneyland East were always mustering low-profile swaps to keep the statisticians at Puzzle Palace amused and entertained. But trying this sort of thing so near Tan Chau village was tempting fate—nothing short of striking at a slumbering dragon's reptilian plates with GI E-tools just to see if the beast was dead. Tan Chau—and, indeed, the entire western fringe of Chau Doc Province in this sector of the Mekong Delta—was the beat of Tri Quoc, hero of the Quang Chang, the South Vietnamese Military Police.

Quoc was a street cop through and through, born and bred in Saigon and bitter at having been reassigned to the boonies after busting an ARVN general's son for running heroin from Bangkok to Bien Hoa. He was no friend of the NVA or VC. Swapping prisoners to save a high-echelon spy's life was one thing, but Quoc had probably heard through the grapevine that this exchange was as political as they came: nothing more than a favor between one crony and another to honor some age-old family legacy soiled by the spilled blood that had been the curse of Indochina for centuries.

Dillon grunted as heat lightning crackled in the distance. Rumor Control had it that Quoc's people would display a show of force halfway through today's prisoner swap to demonstrate the ARVN Military Police's displeasure with what Quoc perceived to be a softening on the part of the Saigon brass. The regular ARVN had an entire battalion posted along the eastern edge of the border bridge in the event that Quoc's renegade troopers attempted to storm the ceremonies. But the CIA's snitch had maintained that any interference would no doubt manifest itself in the form of a solitary sniper drilling the Commie prisoners. Acting out the countersniper role they were so experienced at, Dillon's team was on-station in an attempt to prevent that.

The major who'd briefed Dillon and his men back in Can Tho had treated them like teenage cherries, feeding everyone juvenile propaganda designed to motivate them. The major had claimed that Colonel Quoc was corrupt and well-known for raking in loose change off both the round-eyed GIs and ARVN grunts.

"We're turning over two of their high-ranking officers for a couple of our full birds shot down over Cambodia last week," the West Pointer had declared. "This exchange could help improve relations between North Vietnam and the U.S., gentlemen. One of the enemy officers is rumored to be a distant cousin of Uncle Ho himself, though the man has refused to talk since he was captured at an ambush along the DMZ eleven months ago. Seems everyone in this hellhole is related somehow to everyone else. Anyway, the swap could help bring the war to an end, and ruin Quoc's extracurricular war profiteering."

Nothing could have been further from the truth. Quoc's reputation as a fearless, kick-ass cop loyal to his country above all else was legendary to anyone who'd been in-country a month or more, but Dillon and his men had humored the Saigon commando with hard-core grimaces and a string of gung ho thumbs-up gestures. The major had nodded his approval, and Dillon and his men had sauntered out to the Huey slick that had eventually transported them to the insertion point seventy-two hours before even the ARVN shock troopers had arrived.

Dillon placed his eye against the scope again and brought the powerful lens's cross hairs onto first one NVA official's beaming face and then another. One shot. He could pop off just one. Perhaps two. Anonymously. No one would know. Good guys or bad. Who gave a damn in this godforsaken hellhole? Blame it on Quoc. Blame it on Hanoi Jane. Blame it on Bob Dylan. It didn't matter.

Next year Vietnam would be just another page in the history books, and his team would be stomping the enemy in Thailand or Malaysia. Just another quagmire. Just another splendid little war. They were all beginning to look the same to him—Singapore, Indonesia, Burma.

Lifers tended to view destiny that way after they'd put in their first ten tours on dirty, distant ground. The only important thing was guarding that precious right all soldiers held dear: the ability to choose the time and location and manner of their own death.

Eyes darting only, allowing himself no head movement, Dillon glanced to his left, then to his right, scanning the jungle greens, seeking out telltale signs here and there that spoke of men lying in the reeds and bamboo among the lizards, snakes, spiders and leeches. As he did so, he decided that he didn't want to be with any other group of men in the world more than the death-dealing professionals surrounding him.

To his left, Captain Tate and Lieutenant Nordheim crouched close to the team RTO, Stan Bolecki. Beyond them, in the tree line, were Sergeant First Class Jim Brogan and Sergeant Jeb Stuart. To his right was Frank Jefferson. Out of sight, but surely close enough for instant mind-meld if the bullets began to bounce, were Sergeants Crocker, Carbo, Mendez and Nelson. The only man missing was Ben Cross, whisked away less than twenty-four hours earlier on a Medevac slick to Tan Son Nhut and subsequent relay back to the World. The staff sergeant's parents had been involved in some sort of serious accident on the outskirts of Terre Haute, Indiana, Cross's hometown.

Dillon's ears pricked up momentarily. Was that a dull droning he'd detected in the distance? Tanks, perhaps? Armored personnel carriers? A convoy of reinforcements, or Quoc's brigade on the march? But as quickly as he'd noticed it, the odd buzzing disappeared. An eerie silence settled over the jungle once again. The parrots had fallen weirdly mute, as well. He placed his ear against the rotting muck of the forest floor, expecting to hear the vibration of the heavy vehicles approaching, but sensed nothing.

Dillon glanced over at Tate's outline against the murky blue mist drifting up from the river. At twenty-seven the captain was old for a Vietnam A-team commander. With blond hair and blue eyes the six-foot, 180-pounder was well into his second tour with the Special Forces.

Over the months Tate had developed tiny crow's-feet at the corners of his eyes from squinting so much in the tropical sun's glare. Despite his youth, though, he usually exuded an air of wisdom and confidence, something much appreciated by his men, as was his sense of humor. All in all, Dillon thought, a guy couldn't ask for a better CO.

For a moment the rains died down, and the dark, menacing clouds shifted with eerie suddenness, allowing a solitary shaft of sunlight to penetrate the valley even as silvery, shadowlike downpours continued to pound the steep green-and-brown slopes on either side of the distant bridge. Dillon glanced at

Bolecki just as the RTO shifted in the flattened elephant grass and his radio's whip antenna flipped free, springing skyward. In Vietnam silence shouts. As if a sixth sense had warned him that his fly was open, Bolecki's hand shot up, pulling the antenna back down so that its subdued outer edge was facing the bridge. But Dillon couldn't help but wonder if the split second of flapping aluminum had caught the eye of some alert NVA marksman lying in palm fronds a hundred yards away.

No discharge ripped the air, however. No tracer arced out toward them, seeking to reward a careless mistake with instant mortality.

"Why don't you just flip a mirror in their direction next time?" Dillon muttered under his breath.

"Sorry, Sarge."

"Sorry don't cut it, Stan."

"I know." Bolecki bit into his lower lip, angry with himself. "It won't happen again."

The stress of lying low in the bush so long without a break was beginning to take its toll. They would never have wasted words on anything so frivolous before. Sure, losing the antenna was bad karma, but it was no big deal now. What was done was done.

"Forget it, guy. We're still alive," he told the RTO.

Dillon brought the sniper rifle scope to his eyes again. He was beginning to feel a wariness in his gut—something was about to happen. Something bad. This wasn't going to go down smooth and silent and uneventful. The water buffalo dung was about to hit the gunship rotor blades, as their Intelligence specialist, Dave Nelson, was fond of saying.

It was then that he heard the swiftly growing drone of a lone aircraft approaching low across the treetops behind his position—heading directly for the bridge on what appeared to be a bombing run!

He recognized it as an OD green, American-made OV-1 Mohawk, sporting a tall yellow number 13 on its raised tail and the words United States Army emblazoned across the sides in foot-high black letters. Dillon felt both anxiety and relief: the craft had been designed for reconnaissance and was usually unarmed. But what the hell was it doing so low and in a restricted zone on the Cambodian border?

His ears ached as the plane dropped even lower, banking sharply to the left, its two eleven-hundred-horsepower engines grinding away like out-of-sync buzz saws. Dillon caught a glimpse of the pilot's face and thought it looked Asian.

The craft buzzed the bridge, and everyone—NVA, Americans and POWs alike—scattered toward opposite sides of the river, the Communists careful not to panic as they responded routinely to the aerial threat, treating it as just another intrusion into their long-term master plan of national domination.

Wings tipped downward, first left, then right, as the Mohawk abruptly banked hard in the opposite direction, the craft nearly rolling over, as if taking part in a stateside air show. Maybe, Dillon thought, the guy was trying to impress the ladies in the crowd. But the only females in the audience today were Co Congs, and they began blasting away at the OV-1 with AK-47s and SKS rifles.

"Go, baby, go!" Dillon heard both Jefferson and Crocker cheer as the Mohawk roared up into the menacing thunderclouds, rolling like a giant beetle over the valley's edge before disappearing.

An antiaircraft battery, concealed in the tree line on the opposite side of the river, unleashed a fury of fist-size rounds after the recon plane, but it had already vanished in the eerie haze, and the gunners were aiming at the deceptive sound of its straining engines.

Then, suddenly, a second aircraft shot out from beyond the waving treetops behind Dillon's SF team. This ship flew even lower—as daring as any helicopter pilot had ever brought a Huey or Cobra into a hot LZ—and Dillon found he could even read the white numbers on the A-1 Skyraider's tail: TT206. He made a mental note of that as the single-prop engine labored to pull the ten-thousand-pound craft through hot, sticky air clinging to the river valley floor.

Again, this plane's pilot was also aiming directly for the bridge. Dillon knew the Skyraiders were equipped with four fixed forward-firing 20 mm cannons equipped with up to four tons of external ordnance. They could do a lot more damage than a mere Mohawk.

The Communists had spotted the second craft, as well. Already the big AA guns were swinging around, trained on it, and blasting away with dual five-foot flashes of probing death.

"Hold your fire!" Dillon yelled, anticipating the response of his fellow soldiers and giving the warning even before Captain Tate. It was an unnecessary command: they all wanted to blast away at the antiaircraft positions and cheer on the Skyraider, but for now they would just monitor events and restrain their trigger fingers.

Dillon flinched as a burst of AA flak tore through the Skyraider's right wing just as the plane began unloading on the bridge with a ceaseless stream of cannon fire. Barrels still burping hot lead, the entire starboard side of the craft erupted into flames as the fuselage flipped over.

Glowing white and yellow tracers lanced up into the storm clouds as the miniguns continued to fire and the Skyraider, its nose prop backfiring repeatedly as it struggled to keep turning, limped out over the treetops, tail fins swishing side to side as if the entire ship were about to drop wheelbarrows full of cement.

Dillon realized he was holding his breath now as he watched the pilot regain control of the crippled ship, slowly right it, then begin a slow climb away from the green carpet below to disappear beyond the palm fronds.

"Got to be an American in that mother!" Jefferson called out with a raised fist. "No native could fly that good!"

"You better *believe* that was a round eye piloting that Spad!" Andy Crocker chimed in as he rose up out of the jungle muck on one knee.

"You two knock it off with the noise," Lieutenant Nordheim rasped, gritting his teeth and waving them both back down into the prone position. "What the fuck you think this is—the adventure safari at Disneyland or something?"

"I never had a squad of inch-long army ants eatin' on me at Disneyland!" Bolecki complained as he swatted the back of his neck. Pain from several nasty bites lanced down through his backbone, and he swatted again.

"You guys deep-six the chatter!" Tate demanded, sending Nordheim a knowing glare that said, "They'll revert back to kids' antics every time if you don't keep on them about maintaining the strict discipline necessary to play the soldier's game!"

No one needed more encouragement to flatten faces against the valley floor's rotting carpet when, like a giant pterodactyl on the prowl, a shadow raced over them and the Mohawk returned with a roar as it swung back on a second pass.

This time its pilot threw an ammo box full of stick grenades onto the bridge. They exploded with dull pops that immediately brought Tate's head up from behind a termite-infested log. "Chicoms!" he decided.

"Confiscated?" Dillon wondered aloud.

"Ain't no American in that damn thing!" Jefferson declared.

"An American would've dropped regular made-in-America frags!" Nelson agreed. "You know that!"

Carbo nodded. "They pack a better punch!"

Dillon glanced over at Juan Mendez, the heavy-weapons specialist. "Those two renegade pilots had to be Quoc's men!"

"But where would a bunch of MP types snatch a fixed-wing aircraft?" Mendez shot back.

"ARVN MPs are better scroungers than U.S. jar-heads," Jefferson told them both as he slapped a 20-round magazine into his M-16, testing its seal.

"Knock it off," Tate muttered. His narrowed eyes scanned the jagged tree line, but the Mohawk had already vanished. A tight, silver spiral of smoke clinging to the valley's rain-swept contours pointed to the path the crippled Skyraider had taken.

Nordheim's lips parted, but before he could issue a command the sound of the plane crashing several hundred yards away reached their ears.

Dillon flinched again at the grinding roar of metal tearing against metal as the earth devoured the exploding debris until an odd silence settled over the rain forest. In the distance a greenish orange fireball rose into the sky, and moments later the crackle of secondary explosions reached them.

"It dumped right over that ridge," Tate said, motioning toward the high left while he scanned the bridge below with his binoculars. None of the enemy had emerged from the water. "Let's beat feet over there before Charlie or Marvin the Arvin can kick ass."

"And see if we can snatch us some Red Baron bozo for a little session of truth-or-consequences," Nordheim added.

Frank Jefferson glanced at him questioningly. "What?"

"Just get your black ass in gear and double-time after that smoke trail!" Dillon growled.

"Roger your last, Sarge!" Jefferson was up and bounding over the fallen logs, zigzagging down through bomb crates and booby traps with seeming abandon.

2

BLUE BAMBOO BAR
TERRE HAUTE, INDIANA

Sergeant Ben Cross stared deep into the eyes of the Dragon and didn't blink. Slowly at first, small streams of silver smoke began boiling forth from the crimson serpent's nostrils, then a ball of rolling smoke engulfed the Special Forces NCO, and he backed away, gagging and coughing.

A roar of laughter—not reptilian outrage—filled the cramped lounge, and scattered applause shortly followed. Someone slapped Cross on the back after he staggered over to the nearest stool and collapsed onto it, eyes watering.

"You lose, hero!" the tall, stocky man said, laughing loudest, a thundering bellow that made Cross's ears ache. "But don't feel bad, brother. No one's beaten the Dragon yet. Old Man Phuc over there fills his mechanical gut with an illegal concoction of Army-issue CS tear gas and stale *nuoc-mam*."

Another vet staggered up on Cross's other side. "The kid lost to the Dragon! That means he buys a round on the house for everybody!"

"He's new here," the first soldier said, tilting his head to one side. "How was he supposed to know nobody sits in front of the Dragon unless he wants to challenge the big beast?"

"It was the only stool open in the...whole... damn...place," Cross muttered slowly, his head starting to clear.

"I'll buy on his behalf, asshole," the first vet stated loudly. "Now go over there and sit the fuck down and shut the fuck up before I slam-dunk your REMF face into one of them plugged-up latrines back there in the head."

"Bullshit," the second soldier growled, puffing his chest out importantly. "*I'll* buy before anyone will."

Cross stared at the two men: both white, in their early thirties, wearing civvies. He glanced around the bar—nearly everyone else in the room was white, as well. Things hadn't really changed in his absence. Through the swinging front doors, out across the street, soul music blared from the Plantation Lounge, where most if not all of the black vets congregated. It reminded him of Saigon, and the self-imposed segregation over there. It was funny, he thought, how they could die together, but seldom drank with one another. Cross shook his head and thought of Frank Jefferson back in Vietnam with his A-team. Frank and he were good buddies, but he wondered if he would be comfortable with the big black dude in this bar.

Bottles of beer were placed before him—the same brands that filled ice chests from the Mekong Delta to the DMZ and were rumored to be provided free by the stateside breweries. He felt himself being squashed by the shoulders of the two big men on either side, but he wasn't claustrophobic; these men were brother warriors who knew what it was to be sent by your government to a faraway land while the sons of richer men sat out the war on college campuses or in the National Guard.

Cross glanced up at the big man on his right, who'd relented as wallets were produced, allowing the first vet to buy beer for soldiers whose veins now ran golden with it. "Have another." The man plunked down a pitcher bearing a skull with a green beret labeled Fifth SF Group. The big man's face was a combination grimace, growl and satisfied grin. His eyes were mere slits beneath brows that came together over a flattened nose. His head was shaved clean and a wicked scar ran down the middle of it—a souvenir of a bar fight in Saigon's Xin Loi Bar.

Cross was impressed. He decided not to argue. The man was a monster. Probably Special Forces, as well. The Blue Bamboo Bar was known to be a Green Beanie haunt. That was why he'd searched it out.

Previously he hadn't had enough balls to enter the place, feeling he hadn't earned the right. Now, fresh back from Nam, the place felt like home. More like home than the cozy stucco house two miles away that he'd grown up in. He stared up at a proclamation in Oriental mother-of-pearl across three slabs of polished black-lacquered wood: You Have Never Lived Until You Have Almost Died. For Those Who Fight For Freedom, Life Has A Flavor The Protected Will Never Know.

Perhaps *that* explained his preference for the SF bar over his own home.

He wished he could shake hands with the man who'd dreamed that one up. Probably some Saigon commando who felt guilty about being stationed in the rear but needn't have.

"Here's to you, bub," Cross muttered, lifting his glass of beer.

"Huh?" the big man next to him said, nudging him with an elbow.

"Aw, nothing."

"Right," the guy agreed as he downed an entire mug of brew. "Fuck it. Don't mean nothin'."

"A native, are you?" the soldier on his left asked.

Cross blinked. "Huh?"

"Born and raised in the U.S., eh? Born right here in good ol' Terre Haute?"

"Uh, right." Cross had to think for a moment. Most of his brain was still in Vietnam.

The hulking soldier who'd bought the last two rounds stared long and hard at Cross, sizing him up. The NCO looked under twenty-five, had red hair and was something of a runt. The freckles splashed all over his "aw-shucks" face reminded most people of Archie Andrews from the comics.

The big guy sitting beside Cross knew redheads didn't tan well. Perhaps that was why this kid didn't have the bronzed look of most vets fresh back from Nam. But there was a look in his blue eyes, one that said the man had stared death in the face more than once. He was willing to give the kid a break. "Drink up, hoss. You're falling behind the rest of us."

"Yeah, sure." Cross glanced up into the vet's unblinking bullet gray eyes.

"What's that?" the towering, bald Green Beret growled.

"You gotta speak up. This here bar's noisier than a Bangkok cathouse on a hot Saturday night. Hey, I got it. Maybe it's your lack of altitude." The guy grabbed Cross by the collar of his jean jacket and started to lift him off his stool, then he noticed the patch on his right shoulder: Vietnam 1968: Sure To Go To Heaven 'Cause I've Spent My Time In Hell! "Yeah, this guy's a fucking vet." The big man released his hold on Cross and slapped the combat engineer on the back again. "Pitchers of suds on me all around!"

An explosion of cheers erupted in the bar, all but drowning out the jukebox music: Johnny Cash singing something about how prison life sucked. A short, scrawny Asian man appeared from behind a wall of shimmering imitation jade beads. He had an evil grin that stretched from ear to ear, and the name tag on his bartender's OD green smock read, Mr. Phuc-Off.

Cross smiled back. He knew "Phuc" was almost as common a name in Vietnam as Smith and Jones in the U.S. It was pronounced *fook* by the Viets, but few GIs were so polite. Cross wondered if the bartender had designed the name tag, or if someone else had dreamed it up.

"Howdy, Sammy!" the generous vet said, giving the bartender a light punch on the collarbone.

Phuc's smile grew as he recognized the men seated on either side of Cross. He set a pitcher of beer down and whirled as if to throw a Bruce Lee martial arts kick, but held back at the last moment, reconsidering. "Howdy, mates."

"How's the bartending business?" the bald vet asked.

Sammy shrugged. "Sometimes fast, sometimes slow."

Cross got the impression Sammy Phuc owned the establishment. He glanced beyond Phuc's shoulder to a liquor license hanging above a mirror that ran the length of the bar. The name listed was Tina Tran.

Someone pulled the plug on the jukebox, but groans of protest quickly turned to howls of delight as the lights suddenly dimmed and purple strobes began pulsating in their place. Three scantily clad women sauntered out onto the long countertop: one white and two Asian. They wore glittering G-strings and black bikini tops, which were quickly discarded.

Cross knew one Oriental was Japanese, but he wasn't sure if the other was Khmer or Vietnamese. Then there was an unexpected cymbal crash, and three band members—two guitarists and a drummer—appeared on a tiny stage.

The band played an instrumental version of the Rolling Stones' "Paint It Black," and with each drumbeat the three women whirled and gyrated until tiny beads of perspiration slid down their upturned breasts, driving the men wild. The Japanese dancer maintained a plastic smile but stared off into the distance as if in a drug daze. The white woman's eyes wandered around the crowd, as if searching for someone special. Her eyes passed over Cross and the men around him without apparent interest. Only the Cambodian girl—he was sure of her origin now—was really smiling, a faint, almost taunting grin and her eyes had locked onto Cross's. She was literally devouring him.

Cross stared back, feeling a sudden heat sear his crotch. It had been nearly fourteen months since he'd had a woman outside the war zone. He hadn't bargained on being attracted to an Oriental, but there was something definitely seductive about this woman. Was it hunger he read in her eyes? Or arousal? Or just the loneliness that veterans of war—both men and women—could heal only among their own kind?

Cross winked up at her, but his acknowledgment broke the spell, and she looked away. He didn't see her join the band, but soon another woman's soulful voice complemented the mellow guitars and understated drumming. The song was now "Piece of My Heart."

His eyes remained fixed on the Cambodian girl, though, taking in her slender hips, firm thighs, flat belly and jutting breasts, which peeked out from behind strands of long black hair. Looking at her, he knew he wanted more than just a piece of her heart. He wanted to climb the counter, pull her down into his arms and eat her alive.

The big bald vet clamped a hand onto his shoulder and forced him back down before he could make good on his fantasy. "Down, boy, down. What d'you think this is—a candy store?"

At that moment the dancers moved closer, and the Cambodian girl dropped into a squat and flipped her mahogany brown breasts against Cross's nose as if massaging him. "Hi, handsome," she whispered.

Cross was sure his heart was about to give out. The band had moved into a faster-paced song—Jefferson

Airplane's "White Rabbit." The red-haired NCO could feel sweat prickling his forehead.

"What's your name, soldier boy?" the Cambodian girl asked as she straightened up.

But the dancers moved away before he could answer, and all he was left with were billowing clouds of cigarette smoke.

"I'm gonna bed that broad if it's the last thing I do," the bald vet swore.

"I had first dibs on her," Cross protested, slightly irritated but maintaining his smile. No woman was worth fighting over.

The soldier laughed. "Not the Khmer bitch. She's too tiny. I wouldn't wanna split 'er down the middle, pal. I was talkin' about that white babe."

"Jesus," Cross muttered, happy not to get on the wrong side of the heavyweight Green Beret.

He turned to his left, searching for the bartender, and froze at the sight of an older man in his late fifties. A chill went down Cross's backbone, but he knew it couldn't be true. The man couldn't be his father. And then the clouds of cigarette smoke subsided, his vision cleared somewhat and the man's face changed. The guy was just another stiff in the bar. Cross's father was dead. All of a sudden the freckle-faced NCO forgot about the Cambodian dancer.

His mother had died in the car accident, too. A head-on crash that had turned their Ford into a heap of scrap metal. The pickup driver who'd been speeding the wrong way down the divided highway was in the hospital's critical care unit, paralyzed from the waist down. His blood-alcohol level had been three times more than the legal limit in the state of Indiana.

At first Cross had wanted to race to the hospital ward and pay the man a .45-caliber visit. But then he realized the guy would be a paraplegic for the rest of his life—punishment enough, perhaps. And besides, there would no doubt be a police guard watching over the dirtbag, waiting for his condition to improve so they could transfer his no-account ass to the jail ward. Cross didn't need that kind of grief. He was already in a certified world of hurt.

His uncle had met him at the airport. Cross was glad he'd taken the advice of vets returning from the R and Rs in Hawaii. They'd told him to exchange his uniform for civvies, which he'd done. He hadn't liked the determined look in the eyes of the war protestors in Chicago or Terre Haute itself, and hadn't been in the mood for a public confrontation with Peaceniks.

He'd visited the funeral home that afternoon. That was why he was purging his soul with booze tonight. It would have to be a closed-casket affair. His uncle, who had fought in Nam, too, and Korea before that, had identified them both. But Cross had insisted on seeing their faces for himself. He would always regret that decision. Not even a thousand buddies' faces split down the middle by machine-gun bullets could prepare him for the sight of the decapitated bodies of his mother and father.

The mortician had sewn their heads back on, of course, but there was no hiding the grotesque disfigurement. Scenes like that were only supposed to happen in Vietnam. Not Hometown, U.S.A. Not here in good ol' Terre Haute.

Cross coughed. His temples throbbed and his belly gurgled. Just thinking about the funeral home made him feel as if he was going to puke.

They were still trying to find his kid brother. Perry was trudging through the cloud-cloaked mountains of Nepal or Burma or some godforsaken place at the edge of the world. He was trying to prove himself as a free-lance photojournalist for *Valor* magazine ever since the Army had refused to accept him because of poor eyesight. The kid was just about legally blind— you *had* to be for Uncle Sammy not to show an interest in your ass. Poor Perry. Cross's mother had branded him with that godawful name because she was in love with Raymond Burr's TV-show character. And the kid had spent the rest of his life trying to prove to the world he wasn't a mama's boy. Now he was off chasing mountain goats in Kathmandu or some such place, and the funeral would have to wait until he'd been returned or the summer heat set in— whichever came first.

In the meantime Special Forces Sergeant Ben Cross would spend his nights haunting the bowels of the Blue Bamboo Bar, or any other after-hours dive that would have him. He wasn't afraid of Charlie or jungle punji stakes or even rain forest ghosts, but he couldn't spend another night alone in his parents' empty house. He'd rather die first.

3

Lieutenant Nordheim was thinking trip wires and booby traps, not mobile death. That was why the brilliant flash of fangs nearly froze his heart as the Bengal tiger sprang at him from its lair in the razor-sharp reeds at the swamp's edge. The big cat bowled him over, roared on in Tate's direction, pivoted as soon as the captain raised his M-16, then disappeared like a giant ball of rolling fur into the elephant grass.

"Holy shit!" Frank Jefferson exclaimed, still face-down in the muck.

"Damn!" Dave Nelson slapped his thigh hard. "That damn thing was up and outta here before I could even blink an eye."

"Didn't think there were no goddamn tigers this far south, Captain," Stan Bolecki said. "Thought they were all up in the Highlands."

"This is Nam, Stan," Master Sergeant Joe Dillon said, allowing himself a muffled laugh. "From top to bottom it's got everything from cobras the size of Rhode Island to an elephant graveyard that'd put Hollywood's best African epic to shame."

"Cut the chatter," Tate muttered. His gun hand pointed westward. A thick column of smoke rose from the Skyraider's crash site. "I wanna get over there and nab those bastards before Charlie does. Otherwise Hanoi'll have 'em singin' for the press corps, and every pinko rag from Singapore to Seattle will be playing this party crash episode for every cent it's worth."

Dillon cocked an eyebrow. "You mean it could actually wreck the overtures of peace offered by Uncle Ho?"

Tate cast him a glare that could melt steel. "Let's just get those fuckers, okay?"

"Last one to the Spad is a VC turd!" Andy Crocker, one of the team's engineers, called out. He began high-stepping through the elephant grass like a high school majorette.

"What's with these guys this morning?" Tate asked, looking over at Nordheim, obviously miffed by their behavior.

"I'd say that last two or three days lying low in the rain waterlogged what few brains they had left, Captain." The lieutenant forced a tight grin, and then was off into the grass in a flash.

"Jesus," Tate muttered, struggling to keep up with the younger man.

Eddy Carbo, one of the team's two radio operators, was suddenly beside him. "Sir, I've got Kingpin on the commo."

"The general?"

"Roger that."

"What the hell's he want at a time like this?"

"He says no aggressive action on our part. And no defensive action unless our asses are really in the wringer."

"He actually said that?"

Carbo held out the Prick-25's handset, but Tate made no move to grab it. "Well, my choice of words was a little kinder than—"

"Are you trying to tell me—"

"He's trying to tell *you*," Nordheim cracked, returning to Tate's side, "that they're dancing with the devil back there on that bridge and they don't want us zapping any trigger-happy Commies and messing up their game plan with Hanoi."

"I knew that," Tate snapped. "Shit!" He glanced over at the bobbing heads of his men as they raced through the shoulder-high reeds. "Christ Almighty," he muttered as the pith helmets of a hundred NVA shock troops emerged from the distant tree line and began converging on the crash site.

"We can still make it in time," Jeb Stuart, the Southern medic whispered as they located a trail through the sea of deep grass. "If we just double-time it."

"No trails," Nordheim warned.

"We don't have the luxury of time, LT," Tate countered, tightening the loose webgear harness of the man crouching in front of him.

"Booby traps," Nordheim reminded him.

"I know that, Pete, but this whole goddamn country's a booby trap for Christ's sake!" Tate brushed past Mendez and Brogan, taking the lead as secondary explosions rocked the Skyraider's vertical stabilizer, which jutted up through the blanket of smoke a hundred yards away.

No booby traps slowed them down with casualties. Within a few seconds they were wading through the dense black smoke, and then part of the Skyraider's fifty-one-foot wingspan blocked their path. The plane had survived the crash relatively intact, though the nose had been badly smashed in the impact. Then the left wing began to tip—someone was dragging himself down it from the caved-in cockpit!

Tate instinctively gave hand signals, sending his men to the left and right beyond the craft's fuselage. But they had already sought cover on their own and were training their rifles on the demoralized shape moving facedown along the bullet-riddled wing. Tate reached out and grabbed the pilot by his smoldering collar and jerked him to the ground just as the first green tracer sizzled past a few inches from his earlobe.

"Goddamn it!" Tate slammed the semiconscious pilot into the mud and flipped the safety off his carbine. Another burst of green tracers flew past—this time a few feet above their heads.

Tate sniffed the air. Fumes from the aircraft fuel were heavy in the area. He had no idea how much the plane had been carrying, but it didn't matter. If the thing blew, they'd never know what hit them. And the North Vietnamese would get one fine fireworks show.

The captain could hear shouting in rapid-fire Vietnamese now, and the sporadic shooting had ceased. One of the NVA commanders was telling his men to knock it off unless they wanted to visit their dead ancestors by riding billowing balls of flame from the Skyraider's exploding fuel tanks.

Tate glanced down at the groaning pilot. He wore a gray flight suit and had Asian features. The monogram on his white silk scarf was the dual lightning bolts and black beret of a South Vietnamese Military Police antiterrorist unit. One of Colonel Quoc's men.

"Come on!" Tate ordered as the elephant grass all around them began to bend and shimmer. "Get his ass up. We've got to hustle the bastard over to the extraction point before—"

"Not so fast, my American colleague."

The Vietnamese-accented English turned Tate's blood to ice. He whirled, weapon at the ready, but there was nothing he or any of his men could do. They were completely surrounded by several dozen NVA infantrymen with AK-47s extended, their fixed bayonets gleaming in the harsh tropical sun.

But Tate's A-team was as startled by the sudden descent of several Huey gunships as the platoon of NVA regulars encircling them. The helicopters roared onto the scene, emerging from the tree lines in all four directions, with earsplitting turbine whines and a rotor blade downblast that fanned the shimmering sea of elephant grass like a killer typhoon. Faces flinched and hands shielded eyes as one of the choppers flared in for a rough landing, bouncing across several gnarled tree roots. The other Hueys, however, remained in stationary hovers overhead.

The resulting blast of steady wind was sufficient to topple the Skyraider's vertical stabilizer fin. By now Tate's men had their weapons poised for gunplay, as well, but it wouldn't be necessary. The two officers bounding out of the Huey wore the uniforms and insignia of both the U.S. and North Vietnamese armies.

Nordheim cringed at the sight of the NVA officer rushing out of the olive drab bird as if he owned it. But before he could put thoughts into words General Gordon L. Sherwood, big and stocky like a Sherman tank, stormed up to the laager of frozen combatants, pushing several of the Communist soldiers out of his way before halting in front of Tate. He ignored the captain's casual, two-fingered salute, which could cost an officer in the sticks a sniper's round between the eyes. The NVA officer kept up with the general like an out-of-breath shadow.

"Well?" Sherwood demanded.

Tate cocked an eyebrow. "Sir?"

Sherwood rose on tiptoe, trying to see over Tate's shoulder. "Damn it, man, the pilot! Have you got the pilot!"

"Is the pilot alive?" the North Vietnamese officer asked, appearing more worried and bewildered than angry.

"Sir," Tate said, ignoring the Communist, "if you turn our boy over to this lynch party, we'll never get word one outta—"

"Lynch party?" Sherwood bellowed effectively over the noise of the helicopters hovering around the crash site. "Hell, son, I'm pissed off enough right now to execute the bastard here on the spot. Do you know how close he came to—"

"He's ARVN, sir," Nordheim cut in. "A QC officer."

"Is that supposed to make a difference? I don't give a puckered rat's ass if—"

"We want him for . . . interrogation," the NVA officer announced calmly.

Tate glanced up into the black goggles of a Huey door gunner hanging in the gray sky only a few dozen feet away. Then he stared at the NVA officer. "Well, you can't have him. As the first officer on-scene, I—"

"This ain't a goddamn flophouse burglary, mister!" Sherwood reminded him. "But it could very well be the scene of your own untimely demise if we piss these Commie hotshots off any more than we already have. We're in *their* territory, you know."

"I thought we were still in *South* Vietnam, General."

"Don't piss me off, son." The general rose on tiptoe again. It was the only way he could be taller than Tate. "We're in fucking Cambodia here, and you know it."

"But, sir—" Nordheim began.

"Besides," Sherwood said, waving him silent, "I'm not turning this guy over to nobody. We all go back together, aboard that same UH-1 we just dismounted."

"Back where?" Tate persisted. Mendez and Brogan now had the semiconscious pilot propped between them. They were both looking at Tate for guidance.

"Back to the joint coordinations center at the bridge," the general replied. "Back there we can all take turns asking this first-class asshole who he's working for and why they deemed it necessary to buzz one of the first attempts at peaceful negotiations in the field that we've been able to arrange with our North Vietnamese 'buddies' here."

"'Buddies'? You don't mean that, sir," Nordheim rasped.

"Of course I don't, Lieutenant. But for now, with about twenty or thirty AKs pointing at my close-to-retirement butt, we play the game, soldier. Now I haven't got any more time to flap my gums. If you don't mind..."

Every man in the clearing dropped into a squat as a prop-driven plane suddenly barreled from the sky, dived between two of the hovering helicopters and nearly put a crease in Sherwood's silver crew cut.

"Jesus *H.* Christ!" The general drew his .45 pistol and popped off eight quick rounds at the Mohawk's silhouette as the craft climbed back into the sun. It was a useless effort, though—the plane was already out of the automatic's maximum effective range. But the general's action was impressive: it was the first time either Tate or Nordheim had ever seen a general officer engaging potential "hostiles" with a handgun.

"It's his buddy!" Brogan whispered in awe. "The Spad's buddy came back to check on him."

Sherwood rushed between elbows as he ejected the spent clip, slammed a fresh magazine home, holstered his Colt and grabbed Carbo's handset. "Don't just hang there looking pretty!" He made eye contact with the nearest gunship pilot, seeming to stare through the warrant officer's black face mask. "Run that Mohawk down, mister! And clip its goddamn wings!"

"It carries markings of a friendly, sir!" came the static-laced reply.

But Sherwood was already hustling back to his own Huey. He turned and glared at Tate as if engaged in telepathic instructions. The captain nodded and grabbed Carbo's handset again. "He says screw the markings. Blast that bird outta the sky. You copy my last, Headhunter?"

"Roger that. Wilco, Zulu Six."

Before he joined Sherwood aboard the C and C Huey, the NVA officer rattled off some directives to his own men. Somewhat grudgingly they lowered their rifles and, one by one, melted into the bamboo, never turning their backs on Tate's men nor breaking eye contact until they became one with the elusive jungle shadows.

Two slicks flying ammo support flared in, flattening the shoulder-high elephant grass. Tate and his team scrambled aboard, and the two Hueys ascended despite vibrating floorboards and protesting rotors.

Within a few minutes they caught up to the action. The Mohawk was flying tight circles over a hidden runway secreted deep in the heart of the rain forest less than a klick east of the Cambodian border. Several gunships, including a sleek two-man Cobra, were darting about, taking turns pouncing on the recon ship. It was riddled with bullets but still refused to drop from the sky.

On the ground below, several QC gun jeeps waited on either side of the runway, the M-60s trained on not the Mohawk but the helicopters pursuing it. Obviously they were Quoc's men.

Tate's people sat almost sidesaddle in the open hatches of the choppers they rode, hanging against the craft's momentum by canvas straps or lifelines as they trained their rifles on the ARVN MPs waiting brazenly below.

"I don't like the idea of firing on our allies, sir!" Dillon called forward to Tate.

"Even if they're MPs?" Mendez asked, chuckling above the din of the rotors.

"They aren't allies!" Tate shouted back. "They're renegade cops—that bastard Quoc's boys!" he reminded them. "Besides, we haven't fired any shots yet at all."

"Yeah, the flyboys are getting all the fun!" Nordheim pointed out just as the Cobra gunship swooped low to the ground, clipping several palm fronds. It ascended sharply again toward the gliding Mohawk on a collision course with its underbelly.

"They've been giving it orders by radio to land back at Tan Chau," Carbo said as he held a headset clamped tightly over his ears. "But the pilot responds only with insults about the NVA officer's cultural lineage."

"What?" Tate growled.

Nordheim grinned. "Translation. Taunt and tease in Vietnamese. Works every time. They learn it from the bar girls."

"Jesus," Tate muttered.

"Works to get everyone pissed off," Dillon said just as the Cobra unleashed two of its rocket pods. Both projectiles ascended in silver streaks, their brilliant plumes of smoke obscuring the ghostlike outline of the gunship that had launched them.

"That's prettier than an eighteen-year-old Hue City cherry girl droppin' her silk pantaloons for the first time," Mendez decided.

The recon plane tried to bank sharply, but both rockets struck its underbelly at the same time. The craft separated just behind its wings, ceased nearly all forward momentum and suddenly dropped to earth, one wing cartwheeling after the smoking debris, the other floating along on the air currents for a while before disappearing beyond the tree line.

"Follow the bastard down!" Tate ordered.

There wasn't much to follow. The pilot attempted to eject midway, but he was too close to the ground for his parachute to deploy effectively, and they watched with open mouths as his body splattered on the ground like a rag doll.

Nordheim was concentrating on the gun jeeps. Their menacing-looking M-60s and 50-caliber machine guns were trained on Sherwood's Command and Control ship. Would they shoot? If he were in their position, Nordheim decided he would. What did they have to lose? Colonel Quoc faced a summary court-martial over this fiasco, no doubt. But had anyone actually seen the South Vietnamese MP colonel's ugly mug? Nordheim didn't think so. It was all rumor, innuendo, which was probably enough to convict a QC in the combat zone. There was no love lost between swaggering inflictors of jungle justice and the infantry leaders who resented REMFs extending their territory into the field.

"Can we shoot now, sir, or do we have to wait for those bastards down there to fire the first shots?" Brogan demanded.

Tate glanced over at the light-weapons expert. The man's trigger finger was white with tension. "Stand by," he decided.

"If they've got the balls to fire on an American gunship," Nordheim shouted over the whine of helicopter turbines, "They'll take out the general's bird first."

"Hell, they've got enough gun jeeps down there to take us all out with one concentrated blast," Dillon observed.

"They wouldn't dare," Brogan said, his eyes blinking nonstop as sweat streamed down his forehead. "The bastards wouldn't fucking dare."

An earsplitting roar of slow, thumping discharges lured all eyes to the west, and Dillon cheered as the Cobra appeared in a break along the dense tree line. Once again it was racing low, its landing skids skimming through the reeds as it unloaded with its snout cannon. None of the gunship's rounds were aimed at or struck the QC gun jeeps, however, and slowly, one by one, the South Vietnamese military policemen lowered their machine-gun barrels and backed away from the smoking craters, vanishing from sight beneath the tree branches.

"Engage?"

Tate monitored the Cobra pilot's request for some joy time with the ARVN MPs.

"Negative," came Sherwood's unenthusiastic reply. "You did good, Sharkshooter. Return to base and gimme an after-action on what you eyeballed down there. Copy?"

"Roger, out."

"What the hell does all that mean?" Brogan asked.

"You're no buck private. You know better than to ask a stupid question like that," Nordheim said, taunting the light-weapons sergeant.

"What I meant was—"

"Don't we get to bust some caps on those bozos just for good measure?" Dillon translated.

"Maybe next time." Tate glanced out the open door in time to see Sherwood's chopper banking hard to the left as it headed back to Tan Chau and the cold LZ beside the border bridge. "For now we let the politicians and diplomats call the shots."

"What shots?" Brogan flipped on his M-16's safety and grumbled all the way back to the bridge. The thought of a North Vietnamese officer riding inside one of the Hueys ahead of them without benefit of his wrists handcuffed behind his back turned the Special Forces sergeant's stomach.

4

BLUE BAMBOO BAR
TERRE HAUTE, INDIANA

Cross didn't know the man's name. He was an Army
MP who'd just returned from less than four months
in-country, his tour cut short by a bout of dengue fever that couldn't be cured at Third Field Hospital
outside Tan Son Nhut. But the guy seemed blessed
with an endless amount of money and was generous
with it, too, buying a round of drinks for the whole
lounge—ten or eleven wary-eyed warriors last count.
As long as the man was free with his money, Cross
would listen to his chatter. This was his second night
in the Blue Bamboo, though it felt as if he'd been
coming here for a month.

The MP buying the drinks had been sufficiently
impressed with Saigon, City of Sorrows and onetime
Pearl of the Orient. He was so impressed that he swore
he would write ten million words about the place before he died. And someday he'd go back—to die. Saigon had become home to him. He was a self-
proclaimed adventure novelist in search of a publisher, with over thirty unpublished manuscripts to his
credit.

"All about Vietnam," he told Cross. "Nothing but Vietnam. Oh, I've tried detective mysteries and Gothic horror, even science fiction, but I always come back to Nam. Always. It's just that none of those god-damn editors in New York are interested."

Cross laughed softly. "No one's interested in Nam. You oughta know that. People wanna read shit by Jerry Rubin or Abby Hoffman."

"Or Norman Mailer," the MP said.

"Too bad the guy sold out," one of the patrons spoke up, shaking his head. "He used to be one of the good ones."

"Books are for saps," Cross muttered into his beer.

"Books are my life," the MP intoned. "I'll always be writing them. They keep me alive. I won't stop until I've finished one book for each day I spent in the Pearl of the Orient."

"Crazy," someone muttered.

"Go back as a civilian," someone else suggested. "You could clean latrines or something."

"Life without love and war," the MP said, "sex and violence in the tropics is insipid, cancerous in comparison," he went on, blocking them all out, listening only to his memories. "How can I explain to you? How can I possibly try to convey the job satisfaction, the adrenaline rush that came with six days or nights a week, twelve-hour shifts, chasing VC across the rooftops or battling balcony snipers while pinned down in a maze of sleazy back alleys?"

"Oh, brother," Cross mumbled.

"Here I was—this nineteen-year-old kid from a steel-mill town in Colorado, cruising a teeming, steaming metropolis of two or three million potential hostiles, a .45 strapped to my hip, racing down Tu Do or Le Loi or Le Van Duyet in a souped-up gun jeep, answering an MP-needs-help call or robbery-in-progress or possible murder-suicide.''

Cross glanced at the kid with a sudden sense of appreciation. Maybe the guy wasn't just a talker. Maybe he did know the score.

''My partner was a buck sergeant from my home-town. Can you believe that? He taught me to survive not only the Vietcong lurking down every dark street, but the ladies of questionable virtue waiting to pounce from the shadows of cheap bars and down-and-dirty strip joints.''

''You're truly destined for literary excellence,'' a nearby vet muttered sarcastically.

''My partner was a great training officer. Hell, we were Matt Dillons patrolling the toughest beat in the world, and damn fucking proud of it. Do you know, he felt an MP wasn't out there doing his job if he didn't come off his shift drenched in blood from the last bar brawl before end-of-watch?''

''I can imagine.'' The guy had Cross's full attention now.

''Shit, we'd wear those bloody fatigues on night shift or khakis on day shift like a badge of honor. You'd make your appearance just before going off duty, listening to the desk sergeant or provost marshal briefing the troops on the latest threat from Uncle Ho's boys or which whorehouse the medics were requesting we crack down on or whatever, then hop onto the back of a motor scooter or jump in a cyclo and cruise on down to your favorite whore, feeling good about the heat of the city, the perfume flower stalls, the smell of boiling noodles and ginseng soup mingling with the ripe stench of the waterfront.

"Working cover shift and getting off around midnight was best, of course. You could race home under an orange crescent moon and watch the countless formations of flares drift across Saigon, the aroma of shrimp and noodles drifting out from endless all-night sidewalk cafés. The stink of dead bodies would drift up from the banks of the Saigon River, mingled with the weirdly invigorating smell of joss smoke everywhere as you passed below the dragon spires into your housing project off Thanh Mau Street, smiling at the teenage militiaman who saluted you because he was impressed by your legendary paycheck, not the arm band. Even an enlisted man could live like a king in South Vietnam, my friends.

"You'd remove your web belt, slide it over one shoulder and make a mental note not to let your whore sleep on your right arm so you'd have it handy in case of emergencies—because anything could happen in the City of Sorrows. Then you'd slip off your jungle boots at the third-floor stairwell, and your woman would meet you at the door and help you remove your shirt, fatigue trousers and olive drab GI shorts. She'd drape you in a red silk robe emblazoned with a golden dragon, then sit you before a rice cooker and stuff you with its delights.

"After dinner, she'd give you an hour-long massage, walking on your back until you reached the edge of dreamland. Then she'd coax you into a dozen different exotic positions for two hours of the most intense lovemaking a guy could ever want. And finally, naked together, side by side on the blue satin sheets you'd rest as the ceiling fan twirled slowly overhead. Still unable to sleep, you'd snuggle against your woman's warm curves, immersing yourself in the flowerlike fragrance of her silky, midnight blue hair, the strands falling below her shoulders, framing the contours of her breasts in jet black. Far away you'd hear Phantom jets racing their engines at Tan Son Nhut as heat lightning rolled over the land in the distance, mingling with the nearby rumble of outgoing artillery.

"Then, ever so gently, you'd place your ear against her breast and listen to her racing heart, wondering what she was dreaming about, wishing you could join her in those dreams, knowing you couldn't. And, lying there, you'd feel passion for this city girl with the smooth-soled feet, she, your Saigon city girl, whom none could compare with, just like the city, this town without pity, the city of pain and ecstasy packed tighter than a rucksack and ready to explode with the force of a claymore.

"That's why every second with her was so precious, why you were unable to sleep despite twelve hours working the street and all the lovemaking and food that followed. The intensity that was Saigon made all other cities of the world as boring as Des Moines.

"You didn't want to fall asleep, for fear it would be over too soon. You'd rather lie awake against her breast, listening to her heart race as the VC chased her, your GI whore, through nightmares that brought stress lines to her high cheekbones as she threw her head back in silent cries of terror, the skin along her throat tight as tears welled up along the edges of your own eyes, rolled down your cheeks as you cried quietly for this godforsaken place that had become your refuge from the games and phoniness and insanity of life in America.

"Relief flooding you as her nightmare ended and she whispered your name, you'd hold her close, feeling her breasts, her thighs, firm and strong from a childhood spent squatting instead of sitting. Thighs that put her Western counterparts to shame, thighs that were magical in their ability to squeeze the guilt from a man, purge his pain, raise him above his troubles, propel him above the war and make him forget the woman an ocean away who'd sent him letters proclaiming their engagement dead."

"Hey, I can sympathize with *that*," a nearby vet said, nodding solemnly as bad memories returned to haunt half the men in the Blue Bamboo. But the MP didn't seem to hear, or care. His eyes had misted over long ago as he stared into a reflection behind the bartender, a ghostly version of a man he no longer recognized as himself.

"This Saigon city girl who didn't care about a car or a house or money in the bank," he continued, "but only wanted her man home at night, in her arms, sharing her dreams beneath the slowly twirling ceiling fan as golden flares floated past the balcony railing outside and rats raced across the rooftops."

"Give this kid another pitcher of beer on me," Cross cut in. "I don't want him to stop."

The kid didn't. "And you'd listen to the jets taking off seven miles away, kicking in their afterburners, unleashing sonic booms to roll across the land, rattling the windowpanes, knocking cockroaches and lizards off the walls. And then the eerie Saigon silence would close in—eerie, for there was never really silence in Saigon at night, not even with the curfew. There were always the sounds of war and the noise of soldiers preparing for it, praying for it, dreading it.

"The building would rock as a bomb went off somewhere down the block, and the woman in your arms would hug you tighter and you'd move ever so softly, so slowly, checking to make sure she was still sleeping, that the sounds wouldn't turn her dreams back into nightmares.

"Your eyes half-open, you'd realize, as you anticipated the mournful wail of the air raid siren, waiting for the solitary VC rocket to come crashing down on your rooftop, that your Saigon hooker had heard those same sounds all her life. You'd realize she was the real veteran. Not you, not anyone else you knew, but her."

"There it is," Cross agreed.

"Most definitely," a nearby vet added with glazed eyes.

"Do you know how many times I've responded to a Ten-39 call where Vietnamese women placed a grenade between their breasts and held on tight to their sleeping American GI boyfriend when they discovered he was about to leave Saigon for the Land of the Big PX and round-eyed blondes?" the MP asked without taking a breath. "It happened, pal. More times than I care to recall.

"My favorite shift with the six-to-six downtown goon platoon. You saw everything. There was no such thing as 'routine patrol' in Saigon during Tet. The South Vietnamese were desperate. I was so naive. I had no idea. And yet I didn't really worry about the country's fate, or the world's for that matter. I was convinced our government would always be there for the South no matter how bad things got. After all, LBJ promised Nguyen Van Thieu, didn't he?

"All that mattered, at first, was the brotherhood of the badge. The gun and the street. The Military Police Corps was my world, my life. Until she came along. And then racing through the night in search of robbers and rapists and the sleazy side-street denizens of Saigon's underworld no longer seemed so important.

"Watching the tracer light show from her apartment balcony became preferable to seeing the flash of discharges from behind the shattered windshield of a gun jeep under enemy ambush. The adrenaline rush of a high-speed chase through Cholon or Gia Dinh was replaced by orgasms and the countless ways she could show you to capture them."

"Take that man's beer away," Cross said, issuing a mock order as half the men at the bar seemed to sober suddenly at the MP's words.

"After all, we'd given our most vulnerable years to Vietnam, hadn't we?" the guy continued. "Explorers to those shores long before even the French had written in their journals of having been bewitched by the tears of Oriental witches with dark almond eyes and silky hair so radiant and jet black as to appear blue in moonlight.

"We've always tried to bury our Vietnam experiences beneath the boring facades or everyday life lest the phonies in our midst accuse us of living in the past. But I've learned that all men experience only one or two truly important events in their lifetimes—and all other facets of their future are formed or affected in some way by that experience. All their war stories return to that unforgettable prologue.

"The short time I spent in Vietnam was the most intense period of my life. Now I've come to accept that Vietnam is my legacy and, for that, I have no apologies."

Cross cocked an eyebrow at him. "No apologies?"

"None whatsoever."

"Glad to hear it." He extended a hand. "Cross is the name. Ben Cross, Fifth Special Forces, A-410 outta Four Corps."

"Thornton. Jeff Thornton. Just a Rear-Echelon Motherfucker from Saigon—716 MPs, to be precise."

"So, are you finished?" Cross took a deep breath. "About the girl, I mean."

"I'm finished," the MP said, nodding slowly.

"Then I take it that means you're going back someday to look for her."

"Yeah, someday."

"Sounds like she was quite a gal."

"She . . . yeah, she certainly was."

"Then I think we should drink a toast to her, pal."

"Yeah . . . yeah, we should, bud."

"What was her name?"

"Mai."

"Mai . . ."

"Or Kim."

"Kim?"

"Or Khanh, or Tamminh. What does it matter? They were all so beautiful."

"Yeah, beautiful..."

"Righteous." The MP lifted his empty mug.

"To Miss Saigon," Cross proclaimed, raising his mug of beer toward the others until a bell-like, clinking sound filled the Blue Bamboo.

"To Miss Saigon!" they all chanted.

5

TAN CHAU
CAMBODIAN BORDER

North Vietnamese General Ho Van Tho pounded the tabletop with a clenched fist, then shook an extended forefinger at the South Vietnamese MP captain, who was clad only in baggy white shorts and handcuffed to a chair in front of him and General Sherwood. "You dare jeopardize these prisoner negotiations for purely personal reasons?"

An ARVN interrogator translated Tho's excellent English into Vietnamese for the detainee. Tho enjoyed impressing American officers with his ability to speak more than passable English. He'd spent six years at West Point in the mid-forties when his cousin, Ho Chi Minh, was assisting United States OSS agents in the mountains overlooking Hanoi. That was back when the Americans considered Ho Chi Minh an ally, of course. Now things...circumstances, had changed drastically.

"Was Colonel Quoc behind this brazen display of stupidity?" Tho demanded, again pounding the tabletop.

The MP captain remained silent.

"Was Quoc out there this morning, among that caravan of gun jeeps?"

Again the captain, whose name was Nguyen, remained silent.

The ARVN interrogator lunged forward and slammed a rubber truncheon filled with lead against Nguyen's nose. The QC captain's head flew back as if he'd been struck by a baseball bat. Blood sprayed across the wall behind him, and a policewoman in khaki sidestepped it before she was hit by the crimson drops.

"I don't think that's necessary, soldier," Sherwood said, shaking his head in disgust as he glared at the interrogator.

General Tho smiled. "You don't understand these QCs or Quoc. They're ruthless, General. They're trained like attack dogs. This slap in the face means nothing to him. A punch to the solar plexus—" Tho reached forward, delivering a devastating blow to the captain's chest that sent the wind rushing from his lungs and made his eyes bulge "—only tickles the bastards. Is that the correct word—tickles?"

"I hardly think so," Tate piped up.

"You may be right." Tho produced an ear-to-ear grin. "Perhaps I meant something else." He reached forward again, rising from his own chair, and grabbed the QC captain's hair. With a blinding maneuver he rammed the MP's face on top of his knee, which he'd brought up with crushing force.

Both Sherwood and Tate could hear bone cracking, and a trickle of blood began streaking the prisoner's white shorts.

"I know nothing," the MP captain muttered.

Tho frowned. "You knew enough to pilot that plane all the way out here from Saigon, or wherever you stole it, and buzz our prisoner exchange ceremony this morning."

"It was an accident," the captain mumbled, blood bubbling between his lips. "I . . . got lost."

Tho laughed harshly. "Accident? Just like this, perhaps." He made as if to sit down, but delivered a grazing side kick to the prisoner's temple instead. Nguyen flopped over sideways and struck the floor, taking the chair with him.

"General, this is getting us nowhere," Sherwood protested.

"Excuse me," Tho apologized with mock sincerity. "Sometimes I get carried away." He helped the guard right the chair and lift their prisoner back up into it. "Get some straps," he directed in Vietnamese to two nearby guards. "Tie him to the chair, elbows pulled slightly back."

Tho dropped to one knee and moved to within inches of the prisoner. Gently he took Nguyen's chin and lifted his face until they were nose to nose. "The other pilot," he said softly. "Who was the officer flying the Mohawk?"

The Mohawk pilot's face had been smashed beyond recognition, and there was no name tag on the uniform or dog tags on the body.

"What Mohawk?" Nguyen asked without expression.

"Hmm. So you have a sense of humor. Such a talent should be rewarded." Tho threw his head back in wicked laughter, and Sherwood and Tate tensed, sensing another sudden physical assault on the prisoner. None came, however.

"It has come to my attention," Tho began, "that your leader, Colonel Quoc, fears a drop in his profit potential should this nasty war between Vietnam and America come to a halt.

"Between *North* Vietnam and America," Nguyen rasped as he slowly raised his swollen face and locked eyes with Tho. In brazen defiance he spit blood at the NVA officer.

"Ah, yes." Tho produced a white handkerchief from within his brown tunic and wiped the bloody spittle clinging to his cheek. "They warned me that Quoc's officers were a tough lot. Well, we shall see. We shall see...."

"I won't tell you anything," Nguyen said. "So you might as well kill me now. I'd rather die on South Vietnamese soil."

"I wouldn't waste the effort it would take to have you transported north," Tho assured him. "But these games Quoc and his boys are playing must come to a complete halt, young man. You must see beyond your close-minded shroud to the bigger picture—the *world* scene. What happens here along the border between puny Cambodia and inconsequential Vietnam could have earthshaking ramifications. Do you understand?"

"I understand enough to know when a donkey is passing gas," Nguyen said.

Tho lashed out again, bruising his own knuckles as he struck Nguyen's brow with enough force to snap the man's head back.

"Sir, I protest this treatment," Tate said, getting to his feet in a hurry. His words were directed to Sherwood, while his glare burned into Tho.

The American general waved a hand at Tate calmly. "Sit down, Captain. This doesn't concern us as much as you might think it does."

"It concerns me, sir, when I see one of our allies being beaten by an enemy," Tate insisted.

"And right in front of us, for Christ's sake," Nordheim added, gritting his teeth.

"I don't care what the son of a bitch has done," Tate said, indicating Nguyen. "It isn't right for us to stand around here with our thumbs up our butts while Uncle Ho slaps this MP around."

"That'll be enough, *Captain*," Sherwood rumbled.

"*You*," Tate growled, pointing at Tho, "knock it off."

Sherwood inhaled loudly but said nothing. Nordheim and the rest of the men exhaled with just as much noise. Tension filled the room, making the atmosphere seemingly unbearable. But Tho merely nodded.

"Please excuse my rather overenthusiastic response to this man's disrespectful display of insolence," the North Vietnamese officer said, enunciating his words carefully.

"I think it's time I cracked open my fucking pocket dictionary," Jefferson muttered under his breath to his fellow medic, Jeb Stuart.

"Knock it off!" Dillon warned them.

"I'm sure you wouldn't have been able to restrain yourself, either," Tho told Tate and Nordheim, "if one of my men spit in *your* face."

"So what's the story on this guy?" Nordheim asked, motioning toward Nguyen as he spoke to the NVA officer in spite of Sherwood's growing frown. "When do we transfer him to Saigon?" His tone told Tho there was no other option.

"He goes north as soon as possible," Tho decided, contradicting his earlier comment about Nguyen not being worth the trouble.

"Bullshit," Tate said.

"Captain—" Sherwood began.

"Sir," Nordheim interrupted, "the purpose of this fiasco today was to swap POWs, but now you're letting them add another prisoner to their roster of booty."

"Yeah, what about that, General?" Brogan butted in, demonstrating the rash pugnacity he was semi-famous for.

"Speaking of POWs," Dillon interjected, folding his arms across his chest, "what's the word on those guys you were all going to swap on the bridge this morning?"

Sherwood glared at Brogan, filing his face away for future reference. Then he looked at the master sergeant. "Our people sank back into the shadows when the shooting started, their catch in tow."

"And my comrades retreated back into the bamboo, as well," Tho revealed, "as soon as it was evident you Americans had set up some sort of trap."

"It wasn't a trap, General," Sherwood snapped. "You know that. This Quoc bastard is a loose cannon. Otherwise I wouldn't have invited you aboard my chopper when we went out hunting for the Sky-raider."

"I'll give you credit for that, but—"

As Tho was engaging in the verbal sparring he enjoyed so much, Nguyen rose to his feet, the chair still strapped to his back and elbows. Leaning hard to his left, he kicked out with his right heel at Tho.

The QC's foot caught Tho in the chin, and he went down like a water buffalo blasted by an elephant gun. Instantly Sherwood lunged forward and kicked Nguyen's feet out from under him. The NVA guards in the doorway rushed forward, AK-47s bristling with bayonets. More guards rushed in from outside.

Slowly Tho rose to his knees and massaged his jaw. None of the Americans made a move to assist the NVA general. Neither did his own guards. They kept their rifles trained on Nguyen and the Americans, expecting some type of diversionary tactic. Tho slowly raised a hand, waving them back, silently ordering restraint.

Tate glanced around the room. They were packed into the room like sardines, with three open doorways. Those on the side led to small porchlike platforms with steps leading down to clearings along the riverbank in which jeeps and V-100 assault tanks were idling with clouds of smoke collecting between tailpipes. The rear doorway led to a wooden plank stairwell that dropped into the river itself and led to an old, sunken, termite-infested pier where several camouflaged sampans were tethered. They reminded Tate of stoop-backed burros tied to a hitching post.

Nordheim was the first to flip the selector mechanism on his M-16 to auto. Then Tho issued a directive in muffled Vietnamese, but his men didn't seem to hear. They failed to lower their carbines. Brogan and the others slowly brought up their own rifles until both

Americans and Vietnamese were looking down the flash suppressors of each other's weapons.

It was a standoff, and nobody involved liked the look of it. But it was too late to turn back now.

"Mr. Nguyen here ain't goin' nowhere, General Pinko," Brogan announced. He met Sherwood's glare. "Sorry, sir..."

"But we ain't about to let the Commies take Nguyen for a ride north, General," Bolecki said. "He might have acted irresponsibly today, and downright illegal in fact, but he didn't zap anyone when he could—"

"Put a lid on it, Sergeant," Sherwood ordered.

"Yes, sir."

The American general reached down and helped Tho up. "You'll have to forgive my men, General. They're young and—"

"They know not the ways of peace pipes and diplomacy, eh?" Tho forced a laugh as Tate assisted Sherwood, resisting the urge to deliver an "accidental" swinging elbow to the NVA officer's jaw.

Tho seemed to have regained his senses. He brushed himself off and stared long and hard at Nguyen, whose eyes burned back, refusing to glance away. "Perhaps something accommodating can be arranged," he said at last. "Since we are, after all, *south* of the border."

"I'll make sure Nguyen here gets an armed escort to Chi Hoa Prison in Saigon for interrogation," Sherwood assured him. "Right, Captain?"

Tate nodded. "My men'll take care of it, sir."

Without warning, the room filled with powdered sugarcane and splintered bamboo as numerous bursts of red and orange tracers ripped through all four walls of the building along the roofline. Everyone inside dropped to the floor. Nordheim flipped Nguyen's chair over on the way down, but none of the bullets from outside dropped to chest or even head level.

Tate rolled toward one of the side doors and glanced out into the furious activity taking place near the parked gun jeeps. The sentries they'd left posted outside—both South Vietnamese and NVA—were scrambling for cover as a superior force converged on the tiny border outpost.

The renegade ARVN MP leader, Colonel Quoc, had returned with over a hundred of his men, and they were ready to kick ass.

6

BLUE BAMBOO BAR
TERRE HAUTE, INDIANA

Ben Cross sat at his usual corner table, back to the wall, and began working on his seventh beer. He'd stopped sitting at the counter. The dancers had proven too hard to resist, the Cambodian one especially. There was something mesmerizing about her. She seemed to seek him out whenever the dancers came out onstage and climbed onto the counter.

Cross wasn't ready for a woman, not even a Khmer whore, which he was sure she was. She'd probably married some CIA agent in Phnom Penh, he decided, and ditched the son of a bitch as soon as she'd made it to the Land of the Big PX.

Still, there was something innocent about her, something special in her look, the way she carried herself, even when she was naked. Perhaps it was the exotic cast to her features, or the sophisticated way her hips moved, the submissive curl to her lips when she blew a kiss across the room to him.

One night he waited outside in his car until nearly four in the morning. Parked across the street and halfway down the block, he waited and watched, lying low for the Khmer whore. Just waiting and watching—not in ambush, but curious, wanting to see whom she went home with, what kind of car she drove, or he drove. Wanting to see the man who would be between her legs in thirty minutes.

Wearing an ankle-length trench coat the color of red Cambodian mud, she exited the Blue Bamboo alone and walked uphill several blocks until she came to the library. And there, padlocked with a thick chain to the bicycle racks, was a small three-speed bike. Glancing around before concentrating on the combination lock, she mounted the bike and pedaled uphill another ten blocks before disappearing down a side alley.

Headlights out, he followed her, cutting the engine upon entering the alleyway and coasting down behind a bowling alley and supermarket into a housing project, nearly knocking over a row of trash cans before he spotted her by the light of an orange crescent moon.

He swerved behind an abandoned bus with flat tires and multicolored flowers painted all over it before she could spot him. There he lit up a cigarette and, feeling like an underpaid undercover cop, watched her dismount with casual ease, walk the bike up to a deteriorating cinder-block duplex and park it inside a shed. The same padlock she'd used earlier on the chain she now used to secure the shed door.

He watched her walk up an outdoor stairway to an attic perched atop the building. She was inside for several minutes before a single dim bulb began burning inside.

He focused his binoculars on the windows, but could see nothing for quite some time. Finally the light was extinguished, but he didn't start the car up. A moment later she drew the drapes back and stood in the narrow window, naked from the waist up, her breasts jutting out, proud and flawless.

He felt suddenly aroused but, even more, curious, as she worked at opening the windows. He slid down a few more inches in the front seat of the car and refocused the binoculars again, spotting the tiny wisp of incense floating out from the attic for the first time.

She leaned out onto the slanting roof and placed a joss stick on a small altar bearing a porcelain Buddha, brought clasped hands to her forehead and bowed in Cross's direction. The predawn chill forced her nipples taut and erect.

He wondered if, in her odd sense of wisdom, she knew he was down there in the half light, watching, waiting....

Eventually she finished her silent prayers. As she closed the window and vanished in the gloom, his erection subsided and, a few minutes later, he started the car and drove off, thinking about her smile and the way her lips curled out away from her teeth when she blew a kiss across the bar to him.

ONE OF HO VAN THO'S lieutenants jabbed Tate with an AK-47 as tracers danced across the floor between them.

"What d'you think you're doing?" the SF captain demanded, slapping the rifle away.

"Those bastards out there are shooting at *all* of us!" Nordheim cried out. He switched to his best pidgin Vietnamese and repeated the exclamation for the Communist cadre, but the NVA seemed convinced Tate and his men were somehow in on the surprise assault.

Tho himself scratched at the wisp of gray hair below his chin. "I'm almost beginning to wonder myself," he said, staring through Tate as another burst of shells roared in from Quoc's hidden ranks outside. His glare turned into outright anger. In Vietnamese he ordered, "Relieve the Americans of their weapons! *All* of them!"

Nordheim whirled. "No way!" He knew enough of the local lingo to realize their numbers were nearly up. The NVA lieutenant's AK-47 erupted with a 3-shot burst, but all the rounds flew several inches over the American lieutenant's head, and he responded with a single shot to his opponent's face that tore the man's lower jaw away.

The young NVA officer dropped onto his back, arms and legs jerking spasmodically, bulging eyes unblinking as they stared up at the ceiling, suddenly lifeless.

Tate threw a wild roundhouse punch that knocked Tho off his feet. "Sorry about that, General," he muttered, "but you should've rescinded the order."

"What a chump," General Sherwood said as he crouched beside one of the side doors, his .45 automatic drawn again. He was referring to Tho. On either side of him North Vietnamese soldiers stood or crouched or wavered on one knee, wide-eyed, unsure what to do next.

"Grab Nguyen's webgear over there and see if he was carrying any handcuffs," Tate directed. "Or a handcuff key at least. We'll need to get that pair off his wrists, too."

"Then we can use the ones he's wearing," Nordheim said, nodding.

"For what?" Brogan asked.

"To cuff ol' Ho Van Tho there," Nordheim replied.

Brogan frowned. "I knew that." He moved sideways through dancing ricochets, leaned out the side door opposite Sherwood and cut loose with a 20-round blast from his M-16 on full-auto. The return fire from outside only seemed to double.

"Got it!" Frank Jefferson held up a rusty handcuff key. "No cuffs, though."

Nordheim grabbed the key. "Never mind that." Within seconds he had the handcuffs off Nguyen and on Tho's wrists.

"Sorry, sir," he said, his words soaked with sarcasm as he stared down at the NVA general. Nordheim then turned and gauged the expression of the Communist soldiers crammed into the small building. They were all young and inexperienced, for the most part, yet somehow they'd sensed their commanding officer had acted irresponsibly when he turned on Sherwood and his men. The hostile force outside was obviously gunning for everyone inside the building. The bullets weren't discriminating today. A few NVA kept their muzzles pointed in the Americans' direction, of course, but they were too petrified to shoot first.

Tate was breathing hard and counting his blessings. The situation inside the building could have exploded into a close-quarters gunfight that would have resulted in a mutual massacre. As it stood now, all they had to worry about was whether or not Quoc seriously intended to continue his assault until he'd cleaned out their makeshift lair. The QC colonel had directed his MPs to lower their aim on the bullet-riddled building, and its occupants were now pressed flat against the floor. Overhead the tin roof, layered with straw thatch, was smoldering where a few tracers had started small fires.

Tate glanced over his shoulder at Sherwood in between bursts from a 20-round clip. "Any suggestions?"

"Lieutenant!" Sherwood yelled across the room at Nordheim.

"Sir?"

"You speak passable Vietnamese?"

"Passable's a good word for it, sir," Nordheim replied, leaning out the back door. He surveyed the river below, decided none of Quoc's men was lurking out there, then rolled toward one of the side doors crowded with NVA and began firing single shots at muzzle-flashes in the distant tree line. "With Vietnamese," he said calmly between discharges, "you've gotta worry about pronunciation. The same word can have five different meanings, depending on how you accent the damn thing, where you *place* the accents, I should say."

"Never mind all that superfluous crap!" Sherwood growled. "Just tell those NVA bastards huddled around you, and the ones by me here, too, to grab some free space by either doorway and start firing at Quoc's positions. I don't care what they aim at, or even if they aim! Just have them point their damn AKs toward that firepower out there and start pulling triggers!"

"Yes, sir!"

"I want Quoc to know we've got a sizable force in here—and that we mean business!"

"Right, sir!"

Nordheim had only uttered a few words before the North Vietnamese soldiers got the message. They crowded the doorways and began unleashing long 30-round bursts from their banana clips.

The firing went on for a good two or three solid minutes before it tapered down to sporadic shooting—and one-sided at that. Nordheim and Tate noticed at the same time that no more incoming rounds were making shards of sugarcane float through the air.

"Cease fire!" Nordheim called out in Vietnamese.

Still bitter that their commander had been cold-cocked, a few of the Communists failed to respond immediately out of sheer principle. They popped off a dozen or so more shots before eventually lowering their rifles and fixing cold glares on the American lieutenant.

Finally an eerie silence settled over the small border encampment, eerie because no birds chirped and no monkeys chattered.

"Half the damn rain forest's probably gone deaf," Tate decided, surveying the perimeter through the ground-clinging blanket of gun smoke.

"I demand you release me!"

Sherwood stared long and hard at Tho. "What do you think, Tate?"

"I say feed his ass to the tigers out there."

"The tigers are probably shell-shocked," Sherwood said, producing a light, uncharacteristic chuckle. "Shell-shocked and shit faced."

"I *demand* you let me go!" Tho insisted.

"All in good time, my friend," Sherwood said, scratching the stubble on his chin. "All in good time."

"You're jeopardizing the entire peace process, what little progress our two sides had made before Quoc and his band of cutthroats came along!"

"I think I should take you into protective custody," Sherwood threatened. "You're hotheaded and trigger-happy and a danger to your own men."

"And you're a fool!" Tho snapped, jutting his chin out at the American general.

"Maybe," Sherwood said, nodding, "But I kinda doubt it, chump."

Tate and Nordheim stared at Tho's men. They'd all lowered their weapons, the fight drained from them. Nordheim was translating the verbal exchange, but most of them didn't seem interested. They all had the thousand-yard stare, as if they'd been humping the boonies for the past six months, dragging hundred-pound rucks down the Ho Chi Minh Trail perhaps. They weren't in the mood for anything right now. Not for Tho, and not for Sherwood. Tate had seen the look before: what these men needed was a three-day R and R in Saigon, sucking tit and letting moist ladies of questionable virtue sit on their faces.

"I'll tell you what I'm gonna do," Sherwood told Tho. "You call in your boys from the jungle out there—the ones who've got our POWs stashed deep in the bamboo—and I'll consider this clusterfuck history. We can start all over again from step one."

"Never!" Tho shouted.

"Suit yourself," Sherwood said as he ejected the spent magazine from his .45, inserted a fresh clip and flipped the slide's safety lever down so that a hot round was slammed forward into the chamber. He walked over to Tho and placed the barrel against the NVA general's temple. "Then I guess it's happy trails for you. Nice knowin' ya."

"Wait," Tho gasped.

"I'm waiting, General, but I've gotta warn you. I'm short on patience today and my finger's itchy."

"I can't guarantee anything," Tho said, choosing his words carefully.

"And I understand that," Sherwood said, flipping the thumb safety up and holstering his weapon. "Now, mister, how about you sweet-talk me real good?"

"Take off these handcuffs, release me and my men—"

"Your men are free to go," Sherwood interrupted, waving at them. "Hell, are you blind, man? They've still got their weapons. And I'd say they're a bit perturbed at you."

"Then what do you suggest?"

"Beat feet out there into the rain forest and have a talk with your junior officer, Major Mot or whatever. Tell him what a nice guy I am. Tell him I want my POWs as originally scheduled."

"And the NVA agents you were going to trade for them?"

"I'll get their butts back over here most expeditiously, believe me!" Sherwood took the handcuff key from Tate and released Tho from the iron bracelets.

"I'll see what I can do," the NVA general said.

Sherwood grinned. "It'll be to both our benefits."

"I'm sure it will."

"We should *all* just be glad no news media maggots got wind of any of this," Tate said. "We were damn lucky."

"I think those two clowns from network TV are still over at the Spad crash site," Nordheim added.

"Not many photojournalists out this close to the Cambodian border," Tho said, chuckling, but he wasn't smiling as Dillon and Brogan helped him to his feet. "Am I free to go now?"

"Be my guest," Sherwood said, waving him slowly toward the open doorway.

"I'll be back."

"I'm sure you will."

Tho paused halfway across the room. His eyes scanned the bodies at their feet, coming to rest on a dead youth.

"We'll have some men body-bag your dead and airlift them over to—" Sherwood began despite the glares of contempt from Brogan and the other sergeants.

"Permit me to see to this one...personally," Tho said slowly, extreme pain evident in his tone. "My wife...his mother...wouldn't forgive me if I left him to foreigners."

Tate and the others watched in silence as Tho lifted his dead son into his arms, stumbled down the teak steps and walked, step by agonizing step, through the mist and swirling gun smoke until he disappeared into the shimmering stalks of bamboo.

7

BLUE BAMBOO BAR
TERRE HAUTE, INDIANA

"I lived in Thailand for two years before coming to America," she told Ben Cross. Her name was Dawn.

"In the refugee camps?" he asked, sipping slowly at his beer, his eyes darting now and then to the giant black-and-white TV mounted over the bar. Its sound was turned off, but the images were of the war in Vietnam, an entire world away.

"No." Her dark eyes looked into her coffee cup. "My husband was in the Cambodian army. His unit fled into Thailand and we were jailed as illegals."

"I don't understand."

"I left him. He was a coward. Most of the men in his unit were. I became friendly with one of our guards—a Thai policeman. Eventually I got out of the detention center."

You prostituted yourself for freedom, Cross thought, but he said nothing.

"The Thai policeman was working until midnight. I sweet-talked him, and he gave me his address and key, let me out a back gate. I flagged down a bus, paid my fair, told the driver where to take me. He told me he'd meet me there in a couple of hours. I suppose he expected a good time."

"And so how many months did you live with him?"

"I didn't."

"Oh?" Their eyes met.

"I went into his bungalow, tore up all the floorboards until I found his life savings, then left with his portable TV set and anything else of value I could get my hands on."

You're a thief, too, Cross thought. A whore and a thief. Probably a liar, too. And yet why was he so attracted to her? "You've got *cojones*...for a woman."

"I sold the TV on the black market and hired a scooter driver to take me south."

"Across the border into Malaysia?"

"No. Sattahip, a little place south of Pattaya called Kilo Sip Et."

"Kilometer Eleven," he translated, recognizing the Thai way of identifying villages in the southern provinces.

She was obviously surprised. "You've been there?"

"A short TDY at Utapao," he replied. "Nothing much."

"Utapao," she echoed. "It sounds—"

"Where they launch the B-52s from to bomb Vietnam."

"Ah, yes."

"Great place to visit with its first-class USO and all, but I wouldn't want to—"

"Kilo Sip Et was nice. Bungalows on stilts, half on the beach, half submerged in the coral reef of the South China Sea. Very cheap. I made money...." She hesitated. "Sewing fishing nets for the Thais and peddling T-shirts to the tourists. I caught my own fish for meals. Just fish and sugarcane. It was paradise while it lasted.''

"Paradise," he repeated softly. "You're pretty damn fluent for a bar dancer."

"I read a lot," she said coldly, her smile fading.

"What's your real name?" he asked, reaching for the Vietnamese-style brewing contraption and pouring her some more potent coffee.

"Dawn."

"Your Cambodian name."

"Dawn," she repeated.

"Come on," he insisted.

"At Kilo Sip Et I'd wake up every morning with the sun, row out a mile or two in my little dinghy, then fish until my shoulders burned. Sometimes I'd go to sleep at five o'clock in the afternoon, or three in the morning. But I always awoke at dawn. When I first heard the term, I fell in love with it. It just sounded right— like part of me. And so it became my name. Can we leave it at that?" She locked eyes with him again.

"I was just wondering what name your parents gave you."

"My parents were killed when I was one. I don't remember them at all. As a child I was shuffled from relative to relative until most of them were killed off by the wars. Always wars . . ." Her face became grim. "You . . . *men* and your games."

"Yeah," he said, nodding in resignation as he stirred the rich cream at the bottom of her coffee cup. "It's what keeps the globe rotating, I guess. War and money and power and sex."

"I've forgotten much about my life in Cambodia. I'm still trying to forget the arranged marriage to that soldier who turned tail and ran when the Communists surrounded our ville."

"And so you eventually made it across the pond to the Land of the Big PX," Cross said, suddenly no longer feeling sympathetic.

"It was easy," she said, unmasked pride molding her dark features. "With the right amount of cash a person can acquire just about any sort of document or papers to travel wherever they want. Corruption is everywhere, you know."

"You sound bitter."

"I am. And now I'm trying to forget about it." She turned and looked up into his eyes once again, then took hold of his chin. "Why is it all you . . . *vets* always want to know about the past lives of little worthless Oriental girls like me?"

She'd posed the question with such a matter-of-fact lack of emotion that Cross was taken aback. "I was just—"

"Isn't it enough that we find you attractive and want to gift you with a night spent holding our exotic little dark-skinned bodies?"

"What?" he said, laughing aloud again, then glanced away, suddenly nervous.

"Come home with me tonight, Ben Cross," Dawn said, running her long amber fingers through the hair on his forearm.

"But—"

"In Cambodia the Green Berets called us LBFMs," she told him boasting.

"What?" he asked, even though he was quite familiar with the term.

"Little Brown Fucking Machines," she explained.

"Oh..."

"At first the title offended me, but then I realized it was true. I like to go to bed with foreign men. Foreign men with big, long..."

Dawn's challenge tapered off as a waitress making the rounds stopped at their table to ask Cross if he wanted another beer. She had almond eyes and a golden tan, but Cross knew she was Hawaiian from an earlier conversation they'd had. "Another one?" she asked him.

"Sure," he answered with a tight grin.

"Aren't you dancing tonight?" the waitress asked Dawn with a wink.

"Night off," the Cambodian replied.

"You?" the Hawaiian woman said, snickering. "But *you* never take a night off, honey. Who are you trying to kid?" Her eyes shifted, and she stared through Cross. "Be nice to her," she taunted. "Dawn's a cherry girl, you know. Not many... *new* girls left here in Terre Haute, not many who hang around the Blue Bamboo, anyway."

Cross nodded slightly. He knew "new" girl meant "virgin" to the streetwalkers of Saigon and wondered where the Honolulu native had picked up the term.

"You should be up there flapping your tits for the customers," the waitress said.

"Come home with me, Ben Cross," Dawn said, taking his hand and leading him from the table.

"Have fun, honey," the waitress jeered, chuckling softly, trying to lock eyes with Cross. "He looks like a live one."

TATE AND NORDHEIM stared at the slowly rotating chopper blades of the Huey parked on a helipad fifty yards away. The craft's turbine began to whine, and as the pilot pulled pitch, the rotors began whirling with double intensity. The helicopter rose a few feet off the ground. Then its boom tail swung around, the nose dipped slightly and the craft roared off into the purple mists of a tropical dusk.

Andy Crocker slowly waved at the halo of light following the gunship's reflection of bright sunlight.

"Bye-bye, Saigon," Brogan said, frowning. "I know it would have been fun to screw ya'."

"Sorry, guys," Tate said. He didn't sound sincere. "But duty calls."

"Screw duty," Frank Jefferson muttered. "I was in the mood to make babies tonight."

As Dillon watched the Huey abandon its deceptive halo and disappear into a black wall of approaching storm clouds, he recalled the debriefing they'd squatted through beneath the hot afternoon sun a few hours earlier. Sherwood had told them Quoc was still at large. The QC captain was refusing to talk. NVA General Ho Van Tho hadn't been heard from. And the American POWs were presumably back in their tiger cages in some godforsaken VC tunnel, possibly directly under the feet of Dillon's squad at that very moment! The thought made an irritating queasiness return to the master sergeant's stomach.

Tate had hoped to reward the men's recent efforts with a free chopper ride east into Saigon, but moments before they were to board the First Cav Huey an MP gun jeep with two lieutenants in the back seat had roared up and delivered a rush set of sealed orders for the A-team.

Their R and R would have to wait. Sherwood wanted them back in the sticks before sunrise. One of the corpses from the slaughter at Tan Chau Bridge was no corpse, after all. The NVA private had regained consciousness on his way to a mass grave on the outskirts of the ville, compliments of the Army Corps of Engineers, and had begun talking about defecting. The guy was a regular nightingale and had told his former enemies about the closely guarded river route General Tho was fond of taking whenever he returned to his hidden fortress deep in the Cambodian swamps. The private had also told them that Tho had never planned on releasing the American POWs. In fact, they weren't Americans at all, but East German imposters. Tho only wanted a chance at snatching the high-ranking NVA prisoners the Americans had been willing to trade.

Sherwood wanted Tate's team inserted upstream about fifty klicks. His orders were to get Tho, back dead or alive.

Tate squinted at the papers, rereading them. As he reviewed Sherwood's orders, two Cobra gunships roared in over the tree line and flared into a hover almost directly overhead. A few seconds later three heavily armed Huey gunships, bristling with door hatch 60s and rocket pods, dropped out of the sky and pranged across the helipad's interlaced metal tarmac plates.

"That our ride?" Dillon asked, tugging at a black leather pouch about the size of a lollipop dangling around his neck.

"Looks like it," Nordheim grunted. He waved them toward the choppers. "All aboard who's goin' aboard."

"You mean we've got a choice?" Jefferson cracked.

"Funny man," Tate said, giving the medic a good-natured shove toward the nearest Huey.

Dillon continued to rub at the pouch as he allowed the other men to move out in front of him. The pouch was a good-luck charm presented to him by his wife, a full-blooded Cherokee who still lived back on the reservation. Though he carried a wallet photo of the woman—she had shoulder-length black hair and high cheekbones that gave her pretty face an Asian cast— none of the men could ever remember the master sergeant telling them her name. He always referred to her simply as "his lady."

The pouch contained a deceptively heavy piece of onyxlike stone, which, when removed, was only the size of a small pitted marble. Dillon kept it immersed in some secret "Power potion" his grandfather had prepared for him the week before he'd left for the Army. It contained bits of eagle feathers, wolf fangs, bear claws and diamondback rattlers, or so the old man had claimed. But Dillon considered the stone the pouch's most powerful ingredient, for it was a gift of the gods, a fragment from outer space, a piece of some great falling star that had exploded on the earth less than six years earlier amid great fanfare from the tribal chieftains who claimed they knew it was coming.

Dillon believed the chunk of space rock was vital to his survival. In fact, when combined with the other ingredients of his Cherokee power pouch, it helped him believe he was, if not immortal, at least harder to knock off his feet with mere bullets than the average Special Forces trooper.

"You coming along for the ride or not?"

Nordheim was reaching down out of the chopper hatch now, his grating officer's voice intruding into Dillon's thoughts. The Indian-Irish master sergeant reached up, and Nordheim pulled him in.

Inside the cockpit the Peter_pilot began singing, "Heigh-ho! Heigh-ho! It's off to work we go!"

8

CHONG KHOA RIVER
SOUTHEASTERN CAMBODIA

The moon had risen, and still they hadn't seen any sign of Ho Van Tho or his rumored string of sampans. They were supposed to be making their way up a concealed tributary of the Mekong, but so far the Americans had intercepted nothing more lethal than a traveling family of chimp-sized gibbons that ganged up on Jefferson without warning and had to be scared off with machetes.

"Damn you, Vietnam," Nordheim muttered at the tree line. "Damn you to hell!"

"Say again?"

Tate's voice jabbed at Nordheim like a bayonet against the ribs. He felt himself flush, and was glad it was too dark for anyone to see. "What?" he responded.

"You say something?" Tate asked, lying on his side a couple of yards away.

"Sorry about that."

"Sorry about what?"

"Muttering nonsense to myself." His whisper was so low that he didn't think Tate would be able to hear him.

"You know better than that."

"Yeah, I know."

"Boonies finally gettin' to you, Pete?" the captain asked.

"Yeah, something like that."

"Well," Tate said slowly as he moved closer through the thickening gloom, "before you know it we'll be back in Saigon and—"

A sizzling green tracer burned through the stillness between their faces and impacted against a nearby tree trunk. Half of it disappeared into the rotting bark, the rest exploding with a shower of glowing sparks.

"Jesus!" Nordheim called out as the thundering discharge reached their ears. He rolled away from Tate, seeking cover at a different angle.

"Incoming!" Jeb Stuart called out as two Chicom stick grenades floated end over end through the trees, bouncing along the jungle floor in the group's midst. Like giant crabs, Stuart, Jefferson and Crocker scrambled sideways through a break in the reeds, seeking out depressions in the earth.

Nelson and Mendez sat up, their rifle butts against their hips, brilliant halolike flashes erupting from the muzzles as they returned fire.

Dillon flew through the air between Bolecki and Brogan. He landed roughly on the ground with a loud grunt, and Carbo flattened as much as he could the moment he saw the master sergeant pounce on one of the grenades, punching the other out over a fallen tree where it exploded with muffled intensity.

However, the Chicom pressing against Dillon's sternum failed to detonate.

Tate and Nordheim, frozen for that odd split second when everyone else was watching to see how badly the explosion would tear Dillon to pieces, were both up on one knee now, laying down a side-to-side spray of hot lead in opposite directions until the rest of the team could get their bearings.

"How the hell did they do it?" Brogan muttered to no one in particular. "How the hell did Charlie get behind us like that?"

"Without us knowing!" Nelson said beside him, screaming into his ear as he blasted away at the half-dozen muzzle-flashes less than fifty yards away. He was clearly irate with himself more than anyone else.

"Bastards must've low-crawled all the way up through those reeds there!" Mendez said, gesturing with the barrel of his M-16.

No one heard his words, though. So many bullets were peppering their position that every man's ears were ringing, and it was difficult enough just trying to monitor the advance or retreat of the enemy sappers moving about in the dark tree line.

"Try to keep an eye on the river!" Tate shouted at Nordheim. "I want to know if that sampan caravan floats past while—"

"You've gotta be kidding!" Nordheim said, eyes wide as he ejected a spent ammo magazine and slapped home a fresh clip of twenty white tracers.

"This fiasco might be a diversion!" Tate said. Then a slug slammed into his flak jacket, knocking him backward.

"Christ!" Nordheim rasped, shifting slightly as he switched his selector to auto and unleashed the entire magazine in a blazing horizontal arc. Like twirling baseballs of white-hot light, the tracers smoked through the inky blackness, delivering blinding flashes of death. Several North Vietnamese screamed as the tracers ripped open bellies, tore through throats or cracked foreheads like cantaloupes.

"Rick," Nordheim called out to his captain, "are you okay?"

He dropped beside Tate and was relieved to see the captain's eyes bulging and his chest heaving. Nordheim ran his gun hand over Tate's chest, probing the smoking hole above the SF captain's right breast pocket. The armor plating beneath the fabric had stopped the slug.

"Stuart! Jefferson!" he called to the two medics. "One of you guys get your ass over here!"

"I'm . . . I'm okay," Tate croaked. He was regaining his composure. "It . . . just knocked the wind out of my lungs."

"You're lucky," Nordheim muttered as he ejected another spent clip and rammed home a magazine filled with soft-nosed rounds.

"Lucky, my ass!" Tate sat up and was promptly knocked back down by another chunk of lead flying through the air—this time a ricochet off a nearby boulder. The glowing sliver struck his dog tags—they were taped together to prevent clinking sounds while out in the field—but didn't penetrate the two layers of thin aluminum, perhaps because most of the round's momentum had already been spent before it ricocheted.

"I'm beginning to think you better sit this one out, Cap!" Nordheim said, spotting the jagged hole in the top dog tag immediately. He lifted the set and inspected the bruise swelling over Tate's left nipple. "You're lucky that punch didn't stop your ticker cold!"

"Bullshit!" Tate growled, rolling to his left this time rather than make himself a target again. And just in time—for a burst of green tracers stitched the ground where he'd been lying seconds earlier.

Nordheim rolled to the right, firing off two bursts as he slammed into a tree trunk. Shaken, he tried to sit up but slipped on a root and jerked off a final red tracer that soared skyward, tearing a branch free two hundred feet up.

"LT, you get an eyeball on the bad guys yet?" Dillon yelled.

"Naw. Dozen of 'em in the tree line to your whiskey there, tops."

"Yeah, that's what I figured, too."

"Wanna rush 'em?"

"Wait one."

"Roger." Nordheim saw a roundish shape the size of a football racing toward him beneath the carpet of dead leaves on the jungle floor. The rat bounced off his hip and changed directions, flying off on its hind legs toward Brogan.

"Son of a bitch!" he heard Brogan growl, then saw the flash of a survival knife as the NCO stabbed at the giant rodent, ripping its chest open before flinging it to hissing monkeys waiting eagerly in the trees.

Nordheim chuckled to himself. He couldn't help it. This was insane—an Alice's Wonderland turned deadly. Shaking his head in resignation, he sat up again, brought his rifle butt to his shoulder and began firing off rounds on single-shot every time he spotted an enemy muzzle-flash.

One by one the riflemen hiding in the distant tree line dropped where they crouched or withdrew into the bamboo until only two or three determined snipers were still shooting at the Americans.

"I'm gonna pop a flare!" Jefferson announced.

"No flares!" Tate countered. He was back on his feet now and concealed behind a tree trunk.

"But, Cap!"

"No flares, damn it! Last thing I need is a fucking forest fire or—"

"Too wet for that, Cap!" someone called out.

"Too late!" Jefferson cried before Tate could recognize either voice.

The flare shot up into the triple canopy, arced gently through several branches, missing any and all obstructions, and popped its white parachute. All firing ceased on both sides as the flare drifted down over the battlefield, trailing a silver plume of smoke.

Tate and every man in his squad kept their gun eyes closed, protecting their vision until the flare burned itself out. Shielding the other eye, each man shifted back and forth across the field of fire, picking shapes out, waiting for the captain to fire the first shot.

That was when she appeared—a woman warrior clad in black pajamas and tire-tread sandals, brandishing an AK-47 with fixed bayonet, her hair waist-length and black as coal. She was obviously leading the ragtag band of insurgents who had surprised the Americans. Her features were striking—high cheekbones and flaring eyes more round than narrowed. There were no bangs covering her forehead. She seemed to seek out Tate's gaze, and hiss.

The captain brought his front sight to bear on a depression between her modest breasts and, just as the flare struck a tree and fizzled out, he eased the trigger in, felt the M-16 discharge and saw a male VC standing beside her drop over with a belly wound.

"Damn!" Tate cursed as he vainly examined the rear sight by probing with his fingers. It was too dark to see now, but he already knew the weapon had somehow been damaged during the earlier skirmish. Already Nordheim and the other men were unleashing an endless barrage of automatic-weapons fire on the spot where the woman in black had been standing.

Had. She'd since vanished.

The clouds pressing down against the triple canopy parted for an angry moon, and silver beams splayed down through the trees, marking the men in black pajamas, illuminating their jungle graves as first one and then another flopped over with mortal wounds.

"Let's go! Let's go! Let's go!" Brogan yelled as the last of the VC guerrillas screamed his life out. The NCO was across the clearing in a heartbeat, zigzagging down a narrow trail that lay hidden behind the tree line and scattered bodies.

"Wait a minute!" Nordheim countermanded above the staccato roar of Brogan's M-16.

"I ain't got a minute, LT!" Brogan screamed back. He disappeared down the winding, mist-shrouded trail just in time to see the woman clad in pajamas drop into a spider-hole fifty feet away.

"But what about the river, the sampans?" Nordheim demanded as Nelson and Dillon crowded him on either side. "What about Tho?"

"Screw Tho!" Tate said, rushing past Brogan and the others. "I want that bitch! Dead or alive!"

The captain was spurting blood through a flesh wound on his upper bicep, courtesy of the woman in black.

9

Brogan was the first into the void.

It wasn't that he'd misjudged the spider-hole's size, or that he'd abandoned his senses, casting caution to the tropical breeze. It just so happened the ground at the tunnel entrance's edge had given way under his weight and he'd lost his footing, dropping straight down.

"Jesus," he grunted when he landed, certain the Co Cong would be standing over him, plunging her bayonet or machete into his heart at that very moment. He wanted to open his eyes and meet his fate like a man, but he was still groggy.

His head, neck and upper back throbbed with pain, and there was an odd, far-off ringing in his ears, but no cold steel pierced his rib cage. In the distance he could hear the pitter-patter of sandaled feet—the woman. And directly overhead there was a voice—Nordheim calling down to him.

"Jim? You okay, Sarge? Yo, Brogan!"

Bits of dirt and twigs fluttered down into his face. Finally Brogan was able to open his eyes. He realized he was holding his M-16 at his side, the barrel pointed down into the gently sloping tunnel. The NCO glanced up. Nordheim's face smiled down at him. The lieutenant appeared to be about fifteen feet up, a pale halo of dim light around his face. Brogan didn't respond verbally. Instead, he placed a rigid forefinger against his lips, motioning for silence. Then, with his other hand, he used the carbine to point down the tunnel in the direction the Co Cong had fled.

"Jim!" Nordheim yelled again. He obviously couldn't see the SF sergeant. "Yo, Sarge! Gimme a sign, or we're gonna presume your ass is dead and lob some frags in after the chick!"

Brogan glanced to his left and noticed that a ragged wooden ladder was nailed to the earthen walls with long spikes. Dust particles floated down, caught by a solitary shaft of light, and he shifted on his haunches so that the flashlight beam could play across his face.

"There he is!" Jefferson cried out.

Again Brogan brought his finger to his lips. This time they got the message. He pointed to the ladder and motioned them down. One by one the men descended into the Vietcong lair.

"Wish Cross was here," Mendez muttered.

"You can say that again," Jefferson said, nodding as his turn came to climb backward down through the spider-hole.

"Knock it off!" Tate snapped.

"But Cross is back in the World," Jefferson mumbled under his breath so that only Mendez could hear.

"Probably...fucking," the Puerto Rican whispered.

"Some guys have all the luck."

Cross was well-known for his "talent" of stalking tunnel rats on their own terms. Stripped to the waist and armed with only a .45 handgun and an L-shaped flashlight, he'd crawl down into the narrowest, tightest holes in search of Charlie, and remain beneath the surface until muffled shots signaled he was ready for someone to help him drag the corpses out.

"Jesus!" Stuart muttered halfway down the ladder. He released his grip on the bamboo support poles and dropped back into space as a portion of the wall collapsed and a huge rodent the size of a mongoose popped its head out. The Southerner landed with a grunt at the bottom of the tunnel entrance a couple of inches from Brogan. Dillon threw a vicious punch at the wide-eyed rat, but, startled by the intruders' appearance, it had already retreated deeper into its sub-tunnel.

"Follow my lead," Brogan whispered to Stuart, who motioned for silence from the others and waved the first man down the ladder. Hunched over, they started down into the dark. They were equipped with flashlights, but Brogan preferred to flick his lighter every few seconds, holding it at different positions and away from his body each time.

Trouble struck at the first bend. Brogan heard the trip wire snap, though he was unsure who'd set it off. He dropped to his hands and knees as the post laced with urine-coated spikes flew past in a loud horizontal swish, splitting the air where his chest had been moments earlier. It also missed Stuart by inches.

The thud of wood against dirt was still echoing along the narrow walls when the burst of tracers passed over Stuart's right shoulder and tore off Jef-

ferson's boonie hat before all the men flattened out
behind Brogan's jungle boots.

"Damn bitch sure knows how to lob complexities
into an easy search-and-hurt mission," Nelson muttered, wiping dust out of his mouth.

"Goddamn fucking Cross," Jefferson growled over
and over. "Goddamn Cross is back in the World
havin' a good ol' time while we're down here half a
foot above hell, chasing some crazy broad armed with
a machine gun."

NAKED AND DEFENSELESS Cross tensed as the VC
captain tightened the chains attached to his wrists and
ankles. He fought hard not to cry out, but the pain
was unbearable, and he knew it was only a matter of
time before he told the Communist what he wanted to
know. The man had already peeled long strips of flesh
from his back and chest. But so far Cross had given
only his name, rank and serial number. Nothing else.
And the Communist had only laughed at his bravery
and resumed peeling more skin. Now the bastard was
attaching the field phone wires to Cross's testicles
again, and motioning for a buck private bent over the
hand generator nearby to crank at will. Cross was
convinced his bladder would give out this time.

The pain caused by electricity zapping the scrotum
was enough to make even a martial arts master weep.
Cross turned to the crimson-coated wall, seeking sol-
ace, support, encouragement from the men of his
A-team—Nelson, Brogan, Nordheim, Tate and the
others. But their severed heads just stared back down
at him from atop the long teak shelf.

Dead. All of them. The entire team.

The jolt of electricity didn't come and, feeling a warm, gentle hand caressing his belly, Cross looked down. Terror filled his gut when he saw the young woman standing before him. She, too, was nude. Her long silky hair shone midnight blue by the light of dungeon lanterns. Her breasts were modest but firm, the nipples jutting taut and purple, oddly arousing even under these conditions. But the terror in his belly prevented a stimulation in his loins, for Cross had heard about these Co Cong and their devious methods of torture. This one obviously knew he knew, for she took him into her mouth, forcing him erect against his wishes, against his senses, fondling his testicles with her left hand as the right hand rose into the air and flipped open the longest, sharpest, most wicked-looking straight razor Cross had ever seen.

As the glistening blade began to fall toward his crotch, he opened his mouth and tried to scream but found himself being smothered by a woman's lips as she pressed her mouth roughly against his, her eyes changing to an eerie neon green.

Cross sat bolt upright in the bed, gasping for breath. An imagine of the Cong whore, squatting at the foot of his bed, grinning and pointing at him accusingly as her breasts fell off to expose the ribs underneath, seemed to shimmer and ripple and flutter before him until it finally vanished right in front of his eyes.

An older man's static-laced voice startled him, and he twisted to the left until Richard Nixon's image came into focus. Instantly he realized the TV was on, providing the only light in the bedroom. There was no interrogator. No torture chamber.

"And if you grant me and my team the privilege of representing you in the White House," Nixon was saying, "I can honestly guarantee you a positive change in this great country's foreign policy and, before long, peace with honor in Vietnam."

Cross glanced down at his chest and felt a cold chill run up his spine. A woman was lying across him, her long black hair fanned out on his flat belly, her hand cupping his crotch, her right leg draped over both his knees.

Asian . . . but who was she?

He couldn't see her face, and hesitated lifting it for fear the demon with glowing green eyes would pounce and sink her fangs in his throat. But then he remembered the flesh peeling from his back, and the memory caused him to start violently. The woman moaned as if being coaxed from her dreams against her will.

Dawn. He remembered now.

"I'm sorry." He stroked her hair. "Go back to sleep."

He smiled as she sluggishly kissed the nipple over his racing heart, turned away and sighed long and loud, shifting her slender frame this way and that, rubbing her haunches against the hollow of his side before sighing seductively one last time and finally nodding off again.

Cross concentrated on the newscast. Nixon had been replaced by an American woman with short blond hair and a desperate need for makeup. She was reporting from somewhere in Europe.

"And here in Paris the North Vietnamese delegation has made a final offer to representatives of the U.S. government regarding the rumored POW swap that has been making the rounds of political circles these past several weeks. Officials aren't commenting on the reports, but our source close to the Administration claims the Hanoi regime is willing to release a key high-ranking American prisoner of war for an infamous North Vietnamese general known only by the code name of Zebra, a man the Communists allege has been held in a secret underground chamber at Saigon's Chi Hoa Prison since the days of the Veitminh. According to my calculations—'' the reporter glanced at her clipboard ''—that would be just about fourteen years now.''

Cross grinned inwardly, well aware the reporter wasn't that far off base. The Special Forces sergeant happened to know whom the negotiators were referring to—NVA General Tran and his private little jail cell, known affectionately as the Zebra Cube due to the cramped cell's mind-disorienting black and white stripes.

The Thieu regime continually moved the Zebra Cube to different underground fortresses throughout South Vietnam, just to keep one jump ahead of any possible Communist sapper mission to free Tran, who had become a national hero at the defeat of the French colonialists at Dien Bien Phu in 1954. Currently it was rumored that the cube was in a deep maze of catacombs near the Delta community of Long Xuyen, a longtime anti-Communist stronghold staunchly loyal to the Saigon regime.

Cross laughed, wondering if his old team would somehow get involved in the action. He squinted, trying to make out the unit number on a helicopter gunship floating across the TV screen as the news shifted to American casualties in Southeast Asia. An over-whelming sense of pride in being part of the Special Forces rolled over him.

Cross didn't notice that Dawn had awakened until she was on top of him, her thighs apart, the insides of her knees gripping his hips. Her lips were against his, smothering him until he remembered to breathe again. Her breasts pressed against his chest, her pelvis grind-ing into his.

Smiling, Cross leaned against his pillow and al-lowed her hair to fan out across his face, covering his eyes until the walls and ceiling disappeared and his world was reduced to intense sensation and the sound of Dawn moaning in the night.

10

LONG XUYEN

General Sherwood stared at the small black-and-white TV set sitting on the teak bookcase. He felt like saluting the Republican presidential candidate, Richard Nixon. God, he loved the man. But he decided against it for fear of alienating his public information officer, who was a liberal at heart despite volunteering for Vietnam one month before Tet.

Nixon's chief military Intelligence adviser was shown preparing a key briefing for the senior politician, a briefing involving the upcoming prisoner swap and his political opponent Hubert Humphrey's inability to use the Vietnam War to his advantage. An aide's suggestion to Nixon was simple: "Tell the American people you'll begin a troop pullout from our Indochinese quagmire, with light at the end of the tunnel in the form of peace with honor. Now that ought to please everybody."

"Christ, do those guys know there's a TV camera documenting everything they say?" Sherwood muttered.

"Sounds kind of catchy to me," his PIO aide said. "Light at the end of the tunnel and peace with honor. Yeah, I like that."

"Gentlemen," a South Vietnamese officer said, clearing his throat. He motioned toward the doorway, plastic smile intact beneath thick black sunglasses. Sherwood turned from the TV set. "The representatives from the North Vietnamese government..." Four elderly, smiling Asians in stiff tunics entered the room, arms extended for handshakes.

The meeting began immediately, and Sherwood wasted no time with political games. "Gentlemen, three of our U.S. airmen were released by Hanoi and we responded by releasing fourteen North Vietnamese sailors. Now, if talks are deadlocking in Paris, that doesn't mean we have to remain tight-lipped here on the battlefront, does it?"

"And just what exactly are you suggesting?" an eighty-year-old Communist asked, tugging at his goatee.

"Hopes were raised at the Paris peace talks that there would be more POW exchanges. The deadlocked talks were revitalized when we agreed to stop bombing the North in return for your agreement to respect the DMZ and stop shelling cities in the South. The talks were expanded to include Saigon and the Vietcong, a development that promised to give Humphrey's campaign a major boost. But only one day after the bombing ceased Saigon refused to participate in the talks, thus wrecking the initiative. And, quite frankly, I hate to see it end at that."

"And just what exactly do you propose?"

"You've expressed an interest in the Zebra," Sherwood said, smiling slightly.

The eighty-year-old NVA officer grinned in reply, but didn't immediately say anything. There was a gleam in his eye that gave Sherwood an odd sense of satisfaction.

BROGAN WAS the first man to reach what appeared to be a dead end in the tunnel—a solid wall of old warped and mortar-riddled runway tarmac.

The female guerrilla had vanished. First she was firing at them nonstop with an AK-47, then she was gone.

"Trapdoors!" Tate decided. "Start searching for trapdoors!"

"And air vents!" Nordheim added. "Maybe she went up an air vent!"

"Maybe she was a ghost," Dillon said softly, rubbing the leather pouch around his neck.

"What?" Jefferson rasped. He didn't sound very happy.

"A rain forest ghost," Dillon added.

"More like the ghost of a tunnel rat killed by some past B-52 raid," Brogan said, spitting.

"Ghosts don't bleed," Nordheim snapped as he dropped to one knee and ran his fingertip through several drops of blood forming a trail on the tunnel's earthen floor. "What are our chances to get some dogs down here and try to catch a scent?" he asked Tate.

"Don't know till we get topside and I play with the commo," the captain responded. "Depends on whether or not the Blues have a scout team in the area. But we'll give it a shot."

"Does that mean we can all get the hell outta here, sir?" Jefferson asked, already heading for the bamboo ladder.

"I guess it does, Frank," Tate said, grinning.

The First Air Cav brought in two German shepherds an hour later. The dogs located a hidden trapdoor that descended into a lower labyrinth of tunnels. As soon as the infantrymen searching the maze took their first casualty, thanks to a hidden punji stake pit, Tate called an end to the mission and ordered gasoline to be poured into the tunnel complex. The entire plateau was transformed into an inferno as hidden air shafts everywhere erupted with puffs of smoke and flame.

The female guerrilla was never located, but Tate and his men knew they hadn't seen the last of her.

COLONEL ALAN RICHARDSON filled General Sherwood's coffee cup as they both listened intently to Intelligence Specialist Dave Nelson's briefing of Tate and the other members of the A-team concerning the potential POW swap and Hanoi's desire to see the infamous General Tran top the list of trades.

"But isn't Tran dead?" Nordheim asked.

"That's what we were led to believe," Nelson said.

"Until now," Richardson added with a tight grin.

"Ever hear of the Zebra Cube?" Nelson asked, narrowing his eyes at Nordheim.

"Just rumors dripping down the wait-a-minute vine," the lieutenant replied. "Something about an underground secret jail located in the catacombs beneath Saigon, a place were they keep the most-valuable enemy prisoners."

"Well, Rumor Control over at Puzzle Palace claims President Thieu has Tran in the Zebra Cube and refuses even to consider trading him for anyone," Nelson told them.

"But the ambassador is trying to soften up the South Vietnamese president," Richardson said.

"In the meantime you men will be pulling some extra duty," Sherwood announced.

"Sir?" Tate piped up, frowning.

"General Tho is apt to surface in the most unlikely places," Richardson said, scratching his chin, "and I'd lay my bet on the senior NVA giving the Zebra Cube a shot for his next trick."

"Does that mean that we—" Brogan began.

"Get to bird-dog the mission. It'll be a waiting game."

"In Saigon?" Jefferson asked hopefully.

Richardson's grin grew. "Negative."

"They rotate the Cube in-country," Sherwood revealed. "At present, it's right here in the stinking Mekong Delta."

"Long Xuyen?" Tate asked.

"A stick grenade's throw to the whiskey."

"Underground? In a tunnel, you say?"

"Yep," the general replied.

"It's times like these I wish I'd become a bank robber like my daddy," Jefferson groused.

CROSS KNEW Dawn was holding his hand, clenching it tightly, in fact, but he couldn't feel anything. He believed his heart, soul and mind had turned to stone. Stone layered in ice. He had no feelings. He could feel no pain, no sorrow, couldn't feel Dawn squeezing his fingers as she stood beside him in the drizzle, crying though she'd never known his mother and father. Crying simply because they *were* his mother and father...had been...

He stared at the World War II veterans who were slowly lowering the two caskets into the side-by-side graves. On the hilltop an honor guard wearing dress uniforms and chrome helmets fired off a salute with M-2 carbines, his father's favorite weapon.

"I miss you, Pop," Cross whispered as a long-lost aunt dropped flowers onto the casket. "I love you, Mom."

He glanced over at his kid brother, Perry, who'd arrived the night before. They'd emptied a half-dozen pitchers of beer with Dawn at the Blue Bamboo, staying out until sunrise, then walking all the way to the church ten minutes before the mass had begun. Now they didn't even glance at each other, guilt ridden perhaps, frightened one might be able to read the other's thoughts.

Cross's ears pricked up as something attracted his attention. In the distance he could hear the angry yells of an antiwar protest, which he decided to investigate.

Instead of the expected college students, Cross and Dawn came upon a dozen men dressed in fatigue jackets and mismatched military uniforms. They carried a banner that read Vietnam Veterans Against The War and were throwing their medals up onto the steps of the city hall near the cemetery.

"I want to talk to them," Cross said, starting to climb the chain-link fence.

"No, Ben," Dawn pleaded, holding on to his wrist.

But Cross pulled his arm free. He was angry. "I have to see what the bastards are all about, what really makes them tick," he explained, refusing to look back down at her.

"I'm coming with you!" she said, jumping onto the fence. It was a good six feet high, and she ripped several buttons off the front of her blouse.

On the ground on the other side he turned to see her zipping up her knee-length jacket.

"Just calm down!" one of the vets yelled, his hands pressed gently but firmly against Cross's chest.

"My parents are being buried over there, maggot!" Cross shouted, rising on tiptoe, nose to nose with the older vet. "And you assholes are over here chanting about the war being wrong and everything. Don't you have any respect for the dead?"

"Hey, mellow out, brother," a shorter vet with a blond Afro said, holding up two fingers in a peace sign. "We're sorry. We didn't think about it, the cemetery and all. We're sorry if our chanting interrupted anything, but we've got to make ourselves heard. Surely you can understand that—"

"No, I can't!" Cross interrupted as he watched a black vet toss a handful of medals up over the police barricade and onto the city hall steps. "What the hell's gotten into you clowns, anyway?"

"Just calm down and come to one of the vets' meetings," the blonde told him. "There's one scheduled to take place tonight after Nixon's speech in Indianapolis."

"It's going to be held over at Rob Findlay's house," the other vet said.

"Rob *Findlay?*"

"Yeah. Know the guy?"

"We went to high school together."

"Good. Then you should get along just fine. If anyone can convert ya, Rob can."

"I kinda doubt it, slick."

"We'll see," the blond vet said. He told Cross the address. "Rob couldn't make it to the rally this afternoon. He had a little trouble with the law. But we're raising the money to bail him out. Wanna contribute?"

"Sure." Cross dug out a ten-dollar bill, his attitude softening somewhat. He still couldn't believe it: he and Findlay had been good friends all through high school, and he remembered the guy being gung ho when they both volunteered for combat duty, only to be sent to different parts of Vietnam after basic training. "What time?"

"Ten sharp. Be there or be square."

"I'll be there."

"Can I come?" Dawn asked as they walked away.

Cross stared at Dawn. "You can come, all right," he said, his grin returning. He dropped his hand and gently caressed her bottom as they walked.

"I want to go home right now, Ben Cross. I want to speed all the way. And *do* it."

"Me, too," Cross said, fondling one of her breasts. "Me, too."

11

LONG XUYEN

Tran Thi Hoa held the pressure bandage to her breast and closed her eyes tightly as the VC doctor treated a long line of puncture wounds across her shoulder blade with Cuban-made disinfectant. A ricochet had splintered and struck there.

"What about here?" Hoa asked, motioning toward her chest, but the doctor didn't seem excited or hurried. He stood behind her in the dim lantern's flickering light, patiently dabbing the slowly oozing wounds with a long brown swab.

"Presently," he said. "Just hold the bandage in place."

"I need my breast stitched up before it falls off, or I bleed to death," Hoa insisted. "Whichever comes first."

"You aren't going to bleed to death as long as you keep the bandage in place," the doctor maintained with a sly grin. "And I'll be done shortly. Didn't your parents ever explain to you that patience is a virtue?"

"I never knew my parents," Hoa snapped.

"Nonsense," the doctor said, his smile fading. "Your father's a very important officer in the North

Vietnamese command. You should use more respect when you speak of him. He's a very famous soldier, a much *revered* soldier."

"Then why am I fighting in the mud with foreigners like some frontline coolie?" Hoa demanded, wrinkling her wide, flat nose at him.

"You volunteered to fight with us in the South, Comrade. You should count your blessings."

"Count my *what?*" Hoa muttered.

"You *could* be building bridges beneath the waterline along Honorable Ho Chi Minh's Trail."

"But, Grandfather..." she grumbled.

"It's true," the old man said, nodding confidently.

Hoa sighed and shook her head slowly. "I give up on you. On *all* men."

"Oh?" the doctor said, jabbing gently with the swab, causing her to wince.

"Well, maybe not *all* men," she reconsidered, her eyes darting toward the earthen ceiling as the walls began to shake slightly and dust swirled down on them. One of the American V-100 assault tanks was rumbling past twenty or so feet overhead.

They both remained silent for a moment. Then, after the small convoy of tanks passed, the doctor stared down sadly at his nineteen-year-old granddaughter. "Not *all* men?" he asked.

"No," she said softly, eyes downcast now as she examined her slender frame, hopeful her boyfriend would still want her despite all the weight she'd lost over the past several weeks.

"And have you heard from Van lately?"

"A letter."

"Oh?"

"Kim brought it to me last week."

"You didn't tell me."

"It was stamped two months ago." A tear welled up at the edge of one eye, and she lowered her head again. "His letters are becoming...cold," she revealed.

The doctor's eyebrow arched slightly. "Oh?"

"Not...not as if he's found another girlfriend. Just so political. They're no longer love letters, Grandfather. They're propaganda."

"Propaganda?"

"Yes," Hoa said, flinching again as he placed a large gauze sponge across her entire back, then began tying it in place with twine. "Communist propaganda."

"That's not like Van."

"Yes. He was always a nationalist first. We were never interested in Communist doctrines. Not really."

The doctor chuckled slightly. "I wouldn't let your father hear you talking that way about the cause."

"It'll only bring more suffering and hardship on our homeland," Hoa sighed. "If the North succeeds. You know that, Grandfather. That wasn't why we joined the movement."

"You only wished to see the North and South reunited into one country."

"Yes. Too naive?" She turned her head and glanced into his gleaming eyes, the eyes of a healer and peacemaker.

"Perhaps. But we all have our hopes and dreams, child. Without them life would have no flavor, no purpose."

"And you, Grandfather? What do you wish for?"

"That I may someday return to Dak To and visit your grandmother's final resting place."

Hoa's frown deepened and her brow furrowed. "I still can't understand why that province chief up there put a bounty on your head."

"Dak To is controlled by the Saigon regime's puppets."

"But the people know you're a good man, that you help people, make them well again."

"The people aren't in charge of who comes and goes through the gates leading to Dak To, child."

Hoa's face brightened as he began cleaning out the gash between her breasts. "You could go at night. *I* could escort you."

"Nonsense."

"What nonsense? I'm serious."

"Yes, I can tell that you are," he snorted.

The doctor probed with a new swab, hoping the pain might silence the child of his dead daughter. Again she winced, but the questions continued to roll off her tongue.

"Will the foreigners ever leave Vietnam, Grandfather?"

"Which ones?" he asked.

This elicited a quiet laugh from Hoa, but she didn't glance back up at him. "The long noses—the Americans."

"Ah, they'll leave, child. In due time."

"Will they win the war, do you think?"

"They just might, but then we'll just win the country back eventually. That's the way it's always been for as far back as I can remember. There is always someone trying to rule us. They take. We take back. We make new friends like Moscow, fight some more and win back lost real estate. Over and over. It'll continue long after you and I are mere dust on the breeze, my child. The greedy will always be with us."

"No," she said, shaking her head and beginning to cry again.

"You must stay tough, my child. We must all be tough so that we can continue—"

"I'm not crying for myself, Grandfather. I cry for Van."

"Van?"

"Someday he'll come home to us."

"Yes, he's a good boy. I light a joss stick for him nearly every night," the old man reminded her.

"He'll come home to a woman whose body is young and firm yet disfigured like the old beggar women who squat in Saigon's central market with their withered palms extended for charity and their breasts dried up and—"

"Don't insult yourself," he chastised her.

"It's true."

"You must be thankful to Buddha that you're alive," he said as he finished stitching her wound.

"There is no Buddha," she snapped.

"No need to talk that way, child," he told her. "Be careful what you say. The jungle is a mystical place, you know. There are more gods here than in the city, and they all have ears. Some have dozens of ears. And a mean disposition."

"I don't believe in your silly superstitions."

The doctor laughed as he lifted her arms and began wrapping a bandage around her upper torso. "You have a short memory, my dear."

"What are you talking about now, old man?"

"Oh? Old man is it? Five minutes ago I was your precious, beloved grandfather. Now I'm an old man."

Hoa remained silent, fighting the strong urge to insult him again.

"When you were six or seven," he continued, "you wandered out alone into the swamp one night during a fierce rainstorm. Your mother had just bathed you. You were naked and defenseless."

"There is a purpose, I suppose, to retelling this fable for the thousandth time?" she asked, folding her frail arms across her chest defiantly, then wincing noticeably at the pain the contact caused her.

"It was back during the time when a pride of man-eating tigers was roaming the delta, terrorizing villagers. The big cats found you sitting beside a pond, crying your heart out."

"You made it up. I don't remember anything like that ever happening to me."

"The tigers were closing in on you when a huge elephant with tusks the size of tree trunks charged through the bush, trumpeting its alarm as it rammed the roaring cats with its ivory sabers. And after it frightened off the man-eaters, and potential *child* eater, the elephant dropped onto its front knees and gently picked you up by its long snout, hoisting you onto its shoulders. And you cried and screamed like a demon."

"Yes, I did," Hoa agreed, almost childlike now, her eyes moist and glued to his face as he recreated the scene for her.

"But you hung on for dear life, and the elephant lumbered to the edge of a nearby village, placed you on the ground and trumpeted its farewell. Then it nudged you on the ear with its long trunk, turned and crashed back into the jungle."

"I dreamed it."

"There were witnesses."

"It proves nothing."

"It proves there are gods, that Buddha exists."

"If the elephant was guided by gods, he would have returned me to the right village."

Taken aback, the old man scratched an earlobe. Finally he laughed. "You'll never change, will you, child? Tran Thi Hoa, forever the skeptic. You'll never change."

"Probably not," she agreed. "It's in my genes."

"Eh?"

"The urge to fight. I'm a woman warrior," she said. "I know nothing else, care for nothing else." Hoa ran her fingers over her stitches, counting the bumps, grimacing at the bolt of pain yet remaining silent. "I hate the Americans who did this to me," she snarled viciously. "I should have killed them all."

"Another opportunity will present itself, child. Don't be so impatient."

"I hurt, Grandfather. I want revenge."

"And you shall have it. Soon."

Her face seemed to brighten, and she moved closer to him as the old man began replenishing supplies in his medical ruck. "You've spoken to Father?"

"Perhaps. You know I can't—"

"You can tell *me,* Grandfather. I am his daughter."

"And this I understand. What you don't understand is that, should the foreigners capture you some unlucky night—"

"It'll never happen," she muttered, making the stress lines along the edges of her eyes jump menacingly.

"Nevertheless, *should* the enemy have unforeseen luck and happen upon you when you're defenseless, for example, their methods of interrogation would break even a brave fighter such as yourself."

"I'd die first."

"They wouldn't let you. That's what's so terrifying about becoming a prisoner of the round eyes."

"You're repeating rumors."

"I've treated the men who have escaped Chi Hoa Prison. There wasn't much left to treat mentally. Not much at all."

"I want to know."

"Know what?"

"About the Zebra Cube."

The old man's smile faded. "I didn't hear you ask that." He turned away.

"Kim told me word is going around that the Zebra Cube is in this province, in Long Xuyen." She slapped the earthen wall with an open palm. "Perhaps on the other side of this very wall of dirt."

"Perhaps," the old man said.

"When do we link up with General Tho and Major Mot?"

"Soon."

"Tonight?"

"Perhaps."

"And my father."

"You know."

"He's the Zebra?"

"Yes."

"We'll free him?"

"We shall try, child."

"I'd give my life for him."

"No," the old man said, shaking his head. "Make the Americans give theirs."

12

TERRE HAUTE, INDIANA

Ben Cross stared at the scenes unfolding on his TV set:
antiwar protests at a nearby college campus. Men with
shoulder-length hair threw rocks and bottles at the
National Guard. A Molotov cocktail exploded against
a police car, sending a brilliant orange fireball into the
night sky. Windshields were shattered.

"Jesus," Cross muttered under his breath. "What's
this country coming to?"

The scene shifted to a protest earlier that day in
front of the Terre Haute city hall. High school youths
chanted, "Hell, no, we won't go!" and burned their
draft cards.

"Christ," Cross growled, rubbing his throbbing
temples. He stared down at the Colt .45 lying on the
bed and bit softly into his lower lip as he envisioned
himself walking into the midst of the radicals and
suddenly unloading on them point-blank.

He picked up the .45, removed the magazine, pulled
back the slide and inspected the chamber to ensure
there was no hot load seated in front of the hammer.
Then he took aim on the TV faces, inhaled a deep

breath and slowly, gently began bringing in the slack on the trigger.

"Peace pukes," he muttered, easing off on the trigger. He slammed the clip home, then slid the pistol under the mattress. Outraged, he kicked the TV set over and walked outside, slamming the door behind him.

In the driveway the brand-new blue Ford Mustang beckoned. He was still unsure why he'd bought it, but it was something he'd dreamed about having the whole time he was in Vietnam.

He sat behind the wheel, turned the ignition key and gunned the engine for several seconds before popping the clutch and roaring down the street, rear tires spinning, clouds of burned rubber obscuring his taillights.

When he got to the Blue Bamboo, Jeff Thornton was there. So was Rob Findlay. Dawn was dancing, and the patrons were all singing, "We gotta get outta this place." An old man wearing an American Legion cap was throwing darts at an eight-by-ten photo of Ho Chi Minh taped to the wall.

"Drinks are on me," Thornton announced.

"Well, that's mighty nice of you," Findlay said, clapping the Saigon commando on the back.

"It's the least I can do," Thornton declared, "seeing as how I'll be leaving you all real soon."

"Oh?" Cross said. "Heading back to the ol' hometown?"

"Heading back to Nam, brother."

A few heads turned. Cross shook his head. "Get serious."

"I'm about as serious as a man can get, amigo."

"There's nothing waiting for you back in Saigon except a world of hurt," Findlay said.

"She's waiting back there for me."

"Well, *she's* not fucking worth it," Findlay growled, burping as he slammed a bottle of beer against his wheelchair, sending shards of glass flying everywhere. "Nothing's worth going back to that godforsaken hellhole. It's the asshole of the world, hoss."

"What's going on here?" Sammy Phuc demanded, appearing out of nowhere.

"Sorry, Sammy," Dawn said as she tried to pick up the larger pieces of glass with her bare fingers. "He just got a little carried away, that's all."

Findlay glared at the proprietor. "And they'll carry you away in a fucking box if you don't get outta my face, ya goddamn runt!"

"Hey, mellow out," Cross said. "He's just trying to keep the peace."

"Well, I don't like him. What the hell's he doing here in America, anyway? Zips in the wire, man! Where's my M-16?"

"Get him the hell out of here!" Sammy said, leveling a rigid forefinger at Findlay's nose. "Before I call the police!"

"Sammy, please!" Dawn pleaded. "He'll knock it off. I'm sorry." She gently shoved him toward the bar. "Go back to work, okay?"

"Okay! But tell your friend *this* zip became naturalized U.S. citizen five years ago. I've been in this country since 1954! And I didn't swim across no river to get here. I had a scholarship."

"Podunk College of Bartending?" Findlay taunted.

"University of Indiana. Political science major."

"Good for you, Major!" Findlay sneered, saluting the Vietnamese man. "A beer for the slant-eyed American! On me!"

"Jesus, Rob," Cross said, turning his friend's wheelchair slightly aside. "Just cool it before the shit hits the fan in here."

Findlay seemed to run out of steam. "Okay, I'm sorry," he sighed, letting his chin rest against his chest. Less than a minute later he was snoring.

Cross laughed. "What a character."

"I'll send you a postcard," Thornton said suddenly.

"From Saigon?" Cross asked.

"You got it, partner."

"I'll be waiting for it."

"I'm serious."

"Give me one of those VFW matchbooks. I'll write my address on it."

"Shit," Thornton said, refusing the request.

"Changed your mind?"

"I can't go back."

"Why not? It's a free country."

"I don't even know where she is, man."

"Find out."

"Huh?"

"You're the cop."

"Was."

"Did you forget everything they taught you at Fort Gordon?"

"No, I suppose not."

"Then go over there and track her down."

"It's not that easy."

"Why not?"

"I'm scared."

"You?"

"Believe it or not."

"Naw."

"A guy could get blown away over there."

Cross laughed. "In Saigon?"

"Hey, listen up, guy. I was in that town during Tet. Twenty-seven of my buddies gave their lives to protect Saigon from the Cong. Forty-four more got seriously shot up. We're talking Purple Heart serious."

"Sorry. I didn't mean to—"

"Yeah, sorry my ass. Aw, forget it." Thornton grabbed another bottle of beer and began guzzling. "Don't mean nothing."

"I think you need to go back," Cross said softly. "Get it out of your system."

"That country's gonna fall any week now."

"I don't think so, pal."

"And I don't wanna be there when it does. I've got a low pain threshold. I don't wanna become one of Charlie's houseguests at the Hanoi Hilton."

"South Vietnam ain't going to fall."

Thornton grimaced. "That's what you say."

"Go back to her. Bring her out. Get it over with. What would it take you—a week? Two?"

"I'm not sure she's worth the risk."

"What? But I thought you just said—"

"I know what I said. I love her. I think about her every goddamn second of every goddamn minute of every single day and night. But . . ."

"Then forget her."

"I can't."

"Then go."

"I...I don't have the backbone, the nerve." Thornton looked away quickly. "Sometimes I think I'd rather just pull out my gun and eat the damn thing."

"That's crazy talk," Cross said, alarm in his eyes now.

"It's the truth."

"Then do it."

"What?"

Suddenly standing, Cross grabbed the front of Thornton's jean jacket and pulled him out of his chair. "Do it!"

"Do what?"

"Come on!" He dragged Thornton toward the front door of the Blue Bamboo, knocking over tables and chairs.

A rowdy crowd followed, smelling a fight. Cross hauled the flailing Thornton through the doorway and out into the parking lot.

When they reached his Mustang, Cross jerked open the passenger side door, unlocked the glove compartment and removed his father's old German Luger. Placing it partially in Thornton's hand yet refusing to let go completely, he repeated his earlier challenge. "Do it!"

"You're crazy!" Thornton cried, trying to give back the gun.

But Cross wrapped his arm around the Saigon MP, placing him in a chokehold and lifting him off the ground slightly. Then he jammed the Luger's barrel into Thornton's mouth. "Eat it!"

"Come on, Ben!" Dawn pleaded, trying to pull him away. "Let him go."

Thornton was wide-eyed and scared to death, but he refused to fight or beg.

And then Cross froze. Deep in the depths of the former MP's eyes he saw something, an eagerness, as if the man welcomed death.

As if he hoped Cross would pull the trigger for him.

"Jesus!" Cross released his hold on Thornton, letting him drop to the ground limply. A crowd of thirty or forty bar patrons had gathered outside the Blue Bamboo, but no one said a word. An eerie silence had fallen over the entire parking lot.

Cross stuffed the pistol into the waistband of his trousers. "You're a real maggot, Jeff, you know that?"

"You're the asshole!" Dawn spit at him. "How could you do that? How could you humiliate him like that in front of his friends?"

"Screw you," Cross growled as he walked over to his car. "Screw this whole fucking town. You're all a bunch of goddamn phonies."

He started the Mustang's engine, revved it several times, then sped off through the parking lot, spinning his rear tires. He hadn't traveled half a block before the car bucked, sputtered, then ran out of gas. As he coasted to the side of the road, the wheels struck the curb, the glove compartment popped open and moonlight played across the Luger's blue steel barrel.

Cross stared at it for a couple of seconds, contemplating his destiny and the warrior's sacred right to choose the time and place and manner of his own death. Then he laughed and wondered what Jefferson, Mendez, Crocker, Brogan and his other buddies were doing. Kicking ass, no doubt.

13

CAMP FOXTROT
NEAR LONG XUYEN

Thick sheets of monsoon rain fell so violently that the whole world beyond her had become a swirling silver wall of power and energy. Lightning bolts blasted down, making his hair stand on end as static electricity danced between their outstretched hands. But the whirlwind's force was carrying her away, lifting her into the sky, pulling her helplessly into the storm clouds where she would be ripped to shreds by the uncaring forces of nature gone wild.

She called to him, crying out for protection from the storm's fury, but he couldn't even remember her name. Dang or Sang or something like that. All he could remember was that she'd been the best lay to grace his swinging hammock since he'd arrived in Vietnam.

"Jim!"

The woman's voice had become a man's. Nordheim's.

"Jim! Wake the fuck up!"

The swirling storm disappeared, the woman's face vanished and the stench of burning diesel in the air slammed Brogan back to reality. He was alone, lying on his back in a dilapidated ARVN barracks on the outskirts of Long Xuyen.

The woman had been a dream, and he was now staring up into the ugly mug of Lieutenant Nordheim.

"Christ, what's it take to wake your no-account ass up!" the lieutenant complained.

"Sometimes happens when you've gone seventy-two hours without sleep, LT."

"Yeah, tell me about it. Either get your butt in gear or die where you snooze."

"What?" Brogan yelled.

Tate raced past in his baggy OD green Army-issue shorts, dragging a flak jacket, a rifle and wrinkled fatigues. "We're under attack, goddamn it!"

And then the sounds began registering—incoming mortars, screams and inhuman wailing in the distance, the chop and whirl and frantic whir of gunship rotor blades in the courtyard below.

"Jesus!" Brogan jumped to his feet and slid into his uniform in record time. He snapped on his web belt and began gathering up the contents of his ruck, which he'd been cleaning by candlelight before dozing off.

"The Cong are hitting us on three sides!" Nordheim informed Brogan as he crammed extra ammo magazines into the pouches on his stabo gear. "We think it's a diversion."

"A diversion?"

They both raced toward the stairway, which burst into flames as a 122 mm rocket roared in and slammed into several oil drums filled with sand. Both men dropped into a crouch, shielding each other as the sand showered over them and their ears began ringing.

"What?" Nordheim shouted.

"What?" Brogan responded as Jefferson, Mendez and several of the other men raced past them and began working their way down the stairway. "I didn't say anything!"

"Charlie's hitting us with *beaucoup* ordnance!" Nordheim shouted. "But we've only seen a few sappers attempt to breach the wire, according to the commo I've monitored from the Nung strikers."

"So no large-scale ground attack yet."

"Roger that. And you said the key word—yet!"

Night became high noon as the courtyard below turned into a blinding sheet of all-encompassing white. The shock wave threw them both back into the barracks.

"Jesus!" Brogan yelled before the air was sucked from his lungs.

One of the helicopters had taken a direct mortar hit and disappeared in a huge mushrooming ball of golden flame. That left two Hueys.

"Let's go! Let's go!" Carbo cried as he rushed past.

Dillon, wide-eyed and clutching his lucky-charm pouch, stopped to grab both Nordheim's and Brogan's elbows and jerk them to their feet. "Come on, guys!"

"The chopper!" Brogan said, regaining his senses. "Did any of our guys make it into the chopper before it blew?"

Bolecki was suddenly standing in front of them, his face black with soot, his hand extended with the radio mike. "What's our game plan?" he asked Nordheim as a burst of green tracers arced up through the open doorway and missed the men by less than a foot. It stitched the ceiling, leaving behind smoking holes, which every man stared at for a long moment.

"We get in the remaining two choppers and head out to the facility," Nordheim said.

"The facility?" Brogan echoed.

"Yeah. We reinforce the perimeter. The captain thinks this is a diversion so Charlie or the NVA can mount a full-scale attack on the detention center."

"They're after the Zebra Cube," Brogan commented. He yanked his M-16's charging handle back and let it slam forward, chambering a hot round.

"We think so," Nordheim confirmed.

On the ground, as they were scrambling into the two remaining Hueys, Nordheim stood between the birds and took a quick head count before he clambered up over the landing skids himself. His eyes were drawn to the smoldering remains of the craft that had taken a direct hit—three charred and blackened corpses lay amid the debris, flames licking their faceless heads. "Christ Almighty," the lieutenant muttered under his breath.

Crocker and Nelson were missing in action.

SERGEANT PARK SON YEE scanned the dark tree line with his Starlite scope. There was something going on out there in the hostile jungle; he could sense it. Out of the corner of his eye he'd detected movement twice. But each time he'd concentrated hard on the moving shadows, they had frozen.

In the distance he and the other men guarding the White Horse Detention Center, manned by members of the crack South Korean White Horse Division, could hear an endless series of explosions and small-arms fire lighting up the night. The eastern horizon glowed an eerie crimson, and now and then bursts of green and orange tracers arced heavenward. Flares drifted on the muggy breeze.

Park gritted his teeth, preparing for the worst. He'd never liked the POW guard assignment in the first place. He preferred, in fact, to be out in the boonies, stalking the enemy. And ever since the skycrane chopper with its six-Cobra escort had arrived the week before, he'd known they were all in for a lot of pain.

Dangling beneath the crane had been a metal conex cube—painted black and white inside and out and roughly the size of a Dumpster. Inside was rumored to be a high-ranking Communist prisoner. There were no windows in the conex, so it was impossible to tell.

Park's men had watched in awe as a team of rugged Americans clad in black fatigues had manually pulled back a heavily camouflaged thirty-by-thirty-foot assemblage of metal plating composed of tarmac sheets from a nearby abandoned helipad. A deep shaft, reinforced with concrete, was laid open to the harsh sunlight, and the cube was lowered into the black pit without ceremony. Park had estimated that the conex was slowly dropped at least four or five levels before the skycrane's winch had grated to a stop and the cargo was hastily removed so the choppers could leave before drawing sniper fire from the surrounding jungle.

The shaft was immediately covered up, and no one except the officers were informed of the new prisoner's identity. Park understood Vietnamese quite well, however, and had figured out that the famous missing NVA General Tran was the notorious Zebra Cube's latest tenant. And Thieu's Saigon regime had taken to transferring him around the country from military region to military region, trying to keep one step ahead of the enemy lest they attempt to mount a rescue mission and snatch away President Thieu's prize.

"Damn!" Park muttered under his breath as a security flare popped up along the perimeter. It had been tripped by one of the guerrillas attempting to slide under the concertina wire. As the flare's chute blossomed out, it began drifting low over the barbed wire and punji stakes, and Park and his men were aghast to discover more than a hundred pajama-clad sappers working their way through the coils of sharp concertina. The sappers, many carrying satchel charges slung over their backs, froze in place as first one flare and then several more marked their positions.

Park didn't need to give the command. Guards in all four of the raised towers began spraying belts of M-60 machine-gun bullets down into the perimeter. Park himself began firing on semiautomatic, picking off VC one at a time with clean head shots. He took out more than ten of the enemy in a row before his eleventh target was blown backward out of sight by the 5-round burst from another Korean soldier.

In the distance the wonderful beat of chopper rotors reached Park's ears. Gunships. The American cavalry had arrived.

DILLON WAS the first man off the Hueys as they flared in for rough landings on the cratered helipad. "That way!" he said, directing Brogan and Stuart toward a besieged bunker along the northern perimeter. "Over there!" he said, sending Jefferson and Carbo toward a leaning guard tower that was on fire. Its lone sentry was still firing unceasing streams of M-60 bullets down into the attackers. "Help that man get down before—"

But before the master sergeant could finish his order a rocket-propelled grenade destroyed the guard tower's wooden shack. Body parts and pieces of the M-60's red-hot barrel rained down on the SF reinforcements.

Dillon glanced over at the other chopper: Tate and Nordheim, along with Bolecki and Mendez, were scattering for cover as the enemy intruders blew several holes in the concertina and punji-staked perimeter.

"Pop some flares!" Dillon heard Tate order, and several flares soared skyward as soon as the helicopters were out of the way.

The shower of light outlined the small camp's killing zone for Dillon and the other SFers. It wasn't very complex—perhaps fifty yards by one hundred across gently rolling terrain. A main longhouse thirty yards in length and twelve wide was situated in the center of the camp. At either end there was a shack, one for administration, the other for supplies. On both sides they could see barracks for the guards, and adjacent to the makeshift helipad lay the camouflaged and tarmac-covered pit that contained the Zebra Cube.

Dillon could now see NVA pith helmets and brown uniforms among the black pajamas and ancient carbines. Soldiers from Hanoi, armed with AK-47s were joining the fray.

Like a giant bird of prey, one of the Huey gunships dropped out of the sky and sprayed red tracers into the enemy ranks. Dull pops sounded from the gunship's nose cannons as high-explosive rounds were fired into the tree line, answered by the metallic thump of AK rounds, which peppered the chopper's tail boom. Dillon flipped his M-16's selector from auto to semi and began firing solitary rounds at every ground-level muzzle-flash he saw.

Fuzzy shapes danced in his peripheral vision, but he was too busy to worry about the other men right now. His main objective was to provide cover fire for the chopper suspended magnificently overhead.

The air seemed to split as the second Huey appeared, its rotor blades beating madly at the sticky air as if barely able to keep the heavily armed craft aloft. Rockets roared down from extra pods mounted on the landing skids' upper brackets, and the dark tree line was splashed with bright colors as explosions sent dismembered corpses twirling through the night like rag dolls.

The second he saw the 20-round burst of tracer fire rise up from the shoulder-high elephant grass at the perimeter's edge, Dillon knew the Huey was history. The enemy rifleman was good: nearly all of the rounds punched through the ship's thin-skinned underbelly, beginning with the snout and working back along the tail boom.

The craft didn't explode in the air, but heavy smoke poured from its turbine and, the hydraulics disabled, it quickly lost power and began descending toward the earth in a tight spiral. The pilot tried to land upright, but he didn't have enough control over the craft and slammed sideways into one of the guard towers.

"Damn!" Dillon growled, lowering his weapon, mesmerized by the slow-motion free-fall of the helicopter. A fireball rose from its crumpled fuselage, but the crew chief and Peter pilot rolled free of the wreckage before a secondary fuel cell explosion consumed the craft in a white-hot halo of searing heat.

"Over here!" Dillon yelled to the stunned crewmen. He reached toward two nearby corpses and relieved the White Horse Koreans of their M-14s. "Take these!"

Only slightly disoriented despite scalp wounds that allowed streams of blood to pour into their eyes, the chopper crew crawled toward Dillon's position and gratefully took up the arms.

Despite the extra firepower the Americans appeared severely outgunned, however. Enemy sappers were still streaming through the breached segments of concertina, throwing satchel charges into the White Horse bunkers as they advanced. And the remaining Huey had banked away into the night, forced to return to its base camp for fuel and ammunition.

Within minutes of the gunship's departure the Special Forces commandos became pinned down in their respective sanctuaries. Dillon was worried about the enemy's apparently endless supply of bodies to throw at the installation, but one rifleman in particular was earning his attention. The man was firing with the precision of a well-trained NVA marksman and, actually, he wasn't using a rifle, but an M-79 grenade launcher.

The enemy would pop up from one spider-hole position outside the ring of concertina, fire off a lone blooper round, then vanish before Dillon could get a bead on his pitch helmet's red star, only to reappear twenty or thirty feet away inside another clump of reeds or elephant grass. The bastard was obviously using a tunnel system of some sort, and Dillon wondered if they'd just dug it recently, or if the damn thing had been in place for weeks, just waiting for word that the Zebra Cube had arrived at the White Horse Detention Center.

And Dillon found himself wishing Cross, the tunnel expert, were here tonight. Surely Cross would know what to do. The engineer could sniff out the underground chambers better than some canine teams. Yeah, Cross could do it, Dillon thought. Too bad he wasn't around when he was needed.

14

BLUE BAMBOO BAR
TERRE HAUTE, INDIANA

"Another beer for my ol' buddy here, Mr. Phuc," Ben Cross said.

"Sure," Sammy Phuc said, smiling as he ripped the caps off two bottles with an Army-issue P-38. "This one's on the house. I buy. I like it when you two behave."

"Well, thank you, Sammy," Cross said, reaching across the counter and slapping the Vietnamese bartender on the bicep. "Did you know me and Rob Findlay here went to high school together?"

Sammy nodded. "You tell me many times already."

Cross felt good inside. Despite the T-shirt that Findlay wore with its Vietnam Veterans Against the War logo, Cross was enjoying the company of his old friend tonight. Findlay had told Cross all about the land mine outside Pleiku that had paralyzed him for life. So Cross realized that, despite their political differences, his friend had earned the right to protest the war in his own personal way.

Unfortunately Findlay had become an alcoholic. That much was becoming obvious. Findlay could really put them away. And now he wanted to dance with the Hawaiian girl sliding out of her G-string on the bar. Only he'd forgotten about the war and his wound and his imprisonment in the wheelchair.

Or perhaps he hadn't.

"Have you seen Jeff lately?" Cross asked Sammy.

Sammy squinted questioningly. "Jeff?"

"Thornton, the inglorious Army cop."

"Oh, Jeff Thornton, Saigon MP. No, I haven't seen him since last night. Not since you and he—"

"Not since last night, huh?"

"Nope."

"When he went home with Dawn," a feminine voice added.

"Dawn?" Cross's heart began to race.

"Yeah, Dawn, loverboy," the Hawaiian girl sneered as she got off the bar. She pressed herself against Cross, hot and nude, her body seeming to throb against his. "She's been screwing Thornton off and on for a couple of years now."

"What?" Cross growled, setting his beer bottle down loudly. A few heads at nearby tables turned. "What the fuck are you looking at?"

The other patrons ignored him, and the woman continued. "Thornton's a real head case, though. He's always talking about some woman he abandoned back in Saigon. That kind of talk really turned Dawn off. Jeff was on a never-ending guilt trip, and Dawn moved out and was on the rebound when you came along. But you were just a passing fancy, Benny. Dawn always goes back to Jeff, sooner or later."

Cross rushed out of the bar, jumped into his Mustang and sped through a maze of side streets to Thornton's apartment, where a sea of flashing red lights announced the presence of police cars and an ambulance.

Dawn was inside, lying in the bathtub, her throat cut. Thornton was in the living room, his head blown off by a shotgun.

Cross knew one of the cops at the scene, and the man let him into the apartment.

"Did you know her well?" the officer asked him, a combination of suspicion and curiosity playing across his face.

"I . . . I guess I didn't really know her that well, after all."

"Didn't you say her name was Dawn?"

"Yeah, Dawn. That's right. Why?"

"As in the sunrise?"

"Yeah."

"Funny."

"Funny?"

"Must have been a nickname."

"Why do you say that?"

"Because it's not the name on her passport."

"She had a passport?"

The police officer held up a plastic evidence bag for him to see. Sealed inside was a dark green document bearing the seal of North Vietnam, but Cross didn't immediately recognize it.

"May I?" he asked.

A frown creasing his features, the cop glanced over at the dead woman in the crimson-clouded bathtub water. "Guess it can't hurt," he decided. "She's not going to mind." He removed the passport and handed it to Cross.

"Did you know she was Cambodian?" Cross asked.

"Guess again, pal."

"What?" Cross slowly opened the passport and stared at the tiny photo affixed to the first page. Dawn's unsmiling face stared back at him. Her hair was pulled back in a tight bun, making her appear ten years older and a lot more severe. "Tran Thi Hoa? But that's Vietnamese."

"Hey, you're a regular Sherlock Holmes," the cop said.

"But . . ." Cross couldn't finish his sentence. Nothing was making sense. It was supposed to be so simple in the States. It was supposed to be home. But it no longer was home to him. He missed the men of his A-team. They were his family now. Life in Vietnam was simpler. You were either dead or alive, and survival was all you had time to think about. Here, in the States, there was too much time to think, and thinking made you crazy, like Jeff Thornton. "Life sucks," he muttered.

"Tell me about it, pal."

"I feel like I'm gonna be sick."

"Wonder if she's any relation to that fucking bastard Ho Chi Minh," the cop reflected.

Cross stared at the passport notation regarding her place of birth. It was Dak To, in a region where the borders of Cambodia, Laos and South Vietnam met. "Was there a note?" he finally asked.

"You mean from the guy?"

"Or her."

"We're not so sure she checked out willingly. Anyway, there's no note from her. But the guy left a note. Christ, it's more like a book. He goes on and on about some broad he knew in Nam. Doesn't make a damn bit of sense."

Cross stared down at Dawn's lifeless form. "Oh, I don't know about that. Maybe it's the only thing that does make sense."

SOUTH VIETNAMESE MP Colonel Tri Quoc glanced at his watch and shook his head angrily. "Faster!" he demanded.

"We can't go much faster, sir," his driver said, staring at the gun jeep's speedometer. It read fifty miles per hour. "Without risking land mines."

"Blast the land mines, man! We've got to get to White Horse before Tho gets his hands on the Zebra Cube. I don't want to see Tran returned to the North. Do you understand?" Quoc yelled from the backseat.

"Of course I understand, Colonel. But it's not going to do anyone any good if we don't arrive in one piece."

Quoc glanced back at the two dozen QC jeeps roaring down the narrow dirt trail behind his own lead unit. "Pull over," he directed.

"What?" his driver asked.

"Just pull over, damn it!" Quoc shouted as he waved four or five of the other gun jeeps past. When his jeep came to a stop, the colonel reached down, grabbed the radio mike and, over the open net, instructed the drivers to continue on the previously agreed-upon course. "That's enough!" he finally said, motioning his driver back onto the trail. "Now we've got some protection." he grinned. "A buffer zone in case there are any booby traps up ahead."

The driver nodded, and Quoc stared off down the road, loving the rush of hot air against his face, remembering the good old days when he'd been a big-city cop and not stuck out here in the boonies.

"Step on it!" Quoc ordered the driver. "For once *we're* going to rescue the cavalry. And maybe I'll finally get transferred back to Saigon."

DILLON FIRED his last bullet, then jumped out of the foxhole and began swinging the M-16 by the barrel, breaking the jaw of the first Cong he encountered. A second sapper rushed up behind him and plunged a dagger into the SF master sergeant's lower back, but the blade's penetration was halted by the flak jacket's thick lower seam, and Dillon whirled, dropped sideways and kicked out, striking the VC in the throat and snapping his neck.

Most of the other Americans were out of ammo now, too, or down to their last couple of rounds. A few, no doubt, had chosen to save their last bullet for themselves, a tradition the French Foreign Legion had made famous in this part of the world fourteen years earlier. Dillon wasn't anxious to grace a POW camp with his presence. The North Vietnamese had long ago made it known they despised the Green Berets even more than the Air Force pilots who dropped tons of bombs from their B-52s. At least the pilots fought an anonymous war. The Special Forces grunts seemed to make it personal. And the Communists resented that with a passion. Many of the SF troopers had large bounties on their heads, which they weren't even aware of.

Dillon swung his rifle at another shadow moving through the night, felt it break in two, then braced himself for the dozen or so pajama-clad enemy rushing toward him.

Just then Colonel Quoc's QC commandoes burst through the tree line, M-60 machine guns blasting away nonstop. The gun jeeps roared up through the breaks in the perimeter and, tires spinning, took up positions all around the besieged soldiers. By sunrise the POW camp was retaken.

15

Tate had experienced a change of heart about Colonel Quoc, but before he could express his appreciation for the QC officer's intervention, the man had roared off into the jungle, leaving Tate and the others to mop up.

"Giving chase, no doubt," Nordheim decided. "Hard-core."

"Chasing who?" Jefferson asked. "They blew away every bad guy caught in the wire."

"You think Tho was out there somewhere?" Tate asked his lieutenant. "Giving the orders?"

"I don't think so, sir. I *know* so. The way they zapped this place, well, that was Tho's style. Especially the diversion over at Camp Foxtrot. Textbook Tho all the way."

"I think you're right."

Sergeant Park staggered up to Tate and saluted the captain. "Will you now bring in more gunships please, sir?"

Tate returned the salute sharply and smiled. "The battle's over, Sergeant. No need for more Hueys, not at the moment, anyway."

"The Communists will return, sir. They always return. We must be ready for them. We need more choppers before the shooting starts again. And ammo resupply."

"Recommendation noted, Sergeant. Now have some of your men secure the perimeter and give me what's left of your reactionary squad. I want to inspect the Zebra Cube."

"The what, sir?" Park kept a straight face, devoid of emotion.

"He's good," Nordheim said. "He don't know us from Adam. And until he does, secret shit like the Zebra remains secret shit."

Tate walked over to the heavily camouflaged tarmac cover, which had sustained very little visible damage during the ground battle. He stomped on its edge with one boot. "There's a pit under here, Sergeant," he told Park. "Now roll the sucker back so we can have a look at the prisoner."

The Korean's resolve softened. "Yes, sir."

"Bolecki!" Tate yelled.

"Sir?"

"Get me a commo link over to Foxtrot. I want to know if they've located Crocker and Nelson—dead or alive!"

"I'll get right on it, Cap!"

The pit was composed of several walkway levels beneath the ground's surface, and they found five men dead at the entrance to the first level as soon as the tarmac cover was mechanically rolled back. Their throats had been cut.

The overpowering stench of chemical explosives reached the Americans' nostrils at about the same time they discovered the hole in the wall. It was connected to an elaborate tunnel network that ran like a rat's maze down into the bowels of the earth.

"Fucking VC," Brogan muttered. "They never give up."

They rushed down the ramps to the second level and found a survivor sitting in a pool of his own blood. His throat had been cut, too, but the man had maintained the presence of mind to keep an empty ammo bandolier pressed against the wound until help arrived. "Get me a Medevac chopper!" Tate called up to Carbo.

"Yes, sir!"

"Ask the man who did this to him," Tate told Park.

The Korean sergeant translated, but the sentry could only gurgle in reply. Nordheim produced a notepad and grease pencil. "Have him write it out!"

A few seconds later Tate was staring at the blood-stained scribblings. *VC sapper team led by long-haired woman,* Park read, eyes rising to lock with the captain's. "She headed down to the bottom level after the Zebra Cube."

"I got me some good news and some bad new, Cap!" Bolecki said, catching up with Tate's team as they made their way to the bottom level. They still hadn't encountered any hostile fire.

"I'm listening. Bad news first."

"The general's up there in his Loach eyeballing the terrain. He advises he hasn't seen hide nor hair of

Quoc *or* Tho. The good news is that Crocker and Nelson checked in back at Foxtrot. They made it through the sapper attack without a scratch."

"Just like those guys to goldbrick," Brogan muttered, relief obvious on his face.

"There," Park said, pointing at a dangling section of cable.

"There what?" Tate grunted.

"The prisoner conex used to hang from it."

"Over there!" Brogan said, pointing his rifle barrel at a black-and-white metal cube. It was lying on its side, the top peeled back as if a giant can opener had been at work.

Mendez, the team's heavy-weapons expert, cautiously approached the conex, ever vigilant for booby traps, and inspected the sharp, smoldering edges of the gaping hole. "Thermite charges," he decided after a couple of seconds. He peered into the Zebra Cube, then at the ground beside it. "Got a blood trail here, Captain."

Tate tested the seal on his M-16's ammo clip by slapping the palm of his hand against it. "Let's go, gentlemen."

The blood trail led to another crater in the pit's concrete wall—a hole blasted by the tunnel rat Cong while other guerrillas had been fighting the Americans and Koreans topside.

"Any volunteers?" Nordheim asked, peering into the dark cavity.

Brogan stepped through without a word, a satanic grin splitting his face.

"They're probably halfway to Hanoi with him by now," Tate said, shaking his head, the look of an exhausted man in his bleary eyes.

"Ours is not to ponder why," a grinning Nordheim said as he stepped into the black void after Brogan.

"Ours is but to do or die," Jefferson added, surprising them all by going next.

They didn't have to explore very far. The tunnel widened to a good twenty feet and looked as if it had been in existence for quite some time. The VC had even laid down iron tracks. They'd obviously known, or suspected, that White Horse would eventually be used to house the Zebra Cube.

The tunnel rose to a height of nearly ten feet in places, and unlit lanterns were hung here and there. Tate's team produced flashlights and walked on. They'd been stumbling forward for only a minute or two when the murky darkness up ahead erupted into fireworks. The glowing light show revealed a cavernous amphitheater in the near distance.

Two hostile forces were engaging each other with awesome fury.

Tate's men instinctively fell into prone positions and began crawling toward the gunfight, their rifles balanced expertly across their wrists as they slithered toward the action.

The Americans made their way to a wall of boulders at the edge of the cathedral-size chamber, which was rich with stalagmites and stalactites that rose from the limestone floor and dropped from the bat-covered ceiling in brilliant bluish green hues. Tate produced a small set of folding binoculars and trained them on the faces of the combatants.

To his left were General Tho and an elite sapper squad of NVA regulars. To his right were Colonel Quoc and a crack unit of South Vietnamese MPs. Quoc had obviously known about the caves and had gone hunting for the Communists in the most likely spot. Tate only wished the ARVN cop had let him in on the secret. They could have combined firepower. Then again, perhaps Quoc feared the American officer might have tried to take him into custody. But somehow Tate felt the gung ho copper didn't fear much of anything.

Right now his men were engaging Tho in a fierce pitched battle beneath the surface of the earth, with NVA General Tran the obvious prize.

Tate scanned the combatants, searching for the former tenant of the Zebra Cube. He found *her* instead, the long-haired woman who'd led the guerrilla squad against them in the tunnel system on the other side of Long Xuyen.

He brought his rifle sights up and placed the cross hairs over her chest, but then she was darting down through the limestone stalagmites and out of sight, only to reappear again a few seconds later, leading two male sappers through the shadows, men who were holding up a stiff, robed figure.

And they were getting away!

Were they carrying Tran? He didn't know. But he wasn't about to allow the VC woman to snatch the prize away without a fight, even *if* two heavily armed forces were shooting the hell out of each other between his men and the bitch in black!

"Let's go!" Tate ordered, rising to his feet.

"Are you crazy?" Nordheim whispered harshly, urging caution.

"We've got no choice!" Brogan said, instantly beside his CO and pointing at the group of ghoulish phantoms hurriedly escorting what could only be a wounded General Tran into another series of misty tunnels cloaked with drifting gunsmoke.

Colonel Quoc spotted the girl getting away, too, and he wasn't about to let her succeed. "Get them!" he yelled, leaving the cover of a large boulder to lead the charge.

Tho leaned out from the dark mouth of a nearby cave and fired a single pistol shot at the military police officer. Even at fifty yards the lone bullet found its mark, striking Quoc in the throat and knocking him backward off his feet. He dropped into the moist limestone muck and gurgled his life away.

Brogan sent a deafening 3-round burst from the hip at Tho, and two of the bullets caught the Communist's lower jaw, ripping it away with a crimson spray and twirling his body around so that it became impaled on one of the jagged rock spires jutting out of the ground.

Clutching his pouch filled with eagle feathers, wolf fangs and a chunk of meteorite, Dillon sprinted through the gun smoke and struck Tran's escorts from behind with a flying tackle. The general went down as if he were made of balsa wood. The men holding him up rolled to either side and came up firing Soviet-made pistols. Tate and Nordheim were both there to silence the VC's trigger fingers with fatal doses of head lead.

Spinning his body like some kung fu master, Dillon kicked out and caught the woman at the back of her knees. She went down in a heap, stunned and groaning. Dillon was on his feet instantly and flying through the air again. He landed on her back, got her neck into a chokehold and began pulling hard as she tried to twist and jab at him with the bayonet on her AK-47. She became a wildcat despite her wounds, and Dillon had no choice. He jerked once, hard, and snapped her neck.

Quoc's men teamed up with Tate's A-team and quickly routed the remaining enemy in Tho's contingent of subterranean sappers. Tate and Nordheim rushed over to Tran's body, which was facedown and still.

"I'll get on the horn and have the medics standing by," Nordheim said. "Wouldn't want our prize to be damaged beyond repair!"

"Little late for that," Brogan said as they turned over the robed figure to find a mummified corpse with half the skull exposed. Its protruding teeth seemed to laugh silently at the men standing speechless in the dank cavern beneath the jungle.

"How can we be sure it's even Tran?" Nordheim asked Tate as they stared down at the corpse's leering cranium.

"It's Tran," Park revealed. "The bastard's been dead for a couple of years now. They've just been ferrying his bones up and down the country to keep Hanoi guessing." Park met their inquisitive gaze. "I'm only a sergeant," he conceded, "but the ARVNs like to tell us Korean NCOs secrets they wouldn't dare reveal to you Americans. No offense."

Tate grinned. "None taken."

"This one's still alive," Stuart said. He had his medical ruck open and was down on one knee beside the woman whose neck Dillon had broken.

"Finish her off," Park said, drawing his pistol, "or I will."

"Not so fast," Nordheim countermanded, rushing over to the medic's side.

Stuart had rolled the Co Cong over and was holding her in his arms. Eyelids fluttering, she gazed up into his face. "Grandfather..." she whispered in Vietnamese.

"Not hardly, darling," the corpsman said, chuckling.

"Please, permit me," one of the prisoners said as he stepped forward and bowed to his captors. He was an old man in his eighties or nineties, one of the oldest Cong Tate had ever seen.

"Permit you to what?" Nordheim asked.

"She's my daughter's child, or thinks she is," the old man informed them. Hands tied behind his back, he dropped to his knees beside the woman, whose breathing was very faint now. Blood trickled from the edges of her lips.

"I am General Tran's daughter," the woman announced proudly in English. "You must take me... prisoner of war."

"*This* is General Tran, honey!" Nordheim said, dragging the corpse over until its grinning skull was face-to-face with her. "And you know it!"

"No!" she cried out, chest heaving. "It was only a decoy. My father is alive! Up there somewhere!"

The old man used his elbow to knock the skeleton aside. "Forget about your father," he said in hushed

Vietnamese. "Worry only about yourself now, child. The past is dead."

"No," she said, shaking her head, her eyelids fluttering.

"I'm sorry, child. But you aren't Tran's daughter. You never were. You lived a lie your whole life...."

"I know," she said suddenly. "In my heart I knew..."

"Remember the elephant?" A gleam seemed to make the old man's eyes sparkle for a moment.

"Yes," she said, forcing a painful smile.

"The elephant saved you from days of wandering in the jungle after your village was bombed by the French. Tran's number-two wife took you in. That's all there was to it, child. I'm sorry, so very, very sorry that I was part of the deception."

"It doesn't matter, Grandfather."

"You are a child of the jungle, a daughter of the rain forest. You are—"

But the little girl who'd ridden the shoulders of a rogue elephant had closed her eyes for the last time and was finally at peace with her past.

16

"The dead girl in the cave was a stand-in for Tran's daughter all these years," Tate revealed a few days later at the after-action debriefing. "For 'security reasons.'"

"What?" Nordheim asked, his jaw dropping.

"Yep. Apparently Ho Van Tho was about to authorize the release of several American POWs *if* the U.S. government would agree to the safety of Tran's real daughter, who was attending a college in Canada of all places."

"Canada?" Jefferson repeated.

"Yeah," Tate said, "Canada. Until she crossed the border one weekend, ditched her bodyguards, dropped out of sight and got involved with an American, an ex-MP living in Terre Haute, Indiana. She became a stripper in a sleazy bar."

"Her name is—was—Tran Thi Hoa," Nelson, the team's Intelligence expert, added. "Seems she and this American vet were involved in a murder-suicide pact or something. The details are a little sketchy, though.

All we know for sure is that Tran's real daughter is dead, and there goes one mighty fine bargaining chip.''

"What a bitch," Dillon muttered.

"Hey," Jefferson said, "Cross lives in Terre Haute. He's there right now. Think he knew anything about all this?"

"Get real," Crocker snickered. "Ol' Benny's too busy banging the local bimbos. He's out of it now. The Nam's history for him."

"By the way," Tate interjected, "anyone heard from Cross lately?"

"You kiddin', sir?" Brogan bellowed. "What did you expect—loyalty?"

"I HATE WATCHING it on TV," Cross said, staring up at the black-and-white images of Special Forces commandos jumping out of helicopter gunships somewhere in IV Corps, Republic of Vietnam. "I feel like I'm missing out on something important, you know?"

"Recognize any faces?" Rob Findlay asked, motioning toward the TV screen through the drifting cigarette smoke.

Cross was finding it hard to distinguish between the cigarette smoke inside the bar and the gun smoke on the screen. "No," he said after several silent moments. "No, I don't recognize anyone. But I should be there with them, tasting the sweat and the heat and the adrenaline rush."

"Yeah, I hear ya, brother. What do ya say we drive over to the east side of town. Couple of broads I know there are throwing a party tonight. It'll do you good, what with Dawn and Jeff and all. Hell, it'll do us both good. We'll take my new van. Specially equipped for a Nam vet cripple. I'll drive."

"You're too drunk," Cross countered.

"Don't mean nothing," Findlay replied.

"You'll change your tune if the Terre Haute coppers pick you up drunk behind the wheel."

"Still don't mean nothing, chump. I've already been arrested for drinking and driving twice. Even wasted some hick couple here in town. But I'll beat that rap, too. Just like I'll beat this one." He tapped his useless legs.

A jolt ricocheted through Cross's gut like a lightning bolt. "What?"

"Huh?"

"What did you just say?"

And then it struck him: Findlay was the man who'd slammed a pickup truck into his parents' car.

"I got to level with you about something, Ben ol' buddy," Findlay said, slapping his legs again. "I didn't wreck my body over in Nam, brother."

"You . . . you didn't?"

"Got my worthless ass paralyzed in a car crash a couple of weeks ago. Yeah," he said, misreading the shock in Cross's eyes. "Ain't been a cripple for the past five or six years, only a couple of fucking weeks."

Findlay hadn't mentioned the names of the people he'd killed . . . murdered. But Cross knew in his heart that this man sitting beside him, this old high school friend, had ripped the heads off his mother and father.

Cross wasn't sure how to react to the revelation. He wanted to shoot Findlay, just as he had wanted to go hunting for war protestors when he first arrived home.

Instead, he got up and walked out of the Blue Bamboo, leaving Findlay to drown in his misery and self-pity. He went over to his car, remembering Dawn and her pretty face and those upturned breasts and the way she'd wept when they made love. He remembered the war stories Thornton had told about the Saigon woman who had driven him crazy.

He got into the Mustang and drove by Dawn's old attic room, fighting back the tears when he saw the For Rent sign and the tiny Buddha statue sitting in the windowsill.

Pushing the speedometer past ninety, he rocketed the car in the direction of his parents' house. When he got there, he buttonholed his brother, Perry, and handed him the keys to the Mustang. Then, looking the kid square in the eye, he said, "Drive me to the airport."

"Why, Ben?"

"I've got to go home."

Perry stared at his brother, concern obvious in his face. "But you are home, Ben."

Cross looked around the quiet street lined with neat duplexes and bungalows. "No, Perry, I've got a date with Miss Saigon, and she's an impatient lady."

For the eternal soldier, Dan Samson, the battle has shifted to the Mexican-American war in Book 2 of the time-travel miniseries . . .

TIMERAIDER

John Barnes

Dan Samson, a hero for all time, is thrown back to the past to fight on the battlefields of history.

In Book 2: BATTLECRY, Dan Samson faces off against deadly enemies on both sides of the conflict—ready to forfeit his life to ensure the course of destiny.

Available in August at your favorite retail outlet.